From playing leading roles in the theatre to starring in long-running television dramas, Judy Nunn's career as an actor in Australia and the United Kingdom has covered a lot of ground.

She became a household name in the seventies as the controversial Vicki Stafford in 'The Box' and is currently best known to television viewers as Ailsa Stewart in the internationally successful series 'Home and Away'.

Judy began her writing career as a scriptwriter for television and radio. She then co-wrote two top-selling children's novels before branching out on her own to write the best-selling adventure novel, *Eye in the Storm*, which has been published in Europe. Its sequel, *Eye in the City*, is to be published in 1991.

The Glitter Game is Judy's first adult novel.

THE
GLITTER
GAME

JUDY NUNN

PAN BOOKS
LONDON, SYDNEY AND AUCKLAND

First published in Australia in 1991 by Pan Macmillan Publishers Australia

This edition published 1994 by Pan Books Ltd
a division of Pan Macmillan Publishers Limited
Cavaye Place London SW10 9PG
and Basingstoke

Associated companies throughout the world

ISBN 0 330 32519 1

1 3 5 7 9 8 6 4 2

A CIP catalogue record for this book is available from
the British Library

Printed and bound in Great Britain by
Cox & Wyman Ltd, Reading, Berkshire

*To my husband Bruce Venables
who makes me laugh.*

Contents

	PROLOGUE	1
1	NARELLE	11
2	JANE	20
3	PAUL	33
4	GREG AND VICKY	45
5	MANDY AND SIDNEY	59
6	THE FIRST DAY	68
7	SIZING UP	83
8	RELATING	103
9	SUCCESS	124
10	REVENGE	147
11	RETRIBUTION	171
12	POWER GAMES	194
13	MANOEUVRES	220
14	RAPE	248
15	MURDER	276
16	DISCOVERY	299
17	BETRAYAL	325
18	SURVIVAL	349
19	THE LOGIES	375
20	REVELATIONS	382
	EPILOGUE	388

Writers, actors and artists
youse call yerselfs
actors writers and artists
I know youse for what youse are
prostitutes, pimps and pooftahs
and the police has been called for.

Miss Porteous Stops The Party
Barrett Reid

Prologue

Edwina nodded to the waiter who hovered beside her, Veuve Clicquot bottle poised. She'd demand Bollinger in her next deal, she thought. Veuve was too bitter.

She glanced around the table at her co-stars, pleased that she'd kept her distance from them. When one had set one's sights as high as Edwina had, involvement was out of the question. Anyway, they were all riding on the crest of her wave. The show would never have been as successful without her — they had no reason to bear her any ill will.

Well, most of them had no reason. She caught the malevolence in Jane's eyes over the rim of her glass. Yes, Jane had every right to be bitter, but that was the name of the game, after all — only the ruthless made it to the top.

Edwina was no stranger to Logies awards. She had picked up the silver State vote for Most Popular Television Personality in New South Wales for the last five years.

But this year was different. This year was the first time a Logies presentation telecast had been sold overseas. Stations all over the UK had bought the rights — the Logies would go to air halfway across the world the following night.

1

For an hour, while limousines had arrived and celebrities had walked up the red carpet into the Regent Hotel, searchlights had scanned the sky and police had held back the thousands of screaming fans.

Inside the hotel the air was electric with anticipation. The most important award presentation night in the history of the Australian television industry had begun.

And it was all because of 'The Glitter Game' and its star, Edwina Dawling. This was the year Edwina had been nominated for the public vote of Most Popular Actress in a TV series, the industry vote of Best Actress in a TV Drama Series and the coveted Gold Logie, a public vote for the most popular television personality in Australia.

Thanks to the unprecedented success of 'The Glitter Game', the sultry pop singer turned nightshow host was now internationally acclaimed as Australia's leading television actress. She was off to the States to star in a glossy new CBS series especially written around her. But first the three Logies. Just to prove to everyone at home that Edwina Dawling really was the best.

'The Glitter Game' had not only been a turning point in Edwina's career: it had created new stars; resurrected a few has-beens and placed them on the international market; and, in just twelve months of airtime, had made more overseas sales than any other series in the history of Australian television, including an unprecedented American network deal.

The phenomenal success of 'The Glitter Game' had been studied endlessly by ratings surveyors and marketing teams and had been put down to two major factors. Across-the-board appeal was one. Its essence of ongoing drama was exactly what the general viewer wanted — but its edge of satire and mild send-up of the television industry won many fans who otherwise scorned all series as 'soap'. The second factor was doubtless the current fascination that overseas markets seemed to have for Australian television and the fact that 'The Glitter Game' was set in an Australian television station in which the characters were making an Aussie 'soap' gave the show a voyeuristic quality that had proved most popular. Imitative series were already popping up but none of them had that indefinable quality that belonged to 'The Glitter Game' — and, of course, none of them had Edwina.

Edwina felt a light tap on her shoulder.

Alain was standing beside her. 'Good luck, Edwina.'

She snapped out of her reverie to return to the noise, glitter and smoke-filled excitement of the overcrowded Regent Hotel ballroom. 'Thank you, Alain.'

As she watched him weave his way back to his table, Davey put his hand on her thigh and whispered, 'He wants you to lose.'

'I know.' To hell with Alain, she thought. It was a foregone conclusion that 'The Glitter Game' would win Best Drama Series. As executive producer Alain would be up there to collect the award — he should be bloody grateful to her.

On stage, the MC was introducing the next presenters.

Mandy leaned across the table, her ample breasts creasing into a thousand wrinkles and nearly knocking her glass over. The dress she was wearing would have looked good on her twenty years ago. 'Next one up, Edwina. Good luck.'

Another of Edwina's gracious smiles. Yes, Mandy's bonhomie was genuine. She had every reason to be grateful. She was one of the successful resurrections — she'd just picked up the Best Supporting Actress award.

' . . . the Most Popular Actress in a Drama Series . . .'

Davey gripped Edwina's hand under the table.

' . . . and the winner is . . . '

The tearing of the envelope, a flash of perfectly capped teeth and a girlish giggle from the American 'special guest' presenter . . . 'Edwina Dawling!'

The spotlight hit Edwina and there was a roar of applause as she rose from the table. The approval was genuine — she was idolised by the public and admired by her peers. But there were no spontaneous pats on the back or cries of 'Wonderful, darling!' as she made her way to the stage. Edwina didn't invite effusive behaviour. She remembered everyone's name, from actors, directors and crew, to wardrobe, hair and make-up, but no one was ever 'darling' and, with the exception of a gracious handshake, she was physical with no one.

'Congratulations, darling.' The make-up was heavy and the American woman looked fifteen years older close up. Her mane of hair brushed Edwina's face as she kissed her on both cheeks and the air was thick with Patou's Joy.

Edwina kept her smile remote and waited patiently for the woman to break the clinch. What show was she from — 'Dynasty', 'Dallas'? Edwina really couldn't remember, they all looked like barbie dolls to her. Where were the legends this year? Where were the John Waynes, the Mickey Rooneys? Even a Lee

Marvin or a Gina Lollobrigida would have done. They'd all been presenters in the past. This year there was a tired line-up of plastic soap stars from the States — no doubt they were considered 'superstars' by the organisers and the public, but as far as Edwina was concerned, they weren't in the same league as the legends. And 'The Glitter Game' was doing better than all the US series put together.

'You must be ecstatic.' Another girlish giggle and the woman backed nervously away. She was out of her league and she knew it. Edwina felt a flash of sympathy for her as she stepped forward to the podium.

Her acceptance speech was short but not brusque, gracious but not patronising and grateful but not humble. She knew she looked good. Her black hair gleamed, swept up and away from the flawless face. George Gross had done a good job on the gown — it clung to her tall, lean body, a picture of elegance.

There was another burst of applause as Edwina left the stage and the MC walked into the spotlight to plod his way to the commercial break.

Edwina froze. A woman had risen to block her path.

'Congratulations, Edwina.' Even with all the lights now trained on the stage, Liza's prematurely silver hair gleamed and her black eyes shone with a hatred that was tangible. 'I wondered whether I might have a word with you in the commercial break.'

Edwina stood her ground and returned the cold smile. 'I'll send Davey to the foyer. He'll be only too happy to relay any message you may have, Liza. Excuse me.' Edwina swept past Liza and returned to her table.

Liza was seething with fury. Send that bloody little poofter hairdresser! Well, she'd give him a message to relay, all right. She stormed off to the foyer.

Behind her, the MC addressed the audience. 'Ten minutes to do the necessaries, folks, then up on applause when we return from commercial break for the Ron Goddard Dance Team.' There was a thin, perfunctory round of applause as people sprang from their seats and made for powder rooms and toilets.

Jane, Narelle and Mandy offered their hasty congratulations en route to the ladies but Sidney and Davey remained, rising slightly from the table as Edwina sat down.

Sidney's bladder was bursting but sycophancy outweighed his need to relieve it. 'Well done, Edwina, well done.' The fruity voice of the old actor was thick with alcohol and, as usual, flecks of spittle shot out from between his Terry-Thomas teeth. Edwina didn't even flinch as one caught her on the neck.

She picked up her glass of Veuve. 'Thank you, Sidney.' Disgusting old ham, she thought. How in hell could the viewers find him funny? But they did. There was no accounting for taste — well, certainly, not in television. Davey again reached for her hand under the table. She smiled gently at him, then remembered.

'Liza Farrelly wants to have a word with you in the foyer.'

'Oh.'

'Go on, Davey. And don't be long. I want you seated before we're back to air.'

As Davey rose from the table, Sidney took the opportunity to stagger to his feet as well. 'If you'll excuse me, Edwina.'

'Of course, Sidney.'

'Knockout, Edwina!' Edwina looked across at the table where the younger members of the 'Glitter' cast were sitting. Seventeen-year-old Vicky was giving her the thumbs-up. Edwina gave a barely discernible thumbs-up sign back. She liked the kid — she was a hard worker and a damn good actress. Then she noticed Paul and Alain standing beside Vicky. Alain nodded effusively and made a 'mind-if-I-join-you' gesture. Hypocrite, Edwina thought, but smiled and nodded back. At least Paul wasn't being hypocritical. He glared balefully at her and turned his back. She respected him for that — not that he didn't deserve what she'd done to him, but she respected him nonetheless.

Davey hadn't returned to his seat before they were back to air. In fact the dance team had been and gone, two awards had been made and the industry vote of Best Actress was about to be announced when he slid back into his seat, his face ashen.

Edwina shot him a look of reprimand.

'Sorry.'

'People performing, Davey. It's rude,' she muttered.

'And the Best Actress is . . . '

During the dramatic pause Edwina noticed how sick Davey looked. 'There's something wrong, isn't there?'

' . . . Edwina Dawling!'

'No, nothing.' Davey rose and assisted her to her feet.

Once again, Edwina led the spotlight to the stage, accompanied by tumultuous applause.

Again her acceptance speech was brief and dignified but her mind was on Davey. She kept glancing in his direction, but she couldn't see a thing against the glare of the television lights. After leaving the stage, she ignored the smiles and congratulations and made her way straight back to the table to slide in beside Davey.

'What is it? What's wrong? You look terrible.'

Her concern for Davey had not gone unnoticed. But then her concern for Davey never had. Their relationship was one of the unfathomable mysteries of the entertainment world. If Edwina had been an all round 'fag hag' that would have been totally acceptable but her general manner towards homosexuals was as gracious and aloof as it was to everyone else in the industry. Sure, as her personal hairdresser Davey did a great job, but a hairdresser was a hairdresser, surely. One journalist tried to intimate that he was her younger brother but investigation had failed to turn up a thing. It was a mystery, all right.

'Nothing's wrong, Edwina — just the smoke, that's all.' Davey edged Sidney's butt-filled ashtray complete with smoking cigarette to one side.

'What did Liza want?'

'The usual bitchy stuff.' Davey's answer was evasive. 'Why you're ditching the series to go to CBS. She wants to see you after the show.'

'She should chat to Alain. He'd love to twist the knife too.'

Sidney had fumbled around for the ashtray but failed to find it so he lit up another cigarette and started ashing in Davey's sideplate.

'He wants to talk to me after the show,' Edwina continued. 'He'll try it on again, of course.'

But Davey was miles away. 'Who? What?'

'Alain. Another plea to throw the CBS deal. After the show.'

'Let's not talk to any of them, Edwina. Let's leave straight after the Gold.'

Edwina shook her head. 'Appearances, Davey. We'll stay till the end but we'll leave after the obligatory chats, I promise.'

The MC droned on, more awards were presented, including that for the Best TV Series which Alain accepted for 'The Glitter Game', and the audience grew restless with anticipation as the Gold drew near. Then, finally . . .

' . . . the Gold Logie for the Most Popular Television Personality in Australia . . . '

Edwina darted a glance at Davey but he wasn't looking at her.

' . . . *and the winner is* . . . '

Edwina was suddenly aware that she was holding her breath. She'd taken it for granted that she'd win the Gold but now, this instant, she realised how much she wanted it. She wanted it desperately.

' . . . *Edwina Dawling*!'

As Edwina rose to her feet, so did the entire audience. The standing ovation gave her time to regain her composure. As she started walking slowly towards the stage, applause thundering in her ears, she glanced around the tables. This third walk to the podium seemed to take forever and she could distinguish every face at every table she passed, despite the spotlight that followed her every move.

She'd been wrong, of course. There were some who did bear her ill will, and from the sea of smiling faces she could single out the four who most certainly had reason to. She could feel their hatred as she passed. Jane, her brittle smile frozen. Alain, trying to dredge up the enthusiastic bonhomie that always clinched his deals but with eyes as dead as a shark's. Paul, not even attempting to hide his loathing. And Liza, waiting beside the stage with an expression that was strangely gloating. Edwina experienced a chill of fear. Something about the woman unsettled her.

Too late to worry about that now. The stage lights hit her and she turned to face the sea of people. Flashbulbs popped and the moment was hers.

Little did she or anyone else know that the night would spell disaster . . . that in a matter of hours the industry would never be the same again.

Narelle

Narelle was born in a dingy little house in a dingy little street in a dingy little suburb with a pretty name. Strawberry Hills. No vestige of its rural colonial days remained, no picturesque historical farmhouses — even the pocket-sized playground, dwarfed by four blocks of council flats and laughingly referred to as 'the park', had been bituminised by a council with an antipathy to anything green.

Strawberry Hills was an inner-city suburb of Sydney. Strawberry Hills was a disgrace. But Narelle didn't mind. Narelle was happy. Narelle would have been happy anywhere.

There had always been something about Narelle. The nurses at the hospital where she was born thought so. Her mother, Charmane, thought so, as she accepted the blue ribbon for Narelle's first baby show. Her father, Norman, thought so too — at first. Four years later, when every penny he'd earned had been spent on interstate trips to baby shows, he wasn't so happy. A further four years later when he was up to his ears in debt for ballet classes, acting lessons and child modelling courses, he left, swearing if there hadn't been 'something' about Narelle this would never have happened.

Charmane barely noticed that Norman had gone.

If she did, it was only to comment on how peaceful things were without him. Besides, he really wasn't necessary any more. The courses were paying off and Narelle's modelling jobs were bringing in enough to cover the classes and the constant need for a new wardrobe.

So what was the 'something' Narelle had? She was beautiful, certainly. Naturally blonde, fluffy hair, huge blue eyes, porcelain skin — but there were hundreds of beautiful little girls in the modelling game. No, everyone agreed that there was an added something in Narelle. Besides the natural innocence of the child, there was a sort of . . . loving glow. Many other children who were products of 'stage mothers' were either irritatingly precocious or painfully shy. Not Narelle. She remained unaffected, even when Charmane was at her pushy best.

Narelle retained her childlike innocence throughout adolescence. So much so that Charmane began to worry just a little. Was Narelle perhaps simple? Her school marks were a little below average but the only criticism that came from the teachers was that perhaps Narelle could pay a little more attention in class. Even they had fallen under her spell.

She matured early and at fifteen was indeed a great beauty, with a body just a little too full and sensual for a successful haute couture model. A horrified Charmane tried to put Narelle on a crash diet but she declined very gently.

'I'd much rather act and do photographic work, Mum. Really. And I can probably earn us more money that way.'

She was right. A series of television commercials for mineral water made her a household body and her face had already adorned the covers of several magazines when her agent rang and told her she was to test for a new daytime soap.

'Flash trash it is, sweetheart. Tons of nudity.' Narelle liked the sound of that. She was fond of her body and the thought of sharing it with others appealed to her. 'Do you think your mother would agree?' Barry asked.

'Oh yes,' Narelle nodded happily. 'She won't mind.'

Narelle was seventeen by this time and Charmane had been nagging her for several years about the youths who constantly dogged her trail. 'You've got a wonderful career ahead of you, Narelle. Don't you dare go throwing it away on some horny little no-hoper.'

She'd even taken the girl to the family planning clinic and had her put on the pill just in case. She needn't have worried. Narelle always did as she was told. Her only disobedience was in not taking the pill. She'd heard it could put weight on and she knew that would really worry her mother.

Charmane's bid to have the compulsory nudity clause withdrawn from Narelle's contract was really only a token gesture. It was what every good mother would do. But when the series producer, the director, the network spokesman and the agent all pointed out that any nudity scenes would be very tastefully handled and that the nudity clause was mandatory anyway, she was quick to see their point.

Narelle became a daytime soap sex symbol. Her many and varied nude scenes were not handled in any particularly tasteful manner but it didn't seem to matter. Sensual and at times erotic they may have been, but they were never offensive. It was the 'something' Narelle had that saved them. In fact the only complaint the network received was from a representative of the Sound and Light Committee who accused them of corrupting innocence by exposing a trusting young girl to the masses in such a way. It was this same representative who waited outside the staff entrance of the studios each taping day and presented Narelle with a red rose.

What no one realised was that Narelle enjoyed her sex scenes. She revelled in them. Surely they were the next best thing to making love. Charmane had told her not to jeopardise her career. No sex. It had never occurred to Narelle to disobey. This way she was keeping everyone happy.

She did experience one jarring moment with a new young leading man. He was a male model, a woeful actor, and it was his first sex scene. Narelle ascribed his obvious tension to this fact, and tried especially hard to take his mind off things.

'Tell her to leave my dick alone, will you!' Marcus snapped as he jumped out of bed and bumped into Camera Two.

Narelle was stunned. Usually the actors loved it. So much so that they stayed in bed for five minutes after the scene so nobody would notice how much. To the delight of the crew, she hopped out of bed and stood naked and tearful before Marcus.

'But I thought you'd like . . . '

'Well I don't! I don't like you touching me at all. And certainly not on the dick!' And he flounced off. The new director, a kindly middle-aged man who'd just left the ABC and wasn't yet used to daytime soap, gestured to the first assistant for a dressing gown.

'Don't worry, Narelle. Get dressed before you catch cold.'

'Oh. Yes. All right.'

From that moment, every actor cast opposite Narelle had a thorough check run on his sexual proclivities, and homosexuals were barred.

'Passionate Possession' ran for two years before the network decided to kill it. Not that it was unsuccessful. To the contrary, it was rating extremely well but it was much cheaper to run an American soap, purchased as part of a package deal, and make up the mandatory Australian content with sports programmes to which all Australians were addicted.

This was the first of life's bitter blows to be dealt to Narelle. The second happened concurrently. During the final week of taping Charmane died.

It was an ignoble death but it made the headlines and Charmane would have loved that. Bereaved Soap Sex Goddess: Mother Dead. Charmane's life had not been in vain.

It was touching really. Charmane had had a headache that day and had been trying to lift the television upstairs so that she could watch 'Passionate Possession' in bed. She'd never missed an episode. When Narelle heard her mother had broken her neck falling down the stairs of their new harbourside home, she was distraught. She finished the show like a true professional, but refused to go to the wrap party.

It was only a matter of a few weeks before a strange thing happened to Narelle. Deprived of her mother, she sought parental influence elsewhere. Particularly from men. And with gentle guidance, she found that sex needn't interfere with her career at all. In fact, channelled discreetly and in the right direction, it could even enhance her career.

★

It was during one of her fortnightly afternoons with her agent that the subject of 'The Glitter Game' came up.

She'd perched on his office desk, legs apart the way he liked it, swivelled his chair around and given him the customary neck massage. Then it was just a case of pretending to take him by surprise. She quietly knelt down in front of him, unzipped his trousers, eased his swollen penis out and gently engulfed it in her mouth. It didn't take long. It never did.

It was Narelle who'd initiated the oral sex. It meant she didn't have to kiss him. Barry always smelt of cigarettes and Narelle hated cigarettes. She was very fastidious. Anyway, she didn't mind. Barry was a nice man and he liked her doing it. Sometimes she fantasised and played with herself. Barry liked that even more.

He let out a strangled moan and slumped back in the chair. When Narelle returned from the bathroom, he was zipped up and leafing through a mass of files as if nothing had happened. He always did that.

'Take that home.' Barry handed her three pages of script. 'And study it backwards. You're testing next week.'

' "The Glitter Game". What is it, Barry? Another soap?'

'Not *another* soap, sweetheart, *the* soap. In fact it's probably a dirty word to even call it a soap. It's prime time, they're not making a pilot and they think they've already got a presale to the UK on the strength of Edwina Dawling's album.'

'Edwina Dawling!'

Barry nodded. 'She's all signed up. This is the big

one, kid. And The King's producing so you're half way there already.'

Alain King had produced 'Passionate Possession' for Channel 10 and had recently been signed up as Head of Drama for Network Three. His appointment had been considered quite a coup. He knew his television market and had never had a series flop on him yet — his Midas touch had earned him the title of 'The King'.

Narelle remembered Alain, all right. He'd put the hard word on her very early in the piece during 'Passionate Possession'.

'You have your first lovemaking scene coming up, Narelle,' she remembered him saying after he'd told her to strip in the privacy of his office. ('We want to make sure the director knows your best angles, don't we dear?') Then the gentle persuasion that she should rehearse with him ('We'll call it research, shall we?'), so that she wouldn't feel shy during the actual taping. It had taken all of Narelle's considerable diplomacy to dissuade him without offending. Of course, this had been in Charmane's time when Narelle obeyed her mother's ban on sex.

Things were different now and Barry didn't know how right he was. She was far more than halfway there. For a plum role in a prime time big budget series starring Edwina Dawling Narelle would allow Alain King all the research he wanted.

And she did. The following week, during her test at the Channel 3 studios, Narelle lingered over Alain's welcoming embrace, wriggling her breasts against his shirt front and thrusting her groin as close as possible to his without drawing too much attention from the others present.

'Narelle, you know Jim Avalon.' Alain's lust was

palpable as he broke the clinch and turned towards the pleasant-looking man beside him. 'And, of course, Chris Natteros, who'll be directing.' Alain sat down and crossed his legs while Jim and Chris kissed Narelle warmly on the cheek. She was glad to see them. Jim had been on-line producer on 'Passionate Possession' and Chris had directed the pilot episode. She liked them both.

Narelle tested well. Each of the three men was well aware that she was not a great talent, but she had 'something' that could not be ignored. What was it about Narelle? As they watched her, Chris, a happily married father of three, denied himself a sexual desire but found himself wanting to cuddle and protect her nevertheless. Alain, fighting to keep his erection under control, was bemused by the fact that she still had this effect on him. After all she was twenty now and he normally set his sights at around sixteen, younger if possible. Even Jim, a successfully closet homosexual who lived with a woman for appearances only, found himself wanting to stroke her hair and touch her skin. But then Narelle had always had that effect on him.

Narelle was blissfully aware of the attraction in the air, particularly the effect she was having on Alain. And she responded to it. She didn't gloat over the power she had, she delighted in it.

After the test, Alain asked her to stay and talk over the role with him while the others took their lunch break. Chris and Jim exchanged looks. Alain wasn't usually quite as obvious as this. But they left discreetly.

Narelle was not a devious person. Anything other than the direct approach never occurred to her and she had the top three buttons of her blouse undone by the time the studio door closed.

'Research, Alain?'

Alain was breathing too heavily to reply. The role was hers.

Jane

Jane couldn't remember much about her childhood. Oh, she supposed she could if she tried but she never bothered. It had been comfortable enough — middle class, pleasant parents, an innocuous younger brother.

Her mother still rang her from Brisbane every November. 'Are you coming home for Christmas, dear?' And every second or third year Jane would agree. But it was a perfunctory offer to keep up parental appearances and a perfunctory acceptance to maintain the status quo. Neither Jane nor her family had anything left in common. In fact they'd had very little in common since Jane's tenth birthday when she'd realised that all she wanted in life was to be an actress. Her father had agreed to send her to drama school, but very reluctantly. He couldn't understand the theatre.

So, Jane had left for Sydney, aged seventeen. Three years later she had graduated from drama school with above-average passes and managed to find herself an above-average agent who helped her land her first understudy job in an above-average theatre. It all looked very promising. But life in the theatre proved to be not quite that simple. One good job didn't necessarily lead to another.

Perhaps now, though, four years down the track, perhaps now was the time for her breakthrough. Stardom was just around the corner. Jane nibbled at a piece of smoked salmon on rye bread. Quite a step up from sardines on toast. Sardines and baked beans. She must have eaten out several supermarkets over the years. Then there was the weekly treat when she got the lust for meat. Lamb spare ribs. Well, that's what she called them. To other people they were lamb flaps chopped up and baked to a crisp. Other people bought them for their dogs.

And her dressing room. Jane looked around her at the leather sofa, the walk-in wardrobe and the en suite bathroom. My God, she could fit three of the succession of bedsits that she had lived in into this space. And carpet! She wriggled her bare toes in the plush pile and grinned to herself. No looking back now, kid, this is definitely the big time!

But she did look back. She looked back at the succession of auditions and rejections. She looked back at the thrill of landing her first understudy job. She looked back at her first role in the theatre. What was it? A maid? No, that was the second role. Somebody's little sister. And she could still feel the surge of jubilation when her agent had rung and said, 'Good news! You got the job at the Royal. Start rehearsals on . . . '. She couldn't remember the rest.

Of course it hadn't continued. There had been more auditions, more screen tests, more unfulfilled promises. What about that test for *Marching Song*? A big-budget telemovie, and she was perfect for the role of 'Dido' — but her agent hadn't put her up for it. ('You're too inexperienced, Jane, they only want people with a track record.')

Bugger that, she thought. She'd crashed the audition anyway. It was a cattle call. There were fifty actresses, and they hadn't even had the grace to read them separately. Herded together in one big studio, they'd had to get up and spout the words in front of each other. Half the girls only got a dozen words out before, 'Thank you, that's fine. Next.' Pigs. But she'd got through. They cut the numbers down to ten and they made them go through it all over again. Six girls, including Jane, were called back two days later. This time the director worked with each of them individually before they were called on to perform before the producer.

A week later, there was another call-up. It was down to three. After two hours' solid work one girl burst into tears when she was told she was out. Down to two. 'Report back next Tuesday for screen testing.'

As Jane was about to leave, the director took her aside. 'Cut your hair,' he whispered.

'What?'

'Cut your hair. I want you for the part but Merv (producer) reckons Dido should look boyish and he's so goddamn thick he won't be able to visualise it from the test.'

'But . . . '

'Do it and the part's yours.' A conspiratorial wink and she was ushered out the door.

Jane had refused to have her hair cut since she was twelve years old. Her proud boast was that she could sit on it even when it was plaited. And it had taken her nearly eight years to get it that long.

Off it had come and the test went brilliantly. Another private wink from the director when the two girls were informed they'd know next week. Jane had felt triumphant when she told the agent that she was the director's choice. ('See, you wouldn't put me up for it, you silly bitch, and look what's happened. Me, out of fifty!' But she didn't say that, of course.)

A week later the girls were told, all right, or rather the agents were. They were told that neither of them had the role. The producer had decided that he wanted a 'name' after all.

That had been four years ago. Jane had kept the plait. It sat in the bottom of a suitcase of souvenirs on top of the wardrobe.

It was back to the bit parts, back to the understudying. And the actresses she understudied were always so damn healthy! Her big break certainly wasn't going to come that way.

Then she'd landed 'Laura'. It was a role she'd always wanted. *The Glass Menagerie* was her favourite Tennessee Williams play and she knew she was good. Of course it was only fringe theatre but it was good fringe and surely someone would see her. And someone did. Kate.

Tall and leggy, with flaming red hair, Kate looked more like a model or an actress than a director. But a director she was, and one of the best. In fact Pentameter Productions had allowed her carte blanche in casting their big-budget production of Peter Wainwright's latest play and even acquiesced to her insistence that a non-commercial actress be given the lead.

'Peter's name alone will guarantee bums on seats,' was her argument. 'He's the hottest playwright in the country. And this is the role of the decade. We need a fresh face.' The producers gave in when she promised them a piece of the movie action. 'Peter's already started on the screenplay. We should create a new star, from stage to screen.'

And so Kate had commenced the fringe theatre rounds. She liked discovering talent that way. General auditions were suspect to her. She'd been caught out a couple of times in her early directorial days by actors who'd polished up their set show pieces immaculately only to fall apart when they had to start on a new role from rock bottom.

Jane was only one of fifteen actresses that Kate had 'discovered'. She'd systematically read ten of them for the role, then stopped. Jane's was the tenth reading and Kate knew she need look no further. Never one to mince words, she'd told the stage manager to call it a day and asked Jane to follow her to the theatre production office.

Kate closed the door behind them, gestured for Jane to sit down and slung a denim-clad leg over the corner of a desk. She picked up a copy of the play and dumped it in Jane's lap. 'It's his best yet, you know.'

Jane looked down at the play then back up at Kate who seemed to tower above her. Did the woman always move this quickly? Did this mean she was giving Jane the role? What had happened to the normal channels — the phone calls to the agent, the endless seeded auditions? No part was ever won this quickly. And certainly not the lead in a big commercial production of a Peter Wainwright play. Virtual unknowns never got so much as a look-in for such a role.

Kate seemed to read her mind. 'It's yours. Take it home and read it. It's an actor's dream.'

'But . . . '

'I'll ring your agent with all the details and you'll have a contract by the end of the week.'

Jane still couldn't believe it. 'But, Miss Redman . . .'

'Kate. The name's Kate.' Her chiselled features softened as she smiled warmly and leaned forward to put a hand on Jane's shoulder. 'I'm moving too fast for you, aren't I? But don't worry, Jane. I'm not going to change my mind. The role is yours and you're going to be wonderful.' The voice was gentler now as her hand began to caress Jane's shoulder. 'This part is made for you. You have a wonderfully sensitive quality. Sensitive, but still strong, defined — that's what I'm looking for. And your looks . . . ' She pushed Jane's black shoulder-length hair from her face. 'Your looks are perfect.'

Jane sat frozen to her chair. Oh God, no. So that was the catch. A dyke director. It didn't even cross Jane's mind to play the game back. What would be the point? A quick fuck and the role would go to someone else anyway. The sick feeling in her stomach started turning to anger. At least she could give this dyke bitch the lesson she deserved.

Kate was practically purring as she stroked Jane's cheek. 'Classical, great face for film. Peter's writing the screenplay and we —'

Jane jumped to her feet, pushing Kate's hand away so forcefully that the woman had to clutch at the desk to keep her balance.

'That's going a bit far isn't it? If I was going to fuck you for the part you didn't need to throw the movie in too.'

Kate heaved a patient sigh and rose slowly from the desk. 'Jane . . . '

But there was no stopping Jane now. 'How bloody gullible do you think I am? You do the rounds of fringe theatre and think every actor you see will jump into bed at the merest hint of a good job. I've been in this business four years and I've done quite well so far minus the obligatory fucks with directors who think they're tin gods and if you . . . '

'Yes, I've checked your track record. It's not unimpressive. We're certainly not after an untrained actor, just one without a high commercial profile.'

Jane was a little taken aback by Kate's mild, unoffended reaction. Still she'd done it now — there was no backing out. She might as well give herself an exit line. 'So if I haven't had to screw directors in the past, why should I start with a bitch dyke like you!?'

She had the door half open when the peal of laughter from behind compelled her to turn back.

Kate was sitting on the desk again and looked genuinely amused. 'OK, OK. I've learned my lesson. Pity. It could have been fun, but it's certainly not essential.' She bent down and picked up the script that had fallen to the floor at the outbreak of Jane's explosion. Jane remained frozen, her anger spent, as Kate crossed to the door, script held out like a peace offering. 'Take it. It's yours.'

After that incident, Kate and Jane developed an understanding. Their mutual respect for each other's work led to a friendship of sorts, although Jane, with her rigid standards, could never understand how Kate could mix business with pleasure. And the more Jane kept her at arm's length, the stronger Kate's attraction became. Not that there was any great drama involved — she'd laugh when Jane knocked back yet another pass.

For a short time it had given Jane food for thought. This sort of thing had happened before. What the hell was it about her that lesbians seemed to find so attractive? She wasn't particularly 'butch' –

so why had she always been so attractive to women? Then she'd shrugged it off — there wasn't time to worry about it. Rehearsals were well under way.

Not that Jane was asexual. Far from it. She'd had her share of affairs and one-night stands. There'd even been two men in her life who'd started to mean something but she'd rapidly got rid of them when the relationship started to interfere with her career. She still experienced the odd twinge of regret on a Sunday afternoon walk through the park when she witnessed the couples embracing, but it never lasted long.

This role was the biggest break of her career. It was hardly the time to get introspective about her sexuality. Every ounce of energy had to be channelled into her work. There was no way she'd put this God-given chance at risk. And she didn't.

After the dress rehearsal, Kate Redman and Peter Wainwright agreed that the girl was good, very good — even star material. If the play was a hit and they got the go-ahead for the movie, Jane was made.

The play was a hit. Another major success for Peter Wainwright and rave reviews for Jane.

Peter had completed the screenplay, brokers were seeking investment and there was already talk of setting a preproduction date on the movie.

Yes, everything seemed assured as Jane looked around at her theatre dressing room and yet again luxuriated in the surroundings. She'd got used to the trappings and she intended to keep them that way. Surely a hit stage show followed by a smash movie would assure her of ongoing success. But still there was a cynical little voice somewhere saying, 'Oh yeah?'. Then something happened that changed it all, and Jane had to make the biggest decision of her life.

The play had two weeks left to run. It was a Thursday night, one of those rare nights when the audience was thin. They usually played to capacity audiences but Thursdays were always a bit slow. It was late night shopping on Thursdays. Nevertheless it hadn't been a bad performance. Jane was halfway through taking her make-up off when there was a knock at her dressing room door.

The stage doorman popped his head in. 'A Mr Avalon to see you.'

'Oh.' Jane didn't know any Mr Avalon. Probably some stage door creep. 'OK, show him in.' She gave Sam the special nod that meant 'Stay by the door', in case she needed help getting rid of the man.

'Miss Richmond.' A tall mild-mannered man, not unlike Clark Kent complete with glasses, extended his hand to her. 'My name's Jim Avalon. I'm presently producing a television series with Alain King for Channel 3.'

Avalon. Jim Avalon. Of course she knew the name. He was a highly successful television producer and he'd worked with Alain King on a number of series. As Avalon continued, Jane couldn't believe her ears. Mr King would like to see her. The King! The King wanted to see her with a view to one of the leads in his new drama series. Jane's heart skipped its customary number of beats whenever a breakthrough role appeared. Then she checked herself. What the hell was she getting excited about? Old habits certainly died hard. Here she was in a hit play, with a movie about to get off the ground and she was getting clammy hands at the mention of a television soap. Sure, Avalon was calling it a drama series, but wasn't that what all producers called their crummy little soaps? It was probably a daytime one at that.

Nevertheless she agreed to the interview. 'Tomorrow morning at ten. Fine.' Well, an interview wouldn't do any harm, surely. And you never knew when The King might come in handy for the future. Even the top actors filled in time with soap.

'So, what do you think, Jane?' She was seated in Alain's office together with Jim Avalon and the director Chris Natteros and now The King was nodding encouragingly at her from the other side of his huge mahogany desk.

'I think the concept of the series and the role both sound fine, Mr King, but . . . '

'Alain.' Again the boyish conspiratorial smile, but there was something behind the eyes that she felt she couldn't trust.

'Alain. It's just that they're getting a movie together of Peter Wainwright's script. I've been offered the lead, and with the play having been such a hit . . . ' She shrugged. Surely she had said it all — but no, The King was shaking his head sympathetically.

'Oh Jane, Jane. A flash in the pan. One hit play . . .' A dismissive gesture. 'And as for "getting a movie together". Come on, now. You're a smart girl, you know the business better than that. How many movies are planned and never get off the ground? And even if they do get up, how many end up on the back row of the video shelves after one showing?'

'But Peter —'

'Even if they are Peter Wainwright scripts.' Now came Alain's pet theme and he was sure of his ground as he leant forward over the desk, his eyes boring into Jane's. 'It's the brain drip system Jane. You need to be in people's lounge rooms every week,

29

fifty-two weeks a year for three years — that's what makes you a star. Then if you want to go into theatre or the movies, you click your fingers and they all come running.'

Chris and Jim exchanged a look. They'd seen Alain in action before. He won every time. But to their surprise Jane's voice was firm and decisive as she replied.

'I'm sure you're right, Alain, but the movie would be a starring role and I really don't want to let it go.'

There was a few seconds of silence before Alain turned to the other two men. 'Jim, Chris, I wonder if you'd mind leaving us for a few minutes. I'd like to have a little chat alone with Jane.'

At the door, Chris raised an eyebrow at Jim. Surely she wasn't Alain's type and there was no way she'd be in it anyway. Jim gave a barely perceptible shake of the head in return. No, Alain was going to pull a Svengali on her and Jim had never known him to fail, although the girl was certainly tough.

The door closed. Jane waited expectantly. The man seemed deep in thought. Actually Alain was wondering whether he should sit back behind the desk which was deliberately placed with the light behind him so that it was difficult for the interviewee to see his face, thus making him a figure of authority. But no, he decided, this should be a paternalistic approach. He circled the desk and sat in the seat beside Jane's.

'Jane . . . ' His brow was furrowed and his voice concerned. 'This series has presold to the UK on the strength of Edwina Dawling's name alone.'

'So you said.' Jane was confused. Why the worry? 'It can't fail after the overseas success of her album.'

'Ah yes, her album. But what other credits has she got?'

'But she's . . . '

'Oh sure.' Alain was way ahead of her. 'She's one of the most popular on-air personalities in the country. But as an actress, Jane. As an actress! She's never acted in her life before.'

Jane waited. What was the man getting at? They needed a few trained backup actors to boost a non-talent star? What a hell of an argument that was. No, she'd take the movie, thanks.

Alain leaned forward and took Jane's hand. It wasn't a forward gesture but a desperate bid to communicate. 'I intend to get this series off the ground on her name but I need to build another star alongside her. A strong actress, an actress who can take over as the pivotal star of the series. Then we drop Edwina and she can go back to her records and we keep you, Jane. You're our star.'

Alain took a deep breath as he rose to his feet. It was exhausting being genuine and he'd meant every word he'd said. Jim would pick a bloody actress who was proving difficult, wouldn't he? But Jim said the girl was brilliant and Jim was invariably right. Jim had been right too when he'd suggested they'd need strong acting talent to back up not only Edwina but Narelle. What Jim didn't know was that Alain already intended to dump Edwina. He wanted stars he could manipulate, stars that he'd created. Edwina was too powerful.

Alain picked up an armload of scripts from the desk. 'These are the first five blocks. Have a good look at the part of Paulina. You'll see where the build starts in the fifth block, episode ten. She takes over as Head of Drama in episode twenty which isn't here, of course, but the storylines are already finished.' Indeed, Evan Ryan, the executive writer, had been mystified as to why Alain insisted on such featured storylining for a supporting role but Alain had explained it with, 'Conflict, for God's sake, Evan, conflict!' And Alain had been proven to know best.

Jane read the scripts that night after she got home from the theatre, then lay awake for hours tormenting herself with indecision. Damn it, she had to sleep — it was matinee day tomorrow. But as the scripts and the characters whirled through her brain, she knew that Alain was right. Edwina Dawling's role of Christine started in the series as the all-powerful Head of Drama within the fictitious network. By the tenth episode, the strongly feminist Christine was vying for the position of general manager. It was obvious that if, in future storylines, the character were to be promoted, she was destined to disappear in network bureaucracy. This would leave Jane's role, Paulina, already second in line, to come through the ranks and take over as Head of Drama where all the action was. Alain hadn't been lying. How ironic that the star character in the series held the same position as Alain himself did at Channel 3. Jane wondered whether it was deliberate. Yes, of course it was. After all, 'The Glitter Game' was his baby.

It was between the matinee and the evening performance that Jane rang Kate and Peter. They were so shocked that they insisted on taking her out to supper to talk her out of it but she was adamant. She would complete the present season but, in the event that the movie went straight into production, she wasn't available. She was joining forces with The King and signing up with Channel 3 for twelve months.

Paul

'No way! The man can't control his cock.'

Jim Avalon heaved an inward sigh. This was great, coming from Alain.

'We need him, Alain.' A mild plea from Chris Natteros.

Jim gritted his teeth and waited for the explosion. Chris should have known better.

It was a slow-fuse explosion but an explosion nevertheless. Alain rose slowly and threateningly from behind his office desk. 'We don't *need* him, Chris. We don't *need* any actor. They need us.' He had been about to say 'me' but thought better of it at the last minute. 'We make them. We make them or we break them. Don't ever forget that!' His voice had risen a decibel as he leaned across his desk, a megalomaniac gleam in his eyes. 'We never, never *need* them!'

'OK, OK.' Chris backed down. There was no point arguing with Alain when he was infected with his power mania. There was definitely a touch of madness about the man, Chris thought.

Jim came to the rescue, ever the diplomat. 'Of course he's not essential, Alain, but he's a very convenient choice. He's still very popular.'

'Sure. In shopping centres.' Alain sat down again, a dismissive sneer on his face.

'Yes! And don't you see, that's exactly our market!' Jim nodded triumphantly. Chris waited for another outburst but The King was suddenly a captive listener. Jim always knew how far he could push Alain, he also knew how much Alain respected his opinion. 'You can't get into the centres when Paul's booked to make an appearance,' he continued. 'He hasn't lost it, believe me.'

'It's been over a year since his face was on the screen.' Alain still wasn't convinced.

'But he's made non-stop promotional appearances ever since, and that's what we want.' Jim always had the good sense to say 'want', not 'need'. 'We want a familiar actor popular to the general public. We don't want to create a new charismatic star who's likely to overshadow Edwina. At least not until we see how much acting talent she's got.'

Alain was nodding thoughtfully. No, he didn't want a new charismatic star. He already had one in Jane. No point in giving her too much competition too soon. Little did Jim and Chris know that Evan Ryan's storylines, written under protest but nevertheless brilliant, had Jane's character well and truly in the ascendant. He'd sworn Evan to secrecy under the pretext of the damage it would do if future storylines were leaked to the press but, having launched the series on Edwina's name, Alain couldn't wait to get rid of the woman. The prospect appealed to him far more than the normal pleasure of manipulation. He hadn't enjoyed their early negotiations. She was too cool, too remote, too in command of the situation. Edwina was the only performer who had ever given Alain the impression that he was the one being manipulated and he didn't like that one little bit.

Now he looked at Jim and Chris, who were both waiting expectantly for his answer. 'All right. Paul Sorell it is. But you two had better play minders. If his cock gets the better of him again the network's not covering. He's out, and the press can have a field day.'

The girl ripped Paul's underpants down to his knees and giggled delightedly when his penis flipped back and hit her on the chin. She was seated on the dressing room sofa in front of him and now grabbed greedily at his erection and shovelled him into her mouth.

'Mind the teeth!' Paul hissed painfully. God, what had he let himself in for? She'd been to the shopping centre for each of his four scheduled appearances and waited outside his dressing room after every show. She was all of nineteen and he'd tried to resist, he really had. But hell, he was only human. Today, when she'd grabbed him on the cock publicly he'd had to whisk her into the dressing room if only to tell her to stop. But when she'd stripped and stood demandingly before him, what could he do? In actual fact very little — she was only too willing to do it all herself.

Despite his healthy erection (Paul always had a healthy erection) he found her a little off-putting. Paul was proud of his prowess as a lover. He had excellent self-control and liked to take his time. His main pleasure was hearing the woman orgasm at least three times. Then he'd let himself go in an explosion of ecstasy, aware that it had been a job well done.

He withdrew his penis from the girl's mouth and

started to ease her head down onto the cushions. This would have to be one of his rare quickies.

But the girl wedged herself up on one elbow, closely inspecting his erection. 'You've got tissue paper on your dick.' With thumb and forefinger, she painfully pinched a piece of fluff from his knob.

Paul stifled a scream as he gently forced her back on to the sofa and covered her mouth with his own to shut her up. She tasted of chocolate. It was a matter of pride that he make love to her now but she sure as hell wasn't making it easy. And he really must remember to inspect himself after his masturbatory visits to the bathroom, particularly as they were becoming so regular in his attempt to remain faithful to Barbie.

Underneath him, the girl moaned in mock ecstasy. Well, to Paul it was mock. She was really only ecstatic about being fucked by Paul Sorell, not by his performance. Paul felt a grim satisfaction at the moans she'd denied herself by not allowing him to make love to her properly. She gave a howl of orgasmic anguish and Paul allowed himself to let go. A couple of perfunctory thrusts and it was all over. He should have told the girl to go home. He should have made another trip to the bathroom.

The phone rang and the girl lay panting loudly as Paul rose to answer it. It was Mal.

'I think I boobed, old buddy. I just rang home.'

'Oh, shit!'

'Exactly. Barbie said she thought you were with me.'

Behind him, the girl's panting was louder and Paul turned to find her, eyes closed, playing with herself and muttering, 'More, more'. Bloody nymphomaniac, he thought.

'I think you'd better go, honey. I've got a business call here.'

'Oh.' The girl's eyes opened and she gazed at him in disappointment. 'I thought we could ... '

'No. I'm afraid not. Off you go, there's a good girl.'

'But ... '

'Maybe another time.' Over my dead body, he thought, as she started dressing.

'Getting rid of her, are we?' Mal's voice at the end of the line was snide.

'Lay off, Mal. I've been pretty good lately.'

'Not good enough, boyo. You're gonna have to do better than that if you want Barbie to ... '

'OK, OK.' Sometimes Mal overstepped the agent-friend mark, Paul thought. 'Let's keep it to business.' But he knew that it was guilt making him snap. He respected Mal's friendship. He relied upon Mal's friendship.

'All right, business.' Mal wasn't offended. Even over the phone he recognised Paul's guilt. Poor bloke, he thought, he can't help being ruled by his libido and even when he tries to lay off the extra-marital sex, women won't leave him alone. 'Get rid of her and take a seat, Paul. You'll want to hear this one on your own.'

Paul was suddenly nervous. 'Good one or bad one?'

Mal felt a surge of sympathy. Beneath the professional confidence, Paul was so vulnerable. 'Good one, mate. One of the best.'

The girl was dressed and parked by the door as if awaiting a reprieve. Paul gave her a little wave.

'After the show next week?' she called.

'Sure.'

The door closed behind her. He made a mental note to duck out the back way straight after next week's performance. It was his last scheduled appearance anyway.

'OK.' He sat down. 'What is it?'

'Big new series for Channel 3. It's been kept under wraps till now. Already sold to the UK.'

'Presale? Without a pilot?'

'Yep.'

'How come?'

'Edwina Dawling's playing the lead.'

'Shit!'

'Precisely. And guess who's playing opposite her?'

'Who?'

'You, mate, that's who! Edwina Dawling and Paul Sorell!'

Ten minutes later, when Paul put the phone down he couldn't remember much of his conversation with Mal. Edwina Dawling . . . A twelve month contract . . . The King!

The King wanted him! He couldn't believe it. Alain King had sworn he'd never work with Paul again. That awful business with the sixteen-year-old girl during the run of 'Family and Lovers'. She'd been playing his daughter — what would the press have made of that! Of course she'd told Paul she was nineteen but they'd never have believed him.

Paul sat down at the dressing table and started tissuing off his make-up. Christ, when he'd started out as a teenage star they'd had chaperones and tutors, and you were brought up to know what was jailbait. Nowadays fifteen-year-olds looked thirty and were allowed to behave accordingly. Too bad if you took them up on it and got caught out.

When the kid's father had threatened to go public, the network had paid out a fortune to keep it from the press. Not as a favour to Paul, of course. His character was the most popular in the series and he was mid-contract — they couldn't afford to lose him. Which was lucky for Paul. Exposure would have meant the end of his marriage and the end of his career. It hadn't altered the situation much when it turned out the kid's father was really her pimp. They still had the photos to prove it and the kid certainly looked sixteen.

Even without the headlines, his career had taken a dive. He'd been sure Alain had put the word around not to use him; he hadn't had a television offer for over a year. Thank God for his loyal fans, who still flocked by the thousands to his personal appearances.

Paul crossed to the sink and washed off the remnants of make-up. Maybe Alain hadn't put the word out, though. After all, here he was wanting Paul for the role of the season. Maybe it had just been one of those runs of bad luck other actors seemed to cop regularly. It had frightened Paul. He hadn't been out of work since the 'Snowy' series had made him one of the first Australian stars at the age of eighteen.

He finished towelling his face, sat down at the dressing table and reached for the Clarins. To hit the downward slide when you were looking forty in the face was midlife crisis with a vengeance. He'd been terrified. Was he over the hill? And was that all the other side had to offer? What else could he do? Acting was all he knew. In fact, he wasn't even too sure about the acting. It was the industry he knew.

He knew how to be a star, he knew how much warmth and charm the public wanted. And he worked diligently: his camera technique was perfect, he took direction, he made sure he got on with the crew and his fellow actors. (Well, there was the rare actress who didn't welcome his attentions.) What more did they want? He'd agonised over it — was Alain wrecking his career, or was it just that he was turning forty? Was he still leading man material, or was he now destined to hang around till his face caved in and he was ideal character casting?

Paul copiously applied the Clarins rejuvenation cream and grinned with relief. No more. It was over. Alain wanted him. He'd turned forty and the other side looked great. He tissued off the excess cream and inspected the face. It was ageing well. The wrinkles were rugged and masculine and not too plentiful. The teeth? He flashed himself a confident grin. Yes, never a problem there. Paul's dental perfection was a trademark; in fact, some were unkind enough to say he abused it. The hair? Well, it was greying around the temples but surely that would be the look they wanted. After all, Edwina was no spring chicken. She had to be in her late thirties, touching forty. Yes, he'd better not have the hair highlighted until he'd checked with the designer, make-up and hair departments. He had a good tan, too, and it was only spring. He'd look great by the time the show was into production.

He stood up and reached for his underpants on the sofa, checking his torso in the mirror as he did. Deep chest, good shoulders, but there was a definite thickening around the waistline. It wouldn't show up in clothes but they'd be bound to want some bare-chested stuff. He'd better start pumping iron as soon as possible.

The drive home from the western suburbs seemed interminable to Paul. He couldn't wait to tell Barbie the news and he dodged the heavy Parramatta Road traffic with an uncharacteristic lack of caution. He took the Hunters Hill turn-off at the Gladesville Bridge and felt the day's tension start to ease as it always did a few blocks from home.

It was a leafy, green suburb with beautiful old stone houses, expensive as all hell — this last year it had been a constant struggle to maintain the mortgage payments but Paul told himself that it was worth it. The store promotions, the TV panel appearances, the product endorsements — all the things he'd once sworn he'd never stoop to — were all worth it. Barbie deserved the best, the kids deserved the best and he'd milk every last reserve of his star status to give it to them.

He turned into the private drive that wound down the hill to the three waterside mansions. Theirs was at the very bottom, its swimming pool jutting out into the harbour. And the house — Paul loved it! Two storeys, five bedrooms of beautiful old ivy-covered sandstone with a spacious balcony overlooking the water.

Jamie was giving the twins a tennis lesson on the grass court beside the pool. He looked good, Paul thought with a surge of pride. At fifteen he looked exactly as Paul had at that age.

Adam and Vanessa had been a surprise pregnancy six years ago. Medical examination showed no reason for their infertility but, after Jamie, it seemed impossible that Barbie and Paul would conceive again. Then out of the blue, twins — just like that. It had certainly saved their foundering marriage. Barbie had taken all she could of Paul's philandering and had been on the brink of walking out. The twins changed all that. During her pregnancy, she and Paul became closer than they'd ever been before. Paul even managed to be faithful to her for the full nine months. Of course there had been the quick hot fuck with the next-door neighbour on her bathroom floor while Barbie was in hospital, but that didn't count. The neighbour's husband was away, Paul's wife was away, they were both as horny as hell — and it was just a form of masturbation, wasn't it? It was only a release.

Paul had honestly tried to curb his sexual appetite, but it wasn't just that temptation was always there and that his libido responded to it — there was something else. Paul had absolutely no moral sense where sex was concerned. His adventures had no relevance whatsoever to his love for Barbie and he could not, in all honesty, understand why they should upset her.

The one thing he had learned, though, was discretion. He had a feeling Barbie still suspected the occasional lapse but, if he was discreet, she was not going to allow it to wreck her marriage. Thank God the studio had covered for him over the sixteen-year-old, though — that one she would never have forgiven.

Vanessa and Adam had seen him and were racing up the hill to meet him at the front door. He got out of the car, lifted them up, one under each arm, and gave them both a resounding kiss on the top of the head.

'Come and play whales, Daddy. Play whales.'

'OK, OK. But I want to talk to Mummy first. You go and hop into your bathers and meet me down at the pool.'

The twins raced inside. Paul waved to Jamie, who was practising his lethal McEnroe serve and then followed the twins into the house.

Barbie was already pouring his Scotch and water. She had given up a successful modelling career when she married Paul, and at thirty-eight she was still a beautiful woman.

'Thanks, honey.' He nuzzled her neck as he took the drink but she didn't nuzzle back as she usually did and she looked a little subdued.

'What's up?'

'I thought you were having lunch with Mal.'

Oh shit! He'd forgotten about the little groupie. 'No, I stayed back in the dressing room to read through a couple of new scripts.' It was glib and flowed off the tongue so easily. 'I spoke to him, though. He rang after he'd phoned here. And wait for it, Barbie doll, wait for . . . !' He put the glass down, struck a leading man pose and flashed the irresistible teeth. 'Just who do you think you see before you?'

Barbie was forced to smile. What could you do with such a disarming peacock? He probably had been reading scripts, she told herself. She was just letting her paranoia get the better of her. 'I give up. Just who do I see before me?'

'Only Edwina Dawling's leading man in The King's new big-budget series, that's who.'

Barbie stared at him, open-mouthed.

Paul dropped the stance and took her by the

hands. 'It's true. A twelve-month contract and it's already sold overseas.'

'Oh Paul!' she shrieked and threw her arms around him. He lifted her off the ground and whirled her about, sending the Scotch glass spinning to the other side of the room.

'We're headed back to the top, honey. Right back to the top.'

He kissed her tenderly. 'Right back where we belong, Barbie Doll.'

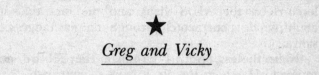

Greg and Vicky

It took Alain no time at all to reach a decision about Greg MacNeil. He didn't even need Jim's suggestion — 'Alain, I've come up with the perfect "Billy" ' — but cut him short with smug satisfaction.

'I know, don't tell me. Greg MacNeil. Get him.'

But with Greg safely contracted, there arose the problem of casting the crucial role of Jodie opposite him. Where did one find a fresh young sixteen-year-old face that would marry well with the eighteen-year-old Latin lover looks of Greg? Not that Greg was eighteen, of course. He was twenty-seven, but the public didn't know that. Just as the public didn't know that the idol of the Australian teenage market was a homosexual and a highly promiscuous one at that. It was one of the best known facts within the industry and one of the best kept secrets out of it. Everyone liked Greg. He was great fun to work with, always sending himself up, professional, efficient and a good actor to boot. Even the gutter journalists saw no reason to threaten his career with 'star's double life' tabloids. Besides, there was no longer any mileage in poofter actor stories.

There had been several incidents at the height of the AIDS scare when actresses had refused to kiss him in the love scenes but Greg himself had quickly rectified that. He collected every bit of information available from the Health Education Department, sat the troubled actresses down and gave them a detailed lecture on the AIDS virus and the fact that it couldn't be contracted through an exchange of saliva.

'Nevertheless, pet, I promise there'll be no tongues.' Hands in the air, a mock-solemn oath. 'No tongues, I swear!'

Needless to say, he won them over every time and spent the next several days assuring the concerned women that yes, he did practice safe sex, and no, he really didn't feel he was at risk.

It was a lie. Greg was secretly terrified. One of his lovers had died of AIDS three years before and although, at the time, Greg's own test was negative, he'd refused to undergo a further one since. If he had the virus he didn't want to know. He was always honest with his lovers, many of whom were in the same situation. They had learned to live with it. They had to.

The only true complication in Greg's life was his family — he'd managed to contain even that complication by simply extending his 'straight' public performance.

An only child, he'd always worshipped his parents and it came as a shock to discover that his 'difference' might be something which would make them ashamed of him. Well, certainly his father. Pat MacNeil was a boxer and a good one. He'd held several titles in his native Scotland and when he came to Australia he opened his own gymnasium and a successful manager/trainer business. His Australian wife, Jill, adored him. A highly capable woman, she ran both the gym and her husband with a firm and loving hand and when their only son was born, their life seemed idyllic. The boy would take over the business and the name MacNeil would become a boxing byword for generations to come.

It was when Greg was ten that he realised he was 'different' and that his father's boxing world was not for him. But he pretended for five years. He worked hard at his father's mandatory training sessions and at fifteen was a worthy sparring partner for Pat's younger protégés.

Just before his sixteenth birthday, Greg stole off and tested for a television series with a schoolmate who'd done two Coca-Cola commercials and knew all there was to know about television. Greg got the part and it was the birth of a successful acting career. The friend made a series of Hungry Jack Hamburger ads and became an insurance salesman.

It was hard telling his father that he wanted to be an actor. Not because he thought Pat would forbid him or try to prevent it, but because of the disappointment Greg knew it would cause. It did, of course. Pat was bitterly disappointed but tried desperately to hide it. What the lad wanted the lad must have and a year later he even put up the deposit for the flat Greg was to share with a fellow actor in the series.

'It's close to the channel, Dad. Saves that bugger of a drive. I'll come home most weekends.'

His father's parting words were, 'Watch out for those poofters, son, there's a lot of them in your business,' and Greg moved in with his first lover just before his seventeenth birthday.

Over ten years later the facade was the same. At least twice a month Greg would go home to Pat and Jill for the weekend, leaving his flamboyance and gay colloquialisms back at the studios. He no longer found it awkward. After all, it was the same butch front he presented to the camera and to the public. He even enjoyed the training sessions at the gym now. As a matter of fact, when the younger, prettier boxers were working out, he enjoyed them very much.

In the meantime, his career flourished — several feature films, a number of award-winning miniseries and now the big, new, internationally sold deal for The King. Greg's future was very secure. He was a little doubtful about the network's decision to find an unknown young actress to work opposite him and had tried to negotiate casting approval in his contract but it was a useless exercise. The King never allowed actors such power. He'd just have to rely on Jim's judgement. It was Jim who'd been assigned to the hunt and only the select few would get through to Alain. Thank God for that, Greg thought. He'd never worked with Jim but his casting judgement was known to be excellent. Brilliant marketing man as Alain was, he tended to cast with his groin when it came to women.

Jim was not having an easy job of it. He agreed with Alain that now they had their commercial stars contracted they should look for a 'real' one. A piece of freak off-the-street casting. A sixteen-year-old star that, a year from now, the network could legitimately claim it had 'made'. But where to look? The character of Jodie was a young rebel, a tough, streetwise kid, and the model and extra agencies didn't have that kind of look on their books. He bumped into one possible, a girl called Sam, who was singing country and western in a Surry Hills coffee basement, but she wasn't really right. True, she was sixteen and there was a rebellious quality about her but she lacked sexuality. She probably led student political rallies and demonstrated for women's rights, Jim thought gloomily. Jodie wasn't that sort of rebel. Nevertheless he lined Sam up for a test and resumed the hunt.

He'd virtually given up when he met Vicky — in the least expected place, of course.

One Saturday afternoon he agreed to go shopping with his flatmate, Sharon, and, after spending a fortune on compact discs at Folkways, she insisted on going for a drink at the pub down the road. The pub down the road was a gay pub and Jim tried to get out of it but Sharon just laughed. She never allowed Jim to take himself too seriously. Theirs was a happy relationship and her sisterly affection was good for him.

He gave a reluctant sigh and followed her into the pub, trying to shake off the uncomfortable feeling that every gay in the bar would recognise him as one of them. He concentrated very hard on his drink and Sharon to avoid eye contact with anyone else and it was only the unexpected female voice from behind the bar that made him look up.

'Same again, two middies? Fosters, was it?'

What was a female bartender doing in a gay pub? Then his eyes met hers. Here was Jodie. How on earth had she conned herself a bar job at all? She couldn't be older than sixteen. And those eyes! Large, framed in jet black lashes, they were the lightest blue. Not icy though — definitely not icy. The sparkle in them was defiant and challenging and held the promise of great sexuality.

'I said, same again!?' Sharon had been so busy talking that she hadn't noticed the girl. Now she paused for a second. 'Oh. Yes, thanks.'

The girl leaned forward, nearly touching noses with Jim. 'And was I right? Was it Fosters?' Now the sparkle was humorous. Maybe she thought his fascination was an instant infatuation, or maybe she'd picked that he was a closet gay hoping to go unrecognised, or maybe it was neither of these. Maybe she was merely amused by his apparent discomfort.

Whatever it was, it wasn't threatening and Jim smiled back. 'Yes, thanks.'

A quick conspiratorial wink and she left. As Jim watched her, he knew how she'd got the job. The self-confidence, the efficiency, the style — she could have been thirty. But no, she was no older than sixteen, Jim was certain. He stood up.

'Excuse me, Sharon.'

'Have you listened to a word I said?'

'No.'

Jim's eyes were upon the girl behind the bar.

Sharon laughed loudly. 'Oh no, love, you've got to be joking!'

She knew he was on a casting crusade, but the little street kid behind the bar! Come on! Sharon took a closer look. Mind you, those eyes . . . She downed the dregs of her beer as she watched him approach the girl.

'I'm producing a new drama series for Channel 3.' Jim proffered his card to the girl who was drawing beer for four glasses and didn't lift her eyes for a second.

'Oh yeah.' There was a perfect half-inch head on each beer as she flicked the handle back.

'Yes. Jim Avalon's the name. I was wondering if I could meet you after work? There's something I'd like to discuss.'

'You wanna make me a star, right?'

Jim was aware of the sarcasm but chose to ignore it and continued in earnest. 'Yes, as a matter of fact. I'm really not trying to —'

But the humour in the steel blue eyes was gone and now they were icy, very icy. And the voice was very loud. 'Trying won't get you anywhere, mister, you've got to make a definite offer. Short time? Long time? All night? Then there's any special —'

'OK, OK, shut up.' He thrust a twenty dollar bill across the bar to her. The girl obligingly shut up and pocketed the note. She served two of the beers to a couple at the end of the bar and returned to shove the other two across the counter to Jim.

'What's your name?' he asked.

'That'll cost you.'

'It just did. What's your name?'

'Vicky.'

'What's happened to the beers?' Sharon had joined them.

Jim handed one to her and continued. 'I'm serious, Vicky. I'm casting a television series and I'd like to see you.'

Vicky had been looking intently from Jim to Sharon and then back again. 'OK, I believe you. When do you want to see me?'

'You believe me? Why?'

'Well, why would you be doing a line? You're gay, aren't you?'

Sharon didn't laugh this time but flicked a look of concern at Jim as he studied his beer unnecessarily closely. That one would have hurt, Sharon thought. No one ever guessed that Jim was gay. She glanced back at the girl. Certainly no hurt had been intended. It had simply been a statement of fact as far as the girl was concerned. But how the hell had she known?

'Would three o'clock Monday afternoon be all right?' Jim took a slug of his beer and looked back at Vicky.

'Sure.'

'Channel 3. The address is on the card. Go to the front reception and they'll direct you to Studio A.'

The girl picked up the card and looked at it. 'OK, Jim.' She grinned back at him.

Jim downed his beer and got to his feet. 'I'll see you Monday.' He left the pub and Sharon had to hurry out after him, leaving her half-finished beer on the bar. That was unlike Jim, she thought.

On Monday, Jim left Vicky alone in the studio for half an hour to study some selected scenes of Jodie's. When he tested her, it was exactly as he'd thought. The kid was a natural. He took her to his office.

'Sit down, Vicky. Tell me a bit about yourself.'

'Which bit do you want to know?'

'How old are you?'

'How old do you want me to be?'

'Jodie's sixteen.'

'So am I.'

Jim congratulated himself. Spot on. He'd always been good at guessing ages. 'So how come you got the barmaid job?'

'She shrugged. 'They wanted me to be eighteen.'

Touché, Jim thought. The kid was quick, defiant and on her guard. But he had a feeling that the tough exterior was purely for protection. The kid was sensual, vulnerable and very young. The kid was Jodie.

'How would you like to be in a television series?'

'I'd give it a go. Something new, anyway.'

Jim decided to leave it at that. She obviously didn't want to talk about herself.

'Right. Well, the executive producer will want to see another test. His name's Alain King. Will tomorrow be all right?'

'Yeah.'

'Eleven o'clock, then — same studio. Greg MacNeil will be reading opposite you. He's playing Billy.'

'Greg MacNeil!' The magnificent eyes shone with excitement. God, the camera was going to love her. 'You're kidding! Greg MacNeil?'

'You're a fan of his, are you?'

'Who isn't! Wow! Unreal!'

Jim couldn't help grinning back. Sixteen? Hell, she could be twelve. 'I'll see you tomorrow, Vicky. And good luck.'

Vicky turned at the door. 'Hey.' Jim waited expectantly as she hesitated. 'I'm sorry if I said the wrong thing the other day. I didn't mean to.'

'Forget it.' He busied himself with a pile of scripts.

'Your secret's safe with me.' He looked up sharply but the returning grin, although cheeky, was sincere. 'I really mean that.'

'I believe you.'

'See you tomorrow, Jim.' And she was gone.

Hyde Park was a mass of spring blossom. The sky was blue and the first bite of a scorching Sydney summer was in the air as Vicky got off the bus and walked back towards East Sydney, but she didn't notice it. Unusual for her. She loved Hyde Park. But now there were too many exciting things to think about. She'd played it cool the whole time with Jim except for the one lapse when he'd mentioned Greg MacNeil. She could kick herself for that. If they wanted a tough street kid, they'd get one — she wouldn't drop the act again. Funnily enough she'd sensed an understanding in Jim. She knew if she ever dropped her guard with him he wouldn't take advantage of her. The others were bound to be sharks though. Don't relax yet, Vicky, she warned herself — not yet, whatever you do.

It was easy for Vicky to play the street kid. She'd been doing it for four years now. After running away from her foster home five times when she was twelve years old, they'd given up looking for her. Never having known her real parents, she'd been fostered out since she was five and, nice as her foster parents were, Vicky had nothing in common with them, just as she had nothing in common with the four other children the couple had fostered. Who the hell wanted to live in Bankstown, anyway? Kings Cross — the seedy centre of the city — beckoned and Vicky ran.

She eventually managed to hide herself away in an East Sydney bedsit, supporting herself with waitressing jobs and learning to avoid the crisis centres, dero hangouts and hookers' beats where the authorities were always on the lookout for runaway kids. She'd managed to scrounge a legitimate living for herself, she'd avoided the drug scene with the exception of the odd marijuana and booze bout, and she had never prostituted herself. Not through any highly moral code but because that was the quickest way to be picked up by the authorities and who the hell wanted to risk AIDS anyway? At thirteen Vicky had figured that prostitution and drugs were for losers.

Not that she was a virgin. She was only fourteen when she discovered that the only way out of a tight corner was to give in.

The Hungarian owner of the coffee lounge around the corner from the old Metro had been the first one. She'd been waitressing there for a week when he asked her to work overtime on Saturday night. He had a group of Hungarian friends coming around for a birthday party and he'd pay double time. Sure, why not? So she closed up at eleven o'clock and waited for the special guests. No such luck. The only Hungarian in sight was the boss waddling towards her, his trousers around his ankles, his huge penis sticking out from under his T-shirt, leading him like a divining rod.

Vicky was frightened. If she managed to push him over it would take him several seconds to untangle the trousers, true, but the door was locked. She'd never get out in time and if he got mad . . .

She tried to brazen it out. 'So where's the birthday party?'

'Here, baby, here.' He put his hand to his groin and waved his penis from side to side. 'You wish me happy birthday, yes?'

What could she do? It didn't take long but it hurt like hell, which pleased the boss even more. She refused to scream, vomit or pass out.

Afterwards, she managed to keep her voice steady as she held her hand out. 'My double time.'

'Sure, baby, sure.' He staggered, still panting, to

the till, counted out her wages and added a further twenty dollars. 'We have another party next Saturday, yes?'

'Sure.'

When she got home to her bedsit she threw up copiously and spent an hour in the bathroom down the hall showering and washing out her bloodied panties.

It had happened to her twice since then. Once with another employer and once in the back of a car when she'd hitched a lift to Bondi Beach to have a swim. Now she always made sure she had the train fare.

It had certainly put her off sex, and from then on she sought jobs in establishments catering to gays. Male gays that is — she had a feeling that rape by some of the hefty bull dykes she'd met around the Cross might be even worse than her previous experiences. Nevertheless it was all grist to the mill and, although it toughened her up, Vicky never thought of herself as a 'street kid'. She was employed, she supported herself, she paid her room rent in advance and, although she never planned too far ahead, she knew that one day things would happen for her. It was just a case of being in the right place at the right time.

And this was obviously it. All she had to do was impress this Alain King bloke. Well, she'd impress him all right.

Alain was bored. Irritated and bored. He watched the anaemic young girl trying desperately to be Jodie.

'What's her name?' he hissed to Jim.

'Sam. Samantha.'

'She stinks. I hope you've got something better than this up your sleeve.'

'I have. Just wanted to give you some grounds for comparison.' Jim felt a little guilty at allowing Sam to get her hopes up when she didn't stand a chance in hell. But he was so desperate for Alain to see Vicky in the best possible light that he allowed himself a rare devious action.

Greg MacNeil was generously giving his all to Samantha, not only in the reading, but in the preliminary chat and introduction. The full-on masculine approach with not a hint of his off-screen theatricality.

Alain brusquely called an end to the test and motioned for the next girl to be brought in. Then he buried his face in some papers and didn't even look up as Jim introduced Vicky to Greg.

'G'day, Vicky. Good luck with the test — I know you'll do well. Jim thinks you're great.' Greg's handshake was firm and reassuring but he hadn't reckoned on the riveting blue eyes that met his and held them seconds longer than most young girls would dare. He flashed her one of his best grins and turned away for his script.

Vicky looked back to Jim. There was a humorous mock-disappointment in her eyes and she gave a barely discernible shake of the head. My God, Jim thought, she's guessed. She knows he's gay. Jim couldn't help it, he grinned back at her, feeling strangely vindicated. If she could guess Greg MacNeil was gay when he was in full butch mode, it was certainly no crime that she'd picked Jim as well. And he knew that was why Vicky was signalling him. It was to make amends and he liked her for it.

'Alain, this is Vicky. Vicky, Alain King.'

'Hello, Mr King.'

Vicky held her hand out. Normally if a young actor had the audacity to proffer a handshake, Alain pointedly ignored it, but he too was not prepared for the eyes. They locked with his and he found himself automatically shaking her hand. He felt an instant stirring in his groin and knew he'd have to sit down soon. Good God, the sexuality of the girl! And she was so young! Just the age he liked them. He released her hand, started to quiver slightly, sat down and crossed his legs.

'All right, Jim. Line it up, let's go.'

As Vicky joined Greg in front of the camera she experienced a slight sinking feeling. She'd recognised Alain's lust immediately. Here we go again, she thought, here we go again. Despite his sophisticated image, Alain reminded her very much of the Hungarian.

She wasn't the only one who'd noticed it. Jim felt his jaw clench as he watched Alain feign indifference. Oh, no you don't, Alain, he seethed, not this one.

'Off you go, dear, let's see what you can do.' Alain leaned back in his chair.

Vicky read well as Jim had known she would and he felt doubly rewarded by Greg's delight at his new discovery.

But it wouldn't have made any difference. The role was Vicky's in any event.

Oh yes, Alain thought to himself, we'll see what you can do, all right . . .

Mandy and Sidney

'We need a couple of old has-beens to play a couple of old has-beens.'

Alain was sticking with his theory of going for the real thing now they had their commercial stars. And who was Jim to disagree? The roles of the two ageing actors in 'The Glitter Game' cried out for the two most famous has-beens in the country and he waited for Alain to make the triumphant announcement. Unfortunately Chris Natteros was with them and Jim winced as Chris now leapt to his feet.

'Mandy Burgess and Sidney Meredith!'

Oh no, Jim thought, when would Chris learn that one had to allow Alain his moment? He must remember to have a word with Chris.

Alain's smile was forced. 'Precisely. Mandy and Sidney. What do you think, Jim? Couldn't get more has-been than that, eh?'

'Good idea. They still have quite a following too.'

Alain gave a derisive laugh. 'Sure, if you're after the infirmary brigade. But they're spot-on typecasting. Line them up.'

Out in the corridor Jim turned to Chris but the director held up his hand in acknowledgement. 'Not a word. I know, I know.'

Jim smiled. 'They'll need to be contacted at the

same time because they'll get their agents to run a check. Of course they'll both jump at it but we don't need to start off with more dramas than necessary. You do Mandy and I'll do Sidney.'

Jim was right as usual. It was common knowledge that Mandy and Sidney loathed each other. Although they'd played husband and wife with monotonous regularity for nearly thirty years, it had been dislike at first sight and had grown ever since.

Sure enough, the agents of both actors rang back ten minutes after the initial contact with the same list of queries. When was the other actor approached? Was the billing equal, the length of contract the same? Simultaneously, Jim and Chris assured them that the billing, the length of contract and indeed the money ('although I wouldn't tell anyone but you') was the same.

The money was, in fact, better than either of them had seen in the past five years, so once their pride was appeased they both leapt at the offer. So much so that the excitement of the impending series outweighed their mutual loathing.

As Mandy sat under the bright lights in her dermatologist's surgery she barely felt the burning pricks of the needle injecting her bi-annual dose of collagen. It had been all she could do to afford the treatments over the past two years. No more worries now, she thought. She'd soon be able to afford her second full face-lift, thanks to the series. But, even more importantly, she'd be back in the public eye! A star! Oh, how she'd missed it. Five years ago she'd been appalled at being offered three granny roles in a row and had turned them down without even reading the scripts. That had been a mistake. In the past two years she'd been forced to accept a series of TV commercials for pensioners' insurance and three episodes of a series set in a retirement village. It was mortifying.

At sixty-two, although she only admitted to fifty-five, and then when cornered — Mandy still wore the vestiges of a once pretty youth. True, the figure had grown blowsy and she dressed like someone half her age, which made her the butt of many a joke, but her bones were good and her eyes were still clear. If Mandy could only have learned to act her age, she would have been a handsome woman.

Mandy squeezed back the tears behind tightly closed eyelids as the needle dug into her upper lip. She thought back to the late sixties and the height of her fame in the four year series that had taken the country by storm. The award nights, the promotion trips, the luxury hotels — it would all be hers again. She'd be able to pay off the mortgage on the Orwell Street flat. God, what a relief that would be. She'd lived there for over thirty years and lately she'd been having nightmares each month as the loan repayment date loomed.

When she and Bill had divorced ten years ago, he'd left her the flat and kept the country house for himself. All very quick, all very civilised and Mandy barely noticed his absence as she poured all the money she'd accumulated from the series into the renovations she'd been wanting to do for the twenty years of their mistaken marriage. And the quicker the renovations were finished the sooner Cindy would move in.

Cindy was the reason Bill had left. He'd known of Mandy's peccadillos with young women for years but, as sex was no longer of any interest to him, he turned a blind eye to them. He supposed it was better than Mandy cuckolding him with men. No one was likely to guess that she was actually bedding her succession of young female companions. But when Cindy arrived on the scene things changed. People guessed, all right. Cindy made sure of that. Cindy had a big mouth and was proud that her lover was a TV star. Cindy was a slut. Bill was mortified and left. Very quickly.

Mandy never thought of herself as a lesbian. Far from it. She was highly sexed, that was all. Indeed, before her marriage to Bill there had been many men in her life. She'd turned to women when Bill had lost all interest in sex. It was quite harmless, just something different to do, really. Well, that's what Mandy supposed. Cindy was something else though. Mandy was besotted.

It lasted till the money ran out. Four years. It would have been three but, after the money from the series was gone, Mandy mortgaged the flat which bought her a further year of Cindy, at the end of which Cindy went off with a highly paid AFL football forward.

Mandy's love life had declined since then. She'd had a couple of flirtations with young women and a pleasant affair with a sixty-two year old farmer who was mildly infatuated with her. She'd had to put a stop to that one though, he was far too old for her (Mandy kept forgetting her age), with a libido active only once every couple of months. Besides, he wanted Mandy to retire and live with him on his struggling wheat farm. Mandy was far too young to retire and she loathed the country.

She breathed a sigh of relief. Her financial situation had been so desperate at the time that she'd been briefly tempted. Thank God she'd held out. Where would she be now? Rotting away amidst horse dung and flies instead of on the crest of international stardom in The King's new television series.

She looked at her face in the mirror that the nurse was holding out to her. Wonderful. She could be a woman in her forties. The camera would love that face. Well, the camera would love it tomorrow when the little red marks had gone. What a pity she had to play opposite that dreadful hammy old fart Sidney Meredith.

Sidney was thinking very much along the same lines as he walked down the street towards the Actors Equity offices. Why on earth did they have to cast that blowsy old tart, Mandy Burgess? Damned shame! He dodged past the dark brick Victorian building which housed Mandy's flat and ducked quickly into the Equity offices. God forbid that he should bump into her now, they'd be obliged to acknowledge one another and talk about the series.

Sidney had lived around the corner in his Victoria Street bedsit for over thirty years and he and Mandy bumped into each other regularly around Kings Cross. Their respective knowledge of the area had led them to the best value butcher, greengrocer and supermarket where they'd avoided each other assiduously for a good quarter of a century now. When they were working together, playing one of the many ageing couples they'd played over the years, they both resented the fact that they were forced to recognise each other over the loin chops, silver beet or soap powder.

Sidney paid his annual Equity dues to the girl at the counter. He paid at the counter every year — it saved stamps. Then he left, deciding to walk around the block rather than pass Mandy's flat again. He didn't want to push his luck and it was a beautiful day.

There was still a touch of spring in the air, although it promised to be a scorching summer. Sidney started perspiring at the mere thought of it. He perspired easily and he hated Sydney summers. In the forty years he'd been in Australia he'd never adjusted and each summer successfully took his system by surprise. So much so that he felt it to be a personal attack. Afternoon siestas, with cold flannels to the temple and Woolworths electric fans whirring all about his bedsit did little to alleviate the heat, and yet other people didn't seem to be affected by it to the same degree. Indeed, many Australians wallowed in the heat. They rolled around on the sands of Bondi Beach like stranded whales. Sidney shuddered. He still remembered with fondness the clean hard pebbles of Brighton Beach and Worthing and Bournemouth.

Sidney was still very much an Englishman. In fact, he would never have come to Australia had he been able to carve an equally successful career for himself in the Old Country. But after twelve years of weekly repertory in the poorer provincial theatres and summer seasons at Billy Butlin's Holiday Camps, he'd felt he was ready for bigger and better things. Of course he hadn't decided on the desperate measure of emigrating straight away. He'd had a bash at London first.

It was when he was at the end of his tether under-studying and playing bit parts in the West End that his agent landed him a six month contract with the National Theatre. It was still the Old Vic then, of course, and the theatrical mecca of the world. Sidney was made. Or so he thought. Six months later, after spear-carrying, miming buglers and announcing that the king was coming, he emigrated.

Australia wasn't his first choice. He'd decided on Canada until he read an article about an actor called Peter Finch who was making an international name for himself. Finch evidently came from Sydney. The name beckoned and the die was cast. Sidney would go to Sydney. Australia would be Sidney's springboard to international stardom. If Finch could do it so could he.

He was thirty-two when he arrived in Australia and he discovered very quickly that his past experience was of great value to the antipodeans. He gained many an introduction with his stories of Larry (Laurence Olivier) and Rafe (Ralph Richardson) and his West End anecdotes went down a treat. Of course he never mentioned that he'd been understudying, blowing silent bugles and announcing that the king was coming. The work started pouring in. A West End/National Theatre actor! He was snapped up gratefully by the humble Australians.

Unfortunately the triumph lasted only a few years. The tragic truth was that Sidney was not a very good actor. Naturally he didn't realise this and put the thin time down to the fact that Australia was starting to find its own identity and there wasn't much call for Pommie actors.

Although he whinged about the heat, the flies, actors' conditions and the lack of cold pork pies, it never occurred to him to go back to England. This was the land of opportunity and he'd soldier on till he made it.

And make it he did. Eventually. With his rather portly figure and prematurely thinning hair, Sidney had always looked older than he was — by the time he reached forty he was eminently castable as the jolly avuncular character who appeared in all the early Aussie soaps.

Delighted as he was with the rebirth of his career, his vanity was a little piqued at the fact that he wasn't playing the leading man, so he took to dyeing black what was left of his hair and combing it all towards the front. It didn't work. He just succeeded in looking a little more ridiculous but nobody dared tell him. Funnily enough nobody wanted to hurt his feelings. Sidney was a bore, certainly, but he was harmless enough — just a bit of a joke, really. Nobody disliked him. Well, nobody, that is, except Mandy.

Sidney had been in the country eleven years before they were cast opposite each other. It was his major breakthrough role as a character actor. They were working on stage at the old Theatre Royal and Mandy, ten years his junior, was appalled to find herself playing his wife. She should have been his daughter, surely. It was she who started the age-old feud. In their first tender scene when she had to place a wifely kiss on Sidney's lips, she shrank with horror from the Terry Thomas teeth.

'Close your mouth, for God's sake,' she hissed.

To which Sidney, surprisingly quick on the rebound, replied 'And you stop flashing those tired old norks at the dress circle!'

It was war from that moment on.

Sidney sighed as he pushed open the front gate and fumbled for his key. He hoped this time Mandy would play it with dignity. He certainly intended to, but if she started in with the snide remarks he'd have to retaliate and it was so exhausting, particularly with summer coming.

He closed the front door quietly, glancing at the landlady's door beside the staircase. Damn, it was ajar. He crept up the stairs to his room on the first floor, praying that Maudie wouldn't hear him and demand tea, bickies and a talk about the good old days when she ran the house as a digs for touring acts. Actually he quite liked old Maudie, and she'd certainly been a stalwart friend during his struggling days but, now that senility was creeping up on her, the good old days were becoming tiresomely repetitive and Sidney had long ago exhausted his own repertoire of theatrical anecdotes.

Maudie didn't hear and Sidney thankfully closed the door behind him, put the kettle on and sank into his armchair beside the window.

Every available area of wall space was covered with photographs from Sidney's stage and television triumphs. In pride of place was a youthful publicity portrait of Laurence Olivier bearing the inscription *To my dear friend, Sidney, with best wishes, Larry.* Naturally Sidney had never told anyone that he'd written the inscription himself to impress the natives when he'd first arrived in Australia. There were times when Sidney himself forgot that he'd written it. The stories had become so embellished that he'd lost sight of what was true and what was fabricated over the years. 'Larry' and the rest of the memorabilia had been very important to Sidney during his lean times. A comforting reminder that he'd worked with many greats, they held the promise that the next exciting role was only just around the corner.

But he didn't need them now. He looked out across Woolloomooloo at the view he loved so much, and thought with mounting excitement of the coming Monday. Only two days to go. Only two days till the meeting of the entire cast and the first read-through of the two hour special. Two days and 'The Glitter Game' would be set in motion.

Outside, a light summer shower started to fleck the waters of the Woolloomooloo docks.

The First Day

It was raining on Monday. It had been raining relentlessly for two days. One of Sydney's torrential downpours which often ended in floods and which invariably invited surprise — 'What about the weather? . . . I don't believe this *rain*!' The rain was a regular occurrence and the only surprise, Edwina thought, as she watched the windscreen wipers, was the fact that people continued to be surprised.

Davey was driving carefully. But then Davey always drove carefully. She glanced at him fondly and he, sensing her look, offered her a supportive smile.

'Big day, Edwina.'

She smiled back, then looked out of the passenger window at the blinding rain, her mind strangely blank.

In the boardroom at Channel 3, a dozen people waited for Edwina.

Jim Avalon and Chris Natteros mingled with the cast, all of whom they'd known previously or had met recently during the casting sessions. Everything was pleasant and informal, although there was a hint of tension in the air, a feeling that this was a gathering of nervous people playing at being casual. Not Alain, of course. This was his day, the birth of his baby and he was going to enjoy every minute of it.

'OK, gang, a bit of shush please.' Instant quiet. Alain smiled benignly. 'I'd like to introduce you to a very important member of our team. Someone most of you won't have met before but someone I want you all to get to know very well and someone who already knows your alter egos even better than you do.' He gestured towards the door and everyone noticed, for the first time, the shy gangly man wearing glasses who looked as if he wished he were somewhere else. 'Our executive writer, Evan Ryan.' Alain initiated the smatter of applause while Evan smiled and nodded self-consciously. 'Now, why don't we all take a seat and get ready for the read-through while we wait for Edwina.'

As everyone shuffled to their places around the boardroom table which was set up with notepads, pencils, jugs of water, glasses and ashtrays, Alain muttered an aside to Jim. 'Where the hell is she? Did you ring her agent?'

'Yes. Rosa called her home and got the answering machine. She must be on her way.'

Alain turned the paternal smile back to the assembled company. 'Put your tea and coffee orders in to Wendy, everyone.'

Alain's secretary bustled about with cups and saucers and the general chatter started up again.

Jane was deep in discussion with Chris Natteros while Paul had made an immediate dive for the chair beside Narelle and discovered that, close up, she was every bit as desirable as she appeared on screen. Even more promising was the fact that she was a fan of his.

'Are you really?' His teeth gleamed his humble appreciation. 'That's very kind of you to say so.'

'Oh I've been mad about you since I was ten. My mother was a fan too. Only she's dead now.'

Narelle's eyes were moist with either adoration or grief. Ten, Paul thought. That hurt! But he tried hard not to let it show.

Greg, one of the few genuinely relaxed people in the room, had dropped all butch pretensions and was whispering asides in Vicky's ear. Wicked, tantalising stories about the others present, all of whom he knew. Nothing malicious, nothing damaging but, hell, the kid was new to the game and she needed some relaxing. And relax she did. Trying desperately to control her laughter, Vicky decided she liked Greg. A lot.

To Sidney's astonishment, Mandy chose to sit next to him. She clasped his hand and placed a moist kiss on each cheek. 'Lovely to be working together again, Sidney. It's been too long.'

So, that's the way she's going to play it, Sidney thought with relief. 'It certainly has, my dear. Far too long.'

The door opened and Edwina stood there with Davey at her side. Evan was busily shuffling through scripts by the sideboard, having refused a seat at the boardroom table, Alain was muttering to Jim to try ringing again, and the actors were all deep in chat. Nobody noticed her.

Davey started toward Alain but Edwina gave a barely perceptible shake of the head and glided silently forward. 'Alain, I'm so sorry I'm late.'

A hush descended. The men rose from the table.

'Edwina!' Alain looked as if he were about to embrace her but stopped at the graciously extended hand.

'You've met Davey, of course.' Edwina released Alain's hand so that he could shake David's. 'David Kennerley, Alain King.'

'Of course. Welcome to the team, David.' Why the hell has she brought her little poofter hairdresser to the reading? Alain was aware that his voice was a little louder and a little more forced than before. The woman had unsettled him again. Why did she do that? Christ, he couldn't wait to get rid of her. 'You've met Jim and Chris and Evan, of course.'

A self-conscious wave from Evan, greetings from Jim and Chris, and Alain continued, 'Let me introduce you to the rest of the cast.'

Edwina faced the boardroom table and offered a general apology. 'Hello, everyone. I'm so sorry I'm late.'

'This is Mandy Burgess.' Alain had started from Mandy's end of the table which gave Mandy a misguided sense of star billing.

She sprang from her seat. 'It's this rain, darling, would you believe it?' Then she planted her cheek against Edwina's, kissed the air and said, 'It's lovely to meet you, Edwina.'

It was Greg who saved the moment. As Edwina's steely gaze hit Mandy and she felt the ground about to open, Greg was at Edwina's side, his hand extended. 'Hello, Edwina, good to see you again.'

Edwina's smile was warm and grateful. She'd sung at several charity concerts and gala events at which Greg had acted as Master of Ceremonies and she liked him.

'Greg. Hello.'

'Sidney Meredith.' Sidney shook Edwina's hand vigorously. 'Amazing weather, isn't it? Absolutely filthy, causes havoc with the traffic.'

Edwina passed on to Vicky. Astonishing eyes, she thought as she shook the girl's hand. Good casting. I hope she can act.

Edwina wasn't the only one doing the 'sizing up'. Jane hadn't taken her eyes off Edwina from the moment she entered the room. Like the others, she was in awe of the woman's presence, but how much of that was simply because Edwina was a star? You'll need more than that, Jane thought. I'll act you off the screen, lady, you can bet on it.

'Hello, Jane.' As Edwina met Jane's gaze, she thought, here's one to be reckoned with.

Narelle was next and she bobbed a half curtsy as she shook Edwina's hand. 'You're my greatest fan, Edwina . . . I mean . . . ' The atmosphere relaxed as everyone laughed.

'I've seen your work too, Narelle.' Edwina smiled encouragingly. 'I'm delighted you're in the show.' Well, they needed a resident sex symbol, Edwina thought, and this one was harmless enough. Certainly no competition.

Alain finished the introductions with Paul.

'Hello, Paul.' Edwina decided a bit more flattery wouldn't go astray — after all, the man was playing opposite her. 'I've been a great admirer of yours. I'm looking forward to our working together.'

Paul had also been riveted to Edwina from the moment he'd laid eyes on her. Strange that he'd never met her socially, strange that singers and actors seemed to mix in separate circles. But he'd seen her many times on the screen and found her fascinating. She was even more magnetic in the flesh. As he felt the firm handshake and looked into the aquiline face, he was overwhelmed by Edwina's sexuality. Bugger Narelle, he thought — she could wait. Here was the challenge. He had to have Edwina Dawling.

Edwina recognised the signals at once. Oh, no you don't, boy, she signalled back. Hands off. But the more she signalled, the more Paul wanted her.

Alain took charge again. 'Right. If you'd all like to take your seats, I'll hand you over to Chris and we can get on with the reading.'

When everyone was settled, Chris stood up. 'One or two things before we start. You've all had your scripts for a while now so you should be pretty au fait with them. Unless there are any objections I'd like to do a straight read-through, no stop-starts, so if you bump into something you want to query or discuss, make a note of it in the pads provided.' There was a shuffle as everyone lined up their notepads and pencils. 'I don't want anyone to give the full performance,' Chris continued. 'Just feel your way for now. I'll read the big print, dailies and fifty worders.'

As Chris opened his own script, Vicky whispered to Greg, 'He'll read what?'

'The stage directions and small parts,' Greg whispered back.

'Everybody ready?' There were murmurs of assent and the reading began.

Chris was a good director. He always started a new production with a casual read-through. It helped introduce the cast, not only to each other but to their characters and relationships. But it never ceased to amaze him that no matter how many times he urged the actors to hold back, not to 'perform', there were always those who simply had to. Today was no exception.

Mandy and Sidney, of course, gave their all. Chris stifled a smile. They really were terrible old hams but the viewers loved them and he'd be able to hold them back. Vicky, out of her depth completely, was also trying to give a performance. The edges were certainly rough, Chris mused, but, with a lot of work she'd be wonderful. Narelle, as usual, simply couldn't help giving it everything she had. Her bottom wiggled in the chair, her breasts caressed the boardroom table, as she draped herself over her script. The girl seemed to be constantly on heat.

Greg and Paul gave good straight intelligent reads. Greg never ceased to astound Chris. The camp act was gone totally and even his appearance changed as he read his lines. He was a stunningly handsome, heterosexual young male heart throb.

Jane and Edwina were particularly fascinating. They weren't giving away a trick. They were not just holding back on performance level — they weren't giving any performance whatsoever. Chris wasn't worried about Jane. He'd seen her in action on stage. But Edwina was an unknown quantity. Hell, this could be a big worry.

Evan barely raised his head during the entire reading but assiduously followed every word of the script, making the odd note here and there.

Alain and Jim, however, watched the actors like hawks. Jim's appraisal was very much the same as Chris's but Alain couldn't resist a flash of triumph over Edwina's reading. It didn't worry him; Chris would somehow get her up to scratch, then Alain would have every excuse to dump her. He turned his attention to Vicky. The girl's rawness and youth excited him and his pulse raced at the prospect of 'research' sessions with her. He wondered how many it would take before he'd be able to get her to bed. He'd have to take it gently, she was a gutsy little number and he didn't want her crying rape. Mind you, she knew the score. That same gutsiness made her aware which side her bread was buttered and there was no way she'd risk losing this job and landing back in the gutter. Yes, she'd probably be an easy lay. He'd allow her three research sessions and then . . . Alain couldn't wait to put her to the test. He was unaware that he was being observed. He was unaware that, to those who knew him, his face was eminently readable.

Jim could feel his anger mounting. You touch her, Alain, he thought, and I'll . . . He caught Greg's eye and realised that Greg was way ahead of him, that Greg had sensed not only Alain's lust but Jim's own reaction to it. Greg gave a tiny smile, a slight shake of his head and returned to his script.

Jim knew that he'd found an ally, that Greg had meant, 'Don't worry, mate, he'll get to her over my dead body too'. He felt his anger subside to be replaced by an overwhelming fondness for Greg. God, don't do it, he told himself. Don't start falling for Greg MacNeil — it'd be the quickest way to blow your cover. A one-night stand with him! Hell, you might as well take out an advert. God, he was attractive though. Greg looked up and again caught Jim's eye. Jim gave a small brisk nod, a professional smile and concentrated on his script, feeling slightly flushed and angry with himself.

After the reading, the heads of other departments were called in to meet the cast. Big Sally was first: Big Sally Cheswick, ex-designer and coordinator for Maggie Mae fashions for large girls. And Big Sally was one large girl. She'd been costume designer on nearly all of Alain's shows, had the top designers in the palm of her hand and was invaluable. She was closely followed by Carol, head of the production department and her assistant Anna, armed with call sheets which she distributed to the cast.

'When you've all got your call sheets,' Jim announced, 'Sally will sort out times when she can arrange fittings for you and discuss labels.' This was with the exception of Edwina, of course, who was to have all her costumes exclusively designed by George Gross.

While the boardroom table was being cleared to make way for the caterer's smorgasbord, the publicity department arrived: Tim Arnold and his assistants, Lois and Val. Tim was a big man with a soft effeminate body and a rabid, cruel wit. He described himself as an evil old queen and he was quite right. Many a Channel 3 star had learned not to cross Tim — it could be very dangerous for one's career.

There was chaos in the boardroom. Tim and Sally drove the production girls mad trying to arrange individual appointments for the actors to fit in and around the rehearsal schedules which had been so painstakingly worked out by Carol and Anna. Besides costume fittings there were photo sessions and publicity interviews and Alain's announcement, 'Don't forget — Liza gets first priority'.

Tim fumed. Liza! Bloody Liza Farrelly! He considered her appointment by Alain to be a total intrusion into his sanctified area.

Liza Farrelly had once been a topline feature journalist for the *Herald* but a bad case of RSI had ended her career. She was still unable to type, or even write by hand and, despite the fact that she was one of their prime writers, the *Herald* had refused to employ a secretary to take her dictation. They'd even tried to give her the sack when she could no longer meet the workload. She sued them, of course, and won the case — but it appeared her journalistic career was over.

Not to be daunted, Liza turned freelance and sold her skills to the highest bidders. She'd concentrated on theatre productions, new art galleries and artists in concert to start with as that was where her interests lay. But it didn't take long before Liza realised that the big money was corporate money, particularly corporation-owned television money. They also provided secretarial assistance, so she didn't have to employ someone to type up her dictation. The work poured in.

Following the mammoth success of Australian television series overseas, the networks were promoting their stars like so many packages of breakfast cereal. Who better to build those plastic images than Liza Farrelly? So Liza started to specialise. Before long she was the best.

And now, not only had Alain hired her to assist with the promotion of 'The Glitter Game', he'd actually instructed that she be given priority over the Channel 3 publicity department. No wonder Tim Arnold was fuming.

'So where's Fleet Street Fanny now, then? Why isn't she here?' he demanded.

'She said she'd rather interview the cast on a one-to-one basis,' Alain replied. 'Which reminds me . . . ' He turned to Edwina. 'Liza Farrelly wants to take you to lunch tomorrow. One o'clock, Jordan's at Darling Harbour. There'll be a limo to collect you from rehearsal and we'll work around you for the afternoon so . . . '

'I won't need the car. Davey will drive me.' Edwina's tone was acid. She didn't like Alain's peremptory manner. She also didn't like the presumption of his arranging appointments directly with her instead of going via her personal manager. She paid the woman twenty-five per cent, after all, that's what she was there for. Edwina reminded herself to pop in and see Rosa after lunch tomorrow and instruct her to clarify the situation with Alain. Awful little man, Edwina thought, as she turned back to resume her interrupted conversation with Greg.

Actually, Alain wasn't little at all. He was 180 centimetres tall and rather overweight but on first meeting him, Edwina had quickly read that, like many men in powerful positions, he had a tendency to megalomania and was a coward underneath. That made him little to Edwina.

Furious at Edwina's snub, Alain decided to seek out Vicky to assuage his anger. He grabbed an open bottle of champagne and two glasses from the caterers who were popping corks and setting up trays of vintage Moët et Chandon and started wending his way to the other end of the boardroom where Vicky was talking to Mandy and Sidney.

Tim Arnold had misread the exchange between Edwina and Alain and presumed Edwina's irritation at hearing about the interview was due to a dislike for Liza. He whispered an aside to Edwina. 'Don't blame you, pet, she's a sour old lemon-lips.'

'I beg your pardon?'

'Liza Farrelly. Vinegar-tits.'

'We get on rather well, actually. What was that, Greg?' And Edwina turned back to her conversation.

Well, up you, dear, Tim thought.

'Like a word with you, Vicky.' It was a very readable command for Mandy and Sidney to disappear. Alain offered the girl a glass of champagne. 'Just one won't hurt, will it, to toast the show?' He raised his own glass. 'To "The Glitter Game" and all who play it.'

Vicky clinked glasses with him and sipped at her

champagne. They were right, she thought. The real stuff did taste better. More bubbles.

'Now, Vicky.' Alain dropped the smile of camaraderie, put an avuncular arm around the girl's shoulders and sounded deeply concerned. 'You're very new to this game. You've got a lot to learn and I'd like to help you.'

'Thank you, Mr King.'

The smile came back, like magic. 'Alain, my dear, Alain. No formality in the family. Now, agents. You don't have an agent, do you?'

'No.'

'I'm going to make an appointment for you with Rosa Glassberg.' Although it was to Alain's advantage to have Vicky represented by Rosa, he wanted the girl to know she owed him a big favour, so he added, 'Normally a reputable agent wouldn't touch you without a few years' experience, but with my recommendation . . . ' He shrugged modestly. 'I'm pretty sure Rosa will sign you up. She's Edwina's personal manager, you know.'

Vicky was impressed. 'Great. Thanks, Mr King. Sorry — Alain.'

'As for performance level,' Alain continued, 'You'll need to put in some hard work. It'll be a learning process for you.'

'I'll work hard, all right. You can bet on that.'

'I'm sure you will, my dear, I'm sure you will. But a bit of help never goes astray. I could probably find the odd hour here and there for a little tuition, a little character research. I thought perhaps . . . '

'Excuse me, Alain.' Jim had been slowly making his way towards them from the moment he saw them clink glasses. Now he stood beside them. 'Could I see you for a moment?'

'Of course, Jim. I won't be long, Vicky — don't go away.'

The two men eased themselves into the corner vacated by Evan, who'd left as soon as possible to avoid socialising.

'What can I do for you, Jim? Good reading, wasn't it? And don't worry about Edwina — I'm sure Chris'll get her up to scratch.'

'Yes, I'm sure he will.' There was a glint in Jim's eyes and his smile was forced. 'It's about Vicky . . . well, the actors in general, but mostly Vicky.'

'Yes?'

'She's the most inexperienced member of the cast and she's very young.'

'So?'

'So, it could confuse her, taking acting direction from two sources. That's really Chris's area and I think we should leave the actors to him, don't you?'

The eyes that now met Jim's were deadly. Dangerous. 'What exactly is it you're trying to say, Jim?'

Jim was a mild man who generally avoided any form of confrontation. In fact, he was a little amazed at his audacity in fronting Alain the way he had. 'Just that maybe you're trying to take too much on yourself.' Jim felt himself back-pedalling frantically. 'You've been involved in every area of the show from the start and now that we're mobile you should be able to take some of the pressure off yourself by leaving the actual production area to Chris and me.' Hell, that didn't sound good – where was his customary diplomacy? 'I mean, you'll have your time cut out with the advertisers and sales and marketing and . . .' That was as far as he got. He knew he'd hanged himself.

'This show is my baby, Jim.' Alain spelt it out quietly, as though reading from a child's primer. Jim didn't know whether it was that which unnerved him most or the chilling smile that accompanied the words, but the combination of the two was lethal. 'It has always been my baby and it will always be my baby. That means every area of it — including scripts, directors, actors and on-line producers, every one of whom are expendable if they don't measure up to my standards.' Alain gestured to the waiter hovering beside Jim. 'Have some champagne.' And he walked off to refill Vicky's glass.

'Don't worry. More than one way to skin a cat.' The voice was two inches from Jim's right ear. He jumped and turned to find Greg smiling confidently at him. 'We'll look after her between us, sport. Now come and have something to eat.'

For one hideous second Jim thought Greg was going to take his hand but he didn't. He took his elbow instead and ushered him towards the boardroom table which was now laden with food. Even so, Jim was consumed with self-consciousness. He wanted to shrug Greg's hand off, yet he enjoyed the warmth of his touch and the pressure of his fingers.

Jane and Chris were still so deeply engrossed in conversation that they hadn't noticed the food, despite the fact that they were standing next to a huge silver platter bearing a huge mound of smoked salmon, Jane's favourite. They'd discovered their mutual background in theatre and the debate was animated and exclusive.

Beside them, Sidney had tried to join in with anecdotes of his Shakespearean season at the Old Vic but Jane and Chris had been saved after the first ten minutes by the arrival of the lobster tray.

Lobster was Sidney's favourite delicacy, but it was far too overpriced for him to ever contemplate buying it. When lobster was offered at someone else's expense, therefore, Sidney made a point of pigging out. Today was no exception and Mandy watched with utter distaste as Sidney devoured lobster by the plateful, cracking the legs with his abominable teeth. It wasn't a pretty sight. But then Mandy was appalled at any public display of people's eating habits. She ate very little herself at public functions, preferring to wait for the refrigerator raid when she got home. Then raid she did: Sara Lee cakes, Toblerone chocolates, Tim Tam biscuits and, if none of those were in the house, bread and jam or Arnott's Assorted. Mandy was a cupboard eater with a sweet tooth.

Paul had cornered himself a bottle of Moët and two glasses early in the piece in preparation for his groundwork on Edwina. But when he looked around she'd gone. She and Davey had slipped out shortly after Evan. Not to worry, Paul thought. There's always tomorrow. So he shared the bottle with Narelle as they fed each other Sydney rock oysters.

'Can I have your attention, please.' It was Alain, standing at the head of the table. 'Stay and enjoy the lunch. There's plenty of champagne and I'll see you all tomorrow when work begins. In the meantime,' he raised his glass, 'to "The Glitter Game". '

Everyone joined in the toast and there was a smatter of obligatory applause. Alain flicked a glance in Vicky's direction but she wasn't looking at him.

He left the boardroom happy with the day's events. Apart from Jim's brief and pathetic attempt to step out of line, everything had gone perfectly. And the girl was coming to his office during lunch break tomorrow. Things couldn't be better.

Sizing Up

Darling Harbour. One of Sydney's bicentennial gifts to the people. It had been a controversial issue and a lot of merchants had bombed out when the shopping complex took a while to get going but it was certainly an impressive development, Liza thought, as she strolled along the left embankment towards Jordan's Restaurant.

After a three-day deluge, the rain had stopped as quickly as it had begun and the sun sparkled on the water.

The tiny harbour was surrounded by a contradiction of architectural design which pleased her. The huge underground aquarium, the Chinese Gardens, the massive exhibition hall and, in front of her, Liza's favourite, the modern gothic complex that housed a colony of bars, grills, coffee lounges, restaurants and tiny shops.

Liza turned into Jordan's on the ground floor. She nodded to the maitre d'. 'A table for two outside, booked for one o'clock, name of Farrelly. I'll have a drink at the bar.' She ordered a campari soda and leaned back against the bar watching the diners and the passing parade of tourists outside.

Towering over the other side of Darling Harbour

was the city skyline linked by flyovers, freeways and the omnipresent monorail.

Liza always arranged her luncheon interviews where the food was good and there was plenty to look at. Television stars were invariably late and, on the odd occasion when she was stood up altogether, at least she could enjoy an excellent meal on her expense account.

Liza was feeling a little irritable. The recent change in the weather had brought about one of the intermittent bouts of pain in her hands. The constant agony she'd suffered before the diagnosis of RSI was a thing of the past and she'd discovered that, as long as she observed the rules, didn't attempt to write or type, and kept up the visits to the acupuncturist, the pain was negligible. But recently she'd found atmospheric changes could give her hell. Bugger it. She was probably getting arthritis on top of everything else.

'Ms Farrelly.' The maitre d' was at her side.

'Miss,' Liza corrected brusquely. She loathed 'Ms'. It sounded like a mosquito and anyway, she was bloody proud of being a 'Miss'. Why would anyone want to be a 'Mrs'? Surely if married women worked under their maiden names there'd be no need for this pretentious 'Ms' shit.

'Your table is ready, Miss Farrelly.'

'Thank you.'

Liza picked up her drink and followed him out onto the terrace. As she sat down, she looked at her watch. Five to one. She probably had another thirty-five minutes to wait. Oh well, it was a pretty day.

Liza was rich, powerful, respected and still the right side of forty — what more could she want? A lot. Apart from the intermittent pain in her hands, there was one major thing wrong. Liza loathed television. She felt the shallow, glittery world of make-believe to be beneath her.

Whenever she was interviewing some soap queen about the break-up of her latest marriage or the new toy boy in her life, Liza would find herself seething with rage. What was she doing with this stupid conceited woman? What did she care about the silly cow's love life? Liza wanted to be back in the mainstream of journalism. She wanted to be reporting from war zones and interviewing prime ministers. She supposed she should have stuck to the theatres, the galleries and the concerts instead of television. At least she'd be mingling with some actual talent, then, but she'd be buggered if she'd take the loss of income now she'd become accustomed to more. She told herself that if she wanted the good life she just had to suffer the television shit.

Liza was wrong. If only she'd looked a little more closely behind the tinsel facade she might have noticed a wealth of true talent. Many writers, directors and actors had opted for the money, as she had, and even the less artistic of them were, in the main, highly skilled at their craft. But Liza refused to recognise this and had become progressively bitter and more vindictive.

She could see Edwina approaching the restaurant from the broad Darling Harbour walkway. Liza checked her watch again. One o'clock. Good God, the woman was on time. But who was that with her? Then Liza realised it was Davey. Of course, she should have known Edwina would bring him along. She was rarely seen without him. What on earth was their relationship? Were they lovers? But surely he was gay. Everyone thought so, and his gentle, effeminate appearance certainly indicated that they were right. Mind you, Liza herself had in the past shared the odd torrid experience with effeminate men who appeared gay but certainly knew how to enjoy women. One must never judge by appearance. So what was it? Here was a story. The true relationship between Edwina and her loyal Davey. It was likely to be the only emotional angle she'd get on Edwina. She knew that other journalists covering the recording scene had dug deep for smut and found nothing. Liza must win Edwina's trust — not an easy task.

'Edwina.' Liza rose, gesturing for them both to sit down. 'How kind of you to be so punctual.'

Edwina smiled. 'I'm only ever late when I feel it serves a purpose. Nice to see you, Liza. You've met Davey, of course.'

'Of course.' As Liza shook his hand she was surprised at the firmness of his grip. 'I'm glad you could come along.'

Edwina smiled to herself, aware that the invitation had not been extended to Davey. But journalists would soon find that, if all appointments were made through the normal channels via Rosa, Davey was always to be included. Not that Edwina blamed Liza — it was Alain's fault. He'd learn. In the meantime, she was prepared to be cooperative with Liza. She'd respected the woman's style during their odd social meetings and she was certainly the most intelligent of the television journalists.

'A drink before we eat?'

Davey opted for orange juice as he always did and Edwina went straight to the wine list.

★

As Edwina's sashimi and Liza's Thai raw fish salad arrived at the table, Vicky knocked on Alain's office door. His secretary Wendy had been told she must go to lunch and stop over-exerting herself even though she was only too happy to work through and complete the backlog of computer input.

'Come in . . . Ah, Vicky.' Alain appeared to have momentarily forgotten their appointment. In fact, he'd been salivating all morning at the prospect. Not that he expected to have her on the first day, but the plan of attack itself was enough to excite him. Alain liked a challenge.

'Close the door, dear. You've brought your script, I see. Good. Sit down, sit down.'

Vicky hadn't said a word but the electric blue eyes studied him unwaveringly.

Alain was a little disconcerted by her assurance. 'Don't be nervous, dear.'

'I'm not nervous.' He's sweating, she thought. And again he reminded her of the Hungarian. Beneath the Saville Row suit his body would be just as gross, his desire just as repulsive as the Hungarian's had been.

'Give me your views on the character of Jodie. You've had a good study of the character breakdown as well as the first five blocks, I take it?'

'Yes, Alain.'

For the next fifteen minutes, Vicky mouthed the character analysis she knew Alain wanted, all the time thinking, shit, why do we need to play games? Can't we just get it over and done with?

Then Alain started to talk about the sexual aspects of Jodie and the scene in which the character loses her virginity. 'Do you identify with that scene, Vicky?'

'Do you mean, am I a virgin?'

'Well . . . '

'No.'

Alain was taken aback by her directness and decided on a slight change of tack. 'The scene will be very tastefully handled, of course, but it will require you to work naked. You're aware there was a nudity clause in your contract?'

'Sure. I read all the fine print.'

'And that doesn't bother you? Working nude in front of a camera crew? Naturally it'll be a closed set but . . . '

'No, that's cool.' Get on with it, Vicky thought.

'Fine, fine. You see, it's the actual disrobing which is the crucial part of the scene. When Jodie decides to give herself to Billy. It's as she slowly undoes her dress and lets it drop to the floor that Billy realises . . . '

'Do you want me to try it for you now? See if I can get it right?'

Alain was dumbfounded. He'd been about to suggest she rehearse the scene in detail at home then talk to him about it next session. Ultimately of course he would have asked her to perform the scene for him. In depth.

'I'll lock the door, shall I?' Vicky jumped up and crossed to the door and Alain felt suddenly deflated. This wasn't the way he was accustomed to playing the game at all. The girl was taking control.

In the canteen, "The Glitter Game" cast and crew were lining up for a choice of burnt chicken schnitzel or fatty pork chops. It was always a choice of schnitzel or chops on Tuesdays — sometimes veal or lamb, but always burnt and always fatty.

The canteen was a very levelling experience. Cast and crew alike joined the queue and no preference was shown — except by the fat lady who made up the sandwiches, who always put double filling in for her favourite stars. Otherwise all suffered equally.

Greg had opted out of the hot food queue and was at the sandwich end of the counter behind Mandy. Mandy always had a sandwich during lunch break. It was the easiest thing to eat delicately. She could see Sidney at the other end of the counter ordering two of the largest pork chops and made a mental note to avoid him at all costs.

The fat lady piled a quarter-kilo of ham into Greg's sesame bun and gazed at him lovingly. 'Mustard?'

'Thanks. English — and whack it on, love.' Greg looked around the canteen. 'Where's Vicky?' he asked.

'With Alain,' Mandy answered. 'No, only a little lettuce dear,' she instructed the pimply assistant.

Greg grabbed his ham roll, handed a two-dollar coin to the fat lady, and made for the door.

'I thought you were eating it here,' she called.

'I'm not.'

'There's ten cents change.' But Greg was out the door.

As he sprinted up the stairs to the offices on the first floor, he nearly bowled Jim over.

'Sorry, sorry. Mercy mission,' and he kept on sprinting.

'What?'

Greg halted at the top of the stairs. 'Vicky — remember?'

'Oh, hell!'

'You going to the canteen?' Jim nodded. 'I'll give you a full report in a few minutes.' And Greg was off.

Inside Alain's office, Vicky was slowly undoing her denim shirt, her eyes boring into his. 'Sorry about the shirt. We'll have to pretend it's a dress but if I do the jeans in the same way you'll be able to get the general idea, won't you? Is this slow enough?'

Alain was dying to look away from the girl but her eyes seemed to have locked with his. It was an uncomfortable feeling and he was aware that the semi-erection he'd been savouring all day at the prospect of Vicky, was turning decidedly limp. Alain's libido was useless unless it was accompanied by a sense of power. It was why he liked them so young. This one was different and he was starting to wish she'd go away. 'Yes, that's very good, dear, but I was going to suggest that you rehearse at home and . . . '

'And when she drops the dress,' Vicky dropped the shirt, 'she walks towards Billy.' Vicky walked slowly towards him, unfastening her jeans.

Alain's eyes finally released themselves from Vicky's and fastened on her breasts instead. The budding breasts of a sixteen-year-old, ripe with promise. He felt a stirring return to his groin.

'And when she's standing in front of him,' Vicky continued, 'she puts her hand on him. Like this.' Her hand suddenly snaked forward and grabbed his scrotum.

'Aargh!' Alain sprang back and clutched the desk in fright more than pain.

There was a loud knock at the door. 'Hey, Alain, is Vicky in there? It's me, Greg.'

'Put your clothes on, for God's sake,' Alain hissed

to Vicky. Then to the door with full-voiced bonhomie, 'Greg! Yes, Vicky's here. Just going through a
few character details. Come in, come in.' Another
hiss. 'Hurry it up, girl, hurry it up.'

'The door's locked,' Greg called.

'Surely not?' Alain looked at Vicky. She was doing
up the last button. 'Sit down,' he muttered, then
crossed to the door. 'Wendy must have put it on lock
without my realising,' he said as he swung the door
open to reveal Greg, complete with ham roll. 'What
can I do for you, Greg?'

'It was Vicky I wanted to see, actually.' Greg
bounded in with his usual lack of inhibition. 'I've had
this great idea for our opening scene, Vick. Want you
to go through it with me right now before I lose it.
Here.' He thrust the ham roll into her hands. 'I
bought you a ham roll so you don't miss lunch. I've
already had mine.' Then an aside over his shoulder to
Alain as he dragged Vicky to the door. 'OK with you,
Alain?'

'Sure, sure. Good to see you so keen.' He was
speaking to the air. Greg and Vicky were through the
reception area and halfway down the corridor. Alain
sank into his chair gratefully. Thank God Greg had
arrived. The girl had been hot for him and there was
no way he would have been able to perform. It was a
pity about those breasts but he'd have to steer clear.
She was definitely not normal.

Down the end of the corridor, Vicky dragged Greg
to a halt. 'I didn't need rescuing, you know. I had it
under control.'

'Oh yeah?'

Vicky stared back at him defiantly. She'd looked
after herself for as long as she could remember and
she didn't like her independence being usurped,

albeit well-meaningly. 'I've handled stuff like that before. Tons of times.'

'Pretty tough, aren't you?'

'Tough enough.'

'Always got out of it before?'

Vicky felt herself weaken a little. The memories weren't good. 'Not always.'

'So how did you know you were going to get out of this one?'

'Because underneath he's a wimp, that's how.'

Greg held her look for a moment, then laughed. 'I think you're right.'

Vicky contemplated the ham roll. 'Thanks, though,' she said and, to cover the fact that she meant it, she took a large bite.

'That's OK. Won't do it again, I promise.'

'Shit!' The mustard hit the back of Vicky's throat and went up her nose and her eyes started to water. 'What the hell have you put in this thing?'

'Give it back, it's mine.' Greg took the roll from her. 'Come on. I'll buy you one without mustard.'

Jim was watching the canteen door as Greg and Vicky entered. Greg gave him the thumbs-up sign and took Vicky to the counter where he asked the fat lady to give her a ham and salad roll with the works minus mustard. Then he slid into the chair beside Jim.

'All OK?' Jim asked.

'Yeah. I thought I'd got there just in the nick of time to start with. Alain had the door locked . . . '

'The bastard.'

' . . . but I'm not so sure who was conning who now.'

'What do you mean?'

'She can look after herself all right, Jim.'

'Oh, I know she's tough, but is she *that* ... '

'Yes, she's *that* tough. Alain was actually relieved to see me.'

Jim looked at him incredulously. 'But he eats them for breakfast.'

Greg shook his head. 'Not this one he doesn't.'

Jim breathed a sigh of relief and looked across at Vicky as she ordered a milkshake with double malt and double chocolate. Just another teenager. He smiled fondly. 'There's something about that kid. She's tough on the outside but ... I don't know. There's something about her.'

Greg patted Jim's hand as it rested on the table. 'You're just an old softie, aren't you, Jimbo?'

Jim withdrew his hand as if he'd been stung and laughed self-consciously.

'We should get together sometime,' Greg continued flippantly. 'We could have a little cry at old movies. I'm a softie too.'

Jim decided things had gone far enough and he snapped brusquely. 'Come off it, Greg. We have nothing in common. Nothing at all.'

'Oh but we do.' Greg's tone was no longer flippant and Jim didn't dare look at him. 'Don't we?' The voice was gentle now and, as Jim dragged his eyes to meet Greg's, he saw the look was one of sympathy. 'Takes one to know one, sport.' A slight smile. 'Old movies can be fun. Think about it.' And he left Jim staring at his coffee cup, his pulse racing.

★

At the other end of the canteen, Mandy had seated herself opposite Narelle and Paul to make sure she had her back to Sidney two tables away. She didn't want her eyes to land on him by mistake. It was just as well as he was into the apple crumble now and a spot of cream rested on the end of his sizeable nose. Mandy would have hated that.

Paul hadn't enjoyed Mandy's intrusion. He'd been on the verge of asking Narelle to dinner that night. He'd already rung Barbie and said they'd be working late. Now Narelle's attention was taken up by Mandy, and the two women were avidly discussing the show and the relationship of their characters. Narelle always enjoyed the company of older people — she warmed to any parental influence and Mandy was playing her aunt, after all.

Mandy couldn't help but find Narelle's respect disarming. What a pity more young things didn't display an equal regard for women a little older than themselves, she thought. She was such an attractive girl too, in the same voluptuous way she herself had been at that age.

'Yes, it's a lovely relationship they have, isn't it? Not like aunt and niece at all, really — more like sisters. I think that's the way we should play it, don't you?' As always, Mandy was working on reducing the age of her character.

'Oh yes, yes I do,' Narelle nodded eagerly.

'I mean Stella's a gift of a role,' Mandy continued, speaking of her own character, 'because she has such convolutions and hidden depths. Take the fact that she's married a man so much older than herself — she obviously has a father complex, doesn't she?'

'Yes.' Narelle hadn't realised Sidney was so very much older than Mandy but obviously he must be.

'Why don't you come around to my place on the weekend and we'll work on our scenes together?'

'I'd love to.' Narelle wriggled excitedly in her seat.

Mandy finished her last sip of tea and looked at her watch. 'Lunchbreak's over. We'll make it four o'clock Saturday, shall we? We can have a bite of dinner after work.'

'Thank you.'

To Paul's annoyance, Narelle also rose from the table. Damn — he hadn't got his dinner invitation in yet.

'Make sure you know all your lines by Saturday, dear. I don't like working with the book.'

'Yes, I will, I promise.'

'See you in the factory.' And Mandy was off.

Narelle picked up her bag to follow but Paul rose and blocked her path.

'Narelle, honey.'

'Mmm?' Narelle's substantial breasts were just brushing his shirt front and Paul shivered with delight at the prospect of burying his head between them.

'I was wondering whether you might like to have dinner with me after work tonight?'

Narelle sighed disappointedly. 'Oh, I'm sorry, Paul. I would have loved to but I have to learn my lines for Saturday.'

As she wiggled off towards the canteen door, Paul fumed. Bloody Mandy.

Davey was savouring the very last mouthful of the very best black forest cake he'd ever eaten as Edwina and Liza sipped their demitasse coffees.

The luncheon had been an unmitigated success.

Liza's tape recorder had been in operation for a good hour now and her intelligent, concise questions were answered in kind by Edwina. The women's growing regard for each other was strongly evident; Davey was pleased that it appeared Edwina had finally found a media person she could trust and relate to.

Liza had been very careful to keep her questions strictly professional. They all related to Edwina's career, her rise to fame, her awards, her ambitions; she'd very carefully kept clear of the woman's personal life. Time enough for that, she thought. She took a final sip of her coffee and turned off the tape recorder.

'That should do it, Edwina. Thank you very much — it's been a pleasure.'

'Yes, it certainly has. I only wish there were more journalists who conducted interviews along your lines.'

Liza put Plan A into action. 'Well, as you know, Alain has given me top priority in his publicity campaign. I'm sure that he'd agree to let me handle you exclusively as far as any feature or in-depth interviews go. It simply means that the magazines and newspapers would have to buy my stories if they want to feature you, which they will, of course. And it would keep the general press away from you.'

'What an excellent idea. I'll have Rosa arrange it with Alain.' There was a brief second as Edwina appeared to come to a decision. She opened her handbag, took out a card and gave it to Liza. 'That's my home number if you should want to get in touch.'

Davey looked up sharply. Edwina never gave her home phone number to anyone. Not even the network. It was unlisted, and the only person who had it was Rosa. All contact was made through her.

'Thank you.' Liza pocketed the card as Edwina rose from the table.

'Time to go. Come on, Davey. I want to call in on Rosa before we go home. Thank you for a lovely lunch, Liza.'

'My pleasure.'

Liza watched them leave, nodded to the waiter for another espresso and sat back, congratulating herself on her coup. She was fully aware that Edwina never gave out her phone number. Plan A had worked. She'd gained exclusive rights to Edwina and she'd started to win the woman's trust. She'd bide her time before embarking on Plan B. Plan B was the inside story on the personal life of Edwina Dawling and she'd need to gain a hell of a lot more trust before she made inroads there.

'Do you think that was wise?' Davey asked as he opened the car door for Edwina.

'The card? Yes, I think it was. She'll want the guts eventually but the more she thinks I trust her the gentler she'll be about it and the more she'll keep the rest of the sharks at bay.' She wound down the window. 'Go the long way to Rosa's. She's not expecting us till three-thirty and I've got some thinking to do.'

'Only too happy to help, my darling, you know that.' Rosa's fleshy face was wreathed in smiles and she glowed with the love she reserved for very special people. A stranger could not be blamed for presuming she was talking to a close member of the family or at least a best friend. Not so. This was the love reserved for producers, casting agents and entrepreneurs.

'Of course, Alain, any time that's convenient.' She cradled the receiver on her shoulder and dug in her handbag for an emery board. 'Friday's fine. You too, my darling. 'Bye.'

Rosa hung up and attacked the offending nail ferociously. It was one of the little ones with a tiny diamante stud pressed into the heart of the scarlet polish. She was annoyed with Edwina for arranging a three-thirty appointment; she'd had to cancel her beautician and her fake nails were long overdue for a touch-up. She looked in the vast mirror which hung on the wall opposite her office desk, bent forward and parted her hair. Yes, the roots would need redoing soon. The skin was looking good, though. Well, it had only been three years since the last mini facelift. She took out a hairbrush, fluffed the platinum hair, smiled at the mirror, admired the perfectly-capped teeth and thought to herself, looking good, looking good.

And for a woman in her mid-fifties she was looking good. She was looking fake, of course, but then everything about Rosa was fake. Even her agency. The plush decor of her Milson's Point office boasted a success her agency had no right to claim. And the harbour views from every window of her four-room business suite impressed the actors she represented to such a degree they felt guilty that obviously the commission on their wages wasn't paying for it. Someone on Rosa's books must be doing well, but who was it? Apart from Edwina, Rosa's stable boasted no one of great importance.

The truth was that Rosa's wealthy real estate husband not only provided her with rent-free office accommodation in one of his many high-rise blocks, but also supplied her with a limitless cash flow.

George didn't mind. The agency was Rosa's baby after all and he wanted to keep her happy. Besides, giving her something to occupy her time left him free to concentrate on his many business affairs. He kept quiet about his input, of course. It would have been a blow to Rosa's pride if people had realised she wasn't making it on her own.

George hated the hype of show business. He was much happier discussing the market share index with a crowd of stockbrokers than the latest premiere or what someone wore to the Logies, so he was only too happy for Rosa to be accompanied by one of her clients to the many showbiz nights she so much enjoyed.

And it was Edwina who invariably accompanied Rosa. Edwina and Davey, that is. It was a constant cause for comment as to why Edwina remained with Rosa Glassberg Management and a further mystery as to why the women appeared to be such friends. Rosa's agency was by no means top of the heap and she and Edwina had very little in common. Rosa was brassy with a streak of the common about her which even her husband's money could not disguise. Edwina had style and breeding. So why were they so close?

Loyalty was the only explanation. Rosa had discovered Edwina as an unknown singer and helped her to land the first lucky breaks. This was surely why Edwina felt compelled to remain loyal to Rosa and her agency. It was further proof of Edwina's class act. Most other performers dropped their early agents and moved on.

Rosa looked at her watch. Three twenty-five. She pressed the intercom button. 'Edwina'll be here in five minutes, Dee, brew the espresso.' Edwina didn't like the Kenyan coffee blend Rosa served up for her other clients. 'And mark in a Friday four-thirty appointment for Vicky Fraser.'

'Vicky who? Never heard of her.'

'Fraser. The King's new discovery. She's doing "The Glitter Game". '

'Oh.' Dee sounded impressed. 'You're taking her on, then?'

'Maybe. We'll see.' Rosa released the intercom button and reached for her highlighter compact. Of course she'd take the kid on, she thought as she touched up her cheekbones. Didn't matter if she never worked again after 'The Glitter Game' but two actors from Rosa Glassberg Management in Alain's show gave Rosa a distinct advantage in the bargaining stakes.

Rosa was a great believer in package deals and constantly used one actor's commercial profile to sell another actor further down the scale. 'You can cut a third off his usual fee if you take her.' Her catch phrase to producers was, 'Two for the price of one, darling, say no more.'

The intercom buzzed. 'Edwina's here.'

Rosa dumped her compact in the top drawer, stood up, checked herself once again in the vast mirror — looking good, looking good — and threw the door open, arms extended for the embrace.

'Darling! Edwina, darling!'

The embrace took the form of Rosa clasping both of Edwina's hands and standing back to admire. Rosa had long ago got the message not to intrude on Edwina's space. As it was, she was the only person who'd made it to the handclasping stage. And for some unfathomable reason, Edwina allowed it.

'You look divine. Hello, Davey.'

'Thank you.'

'Hello, Rosa.'

Edwina sailed into Rosa's office and Davey followed.

Rosa was most apologetic about Alain arranging a press interview directly with Liza. The temerity of the man! She'd get onto it straight away and if anything like that was attempted again . . . 'Just send them to me, darling, send them to me.'

'I've given my phone number to Liza Farrelly.'

A stunned silence. 'You've what?!'

'I trust her. So far, anyway.'

'But, Edwina, you've never . . . '

'Besides, she'll keep the others at bay.'

Rosa sensed that Edwina meant 'end of argument' and, a brief espresso later, they parted company, promising to meet for lunch on Saturday.

'I'll book Eliza's for one o'clock, all right?' Rosa called as Davey pressed the ground floor button. Edwina nodded and the lift doors slid together.

Rosa walked back through reception. 'Brew me a Kenyan, Dee.' God, how she hated that espresso shit. As Dee collected the cups and headed into the kitchen, Rosa looked blankly around the reception walls at the hundred hopeful faces smouldering, scowling, simpering or simply smiling from their ten-by-eights. But she didn't notice them. Her eyes locked on to the lifesize full-length portrait shot of Edwina which she'd conned from the producers of the 'Tonight Show'. It exuded that same elusive sexuality, that same 'you'll never know me but I dare you to try' feeling that Edwina herself generated. Unlike the others on the wall, Edwina never put on a front for the camera. She didn't need to. She was fascination enough.

Rosa closed the reception door and sank into her office chair. Well *I* know you, Edwina, she thought. And don't you ever forget you owe me. It was constantly irksome to Rosa that Edwina never let the barriers down, even with her. The fact that Edwina was closer to her agent than anyone but Davey had been salve enough to Rosa in the past but now there was Liza. Edwina had given her number to Liza. Liza was competition. Rosa seethed.

Edwina was probably the most important factor in Rosa's life. When the agency hadn't proved particularly successful, Rosa would have been happy to throw in the towel and become a society benefactress on George's money, one of those tireless charity workers constantly in the social pages. Then Edwina's career had taken off and with it came the award nights, the premieres, the charity galas. Rosa had the pick of them all. As Edwina's personal manager and companion she was a success. But only as Edwina's personal manager and companion. Rosa was fully aware that this was no business to be in if one weren't a success — if Edwina were to transfer her loyalties to another or, greatest horror of all, leave the agency, Rosa would be finished.

Why had Edwina formed an alliance with Liza Farrelly? Liza was far too clever for Rosa's comfort and certainly wouldn't shy off pointing out the limitations of Rosa's representation should 'The Glitter Game' take off internationally as it was expected to.

Rosa looked out of the window at a boat with a bright red spinnaker. Don't you forget that I could ruin you, Edwina, she thought. The boat slid behind the north pylon of the Harbour Bridge. And don't you ever forget that you owe me, Edwina.

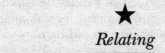

Relating

The fortnight of rehearsals went smoothly as working relationships developed. Chris Natteros was pleased with the general shape the production was taking. The sets were good, the lighting was good, the scripts were good but, most importantly, the performances were good. All, that is, except Edwina's. And that was Chris's one major worry.

It wasn't that Edwina was particularly bad. In a way, Chris wished she was. At least then he'd have grounds upon which to work: 'Not that way, Edwina'. No, her performance was more of a 'nothing'. He'd tried to discuss with her the strength of the character — the drive, the power, the sexuality. Edwina always listened attentively, nodded in agreement, then gave him more of absolutely nothing. The woman's striking social presence seemed to disappear completely when she was called upon to act and Chris was at his wits' end wondering what he could do about it.

Jane, on the other hand, was inspiring to work with and she and Chris were often seen avidly discussing their work at the canteen during lunch hours much to the chagrin of Sidney who thought more attention should have been given to his own performance. He didn't see why Jane should get preferential treatment.

The only definitive production note Sidney had

been given was to stop dyeing his hair. It shocked him horribly. How had they guessed? Actually Chris was very happy with Sidney's performance. It was old-fashioned with a touch of vaudeville about it — exactly the performance required for the character. After all, Sidney was playing an old ham.

Mandy was still a bit of a problem. Why couldn't the woman act her bloody age! 'No, Mandy, yours and Narelle's characters do not have a sisterly relationship. They are aunt and niece.'

But Mandy still couldn't resist an element of girlishness which Chris found grotesque. 'Stop flirting with Narelle! The viewers'll think you're a couple of dykes.'

An injured Mandy gathered her dignity about her and strode from the set. Chris had made the remark good-humouredly, albeit with a touch of frustration and certainly hadn't intended to hurt. Then he remembered the vague rumour years ago about why Mandy's husband had left her. Oh my God! It took him half an hour of placating to get Mandy back on set, only to find that now her performance was wounded little girl. Couldn't she just be an aunt, for Christ's sake!

Vicky and Greg were acting up a storm together. Vicky's early gaucherie was a thing of the past, thanks not only to Chris's tight direction but the response that Greg's performance drew from the girl. They were the ideal teenage couple. The younger viewers were going to idolise them.

Paul was good and professional as Paul always was but, as so much of his work was with Edwina, he was getting nothing to relate to. Chris had noticed that Paul had been trying to chat Edwina up and, as it was obvious the woman didn't want a bar of him, decided to gently point it out to Paul. It wouldn't help their working relationship if he continually annoyed her.

'Only trying to be friendly,' was Paul's defensive reply.

'I know, I know, Paul. But try for not too friendly, eh?'

Paul held his advances in check after that but it didn't make much difference. Edwina either wouldn't or couldn't give him anything in rehearsal.

At the end of the last day's rehearsal, everyone was on a bit of a high. Two days to go till Monday, when the cameras started rolling. Edwina and Davey had left early but the rest of the cast toasted each other with champagne and beer in the greenroom.

Jim joined them and said a few well-chosen words about how hard he'd heard they'd all been working and how pleased Chris was with rehearsals. Jim had kept himself out of the picture to allow Chris space with the actors but he'd been getting daily reports and was also worried about Edwina. Strangely enough, Alain didn't seem too perturbed.

Jim noted Edwina's absence from the greenroom with disapproval. Creating a distance between herself and the other members of the cast wasn't going to help matters. He wondered whether he should have a word with her himself then decided, no, better leave it to Chris. They'd see how things went at the taping on Monday. He downed his champagne.

'Are you going to book the tickets for tomorrow or shall I?' he asked Chris who was chatting to Jane in the corner.

'No, I'll do it. You want to come along, Jane? We're going to the new Nowra play at The Wharf.'

'I'm already going,' Jane smiled. 'I booked last

week.' The play and the female lead — a young girl fresh out of NIDA — had had rave reviews which had given Jane a twinge of envy, but she couldn't wait to see it.

'Mind if I gate-crash?' Greg directed the question to Jim and there was a touch of a challenge in it.

Jim took up the dare simply because he couldn't think of another way out. 'Of course not. The more the merrier.' He delivered the invitation to the rest of the greenroom in a desperate attempt to escape Greg's gaze. 'Anyone else interested in the theatre Saturday?'

They weren't. Narelle had a date with Mandy to work on their scenes together, Paul had arranged an at-home with Barbie and the kids, Vicky wanted to study her lines and Sidney felt that he couldn't afford it.

Everyone clinked glasses and drank to Monday.

Narelle was twenty minutes late getting to Mandy's on Saturday and Mandy had decided to let it annoy her. Who did the girl think she was, anyway? She should have been grateful that an actress of Mandy's standing was willing to give up her free time to help her, let alone cook a meal for her. Mandy looked at the spinach quiche beside the stove and cursed herself for having been overhospitable to the ungrateful little sod. She opened a packet of chocolate digestive biscuits and was on the fourth one when the front doorbell rang. She stuffed the packet back in the cupboard, checked her mouth in the hall mirror and opened the door to a distraught Narelle.

'Oh, Mandy, I'm so sorry, really I am,' Narelle begged, breathless with remorse. 'You must think I'm

terribly rude. I got here early, you see, and I thought
that'd be even ruder than being late so I drove
around the block and then I had an accident.'

'Oh, you poor little thing! Are you all right?'
Mandy's anger had evaporated the instant she saw the
girl's genuine distress.

'Yes, I just drove into the back of someone but he
didn't seem to mind too much.' Narelle gestured to
her sports car parked at the curb with its headlights
smashed.

'Good heavens! I hope you're insured?'

'No, I forgot to pay them this year but the man
said his insurance would cover it.' The man's name
was Burt and she'd also agreed to have lunch with
him the next day. Burt thought his no-claim bonus
was a small price to pay for Narelle's company and
was counting the hours.

'Well, you'd better re-park it, dear, you're illegal
there.'

'No, I'll leave it. I don't want to waste any more of
your time.'

'I really think you should . . . '

'Please, Mandy. I'll pay the fine. It's the least I can
do for keeping you waiting.'

Mandy was now totally disarmed and ushered
Narelle in to the lounge room. 'Honestly, my dear,
you hadn't kept me waiting at all,' she gushed. 'As a
matter of fact I'd just finished cooking us a nice
dinner and I hadn't even noticed the time.'

'Oh, what a lovely home!'

That did it. Narelle couldn't put a foot wrong from
that moment on. Mandy gave her the guided tour
and then they settled down to work.

The rest of the afternoon passed quickly and, in

between bouts of concentrated effort, they giggled and cavorted together like a couple of schoolgirls delighting in each other's company.

Mandy didn't quite know how it happened but, during one of the sisterly cuddles she was giving Narelle, she was suddenly aware that her feelings were anything but platonic. Narelle wasn't quite sure how it happened either but she wasn't particularly surprised when Mandy started caressing her left breast. She'd become used to having that effect on people. She wasn't even surprised at how instantly pleasurable it was. After all, a caress was a caress and Narelle always responded in kind.

She undid the buttons of Mandy's blouse and sank her head between the ample breasts which bulged from the confines of the remedial waist-length corset-bra. Mandy moaned with delight but thought, damn, if she'd only known this was going to happen she wouldn't have worn the bloody thing. With an agility admirable for one of her bulk and years, she twisted her body sideways on the sofa, careful not to disturb Narelle, pinioned her own arms behind her back and in two deft movements released the hook and unzipped the offending corset. It sprang open alarmingly and caught Narelle on the nose.

Narelle giggled with delight and clasped her mouth around the first generous nipple that presented itself. She'd never been with a woman before and she was overjoyed to discover what a delicious experience it could be. Fancy going to bed with someone who knew your body as well as you did yourself! All the little nooks and crannies that were such fun to explore. Nowhere near as fulfilling or exciting as being with a man, she decided. But such fun! You could just go on and on for ever, like masturbation.

It wasn't quite the same for Mandy. After the first heavenly half-hour she was ready to call it a day; when the voracious Narelle was still squealing and giggling and sucking and nibbling two hours later, an exhausted Mandy begged the girl to stop. She crawled off the sofa, her back in agony, while Narelle bounced around collecting the clothes she'd flung off in gay abandon.

'Oh, Mandy, wasn't that lovely? Can we do it again?'

'Not for a little while, dear, no.'

'Soon?'

'I'll just put the quiche in the oven.' Mandy escaped to the kitchen. She was too old for this.

An hour and a half, one quiche and three cups of coffee later, it took a migraine plea from Mandy to get rid of Narelle. Mandy sank into a Badedas bath, creaking wearily. She must never encourage that girl again.

At the theatre, the final curtain came down to tumultuous applause and, when the girl took her bow, it was to a standing ovation.

Jane, Chris, Jim and Greg agreed it had been an exciting night as they walked through the foyer. The three men were elated by the experience — it wasn't often you had a night like that in the theatre. Only Jane was a little subdued. She had seen Kate Redman and Peter Wainwright during interval.

'Isn't she wonderful?' Kate had said of the girl. What was her name? Anna. 'We've seen the show five times.' And there was a trace of triumph in Kate's voice as she told Jane that Anna was the new choice for Peter's movie. 'We start production in two months. It's going to be bigger than *Quo Vadis*, isn't it, Peter?'

Peter squirmed uncomfortably. There was no need for Kate to rub Jane's nose in it. 'How's the series going, Jane?'

'Fine. Great fun. We start taping on Monday.'

Thankfully the bell rang and they returned for the second act.

Jane shook her mood off as they walked into the late-night actors' hangout in the Cross. Don't ruin supper for everyone, she told herself angrily. You're being bloody ungenerous. The girl was terrific, she deserves the role. You made your own bed — now bloody well lie in it.

Half an hour later, the conversation had switched from the play to theatre in general and was at its most stimulating when Kate and Peter walked in. Kate strode straight to their table. 'Mind if we join you?' She already had a chair pulled up and Jane made the necessary introductions. Kate then ushered forward the girl who'd been standing quietly behind Peter. 'And this is Anna, everyone. Anna Bowrey, about to become Australia's newest and greatest star.'

Jane jumped up and warmly shook the girl's hand. 'You were wonderful tonight, Anna — really great performance. We loved it.'

The girl knew the compliment was genuine and smiled gratefully. 'Thanks.' A self-deprecating shrug. 'Gift of a role, of course.'

During supper, Kate didn't shut up about Peter's movie. They'd had to fight the investors off, it was a huge budget, the script was the best she'd ever worked on and the leading role was the greatest starring vehicle any Australian actress had ever been offered. It was all *déjà vu* to Jane.

'Well, you'd know of course, wouldn't you, Jane? You did the stage play for me,' Kate added, as if she'd suddenly remembered.

'Brilliantly, too, I might add.' Peter was wishing Kate would shut up — so was everyone else, as they all agreed that Jane's performance in the stage production had been wonderful.

'Of course it was, darling, we all know that. For the movie role though, I think one really does need an actress a little younger. After all, she's supposed to be nineteen and you can't lie in close-up.' Kate smiled and speared a piece of char-grilled octopus. ' "All your terrible history screams", to quote Alexandra Del Lago.' The octopus disappeared between bright red lips and she laughed delightedly.

What a bitch the woman is, Chris thought as he flashed a look of sympathy in Jane's direction. Everyone at the table with the exception of Anna and Greg knew that Jane had been offered the movie role — indeed, that Kate had begged her to do it. But of course nobody said anything in deference to Anna and Kate just kept slinging the barbs.

Jane wore it well but as soon as supper was over she made her excuses.

Chris also rose from the table. 'I'm off too, I'll never hear the end of it from Helen and the kids if I'm home after one.'

'Henpecked, are we?' Kate smiled.

'Yes, very. I love it. Come on, Jane, I'll give you a lift.'

Outside Jane started walking towards the cab rank. 'Thanks, Chris, it's sweet of you but I'll get a cab.'

'Rubbish. You're in Surry Hills, aren't you?'

'Yes, but you're over the bridge, it's in the opposite . . .'

'And Surry Hills is only two k's away, for God's sake. Come on.'

Jane didn't say anything during the short drive home. Kate's salt was still stinging in the wounds. But when they pulled up outside the tiny terrace house she'd recently rented in halfway trendy Surry Hills, she turned to Chris with a grateful smile. 'Want a coffee?'

Chris checked his watch. 'Half an hour before curfew. I'd love one, thanks.'

While Jane brewed the coffee, Chris admired the picturesque little house with its rough sandstone walls and open grate fireplaces.

'Yes, it's the first house I've ever rented,' Jane told him. 'It's always been bedsits and flatlets with share bathrooms for me. I got it during the run of the play. Maybe after a year in "The Glitter Game" I'll be able to buy it, who knows?'

'Why did you knock it back, Jane?'

Jane took the coffee through to the open-plan lounge room area. 'What?'

'The Wainwright movie. You were totally committed to it that day in Alain's office when I first met you. What did he say to change your mind?'

Jane tossed up whether or not to tell him, then thought, what the hell — she was so pissed off at the moment she didn't give a damn, and bugger it if she was being indiscreet. 'No telling, OK?'

Chris sat back and listened as Jane unfolded Alain's plans for her own rise to stardom and Edwina's demise. He was fascinated. 'It explains why he doesn't seem to give a damn about Edwina's non-performance. But why would he want to risk the show like that? It's sold on Edwina's name.'

'The man's power-happy. Have you seen how uncomfortable he is with Edwina? He can't walk over her and he doesn't like that.'

Chris shook his head incredulously. 'Jim told me the future storylines on Edwina were getting thin but I didn't know Alain was going to phase her out altogether.' He sipped his coffee. 'I must say, going by rehearsal performance it's probably not a bad idea.' A guilty shrug. 'Sorry, I shouldn't say that to another cast member but . . . '

'I'll keep your secret if you keep mine,' Jane smiled.

'It's great news for you, though, and you're terrific in the show, Jane — you know that, don't you?'

Jane grinned back at him. 'Got a good director, haven't I?'

'Does it make up for losing the movie role?'

Jane looked thoughtfully at her coffee cup. 'No, I'm afraid it doesn't.' She sighed regretfully. 'That was a gift of a part and I don't know how I ever let Alain talk me out of it.'

'That's why they call him The King.'

'Anyway, all I can do now is go with his plan. Let him make me a television star, stick with the show till I'm a household name and then go back to the theatre where, according to him, I'll be able to name my price.' She looked around fondly at the little house. 'Hell, what right do I have to complain? I'm earning regular money — I've never had it so good.'

But Chris sensed the regret in her voice. He drained his coffee cup and rose from his chair. 'I think I've been in television too long. I haven't met an actor with your dedication for years. I like working with you, Jane. Very much.'

Jane rose and took his coffee cup, not quite sure what to say. She suddenly felt awkward. 'Thank you.'

Their faces were close together and a kiss seemed inevitable. Jane waited for it to happen; she found herself willing it to happen. Chris leaned forward and, changing direction at the last moment, planted a tender kiss on her cheek. 'Goodnight.'

As Chris got into his car, he felt disturbed, guilty. What was the matter with him? He was the most happily married man he knew. No woman affected him emotionally this way. What was it about Jane? There was a great dignity about her strength and her sense of fair play and yet she was so vulnerable underneath.

Scouring the coffee cups with a vengeance, Jane scolded herself. Get your act together, girl. You never let men interfere with your work and certainly not married ones. Stop playing the femme fatale — it's just director-actor mutual admiration, that's all it is. But deep down she sensed that it wasn't.

At the restaurant, Kate, Peter and Anna had departed and Greg had talked Jim into a second coffee and sambucca.

The sambuccas, along with the sizeable quantity of cabernet shiraz that Jim had consumed during supper, had relaxed him and for the first time he didn't feel on his guard in Greg's company. It was two o'clock, the restaurant was nearly empty, they had a corner table, and despite Greg's probing questions about Jim's closet existence, he was a nice guy, so what the hell? What did Jim have to lose by baring a fraction of his soul?

Greg sensed Jim's one reservation. 'You're quite

safe. I only gossip about the bad guys.'

Jim sucked at his lower lip where the flaming sambucca had taken him by surprise. 'I suppose it started with the family. The straightest parents, the straightest brother, the straightest middle-class upbringing.' Greg nodded understandingly. 'Don't get me wrong,' Jim added hastily. 'They're great. I adore them and they wouldn't have disowned me or anything. It's just . . . ' He shrugged. 'I suppose I didn't want to be a disappointment to them.' His look to Greg was apologetic. 'I still play extra macho when I go home to the family at Christmas.'

Greg laughed. 'It's easier if you're an actor.' He caught Jim's look of bewilderment. 'No need to apologise, for God's sake. I do it too.'

Jim was genuinely surprised. 'But you're always so open about being gay.'

'Never to the public, old dear.'

'I know that, but to every . . . '

'And never to the folks. They get the public performance too.' He shrugged. 'Same reason as yours — I don't want to disappoint them. Bloody stupid of course.' He skolled the last of his sambucca. 'I know once they got over the shock they'd understand.' He acknowledged the slight send-up in Jim's smile. 'Well, maybe not "understand", but then what straight ever does? They'd forgive, OK?'

Jim nodded. 'Let's have another sambucca,' he said. He hadn't felt this good in a long time. He'd worry about the hangover tomorrow. He studied Greg's classic profile as he signalled the waiter. God, he was gorgeous. It wasn't just the looks, it was the style, the humour, the gentleness, the understanding, the . . . Jim realised suddenly just how drunk he was. What the hell, he thought, give in to it for once. And as Greg turned back, he said, 'How can you do it, Greg? Aren't you scared?'

Greg thought of teasing for a second and asking 'what about?', but he saw the desperation in Jim's face. 'Yes,' he said.

'Then why?'

'You want a story?' Jim nodded. 'Six years ago I had a lover. His name was Rod, he was desperately in love with me and wanted us to settle down together. Of course we'd both been around a lot and he knew what a promiscuous old tart I was but he still wanted to.'

The gay-bar slang jarred with Jim but Greg raised his eyebrows in a 'that's the way it was' gesture and continued. 'So we lived together for a couple of years. I was never faithful, of course, and it used to drive Rod wild. We had the most awful fights.' He looked at Jim seriously over the flame of his newly-arrived sambucca. 'I mean awful. We'd scream, we'd hit each other, the police'd be called in by the neighbours.' Greg extinguished the flame with the palm of his hand. 'I'd never known anything like that before. It was possessive, obsessive, destructive, but we did love each other in our own strange way. And I'd never known that before either. I'd never loved anyone before — I'd only had adventures. Anyway,' he took a mouthful of coffee and followed it with a swig of the scalding liqueur, 'we'd been together a year when we decided we'd ignored the AIDS scare long enough, so we went and had our tests. Roddie's was positive.'

He paused. Jim didn't know what to say.

'Mine was negative.'

Jim felt even more nonplussed. He hadn't been about to ask . . .

But Greg continued undeterred. 'It took Rod two years to die. The first year wasn't too bad. He was a stoic little bugger, refused to acknowledge that he was never going to beat it. The next year was a downhill battle, though, and when he was finally hospitalised and it was a matter of weeks, he asked me to call the family in.' Greg downed his sambucca and held the empty glass up. 'What do you reckon?'

'Sure.' Jim downed his too.

Greg looked fondly at his empty glass. 'The one thing I always respected about Roddie was that he never had a closet bone in his body. Wore it like a badge. Even with his family.' He flashed a look at Jim. His voice had an edge of irony. 'Maybe he should have taken a leaf out of our book there. His family were all bastards. The one time he tried to take me home to meet them they wouldn't let me in the house. Then when he was dying, they didn't want to know. Oh, while they could tell themselves and their friends it was cancer that was OK. They sent cards and made phone calls. But when it was the AIDS ward and a month to go, the shit really hit the fan.'

Greg signalled to the waiter for the next round and continued. 'Roddie reverted to childhood a lot at the end. He could only remember the early happy times — I believe it's quite normal. Anyway, he wanted to die at home. His family had a big old country place a couple of hours out of Sydney, they weren't short on money. And the hospital agreed to transport him there and supply a live-in nurse. It all looked as if it was going to happen. And then the family stepped in.

'They sent the older brother up to town to see Rod. That was the only time any of them came near the ward during the month he was there and Rod was so happy to see him.'

Greg paused while the waiter delivered the drinks and collected the coffee cups. 'Then Ian, the brother, gave Roddie the ultimatum. Under no circumstances was he to come home to die. He wasn't to ring home any more and I wasn't to make any contact with the family.'

'My God, I don't believe it.'

'Oh, wait for it, it gets better. Roddie and Ian had an almighty row. I arrived at the end of it to hear Ian screaming stuff like "People in the town are starting to guess you're dying of AIDS — how do you think that makes the family feel?" I raced into the ward.' A slow smile spread across Greg's face. 'Ian was leaning over the bed, his face about two inches away from Roddie's, and he yelled, "The strain of it's killing Mum!" ' Greg threw back his head and laughed. 'And bloody Roddie! He screamed back, "What the hell do you think the strain of it's doing to me!" God, he was a courageous little bastard.'

Jim waited for him to go on. A sip of the fourth sambucca and his world was starting to swim, but he was fascinated. 'So what happened?' he prompted gently.

'Roddie died a week later. The folks at home refused to have him buried in the family plot. I arranged the funeral and of course the family didn't come, but the day after the service someone from their solicitor's office came to take an inventory of the furniture in the flat to make sure I didn't nick off with anything belonging to Roddie.' Greg skolled the sambucca. 'Rod and I had bought the flat together but it was in his name. He'd left it to me in the will but when the family contested it . . . ' he shrugged. 'I couldn't be bothered fighting so I just walked out and left them to it.'

He leaned back and looked at Jim who, despite his fascination, was trying desperately to focus. 'You asked if I was scared. Of course I'm scared. I don't want to go through what Roddie went through. I won't have another test because I know I couldn't be as brave as he was. If I found I had it I'd curl up and die. And I only take lovers who are in the same boat. We practise it safe, of course, but we're all on borrowed time and we all know it.'

'You could always practise celibacy.' Jim wondered why 'celibacy' was such a difficult word to say. 'Like me,' he added with a lopsided grin.

'And live in a state of constant sexual frustration? No thanks.'

'You forget what it's like after a while.' Jim looked at Greg and felt overwhelmed with love. 'Then something happens that makes you want to·break the drought.' Surely he didn't just say 'dreak the brought', he thought.

Greg rose from the table and helped Jim to his feet. 'Time to go.'

'We could get a bottle of that stuff and go to my place.'

'I don't think so, sport — big day on Monday. You can sleep it off tomorrow. Come on, I'll drive you home.'

'Standing by.' The first assistant's voice was crisp with authority. A nod from Chris, who was crouched by a television monitor screen; he always directed from the studio floor rather than the control room.

'Action!' the first barked. It was seven-thirty on

Monday morning, and the cameras rolled on the first scene of 'The Glitter Game'.

The women in the cast had all been called for make-up at six-fifteen, the men at six forty-five. In previous shows, Mandy had leapt into the make-up chair first, considering it was her prerogative as senior female cast member. This morning however, she'd found herself vying for the same chair as Narelle.

'Mandy! Thank you for a lovely time on Saturday.' Narelle wriggled and squirmed provocatively. 'I was wondering if you'd like . . . '

'No time for chats now, hurry along through make-up, there's a good girl. I have to discuss a few things with wardrobe.' And Mandy bustled off to the costume department, wincing not only at the recollection of Saturday, but at the ache still present in her lower spine.

'Oh. All right.' Narelle did as she was told and sat down in the make-up chair.

As Chris watched the monitor, he couldn't believe the difference in Mandy's performance. There was a dignity and maturity about her; she was allowing the space in her relationship with Narelle's character, just as Chris had wanted her to. They must have worked very hard together on Saturday, he thought. Good on them.

A cheer went up as the first scene of the day, between Mandy, Narelle and Sidney, was completed in one take. It was always a good omen for a new series.

The second scene for the day was a long and difficult one between Edwina, Paul and Jane. Paul, playing the station programme manager, was confronted with the newly-appointed and heavily feminist Head of Drama — the character played by Edwina. The sexuality inherent in the writing had never been realised in rehearsal — even the entrance of Jane, who reacted beautifully to a tension which wasn't apparent, had failed to resurrect the scene. It had always been a nightmare for Chris, and now he prayed to the monitor. Give me *something*, Edwina. Just a little bit, but something!

Edwina gave him something, all right. Edwina gave everyone something. To the onlooking cast members gathered behind the cameras it didn't appear to be much — just an extra edge maybe — but to Chris studying the monitor and to Paul acting opposite her, it was dynamite.

Paul dried five lines into the scene. 'Sorry.' He put his hand to his forehead and looked around for the first. 'Line, please. Sorry, everyone.' The first gave him his line, they rolled up and took it again from the top of the scene. This time Paul was prepared for the power that emanated from Edwina: the eyes that locked into his, the defiance of his masculinity. And, halfway through the scene, when Edwina's character was supposed to find herself attracted to him despite herself, Edwina did just that. Paul found himself quivering with desire. It was as if the woman were offering herself to him even as she fought her own beliefs.

When Jane made her entrance, it was to an atmosphere charged with electricity. My God, what have I walked into? she thought as she faced Edwina for her own head-on challenge. The confrontation between

the two women was magnificent: it was the basis for a
battle royal between two protagonists with a strength
worthy of each other, the stuff of which all good
series were made.

Chris let out a whoop of joy. 'Cut. Check. Fan-
bloody-tastic!'

The day went from strength to strength. Everyone
took the lead from Edwina. Even if it was a scene she
wasn't in, the studio seemed to be filled with her
energy and there was a standard and intensity that
every actor had to achieve or be left by the wayside.

It didn't take Chris very long to figure Edwina out.
At first he wondered whether or not she'd been
'cheating' — deliberately holding back to confuse
the other actors. But no, she was taking them up
there with her. She was supportive when she needed
to be, sexual, vulnerable, authoritative. Everything
that the scene and the relationship with the other
actor required, she gave. Then he realised. Of
course. Edwina could only act when the cameras
were rolling.

It was true. She'd been quoted in many articles
about her singing career that she could only sing
when she was confronted by an audience or a microphone in a recording studio. She never sang for
friends or at private functions. Just as Edwina
couldn't relate to people on a one-to-one social basis,
she couldn't relate to them on a one-to-one performing basis either.

At Chris's request, Alain and Jim had kept away
from the studio. Alain had needed some persuasion,
but between them Jim and Chris had convinced him
that the actors' first day nerves didn't need any extra
pressure.

That evening in the control room, as Chris ran the

day's work for them, he could barely contain his elation. He hadn't given them an inkling of what to expect. He had just said, 'Watch this', given the technician the go-ahead, and sat back to study their reactions.

Jim's delight was immediately evident. 'My God, you got it out of her!' He grinned at Chris. 'How did you do it?'

'I didn't. The cameras did.' Chris looked at Alain. His reaction was enigmatic.

'Yes, she's good all right,' was all he said.

Chris concluded he was replanning his strategy. Yes, you can't get rid of her now can you, old boy? In fact, you'd be mad if you didn't start equal storylining for Jane and Edwina, he thought, and decided then and there that he'd ring Evan himself and suggest exactly that.

But Alain wasn't replanning his strategy at all. Well done, Edwina, he was thinking. You've sold the show for us and you've started us on a high. Alain could recognise that Edwina's strength had infected everyone. Everyone except Jane, he thought. Jane had her own strength to start with. And Jane's the one I'll keep. Magnificent you may be, Edwina, but you're out. You think you can dictate to me, but you're only an actor — don't ever forget that. An idea struck him. What a wonderful possibility. I could even kill you off, Edwina, he thought. When the time's ripe, I'll kill you off. Alain smiled. The death of Edwina Dawling! He gloated at the prospect. What a great impact that would make.

Jim saw Alain's smile widen and winked at Chris. Yes, it was going to be a happy show, all right.

Success

It was the end of February. Summer was still at its height, it was the start of the new ratings season and 'The Glitter Game' two-hour special was about to go to air. The whole of the nation was fully prepared. Tim Arnold and his assistants had whipped up a frenzy of publicity. Besides heralding the series in every showbiz magazine and TV supplement, there were newspaper features on Jane: *Star of Stage makes Television Debut*; TV magazine articles on Vicky: *Television's Newest Face*; a pin-up poster of Greg: *Australia's Favourite*; and spreads on the whole cast in every women's magazine.

It was the glossy cover picture of Edwina accompanied by Liza's in-depth story that really did the trick. It was cleverly written, giving the public exactly what it wanted: a secret insight into Edwina Dawling — *The Woman Behind the Mask*. In fact Liza had given the public absolutely nothing — just the image that she knew Edwina wanted to present.

The two women had met for a drink and Edwina congratulated the journalist on the article. Liza started to lay the ground for Plan B. Very gently. 'Yes, I think it read well. I'm glad you liked it, Edwina.' She paused thoughtfully, as though the idea were just occurring to her. 'I'll keep the mystery tack up for a while, of course, but I'm not sure how long I'll be able to milk it before they're going to want a slightly more personal angle.'

'Don't worry,' Edwina promised. 'When the time comes I'll give you something else to go on.'

'Good, good.' Liza smiled gratefully. Yes, everything was going according to plan.

After the press preview, Liza herself had given the 'Glitter' special a rave review. Under a different name, of course. She always wrote her reviews under a different name so that she couldn't be accused of playing favourites with actors on whom she may recently have written articles. She was always very fair in her reviews too. Difficult as she may have been to please and high as her standards were, her criticism was always constructive. If she hadn't liked 'The Glitter Game' she wouldn't have reviewed it at all in deference to her contract with Alain, but it was easy to give the show a rave. It was damn good. Her one criticism that perhaps the characters played by Narelle, Sidney and Mandy were a little stereotyped was followed by the observation that this was bound to be exactly what the general viewing public would want. Bugger it if the general viewing public thought she was talking down to them, she thought. She wasn't lowering her standards for anyone.

The saturation of the press, the on-air promos, the radio coverage and personal appearances ensured that at eight-thirty pm, as the opening titles rolled on 'The Glitter Game', nearly every home which boasted a television set in every Australian town or city had that set switched to Channel 3. And they didn't turn off. They loved it. The general public loved the soap element, the knockers loved the satire and everyone in the country was already picking their favourite 'Glitter Game' characters.

Three days later the ratings came in and the die was cast. 'The Glitter Game' was here to stay.

Behind the scenes, of course, the hourly, daily, weekly, monthly grind of making television continued. The hours were long, the work was hard — but morale was high, as it always was with a successful show. In addition to the schedules for rehearsals, taping and location shooting, all of which came from the production department on different coloured sheets of paper, there were scheduled promotional appearances, publicity appointments, dinners to fete the major advertisers and network 'bashes' where national network heads of departments were invited to impress and be impressed by the stars of the show.

Edwina was the only cast member who was highly selective in her attendance at such events. She refused all promotional appearances, she refused all publicity appointments except interviews with Liza, she refused all advertisers' dinners and, after appearing at the first network 'bash', refused to attend any others. Alain let her get away with it. All the more grist to his mill, he thought. The network could hardly blame him for getting rid of an actress who was proving to be so uncooperative. He'd already instructed Evan to continue phasing Edwina out of the storylines and it would only be a few more weeks now till she realised what was happening. He couldn't wait for her to come begging for a reprieve. And the pleasure he anticipated in telling her there was nothing he could do ('It's beyond my control, Edwina,' he could hear himself saying) knew no bounds. Alain was happy. And he would be even happier when he gave Evan his final instruction – 'Kill her off'.

The first of the network 'bashes', the one Edwina did attend, was held at the end of their second month to air and it was an eye-opener for all but the most seasoned of the actors.

There must have been a hundred executives there; Network Three had stations in every capital city in Australia and all the executives were in attendance. All wore the badge of their tribe, the executive suit; and all spoke executive language and all observed the executive pecking order.

Robert Bryce, the owner of Network Three, was never present at the 'bashes', preferring to leave his executive director, Ray Chaplin, in charge of the television arm of his empire while he himself concentrated on the many other business interests of Bryce Holdings, particularly his corporate mining concerns in northern Australia.

It wasn't that Robert wasn't interested in television. To the contrary, he and his wife, Melanie, were avid viewers when they had the time. It was why he'd added the network to his empire in the first place. Well, actually it was Mellie who had wanted the network and what Mellie wanted, Mellie got. But Robert was a great believer in delegating. He could spread himself only so thin and he'd seen many a mogul go down the drain trying to run an empire single-handed. Besides, Ray was a good 2IC. And if Mellie wanted to mingle with the stars, Robert thought, why should she have to attend network dinners and put up with the boring little people who ran his business with such bloated senses of self-importance? It was far preferable to fly the stars to the Bryce island mansion and have Mellie entertain them on her home ground and in the manner and style to which she was accustomed.

In fact Mellie had already professed a desire to do exactly that and the huge glossy, gilt-edged invitations rested on the table beside the place setting of every member of the 'Glitter' cast. The place settings of the executives were conspicuously absent of invitations, all except Ray Chaplin of course — he was a world apart from the other executives. Alain had received a personal congratulatory telegram from Bryce after the special had gone to air and was horrified to discover that there was no invitation for him. He took it as a personal insult, but he knew there was very little he could do about it. What he didn't realise was that Mellie didn't like him. And she only wanted to meet the stars anyway, particularly Edwina — Mellie had met her once at one of her concerts and admired her enormously.

The cast had fun mingling together in the restaurant bar before being called to table. It was to be a brief respite, as they were seated separately, one to a table of ten executives all trying to outdo each other.

'Better watch out, you know what a cheap drunk you are,' Greg whispered as Jim ordered a second whisky from a passing waiter. Jim grinned as Greg sailed on, champagne glasses held high, to Vicky wedged in a corner with Chris and Jane.

Jim had thought it would be difficult facing Greg the Monday after his drinking bout. The night air had hit him and he couldn't remember the drive home except for a vague recollection of an embrace at the front door. He could recall every word of Greg's conversation in the restaurant and was mortified that, after listening to him bare his soul, Greg might think that it had meant nothing to him.

'Sorry about Saturday,' he'd muttered to Greg in the canteen at lunch.

'Why?'

'Well, I remember everything in the restaurant but when I got home I . . . ' He shrugged lamely.

'Oh. You kissed me and tried to unzip my fly.' Jim searched Greg's face for a spark of humour but it was deadly serious.

'Oh, Christ!'

Then Greg burst out laughing. 'It took you ten minutes to open the front door, then you tripped over an armchair and when I picked you up you said "I wish I'd met Roddie". I left you in the armchair.'

They sat and had lunch together then and it didn't cross Jim's mind to wonder what the rest of the canteen might be thinking. It wouldn't have mattered anyway because they weren't taking a blind bit of notice.

Vicky had quickly adjusted to the publicity hype of the series. It hadn't gone to her head, it was just part of the job, she told herself. But this network bash business, this was an altogether new ball game. After being chatted up by several rather drunken executives with a penchant for the young ones, she'd dived for the refuge of Jane and Chris who were also new to this aspect of the business. Normally directors weren't invited to network bashes so it was a first for Chris and, of course, Jane had never been a 'television star' before. The three of them compared notes and agreed that it was one of the things about a successful network show that they would just have to grin and bear.

Vicky enjoyed the company of Jane and Chris.

They were her kind of people: straight from the shoulder. No bullshit. Except with each other, she thought. It was very obvious to Vicky that Jane and Chris were deeply attracted to each other. What a pity they were both so ethical. But she respected them for it.

Greg arrived with the champagne. 'I think they're about to call us to the tables, gang. Gird your loins.'

Brian Hopgood, head of security for Channel 3 was at the door to the restaurant as everyone filed through from the bar and foyer areas. He wasn't counting numbers or ticking names off lists, just giving a cheery hello here and there. It was amazing the way Brian appeared to know every single employee of Bryce's television network. It was a discreet security check, of course, just to make sure no outsiders crept in to the privately booked dining area.

Brian Hopgood had every reason to know each and every one of the Network Three employees — he held dossiers on them all under lock and key in his security office. He himself, though, was a mystery to everyone but Robert Bryce. It was general knowledge that he'd resigned from the police force ten years ago to take up a position as personal bodyguard to Bryce. It was also general knowledge that when Bryce bought Network Three Brian was ensconced as head of security, but the reasons for such a promotion, his present relationship with Bryce, his personal life — all else was unknown.

He was a big man in his mid-forties with the start of a beer gut but fit nevertheless. He always had a friendly grin at the ready and was available at any time for a chat about whichever television programme the Channel 3 personalities happened to be involved in; he knew them all, the current affairs and sports departments being his favourites. Everyone liked Brian but, despite his jovial appearance, there was a distance about him that made one feel he'd be a good man to have on side, not one to be crossed.

'Hello, Brian.' It was Narelle, wriggling up against him invitingly. She'd always fancied Brian, such a lovely big man. 'I don't know what table I'm at. The waiter told me but I've forgotten.'

'You're at table 3, love.' Brian didn't even consult the copy of the seating plan he had. 'The West Australian contingency, up the end there.' He pointed the way, then turned and nodded to Alain who was passing by. 'G'day Alain, congratulations on the show.'

A disappointed Narelle weaved her way off to find her table; she'd much rather have stayed for a chat. Alain gave Brian a curt nod. He didn't like the fellow's familiarity. He didn't like the way Brian behaved as if he were more than just a security man. But then he'd been personally appointed by Bryce so maybe he was. Alain didn't dare push it.

Edwina was seated at table 6 with the big guns, headed by Ray Chaplin, and Paul was seated at the table alongside with Roy Mansfield, the rather ineffectual Channel 3 managing director, and the rest of the New South Wales contingent. Paul jumped up and pulled Edwina's chair out for her.

'Thank you, Paul.' She smiled warmly and gave him a specially cocked eyebrow which meant 'What are we in for?' Paul gave her an understanding nod and grinned back. It was a friendly workmates' exchange, although Paul felt anything but a friendly workmate. Ever since the first taping day, Paul's lust for Edwina had become an obsession. He'd stopped chatting her up and now played it cool, the way she obviously wanted it. And it had worked. The cooler he played it, the more Edwina dropped her guard and was warm and charming to him. Little did she know that Paul, in his obsessed state, was misinterpreting every move. He read every little friendly gesture as a signal that she wanted him just as much as he wanted her. Soon, Edwina, he thought. Soon.

The truth of the matter was that Edwina had relaxed considerably with everyone. She hadn't realised how tense she'd been about her acting performance. She should have known that once those cameras started turning she'd feel at home. And it had happened. Suddenly everything had fallen into place at the call of 'action'. She was good and she knew it. She could now afford to be at ease with her co-stars, including Paul.

As soon as everyone was seated, Ray Chaplin crossed to the small podium and microphone set up at the end of the room. 'Good evening, everyone.' He waited patiently while the chatter and clatter faded. 'On behalf of Bryce Holdings I'd like to welcome everyone and to congratulate all the sales executives on the terrific job their departments have done since our last dinner. It's been a great two months.' He raised his glass and the dozen or so executives who'd just been given the seal of approval cheered as they waved to each other from their various tables.

Ray was good at his job. He didn't need notes to remind himself of specific names that needed mentioning and there wasn't one department that didn't get a congratulatory word, albeit a brief one. He tried hard to be lightweight and amusing but there was a touch of arrogance about him nevertheless.

He'd been a nice man once before he joined the

network and he presumed that he still was. But he was now an important man too and this had to be recognised. It was recognised all right — every executive in the room knew that Ray was the most important man present. In fact, only one thing could possibly have overshadowed his importance and that would have been the arrival of Robert Bryce himself. And if the obeisance to Ray's position was sometimes interpreted as 'brown-nosing' or 'arse-licking' by those not familiar with corporative structure, like actors, writers, and directors, then it was just proof of their ignorance. This was big business and 'talent' just didn't know how it was run.

Ray moved on to the most important tribute of the evening. 'And of course we'd all agree that Network Three's major achievement over the past two months would have to be the overwhelming success of "The Glitter Game"!'

There was a roar of approval from all present. A hit series made everyone in the network proud and proprietorial. In fact even the most humble executive dined out on the fact that it was his network which had produced the hit show. It made for a good 'happy family' feeling all round.

With only a fleeting glimpse at the card secreted in the palm of his hand, Ray rolled through the line-up of names connected with the show, starting with Edwina, followed by Alain, then through the ranks of the cast, ending with, 'and last but certainly not least, the lovely Narelle!' Ray gave a wave to Narelle who half-stood, blew him a kiss and acknowledged the round of applause.

'On behalf of Network Three,' Ray continued, 'I'd like to welcome all concerned with "The Glitter Game" to the bosom of the family.'

Narelle's ample breasts promised to escape the skimpy confines of her cocktail mini and, as she wriggled her bottom back into her seat, there was a general executive laugh of approval. It was a cheap but deliberate gag. They were all halfway drunk and Ray knew it was what they wanted, just as he knew Narelle wouldn't be remotely offended. She wasn't, but basked happily in the knowledge that her attributes were so appreciated.

'Of course, "The Glitter Game" hasn't been an overnight success. There's been a lot of work behind the scenes to get the show mobile and we'd like to congratulate all those who contributed, including our own Channel 3 publicity whiz Tim Arnold.' There was applause for Tim. 'I look forward to seeing the cast members at Bryce Island the weekend after next — you'll all find the invitations in front of you — where Melanie and Robert Bryce would like to thank you in person for your splendid efforts. In the meantime,' he raised his glass again, 'to "The Glitter Game". Long may it prosper.'

As everyone drank to the show, Chris cast a surreptitious look in Evan's direction but the writer was deep in discussion with Vicky and didn't notice. I wonder if he likes being one of those who 'contributed behind the scenes', Chris thought, aware of the months of sixteen-hour days Evan had put into creating the show, followed by the storyline conferences, the character breakdowns, the sweating over endless script revisions. Chris himself felt overlooked, surely Evan must.

Chris had yet to realise that corporations took scant notice of directors and writers. Their recognition was limited to executive producers and stars. Evan was so accustomed to being overlooked that he hadn't even noticed the omission. Indeed, if he'd been mentioned he would have been hideously embarrassed — he was wishing that he hadn't been invited at all. He usually wasn't and was grateful for the fact.

It was all a lesson for Chris; most of his previous work had been for independent production companies where directors were, if at times overworked and underpaid, at least acknowledged and, if they were good, respected. Oh well, this was obviously the name of the corporation game.

As he looked at Evan, Chris wondered why the writer had been so evasive over the phone when he'd suggested equally strong storylines for Jane and Edwina. 'It'd be good for both women, they bounce off each other,' he'd said.

'Can't do it, Chris, orders from above,' had been Evan's reply.

Orders from above meant Alain, of course, and when Chris had tried to corner him he'd met with an equal blank. 'Sorry, Chris, no way. The writers are already overworked, we can't expect Evan to restructure a whole month of storylines. No time.'

Surely that didn't mean that Alain was still phasing Edwina out? That would be madness. Chris couldn't lay his hands on the advance storylines either. Evan said that they hadn't been finally typed up. Chris shrugged to himself. He'd done what he could, he'd just have to wait and see.

For the first time during the evening Evan was enjoying himself. He was talking shop, of course. He always enjoyed himself when he was talking shop. Evan's mind was a sea of storyline possibilities and he was never happier than when he had an avid listener who appreciated them. Vicky was just such a listener.

'That's a fantastic idea, Evan.'

The blue eyes sparkled with genuine admiration and Evan went from strength to strength. He was outlining to Vicky the new character he was writing into the series: Jodie's brother. Vicky had proven so immediately popular with the young viewers that Evan had decided that her character, Jodie, should be expanded and given more background. 'More springboards to bounce her off,' was the way he'd put it to Alain.

Thank goodness Evan had found another song to sing, was all Alain thought. He was sick of the endless disagreements about the phasing out of Edwina and had even threatened to sack Evan if he didn't shut up and do as he was told.

'Jim's started casting sessions already.' The normally reticent Evan was aglow with the excitement of creating a new character.

'The brother's nineteen, and you haven't seen him for four years, not since you ran away from home when you were twelve. He comes to the station as a trainee cameraman and doesn't know you've been hauled off the streets and given a job. Great scene where you first meet. He doesn't realise it's you but you remind him of his little sister and we do a flashback to when you were kids. Good stuff eh?'

'Great.'

'It means we can give you a background. We can see the parents, see what made you run away, why you bucked the parental ... oh, sorry.' The entree had arrived and Evan nearly knocked his wine glass over to make way for it.

Edwina picked at her entree. Smoked trout was a

favourite of hers but she wasn't really interested. Just as she wasn't really interested in the wine or the company. Davey never said much when they were out socially but his presence was support enough and she missed him when he wasn't there. And of course he wasn't there tonight; network bashes never included partners. Edwina remembered them only too well from her 'Tonight Show' days. Well, she decided, this was the first and last 'Glitter Game' bash she'd attend.

'I'm sorry, Ray, what was that?'

She really must concentrate. What the hell had the man been talking about? It wasn't that Edwina disliked him, it was the others' subservient attitude to him that made her shudder, as well as the feeling that, underneath his pleasant exterior, he expected such subservience.

'I said Melanie's looking forward very much to seeing you again. She's hoping you'll be able to get up there for the weekend.'

'Yes, yes, I'll be going.' I suppose I'll have to, Edwina thought, but she was damned if she was going to say 'I'm looking forward to it' as was obviously expected.

'She's a great fan of yours, you know.'

'Sorry?'

'Melanie. She's a great fan of yours.' Dammit, the woman wasn't listening to a word he was saying. Ray wasn't used to that and it made him feel ill at ease.

'Yes. I'm very flattered. She's a woman with great style.' Edwina caught Paul looking at her and they exchanged sympathetic smiles as he fought his own battle with Roy Mansfield.

Edwina had found herself warming to Paul ever

since he'd stopped putting the hard word on her. She realised he was a little infatuated but that couldn't do any harm. It certainly lent sparks to their work together and, apart from his obvious obsession with sex, he was a nice man, generous and good-natured with a lovely sense of humour. Yes, so long as he kept his distance they could be friends.

Paul felt a shiver of ecstasy at Edwina's smile. She wants me, he thought. He'd take it very gently, he told himself — no pushing, but maybe tonight?

'Yes, she still talks about your concert at The Pavilion.' Ray again. Still talking about Melanie.

Edwina smiled at the compliment and nodded to the waiter who cleared her half-finished entree plate. She wasn't at all surprised that Melanie remembered The Pavilion concert. After all, it was the night of The Pavilion concert that Melanie had made a play for her. Of course she'd been rather drunk at the time, but with a woman of Melanie's style it was difficult to tell how drunk and Edwina was pretty sure that Melanie would remember everything that had happened that night.

So why the veiled messages via Ray? Did she want another bite at the cherry? It promised to be an interesting weekend if she did.

But a boring night, she thought, as the waiter plonked a plate of rare roast beef in front of her. Edwina never ate red meat and she'd ordered the chicken so she shook her head at the waiter who apologised profusely. 'I'm so sorry, Madam, I'll bring the chicken.'

'No, don't bother. The trout was ample, thank you. I'll skip the chicken.'

Paul had watched her every move and, having refused his own main course, waited until everyone had been served and crossed to Edwina's table. 'Excuse me, Edwina. Just noticed you're not into the mains either. Do you want to duck into the bar while everyone bleeds the beef?'

Ray gave a hearty smile as Edwina agreed and excused herself but he didn't approve and a silent black mark was ticked up against Paul. Paul knew it but, much as he'd always made it his rule to play the game, he didn't mind. Edwina wanted to be with him and that was all he could think about.

Edwina, on the other hand, was delighted to be rescued. How kind of Paul. A quick thank you drink and she'd sneak off home.

'I've got an even better idea,' Paul said as they entered the bar. 'Why don't we shoot through and go to Mimi's instead?'

Edwina shook her head. 'I don't think so, Paul. It's getting late and . . . '

'Marcel will give us the back room — it'll be quiet and we can get away from all this bullshit.' Edwina still looked unsure. 'We won't stay long, just one quick drink. Marcel makes the best margaritas in town.'

Edwina laughed. 'All right, you've got me. But just one,' she warned, as he signalled for her jacket.

'Sure, sure. Are you driving?'

'No, they sent a car.'

Better and better, Paul thought. 'Fine. I'm parked right outside.'

'You're right. They *are* the best margaritas in town.' Edwina dabbed at the salt-rimmed cocktail glass with her finger.

'What a shitfight, eh? I wish they'd just let us get

on with making television and stop insisting we play
their marketing games as well.' Paul had always quite
enjoyed playing 'their marketing games' in the past,
impressing the advertisers and talking timeslots and
ratings with network executives, but he knew Edwina
hated it.

'Yes,' Edwina agreed. 'I know it's the actors' popularity that sells the show so I suppose it's fair enough
we cop the advertisers, but why we have to suffer
these in-house pat-on-the-back nights is beyond me.'

They talked shop for a while, then theatre, music
and favourite actors. All the while Paul was giving the
performance of his life. His intelligent comments on
the business, his gentle humour, his lively debate, all
covered an intense desire to grab Edwina there and
then. As he watched her perfect mouth shaping the
words, he longed to press his lips against hers and
force them open. He knew there was no bra beneath
the well-cut silk cocktail dress and he wanted to rip
at the fabric and expose the firm breasts. He wanted
to . . .

'Are you sure you won't have another one?' he
asked.

'No, thanks,' Edwina rose and gathered up the silk
jacket.

Paul took it from her and helped her into it, trem-
bling as he touched her shoulders. 'Come on then,
I'll drive you home.'

'No, thanks. Really. I'd prefer to get a cab.'

Her voice was decisive and Paul knew better than
to insist. All right, not tonight, he thought, but I
know you want me, Edwina. *I know you want me.*

There were a number of vacant cabs in the street
but he walked her near to where he'd parked his car
before he hailed one.

'Thanks for the rescue mission, Paul. It turned out to be a very pleasant night,' Edwina said as he opened the cab door for her. He leaned forward and gave her a gentle kiss on the cheek. She didn't move but Paul read her enigmatic expression as a harnessing of her own desire.

'For me too, Edwina. Goodnight.'

He helped her into the cab and watched for a while as it drove of. Then as it started to turn a corner he jumped into his own car and followed.

As he drove, keeping his eyes on the cab ahead, Paul had no idea what he was going to do. Maybe I'll just find out where she lives, he told himself. He'd never experienced anything like this before. He knew he wasn't in love with the woman; she was a mystery, he hardly knew her. What he felt for her was an unbridled lust of proportions he'd never even known existed in him. In the past when his sexual urges had driven him he'd chatted up the girl, won her, bedded her and that was that. And on the odd occasion that he'd actually suffered a knock-back he'd put it down to experience and moved on. But Edwina! Edwina was teasing him, tantalising him — like a siren she was calling him, perhaps to his very doom, but there was nothing Paul could do about it. He was obsessed.

The cab pulled up outside a small attractive cottage on Cremorne Point and Paul pulled into a side street two blocks away, watching as Edwina alighted and paid the driver. He waited till she'd gone inside before he got out of the car and walked the two blocks to the house.

There was a small gate and a narrow path leading down the side garden of the cottage. Still unsure of what he intended to do, Paul pushed the gate open and started walking quietly down the path. He just wanted to see her, he told himself, he wouldn't do anything. He didn't want to frighten her.

A light went on in one of the side windows. Paul crept past a set of French doors which opened onto the garden and peered in. Through the flimsy curtains inside, he could make out a dressing room: racks and racks of clothes, shoes, hats, with a door on the far side which obviously led to a bathroom.

He drew back into the shadows as Edwina entered from the bathroom, a towel in her hands. The silk jacket was tossed on the sofa, the cocktail shoes kicked onto the floor beside it and now Edwina reached behind her back and undid the zip of her dress. As she let it slide down over her hips, Paul caught his breath. She was magnificent. Small rounded breasts and long perfectly-shaped legs. Satin panties clung, glossy and inviting, to her tight flat stomach and narrow hips.

As Edwina stepped out of the dress she caught sight of his shadow at the window and froze. She didn't attempt to cover herself but stared at the window.

Her voice was clear and demanding. 'Who's out there? Who is it?'

Paul felt a rush of humiliation. Oh God, she'd think he was some sort of Peeping Tom. Then he told himself, no, of course she wouldn't. She'd read his desire for exactly what it was. And she desired him too. He knew she did.

'It's me. Paul. I'm sorry, Edwina, I didn't mean to frighten you.' He stepped in front of the window so that she could see him. It was difficult to read the expression on her face through the dressing room curtains, but she still made no attempt to cover herself, and after a few seconds' pause she called, 'Come in, Paul. Through the French doors to your right.'

Paul needed no further invitation. His heart was pounding as he opened the French doors and stepped into the darkened bedroom. The door at the far end which led to the dressing room was pushed open and Edwina stood there, bathed in light.

'Come here, Paul.' She stepped back invitingly and Paul crossed the bedroom to stand in the open doorway. His eyes caressed her half-naked body.

'You followed me.' He looked at her face. Her eyes were burning into his.

'Yes.'

'You were spying on me.' And now he saw that the eyes were burning, not with desire, but with deadly anger.

'No, Edwina.' He took a step towards her. 'I wasn't spying. I . . . '

But she stopped him in his tracks. 'How dare you, you loathsome man, how *dare* you spy on me.'

Never before had Paul felt such hatred directed against him. 'Edwina, please . . . '

'Time to go, Paul.' Paul spun around at the voice behind him. It was Davey, standing only an arm's length away. He must have been behind the bedroom door when Paul had come in. He was wearing nothing but pyjama pants and, even in his confused state, Paul was surprised at the well-developed body. Then the realisation hit him. My God, they're lovers!

'Davey. I'm sorry . . . ' He turned back to Edwina. 'I'm sorry, Edwina, I didn't mean to . . . '

'You'll pay for this, Paul.' The eyes again, venomous with loathing. 'I'll make sure you pay for this.'

'Please — I didn't . . . ' He turned to appeal to Davey but Davey stepped aside, reaching in to turn on the bedroom light.

'Time to go.'

There was nothing Paul could do. He walked through the bedroom and out into the night air. They both stood watching him as he left.

The next day was Saturday. Edwina put down the phone and turned to Davey. 'She'll be here at one o'clock.'

Davey nodded. 'I'll pick up a quiche from the patisserie, shall I?'

'Thanks.'

'Do you want me around?'

Edwina thought for a second or two then shook her head. 'No, not this time.'

The phone rang. It was Rosa. 'I've booked a table for midday. I thought we'd try Azzurro at Bondi. It's a heavenly day and we can sit outside and look over the beach.'

'I can't today, Rosa.'

There was a moment's pause. 'But we planned it. You told me to go ahead and book — last Thursday, remember?'

Edwina suddenly did. 'Oh, yes, that's right. I'm sorry. I'd forgotten.'

'Azzurro has the most divine antipasto selection, you'll love it . . . '

'I can't. Liza Farrelly's coming to lunch.'

The silence was palpable. It was broken by Rosa, deeply wounded. 'I see. Well, I'll cancel the table.'

Rosa hung up. Wounded? She was livid. Liza Farrelly? Liza bloody Farrelly? Edwina had never asked Rosa to lunch. What the hell was going on?

Liza wondered when Edwina was going to get to the

point. She was fully aware that to be invited to the Dawling home was probably a first for any journalist, but knew there had to be more to the invitation than friendship. After the quiche and a bottle of chilled Frascati she waited patiently for Edwina to come out with it. Finally, over coffee . . .

'I need a favour, Liza.' Liza nodded and Edwina dropped the bombshell. 'I need a story on Paul Sorell that'll make the network drop him. A story that will ruin his career.'

Well, she certainly doesn't mince words, Liza thought. 'Am I allowed to know why?' she asked.

'That's not necessary. Suffice to say I'll make it worth your while.' Liza's mind was racing. This was even better than she'd hoped. Edwina misconstrued the brief silence. 'Very worth your while. I promise.'

'There's only one form of payment I'd accept, Edwina. That is, presuming I can get such a story,' Liza added. Edwina nodded and waited for the terms. 'I'd want the inside story on Edwina Dawling.' Edwina said nothing and Liza continued. 'The child-hood, the parents, early career, love affairs . . . ' Watching Edwina's face, Liza suddenly thought she may have gone too far. 'Well, views on love affairs, marriage, that sort of thing,' she amended.

Edwina thought for a second, then nodded. 'Done. You'll get it.'

Liza had the feeling she was going to regret this. She'd never muckraked in her life before but the inside story on Edwina Dawling was worth it, she insisted to herself as she shook off her misgivings. She'd hold off and sell it overseas to the highest bidder. In six months when the show was to air internationally . . . She stopped herself. Time for that later.

She leaned forward over her coffee cup. 'There was a story around a year ago that could have killed Paul Sorell if it had got out and still would,' she said. 'It involved sex with a minor.'

'How come it didn't get out?'

Liza shrugged. 'There hadn't been many leaks and the network bought off the one or two muckrakers who knew about it.' Liza herself had been one of the few journalists who had heard the rumour, but the network hadn't needed to buy her silence. Gutter journalism had been beneath her in those days. She shrugged to herself. Anybody had their price and Edwina's story was hers.

'Give me a week to dredge up all the details,' she said. 'I'll have to put it out anonymously, of course.' Edwina nodded in agreement. 'But they'll buy it once they check their facts and see there's no libel involved.'

'Right.' Edwina rose and collected the coffee cups. 'I'm away next weekend, so shall we say Monday week? You can show me your copy and then we'll get moving. More coffee?'

Sensing that the meeting was over, Liza refused a second cup, and left.

Edwina watched her drive off with no misgivings. I said you'd pay, Paul, she thought, and pay you will.

Revenge

Jim shifted restlessly in his seat. It wasn't that the actors were bad. To the contrary, there were some lovely things happening on stage but how many times over the years had he sat through *Twelfth Night*?

He was at yet another production given by the final year NIDA students in his hunt for 'Jodie's brother' and he'd nearly given *Twelfth Night* a miss until Sharon told him that it could be just the time he'd find what he wanted. She was right.

He checked out the wimp playing Orsino and heaved a sigh. Act II, enter Sebastian — Jim sat bolt upright. He looked at the leaflet in his hand. Simon Rothwell. Sharon nudged him in the ribs but he didn't take his eyes from the stage. 'OK, OK. You were right,' he whispered.

It was not surprising that Sharon and Jim were impressed by Simon Rothwell's performance. He'd topped his year at NIDA and had already been snapped up by one of the top agents. He was lean and wiry, of average height, with a shock of black hair, a sharp intelligent face and blue eyes. It was the eyes that got Jim. It was unusual to see the combination of black hair and blue eyes. It was the eyes that so reminded him of Vicky. Yes, they could certainly be brother and sister. And the boy could act!

As they waited to meet him in the foyer bar after the show, Sharon teased Jim. 'See? You would have missed out if you hadn't listened to me. What are you going to do when Auntie Sharon moves out next week?'

Jim smiled. 'I'll expect you to ring and nag me at least twice weekly.'

Sharon had recently had a whirlwind romance and was about to move in with her boyfriend. Jim was going to miss her.

'OK, I'll ring. Wednesdays and Fridays, I promise.'

'And a Sunday drink at the Tilbury? You can bring Ted.'

'You're on.'

Simon proved to be just as attractive offstage as he was on although there was a touch of arrogance about him. Not to worry, Jim thought, the weekly grind of television with established actors will soon get rid of that. The boy wouldn't be able to 'bung it on' with the likes of Edwina and company. The boy? Well, young man. Simon was twenty-two although he looked barely nineteen. Perfect age for the brother.

Simon was going overboard at playing it cool. Sure he'd turn up for a test tomorrow morning but he'd like to read through some scripts and check out the role before he accepted anything. He was really more interested in the theatre after all.

Well, up yours, Sharon thought and wondered why Jim didn't tell him where to get off.

But Jim had met this reaction from young actors before, particularly those fresh from drama school. The kid hadn't been out in the big world yet. He'd learn. He was aware that it may even be a cover-up, that the boy's arrogance might be masking genuine excitement at the offer.

It was more of a cover-up than Jim knew. Simon was most certainly excited by the prospect of 'The Glitter Game'. He'd seen a couple of episodes of the show, he'd seen the press and wanted nothing more than to be part of the new hit series. But he told himself not to let them know that. You're a trained actor, they've just seen you on stage, you've got a top agent. Play it cool, man, play it cool.

The truth was that Simon would much rather be a television star raking in the money and the recognition than to have to suffer the grind of nightly performances and two matinees a week in the theatre. Television was why he'd trained to become an actor; it had seemed to him to be a pretty easy way to earn a living.

Simon had always had it easy. His family were wealthy graziers from whom he'd had very little contact but every financial assistance. They'd bought him out of a couple of tight spots during his boarding school days when marijuana was discovered in his locker and in his final year, when he himself was discovered, under a hedge in the school grounds with a girl from S.C.E.G.G.S. The family hadn't been too disappointed when he'd opted for drama school. His older brother was more interested in taking over the property and Simon had always been trouble anyway, so funds for NIDA were made readily available. If only they'd realised that Simon's intermittent bucking of the system was a plea to get their attention they might have saved him from his ever-increasing cocaine habit. As it was, they simply supplied the rapidly growing funds he appeared to need at drama school and never questioned why.

Simon didn't consider his coke habit addictive in any way. In fact he didn't even think of it as a habit.

Just a bit of a social buzz, that's all. And the line he had before he went on stage, well, that just gave an extra lift to his performance.

Jim and Simon chatted a little longer, then agreed to meet at ten o'clock the following morning at the studio. Simon Rothwell was to test for 'The Glitter Game'.

Vicky spread the news to the rest of the cast during lunch break at the canteen. A new young actor called Simon Rothwell was lined up to play her brother. She'd seen Jim at morning tea break just after Simon's test and nagged him incessantly. 'What's he like? Is he going to do it? How old is he?'

'We're talking to his agent now. I'll let you know at lunchtime — bugger off, Vicky.' Jim was actually very pleased by Vicky's excitement over the new storylines. He was also very pleased with Simon's test. His only reservation was a possible personality clash between the two young members of the company. Vicky, gutsy little number that she was, might not take kindly to Simon's arrogance. Jim kept his fingers firmly crossed.

So Vicky galloped up to the cast in the canteen with the news hot off the press. 'His name's Simon Rothwell and Jim and Chris both say he's terrific.'

'Is he straight?' Mandy asked.

'Oh. Yes, I think so.' That hadn't occurred to Vicky but it didn't really matter so long as he was a good actor.

Mandy hoped he was straight. That would give Narelle someone else to concentrate on. Mandy had enjoyed a brief respite when the first assistant had fallen for Narelle's charms but lately the first assistant had taken to ducking home early. Mandy had the distinct impression that Narelle had exhausted him too.

'That's great,' Paul said to Vicky, who bounded away to tell Greg. Paul shared a smile with Edwina. They both liked Vicky and enjoyed her enthusiasm.

Paul had never known a day like the day before. The thought of facing up to Edwina after that awful incident filled him with dread and mortification — mortification as he recalled her loathing, and dread at the prospect of having his behaviour reported to the network. The drive to work on Monday morning seemed to take forever.

'Good morning, Paul.' Edwina's smile was warm and friendly — one of her 'special' smiles and Paul was dumbfounded.

Then at morning tea break: 'Paul, can I have a word with you?' She took him aside to a corner. 'I'm sorry about my behaviour on Friday. I had no right to overreact like that.'

'*You're* sorry!' He couldn't believe what he was hearing. 'Edwina, I can't tell you how mortified . . . '

'No. Please. I said the most ghastly things and I'm sorry. I was frightened, that's all. Can we be friends?'

The relief Paul felt knew no bounds. Neither did his admiration for Edwina. The woman was a goddess. 'Of course. But I really must . . . '

'Then we'll say no more about it.' She gave him a light kiss on the cheek and returned to her cup of tea.

Easy, she thought. When the story comes out he'll have no idea I organised it. Edwina felt comfortable in the knowledge that she hadn't jeopardised her own reputation. She'd be able to offer Paul all the sympathy in the world as she watched his career fail and his marriage crumble. And it served him right.

Greg noticed Jim at the coffee urn. He picked up his ham and salad roll with loads of hot English, gave Vicky a goodbye pat on the bottom and joined him.

'Want to share a table?'

'Sure.'

'I hear you found your man.' In answer to Jim's querying look, he elaborated, 'The brother, Simon whatever-his-name-is. Vicky's told the world.'

'Rothwell. Yes, I think he'll be good. Chris is pleased.'

They sat and, after a pause, Greg said, 'I spent the weekend with the folks.' He took a huge bite of the roll and breathed the mustard up through his sinuses. 'And I did it.' His eyes started to water. 'Oh hell.'

'I don't know how you can eat mustard like that. You're crazy. Did what?'

'It's the pain. I love the pain. I told them.'

'You told them?' Jim looked at him in astonishment. 'You told them you were gay?' Greg nodded. 'Shit. How did they take it?'

'Fifty-fifty. Dad was every bit as shocked as I knew he would be but Mum didn't seem all that surprised.'

To say Pat MacNeil had been shocked was an understatement. Pat MacNeil had been dumbfounded, incredulous. At first he hadn't believed it at all. 'Is this one of your jokes, lad?'

''Fraid not.'

Then had followed the interrogation. When had he decided he was homosexual? And the horror when Greg had said, 'Ten, Dad, I knew when I was ten.'

Then the fact that it must all be a mistake: 'How would you know if you've never tried women?' And finally the justification: 'It's not your fault, lad, it's this bloody business you're in. All poofters, you don't meet enough women. What we've got to do is find you the right . . . '

It was then that Jill had interjected. 'Leave it, Pat.'

'Eh?'

'He's had the guts to front up and tell you. That must have taken some doing. Now leave him alone.'

Jill very rarely stood up to Pat, she rarely felt the need to, but when she did, she invariably won. This time was no exception and Greg left knowing that she'd finally talk his disgruntled father around to, if not condoning his sexuality, at least accepting that it didn't need to destroy the family love and unity.

'I got the feeling she'd somehow suspected all along,' Greg now confided to Jim. 'Buggered if I know how, I never dropped my cover.'

'Why did you do it?'

'What, tell them?' Jim nodded. 'I don't know. Something to do with our talk that night. Thinking about Roddie again.' Greg shrugged. 'I don't know. I just needed to clear the decks.' He took another bite of the ham roll. 'The next step is to turn celibate,' he said with his mouth full.

'The next step to what?'

'Self-improvement programme I've started on. Shit!' He exhaled the mustard fumes.

Jim grinned. 'What a time to tell your folks you're gay, when you're just about to turn celibate. Why tell them anything at all?'

'Because that's what the self-improvement plan is. It's an honesty campaign.' Greg discarded the rest of the ham roll, flashing a look at the fat lady behind the sandwich counter. 'She's gone too far this time, I wish she'd get a crush on someone else. Honesty with others and honesty with myself,' he explained. 'A few months of celibacy just to prove I can do it and then ... ' Greg looked suddenly serious. 'And then I'm going to front up for the test again.'

Jim's smile faded. 'But why? You said you didn't want to know. You said ... '

'I know what I said. I've changed my mind.'

'Why?'

'I don't want to spend the rest of my life tarting around, I suppose.' The flash of a smile. 'I think I'd like to meet Mr Right. Settle down one day.' Then he looked directly into Jim's eyes and the smile faded. 'You made me realise that.'

Jim felt a sudden panic. Surely the depth of his feeling for Greg wasn't that readable.

Greg wrapped his half-eaten roll in a paper serviette and his tone was flippant again. 'Don't worry, you're not expected to be the recipient of my affections.' He rose and neatly lobbed the ham roll into the rubbish bin by the main doors. 'Bullseye.' He turned back to Jim. 'Not unless you want to be.' Then he grinned and left.

Jim stared down at his coffee. He hadn't even had one sip and it would be lukewarm by now.

That Friday night, drinks in the greenroom finished early. After all, the cast would be seeing each other at the airport the following morning. Vicky was excited. Not only had she never been out of Australia, she'd never even been on a plane before — let alone a

154

Citation jet. And she'd certainly never stayed in a mansion on a private island.

At ten o'clock on Saturday morning they all met in the flight deck lounge. All, that is, except Edwina. She loathed airports and the gawking of the general public. Partners were once again not invited and she didn't want to go to the Bryces' at all, let alone without Davey. She chose to arrive five minutes before takeoff.

It was the first interstate trip of 'The Glitter Game' cast and Sidney Meredith had lashed out on a new wardrobe. He arrived at the flight deck complete with wide-brimmed Texan hat, sheepskin jerkin and large dark glasses. It had always been his policy when travelling with a recognisable show to travel as a star. Mandy was disgusted, even though her philosophy was basically the same and she was wearing a blue silk blouse with a very large silver bow at the throat. Sidney downed as many of the free drinks as possible, smoking incessantly as he did so. Flying always made him nervous. Seated beside him, Narelle was swathed in smoke and excused herself to sit between Mandy and Paul. Mandy left for the ladies' loo, Paul was busily hunting the crowded lounge for Edwina and Narelle wondered what she'd done wrong.

Vicky was talking nineteen to the dozen at Jane who was delighting in the girl's excitement but not listening to a word she said. Jane was sorry that only the cast had been invited and was wishing that Chris was there. Not for any special reason, of course. She just so enjoyed their discussions.

Greg was thinking along the same lines. What a pity Jim wasn't coming along. He hadn't seen much of him since he'd dropped the bomb on Tuesday. He really mustn't push the poor bloke too fast, he thought, or send him up too much. He grinned to himself nonetheless. Jim invited send-up and it was why Greg had decided that he loved him. Yes, you'd better watch it, old sport. I'm deadly serious.

The trip was pleasant but uneventful. Sidney drank his fill of the endless supply of free alcohol and Vicky ate rapaciously of the endless supply of food.

'Careful,' Greg whispered. 'No one loves a fat TV star.' Vicky shot a look in Mandy's direction. 'Not a young one anyway,' he corrected.

They were met at the island's landing strip by three Rolls Royce limousines. Greg, Vicky, Jane and Narelle made great friends with their chauffeur called Ron who promised to take them on a guided tour of the island after lunch.

Paul tried to corner the second limousine for Edwina and himself. He no longer heavied Edwina in any way, he simply idolised the woman. But Mandy barged in. She hadn't intended to be intrusive but when she realised she was going to be stranded with Sidney in the last limousine she had no alternative.

Sidney was legless. The chauffeur helped him into the third car and Sidney sank into the back seat, blissfully aware that he had a chauffeured limo all to himself and that he was a star and that everything was the way it should be.

The drive to the Bryce mansion was short but spectacular. As Sidney was helped from the car, he noticed the others piling out of the two vehicles ahead and suddenly realised they hadn't all had limos of their own. No time to think about that, though, he'd dropped his hat. The chauffeur picked it up and put it on his head and they all proceeded inside.

Ray Chaplin was there to meet them with several other senior members of Bryce's staff. The Bryces themselves were absent but, according to Ray, were looking forward to meeting the cast at the formal dinner that evening. In the meantime, they'd be shown to their suites; there'd be a private informal buffet lunch by the pool and the drivers would be waiting in the foyer at three o'clock should anyone want to be shown the sights.

It was a magnificent mansion — ultra modern but in the best of taste. Each suite in the guest wing had its own balcony overlooking the ocean, and was luxuriously appointed and individually coordinated. Vicky had never seen anything like it.

'Wow!' Jane had the room next door. Vicky raced in. 'Is yours as good as mine?' She looked around. 'Wow!' she said again. 'Just as good but different. Unreal!'

'Fantastic, isn't it?' Jane had intended to play it worldly but how could she be hypocritical in the face of Vicky's enthusiasm? After all, she wasn't exactly accustomed to luxury herself. She smiled as Vicky ran out onto the balcony. Whatever had happened to that tough, defiant little kid who had turned up to the first rehearsal not so very long ago? They had all warmed to Vicky's metamorphosis and had learned that they couldn't be phoney with her — the girl was too genuine. Anyway, it was embarrassing if one tried; she seemed to see through any artifice.

Jane and Vicky explored their rooms together, Vicky screaming like the teenager she was and Jane screaming just as loudly. They opened one of their bottles of Dom Perignon and read their personal letters of welcome which were nestling in huge bouquets of flowers. Then they ripped apart their baskets of tropical fruit and Jane taught Vicky how to eat a mango.

Edwina's reaction wasn't quite so exuberant. She'd rather be at home with Davey and anyway the Bryce mansion was too modern for her taste. She gave her welcoming letter a perfunctory look and then noticed the handwritten note beside the fruit basket.

It was from Melanie. If Edwina was a little tired after the flight and didn't fancy socialising by the pool perhaps she might like a quiet lunch in Melanie's private apartments?

OK. Might as well get it over and done with. Besides, Edwina thought, it could prove rather interesting. Melanie was a fascinating woman and, to tell the truth, Edwina was just a little bored with the continual 'Glitter Game' fraternising. Interesting people as they were, there was no challenge left. Apart from acting — and performance relationships were now very firmly established — she didn't feel she had that much in common with the rest of the cast. On the other hand, power was stimulating and Melanie certainly had power. Not all wealth-related either. Melanie had real power.

Sidney carefully packed away the gift bottle of Dom Perignon in the bottom of his overnight bag then attacked the courtesy bar-fridge. Three lethal premixed daiquiris later he decided to have a little lie-down before lunch and passed out.

Mandy took a long time wondering what to wear to the poolside buffet and decided on the apricot chiffon.

Greg and Paul both arrived at lunch wearing shirts and bathing costumes and Narelle arrived with a wrap-around over her bikini.

'Hell, is it OK if we swim?' Vicky asked.

''Course it is. It's a poolside party just for us, stupid,' Greg answered.

Vicky and Jane exchanged glances and raced for the lifts to get their bathers.

Paul was disappointed that Edwina wasn't there but had a wonderful time ducking and bombing the girls and generally letting everyone know that he was a superb swimmer. Greg flirted outrageously with the drinks waiter but inwardly smacked his wrists and told himself not to; and after inwardly agonising, Mandy ate a large slice of wild cherry cheesecake in front of everyone, and loved it.

In a suite of rooms in the 'house' wing things were a little more subdued.

Melanie looked every bit as good as Edwina remembered. Very tall, about the same height as Edwina, slim and elegant with a mane of flaming red hair. The two women sized each other up admiringly.

'It's lovely to see you again, Edwina.'

'You too, Melanie. You're looking wonderful.'

'Champagne?'

'Thank you.'

'Which?' Melanie lifted a bottle of Bollinger from the ice bucket on the table. 'I seem to remember you like Bollinger.'

Edwina noticed the open bottle of Dom Perignon on the table and Melanie's half-filled glass beside it. She smiled.

'Dom'll do fine, thanks.' My God, the woman had a memory. They'd only met once after her concert. Mind you, Edwina recalled, they'd talked voraciously for an hour and only called a halt when Melanie had suggested they go back to her hotel and Edwina had replied, 'I'm not that kind of woman'. But they'd laughed and parted friends.

'How are you enjoying the show?' Melanie asked. 'You're very good. Robert's thrilled.'

'I'm glad.' Edwina decided she had nothing to lose by being honest. 'I was rather nervous to start with. All those established actors. Me with no training.' She shrugged. 'Anyway, it worked out.'

'It certainly did.' Melanie took a sip of her champagne. 'It's an excellent cast. Jane Richmond's wonderful – I love your work together.'

'Yes, she's good, isn't she?' Why did Edwina feel a tinge of animosity towards Jane? Their scenes together were good and she loved acting with her. Was she a touch jealous of Melanie's interest in Jane? Why, for God's sake? Was it because she felt that Jane was competition in the work field? Maybe. Her reaction on first meeting Jane had been 'beware' and in a sense she knew she was right. She knew that Jane was dedicated and ambitious, but surely that could be said of any serious actress worth her salt? So why did she feel jealous, competitive, self-protective? Edwina stored it all up. She'd think about it later.

The afternoon sped by pleasantly enough. They ate eggs Benedict and opened the other bottle of champagne. They talked music, theatre and film. Edwina found that she had a lot to learn from Melanie. Not only did Melanie's interests lie in the arts but Robert's many investments included film and theatre so Melanie had made it her business to know all she could about them. They listened to and discussed avidly the scores of two hit musicals about to have their first Australian productions — Robert had invested in both shows. Edwina had never met Robert, but she made a mental note to work on him when she did. The lead in a big musical could prove interesting if she got bored with the series at any stage.

It was nearly five o'clock before Edwina finally made a move to leave. They'd been sipping their coffees in the rooftop garden which overlooked the ocean.

'It's been a lovely afternoon, Melanie, thank you.'

'It could be even lovelier.' Melanie took her hand but Edwina withdrew it gently and shook her head. 'I take it you're still not that kind of woman.' Melanie gave a wry smile. 'I didn't think so. Pity.' She laughed. 'Robert's going to be pleased.'

'Oh?'

'He knew I sent you an invitation. I don't think he liked it very much. And of course by now he'll have been told you've spent the afternoon with me.'

'Oh.' Edwina didn't look too happy.

Melanie laughed again. 'My dear, don't worry. I don't flirt very often — there never seems to be anyone all that worthwhile. On the odd occasion that I do, though, Robert's most forbearing. We have an understanding.'

'But we didn't . . . '

'Exactly. And I'll tell him just that. Which is why he's going to be pleased.'

'And if he doesn't believe you?'

'He will. He always does. We always believe each other.'

Edwina left with only the slightest of misgivings. If Melanie was lying about the Bryces' 'understanding' and if Robert were to take umbrage, then what the hell? Edwina had never allowed herself to be dictated to by people or circumstances and she didn't intend to start now.

Melanie hadn't been lying. She and Robert had a perfect understanding. Although neither particularly liked the other's occasional peccadillo, they always told each other about them — which, after twenty-five years of marriage, they considered a very healthy attitude.

They'd remained faithful for the first fifteen years. Ever since they'd met at university, in fact, she a vibrant nineteen-year-old first year student and he topping his final year at twenty-three. They married six months later. Melanie and Robert were, and had always been, the best of friends. Their sexual compatibility was still good, if in need of the odd meaningless extramarital fling every now and then, and their personal and work relationship was perfect. Although allowing Robert centre stage, Melanie's input to their vast empire was as important and as committed as Robert's. They were inseparable and totally supportive of each other both emotionally and in the image they presented to the outside world.

There'd only been one shaky episode and that was when Melanie had been tempted to indiscretion. It had been five years ago — by then, both she and Robert had succumbed to several one-night stands, always conducted discreetly and with the other partner's knowledge. Then Melanie had let an attraction get out of hand – she'd let an attraction become an obsession.

His name was Brian Hopgood and he was Robert's personal bodyguard. Brian never succumbed to Melanie's advances which made him all the more attractive. If he'd only agreed to satisfy her, he may have become just one of those nights of passion, but Brian's loyalties remained with his employer and Melanie's obsession grew.

Robert watched with growing concern, aware of what was happening but unsure as to the action he should take. It was unfair to dismiss Brian when it was no fault of his and God only knew what would happen if he forbade Melanie to see the man.

It was Brian who solved it all. Very simply. Bryce Holdings had recently acquired Network Three and Brian applied for the position of security chief at the Sydney channel. His reasons for wanting the transfer were never mentioned. He merely reminded Robert of the rumour that there may have been an illicit business being run by the team of security guards at Channel 3; studio supplies, timber and equipment had gone missing recently. Brian thought he'd be the person to sort it out.

He was. Brian sacked the entire studio security staff shortly after his arrival and personally vetted those re-employed, mostly from the ranks of ex-policemen. The rip-offs ceased immediately.

Melanie got over her infatuation and Robert's gratitude to Brian's loyalty knew no bounds. Now Brian Hopgood, although continuing to serve as security chief, was in essence Robert's undercover 2IC and was remunerated accordingly.

Narelle and Paul had intended joining Jane, Greg and Vicky for a sightseeing drive but the distracting sight of each other's bodies in the pool and their physical contact as they splashed about made them aware of other things. By the time Paul had lined up the girls to stand behind each other down the centre of the pool and had swum two lengths underwater between their open legs, a sightseeing drive was the last thing he wanted.

And when Narelle straddled his shoulders to take on Vicky and Greg in a 'cockfight', the warmth of her thighs pressing against the sides of his face made Paul wish to hell the others would bugger off. Narelle was totally aware of the bulge in Paul's bathers and it delighted her. What a lovely afternoon they were going to have.

And they did. As Mandy excused herself to have a lie-down before the formal dinner and the others left to change for the drive, Paul finally emerged from the pool, covered his embarrassment with a towel and bustled Narelle up to his suite.

As Vicky marvelled at the vivid aqua ocean stretching endlessly into the distance, Paul marvelled at the perfect breast offering itself to his mouth.

As Greg and Jane devoured the panoramic view from the island's highest peak, Paul and Narelle, wrapped head to toe, devoured each other.

As Mandy tucked herself into bed, having arranged a wake-up call with Bryce's housekeeper, Narelle and Paul repositioned three-way wardrobe mirrors and experimented with writing desks and glass-topped coffee tables.

As the housemaid tending the suite next door to Sidney's wondered at the stentorian snores, Narelle and Paul met their perfect match in each other. They sucked, blew, nibbled, chewed, tantalised and heaved to their mutual delight.

It was only when the telephone buzzed in Mandy's suite and the voice said, 'It's six-thirty, Miss Burgess' that, nerves twitching and libidos screaming, they exploded in ecstasy.

★

Narelle and Paul were pleasantly tired when they came down to dinner.

Mandy and Sidney, to their mutual consternation, were the first to arrive and so had to sit together in the lounge chatting to Ray Chaplin as they waited for the others.

Sidney felt refreshed. He was raring to go after his afternoon nap and was drinking brandy alexanders as was his wont when he didn't have to pay. Mandy delicately put a pink satin-gloved hand to her face while she talked to him. Sidney's breath was very stale.

'Hello, Paul, Narelle. Did you have a nice snooze?' Mandy breathed a sigh of relief as they joined the table.

'Lovely, thank you,' Narelle beamed.

Edwina arrived, looking spectacular in a simple black cocktail gown, closely followed by Melanie and Robert Bryce who introduced themselves with a casual charm that immediately relaxed the others.

Greg, Jane and Vicky were profuse in their apologies as they raced in fifteen minutes late but the Bryces were gracious, insisting that it didn't matter at all.

It was difficult not to be disarmed by Vicky's enthusiasm. 'I've never seen ocean that colour! I always thought they touched up the postcards.'

It was a pleasant dinner. Despite the six courses including sorbet and impeccable waiter service, it was hardly formal at all and this was mainly due to the Bryces. Melanie was relaxed and friendly, making sure she chatted individually to each member of the cast. But it was Robert's speech which really warmed everyone to the couple. He made several humorous references to Melanie, which she applauded and laughed at warmly and it was generally noted that this was the top of the pecking order. Unlike the executives at the network dinner, Robert and Melanie Bryce could afford to relax and be themselves and it was charming.

Robert Bryce, with Melanie firmly by his side, had most certainly built his empire but he was not entirely a self-made man.

One of five children, his father had inherited a wealthy farming property in the black soil belt of northern New South Wales. It was this same black belt which proved so successful in the cultivation of cotton and Robert Bryce Senior was one of the first farmers to refuse sale to an American combine and convert to cotton independently. It was an expensive conversion but proved hugely successful. So successful that Robert Bryce Senior became far more than a simple farmer. He bought himself a factory, became a major investor in a cotton manufacturing consortium and took a great interest in all facets of the stock market. Indeed, if the anchovies were not running down the warm Gulf of Mexico he planted soy beans that year in the knowledge that, second to anchovies, soy beans were the source of protein most sought by Third World countries and would therefore be heavily in demand. And, not only did soy bean crops thrive on the black soil belt, but a season of soy beans enriched the earth and ensured a bumper cotton harvest the following season. And above all, it was the cotton itself — white gold, as it was known — that mattered most to Robert Bryce Senior, the Cotton King. How he loved to see the uniform rows of silver-white bolls stretching away as far as the eye could see.

It was a disappointment to him when his eldest son didn't want to work the plantation but one he rapidly overcame when that same son showed an early interest in the investment market and a keen desire to go into business himself. Bryce Senior was a hard man, but fair. His son Robert was to receive no share of the property either now or on his father's death. If he didn't want to work the land, he didn't deserve to reap the benefits. He was, however, presented with $100,000 in stocks and shares and told he was to put himself through whatever business or university course he wished and then see what he could make of himself.

And he did. There was never any looking back for Robert Bryce Junior. It was just the start he needed.

After the dinner, Robert, like Melanie, made a point of chatting personally with each of the members of the cast but it was Edwina in whom he was most interested. He suggested they retire to the bar for a cognac with their coffee.

Edwina eyed him over the top of her brandy balloon. He was a highly attractive man, and looked a decade younger than his forty-eight years. Rather like a young John F. Kennedy, she thought: a thatch of sandy-coloured hair, a strong, slightly granite-jawed face and a devastatingly winning grin which he knew how to use.

'Melanie tells me you spent a pleasant afternoon together.'

Edwina searched his face for a sign of disapproval but there was none. In fact there was something beyond the warmth he exuded — could it be gratitude?

'Yes,' Edwina replied. 'She's wonderful company.'

'She says the same of you, Edwina, and I can see why. I've always admired your work, of course. And now I can admire you in person.' He smiled and extended his hand. Yes, Edwina thought, he's actually grateful. 'If there's ever anything I can do for you, I expect you to come to me, all right?' The smile was still there but there was a ring to the voice that said 'I mean it'.

Edwina took the card he offered. 'Thank you, Robert. I'll remember that.'

The rest of the weekend went by quickly. Paul and Narelle had a rematch that night, Sidney drank four brandy alexanders too many after dinner and passed out again and Jane and Vicky explored every inch of the vast mansion grounds Sunday morning while, surprisingly enough, Mandy and Greg enjoyed a game of euchre.

Suddenly it was three o'clock and they had to leave. During the flight home everyone compared notes and came to the conclusion that the Bryces were a terrific couple, that Bryce Holdings was a great management to work for and that they were all lucky to be in such a happy hit show. This conclusion had, after all, been the object of the entire weekend so Melanie and Robert, who also compared notes, were extremely delighted at the outcome. Robert was pleased too on a personal level. Another possible obsession of Melanie's had been averted.

And Edwina was happy. During the plane trip home, she analysed the events and concluded they could well work to her advantage.

★

The first thing Edwina did when she arrived home was ring Liza. 'I know I said Monday but I'm keen to see it. Is it ready?'

For some reason Paul's obvious cavorting with Narelle had fuelled the fires of Edwina's desire for revenge. While he'd been contrite and continued to pay her homage, she'd regretted having to cripple his career. Not that she'd contemplated reversing her decision, of course, but she had regretted having to do it. Now that she'd witnessed him flaunt his lust with Narelle, Edwina was refired. How dare he forget that Saturday night? He must pay for his intrusion.

'Yes,' Liza said. 'It's ready. Do you want me to call around with it?'

'Thank you, Liza. I'd be most grateful if you could.'

That's what I want, Edwina, Liza thought. Gratitude is what I want. Liza hadn't enjoyed doing the story on Paul but she knew that the sooner it was out and had its desired effect, the sooner Edwina would be forced to fulfil her side of the bargain and Liza would have the inside story that any journalist would kill for.

'Another coffee?'

Liza nodded and watched as Edwina put down the copy and went into the kitchen to fetch the percolator. Nothing was said until Edwina had refilled both cups. Then she handed Liza her espresso blend and sat down.

'It's fantastic. Exactly what I wanted.'

Liza had known it would be. It was lethal. 'I've already lined up the editor,' she said. 'He hasn't seen it but he's taking it on my say-so. He's sworn to secrecy and it'll be printed anonymously.'

'When?'

'He'll run it tomorrow if you like. Morning and afternoon editions.'

'The sooner the better.'

When Liza left, Edwina didn't waste time gloating but picked up her script to study her lines, safe in the knowledge that the following day would see Paul Sorell's life in ruins.

Retribution

Paul felt good as he drove to work on Monday. It was a glorious day. He'd done his five-kilometre jog in record time that morning, cooled off with a dip in the pool — and had gained great satisfaction as he viewed his body in the full-length bathroom mirror. It could have been that of a twenty-two year old.

He drove past a newsagency and glanced at the billboard a man was putting on display. STAR'S SORDID PAST — TELEVISION'S BEST-KEPT SECRET! Some poor bastard was copping it, he thought, and wondered who it might be.

The traffic lights turned red. Good. He'd have time to buy a paper. He dug out a dollar and waved to the boy at the intersection.

'Keep the change.'

'Thanks, mate.'

Paul glanced down at the headlines. STAR'S SEX WITH MINOR . . . *Young Enough to be His Daughter*!

The traffic lights turned green. The driver behind Paul blasted his car horn but Paul remained transfixed, staring down at the picture of himself.

Monday was interminable for Paul. He tried to ring home as soon as he got to the channel but the phone was engaged. Some well-meaning creep ringing

Barbie to commiserate, Paul supposed. The rest of the cast were sympathetic, of course, but it didn't help. They're just thankful it wasn't some shit dug up about them, Paul thought. It wasn't long before the summons came.

'Alain wants to see you at lunchtime.' Carol from the production office interrupted rehearsals.

The moment they broke for lunch, Paul again tried ringing Barbie. Still engaged! Why couldn't they leave her alone? he thought. The bastards.

'We'll be terminating your contract, of course, with the customary four weeks' notice.' Alain leaned back in his chair. 'I've already spoken to your agent but I decided, as a courtesy, to tell you myself.'

As a courtesy, my arse. You're gloating, you smug hypocritical bastard. Paul studied the Pro Hart behind Alain's head.

'There's nothing we can do for you this time, Paul. There'll be a public outcry and the network can't afford to let its moral standing . . . '

'Is that all?' Paul rose.

Alain's eyes narrowed. He didn't like being interrupted and certainly not in that tone. 'There's no call to be offensive. I'm merely pointing out —'

'I said, is that all?'

Alain nodded curtly and Paul left.

He tried ringing home again. Still engaged. He tried several times during the afternoon to no avail. How much commiseration does the woman need? Then he realised. Of course! It would be the press. Poor Barbie, they were probably giving her hell.

'I'm going home, Chris.' There was a touch of defiance in Paul's voice; there were still six scenes to rehearse for tomorrow's taping and it was most unprofessional of him. But Chris understood. He even understood Paul's peremptory manner.

'OK, Paul. We'll fly those scenes tomorrow, no worries.'

The first thing Paul saw when he opened his front door was three suitcases standing side by side in the hall. My God, what sort of drama was this? Was Barbie threatening to walk out on him? That sort of dramatic gesture was hardly her style but he supposed it was possible. Not to worry. He'd talk her around as usual.

'Barbie?'

She was sitting in the lounge room, sipping a Scotch and ice.

'I've been trying to ring you all day but the phone was engaged. Was it the press?'

'No.'

'Friendly advice from the shits, then. Great.' Paul poured himself a hefty Scotch. 'Barbie, honey. I'm sorry.' He looked at her but she remained staring down at her glass, swirling the liquor over the cubes of ice. Hell, this was going to be more difficult than usual. He lifted the ice cube tray from the bar refrigerator. Empty. That was unlike Barbie, she knew how he hated running short of ice. He toyed with the idea of getting some from the kitchen then thought, no, he'd better give her his full attention.

'Honey, whatever those shits said, don't listen to them. It was a long time ago and —'

'Those shits didn't say anything.'

'But the phone was engaged all —'

'I had it off the hook.'

'Oh.' Paul sipped his Scotch, slightly unnerved. He

didn't like the expression on Barbie's face. 'Well, that was a good idea. The press would probably have . . . '

'I had it off the hook because I knew you'd be trying to ring.' Barbie's eyes were tired and drawn as if she were all cried out. And she was. She'd made her decision. It had been heartbreaking but not difficult. In fact she couldn't think of an alternative and nothing Paul could say would make any difference. 'I don't want you to say anything, Paul, I just want you to go.'

Paul was dumbfounded. 'But —'

'I've packed your suitcases. They're in the hall.'

Paul sat next to her but she turned away. 'For God's sake, honey, listen —'

'If it was at all viable,' Barbie continued, 'I'd go myself but it's not. The twins need —'

'Stop it.' Paul put his glass down and took her by the shoulders. 'Look at me, Barb.'

She looked at him but the eyes were hard and unrelenting beneath the fatigue. 'I told Jamie he could go with you if he wanted to,' she said, 'but he's decided to stay here.'

'Oh, come on, Barbie Doll . . . '

He attempted to embrace her but she broke away from him, slamming her drink on the bar. 'Don't Barbie Doll me, Paul! Just get out. Get out right now.'

Suddenly Paul knew she meant it and, just as suddenly, he felt exhausted. Everything was falling down around him and there was nothing he could do about it. 'They gave me the sack. A month's notice.'

There was a glimpse of compassion in Barbie's eyes. 'I'm sorry about that.'

Paul rose. 'Barbie, couldn't we —'

'No. No, we couldn't. Ring and leave a number so I can tell people where to contact you.' She left the room.

Paul knew it was no good following her. He downed his Scotch, considered pouring another one, then decided against it. He took a full bottle from the grog cabinet and put it in his pocket. Better to get drunk on his own.

He walked into the hall and picked up the suitcases.

'Dad.'

He turned. Jamie was at the kitchen door. 'I'll give you a hand.' Jamie took one of the suitcases, opened the front door and they walked to the car together. Paul didn't know what to say. He felt like crying.

'I hope you don't mind my staying with Mum. She'll need some looking after — the twins too.'

'I'd expect you to, Jamie.' Paul slammed the car boot shut and stood looking awkwardly at his son. 'I'm sorry. It was a bastard of a story. It was true, but they made it sound like . . . '

'I know. I can't say I really understand, but you're right. It was a bastard of a story and it was a bastard who wrote it.'

Paul hugged the boy hard, willing away the burning tears that threatened to overcome him at any minute. 'I'll ring as soon as I'm settled. Everything'll work out OK. You'll see.'

He got into the car and drove off, not looking back for fear that the boy would see the tears coursing down his face.

Barbie wasn't crying. Barbie was numb. There were no tears left. She eyed the bottle of Valium in the bathroom as she splashed her face with cold water. No, not this time. She'd sought solace in pills seven years ago when she'd felt she could no longer suffer Paul's infidelities and they hadn't solved anything. This time Barbie wasn't going to go under. This time she was set on a positive course of action. This time was going to see the rebirth of Barbie Nelson, photographic and haute couture model. Barbie was going to become her own woman again.

Not that she'd regretted, in the early years, throwing away her highly successful modelling career in favour of Paul. There was simply no choice in the matter. Her love for him far outweighed any personal ambition and there was certainly never the option of having both. Paul had never demanded she give up her career of course but Barbie knew his ego would demand full attention and she'd been right.

Just as she'd been right when she'd told herself, a little later in their marriage, that his sexual dalliances weren't a threat to their abiding love for each other. But repetition wore her down. Repetition of his women, his excuses, his declarations of undying love, until finally she could take no more. Then the twins. The amazing intervention of the twins and the God-given bond they brought with them. Paul changed. Oh, how he changed: faithful, loyal — a different man. Or so Barbie had thought. But how long had the change really lasted?

Barbie felt sick with the realisation of how self-deluded she'd become. She'd read the signs and she'd ignored them, she'd excused them, she'd deliberately misinterpreted them. She'd even attributed them to her own paranoia.

She supposed she would have continued to do so if this present sex story hadn't reared its ugly head. Mind you, she might have even invented an excuse for that had she not received the phone call that same morning — the phone call informing her, very factually, of Paul's weekend of endless sex with Narelle. She didn't need the gentle but insistent male voice telling her that Paul and Narelle had copulated Saturday afternoon, again that evening and, having spent the night together, presumably Sunday morning as well.

All Barbie knew was that she'd chosen to ignore the age-old signs when she'd met Paul at the airport on Sunday afternoon. The cocky, king-of-the-roost strut (that would have been because Narelle was watching), the tender declarations of love that evening (made not out of guilt, but as an attempt by Paul to cover his tracks). Barbie berated herself. What had happened to her? They were all the old signs she used to read so well and lately she'd been waiting in the lounge every evening with a fresh Scotch and ice for her prince telling herself she was paranoid. No more, she told herself, no more.

Barbie hadn't been idle that afternoon. She hadn't left the phone off the hook. After the call informing her of Paul's weekend activities with Narelle, she'd rung several of her contacts from the modelling world, all of whom were only too happy to welcome her back into the industry with the intimidating words 'You've been a long time away, of course'. But Barbie was not to be daunted. She re-signed with her old agent who was delighted to have her back, she lined up a photo session for new folio shots. (She set it for Wednesday, enough time for the puffiness to go down so long as she didn't cry any more.) She'd lined up a facial, manicure, pedicure and body massage for the next day. And she even lined up her first job. No money, but that didn't matter, there'd be press coverage. She was to compere the fashion parade at the charity preview of the new Harry Who range in three weeks. She had a feeling they wanted her because she'd be hot gossip after today's story, but so what? She had to use everything she had. That was the name of the game.

Barbie looked at her face in the bathroom mirror then thought about the Valium in the cupboard behind it and knew she'd made the right choice. So why did she feel like reaching for the bottle? God, how she loved him. She turned off the bathroom light.

Davey hadn't liked making the call but Edwina had insisted.

'There's a possibility the channel won't fire him, Davey — he's very popular. And I want to make sure he suffers so it'll have to be the marriage.'

Davey knew how Edwina loathed having her private domain trespassed upon and he also knew why. She was angry with Paul and Davey understood that, but he never quite understood Edwina's 'vendetta moods'. There was no obvious venom evident — rather a sort of judicial quality. As if she felt she had the absolute right to mete out justice.

No, Davey hadn't wanted to make the call. But he'd made it. Davey always did as Edwina wanted. He always had and he always would.

The following day Paul was nearly twenty minutes late for his make-up call. His eyes were bloodshot, he hadn't shaved and his breath still stank of whisky.

Edwina was most conciliatory. 'It was a shocking

story, Paul, but you mustn't let it affect you like this. Try and put it behind you.'

'She kicked me out, Edwina. Barbie kicked me out.'

'Oh.' Edwina's face was a mask of sympathy. 'She'll get over it in time. She's hurt and shocked right now but she'll get over it.'

'I doubt it.'

'How did the network take it? Has Alain said anything?'

Paul nodded miserably. 'Four weeks' notice.'

'Oh no.' She clasped his hand, a very forward gesture for Edwina. 'I'm so sorry.'

'Thank you, Edwina.' Paul felt grateful. Not many women would be so understanding about a story like that. Her kindness would most certainly help him through this first horrific day.

And it was horrific. He found it impossible to concentrate and the lines that he'd known so well constantly eluded him. Several times during the day he rang Barbie but there was no reply from either her or the answering machine. He finally got hold of Jamie who told him that Barbie had arranged appointments all day and that she was intent on re-establishing her career. Jamie was sympathetic as he told Paul that Barbie's attitude hadn't changed — if anything she was more adamant than ever that Paul keep well out of her life.

Paul drove back to the hotel in a state of acute depression. He bought another bottle of whisky on the way, promising himself that, with an early morning studio call, he couldn't afford to obliterate himself. He'd just have a nightcap to help him sleep.

By the time the bottle was half-empty Paul's depression had turned to anger. He'd find out whoever had been responsible for the story and he'd kill them. The bastards! He'd kill them!

Over the next few days Paul's anger helped him cut back on the drinking. He'd intended making enquiries of every press contact he had as to who had written the article but it proved unnecessary. The press came to him. The first journalist who rang asking for his reply to the story nearly copped a stream of abuse but Paul suddenly thought better of it.

'I'll give you an interview if you find out who wrote that shit.'

He tried the same tack on the next four journalists who phoned, to no avail. If anyone knew they weren't saying, least of all the newspaper editor who'd sworn blind that the article had arrived on his desk anonymously with backup material proving its authenticity in case of a libel suit — of course, it was too good a story for him to knock back.

'Sorry Paul, no harm intended but I have a paper to sell, strictly business, you —'

Paul had smashed the phone down and knocked back two hefty Scotches.

Jim Avalon and Chris Natteros had worried that Paul's drinking might get the better of him and that he might let the show down or seriously hold up production but, as the days wore on, they decided that he was going to be able to handle it. In fact they both thought it was a mistake for Alain to fire him. He was giving an excellent performance and was proving tremendously popular with the viewers.

They transferred their worries to Vicky and Simon. Simon Rothwell had only been working on the show several days before a major problem presented itself. Vicky couldn't stand him. True, he was an arrogant young man but so were many actors of his age — he'd get over it. And his attitude was professional enough, his performance good. Indeed, there were times when his performance was excellent. There were times when his energy level was magnetic and they couldn't understand why Vicky didn't respond to it.

Not that Vicky allowed her dislike of Simon to disrupt work or cause any form of dissension. But there was no magic between them. When she was working with Greg there was a wonderful rapport but no matter how electric Simon's performance was, it drew no response from her.

Chris tried every directorial ploy he knew to no avail. The more energy the boy gave in his performance, the more Vicky withdrew. Finally Chris pulled her aside during a coffee break and hissed frustratedly at her.

'What the hell's the matter with you? Why can't you relate to Simon?'

'I'm sorry, Chris. I'm trying.'

'No, you're not. The more energy the kid gives you the more you hold back. Now why?'

'Because I can't stand him, that's why.' It was the first time during work that Vicky's rebellious nature had got the better of her and she could have kicked herself for snapping at Chris. He was a beaut bloke and he didn't deserve that but, hell, he just didn't know the score. 'Sorry, I'll try harder,' she muttered and left.

Vicky knew why she couldn't work with Simon. She'd known why the first day she met him.

Simon had snorted an extra line that morning before setting off for his first day's rehearsal and he'd slipped his special little grinder into his pocket in case he needed a bit of a lift during the afternoon.

Vicky hadn't read the signs immediately. Like the rest of the cast she thought he was pushing a little too hard, probably due to first day nerves, and had tried to help him relax. When he suggested that they have lunch together she agreed. The quicker they got to know each other the better. It was then that she'd realised Simon had a problem. He'd had two quick hits from the grinder in the men's on his way to the canteen and was on quite a high by the time he met her.

Vicky wasn't judgemental about social drug users. She'd snorted cocaine a couple of times herself at parties but had quickly stopped when she'd woken the next morning with awful sinus pains. Bugger the pros who said flush your nasal passages out with warm water — it wasn't worth it.

But it didn't take Vicky long to realise that Simon wasn't just a social user. In fact she reached her conclusion about halfway through that first lunch.

'Two lamb chops, veg and lots of chips,' Vicky said to the pimply canteen assistant.

'Same for me,' added Simon, although he had no idea what Vicky had just ordered. He wasn't remotely hungry.

They slid into a booth up the back and Simon started. He started talking intensely, gesticulating wildly and laughing loudly. Everything about him was big and unnatural. Vicky looked at his eyes — the pupils were dilated. What's he on? she wondered. Flecks of spittle were forming in the corners of his mouth and he sniffed loudly several times in mid-conversation. Yeah, Vicky concluded, cocaine — and lots of it too. She'd read the signs many times over the years and knew them well. She didn't want to look at him and tried to concentrate on her chops.

Simon was convinced that he was fascinating. Vicky fancied him, he knew it. In fact, he was sure that she lusted after him. He tried to catch a glimpse of her breasts as she hunched over her plate and toyed with her chips — she had a great body all right . . . that tight little arse in those stretch jeans, how he'd love to get his hands around that.

Vicky was well aware of Simon's drug-induced lust and it disgusted her. She tried to attack her food but gave up. The sight of Simon's chops congealing before him put her off. It was a pity, she rather liked the canteen's greasy lamb loins.

Finally she pushed her plate aside and slid out of the booth. 'I'm going back to the greenroom.'

Simon stopped in mid-sentence. 'But lunchbreak isn't over yet.'

'I want to run some lines.' She lowered her voice as she leaned forward. 'I'd go easy on that stuff if I were you.' And Vicky left the canteen.

The warning meant nothing to Simon. From that day on things only grew worse. In rehearsal, brotherly gestures became an excuse for him to touch her up and he merely laughed when she slapped his hand away.

The situation was intolerable and Vicky didn't know what to do. She couldn't report him to management; she'd been brought up not to grass on junkies. Perhaps Greg might know what to do. But if she told Greg, wasn't she just handing him her dilemma? It would then become his decision whether or not to inform management and, if he did, that would still mean she'd grassed, wouldn't it?

★

Vicky actually breathed a sigh of relief when the day came to tape her nude scene. Nervous as she was, it meant a whole day's taping without Simon. After several morning scenes with Mandy and Narelle, the whole afternoon was scheduled for Vicky and Greg, culminating in the seduction scene.

It was a fun day and went quickly. Vicky was so relaxed that, after rehearsing the seduction scene a number of times, it came as a slight shock when Sandy took her aside and said 'We'll need clothes off for the final rehearsal. You OK with that, love?'

'Sure.' Vicky gave an efficient nod but started to feel distinctly nervous as Sandy ordered the first assistant to check the 'closed set' lights.

When Vicky had read on the advance schedules that Sandy, the second unit director, was to be handling her nude scene she'd been disappointed. She wanted Chris – she knew him and felt safe with him. Then she'd realised that Jim had deliberately scheduled a female director for her and she was touched. It was typical of Jim's sensitivity.

And now that she knew Sandy she was doubly grateful. She admired the woman's no-nonsense, direct approach to her work and there was a tough motherliness about Sandy that Vicky responded to.

Sandy was tough, all right. A big woman in her mid-forties, she had fought discrimination in the days when there were few women directors. She was aggressive and had a tendency to be bossy which didn't endear her to the crew. In fact, many crew members openly disliked her which didn't bother Sandy at all. If they slacked off then she whipped them into shape and bugger them if they didn't like it. She positioned herself beside a monitor and nodded to Ken, the first assistant.

'Final rehearsal, quiet please,' she called. A pause. 'Standing by.' A pause. 'Action.'

Vicky concentrated hard, trying to block out the studio and crew as she slowly undid the buttons of the cotton shift and let it drop to the floor. She tried to focus on Greg's eyes as she started the interminable cross toward him. But it was no good, she could feel nothing but the fifteen pairs of eyes, mostly male, boring into her flesh.

'Cut,' Sandy called. She nodded for the towelling robe and helped Vicky into it. 'Tell the crew to take five,' she said to Ken.

'Take five' — I must have been terrible, Vicky thought. Unscheduled coffee breaks are only ever called when things were definitely wrong.

'Feeling self-conscious, are we?'

Vicky nodded miserably. 'Does it show that much?'

'Of course it does. You're supposed to be offering yourself to the man you love. Giving him your body.'

'I know, but . . . '

'You look as though you're offering yourself to an orthodontist. Giving him your root canal problem.'

Vicky felt like bursting into tears. What was wrong with her? She'd never been particularly prudish. Why on earth should it bother her so?

'I'm sorry, Sandy, but I can't seem to help it. I —'

'Of course you can't. You're sixteen, for Christ's sake.' Sandy stopped barking but there was still an efficient edge to her voice as she continued. 'Now you listen to me, Vicky. All those guys are working, they don't have time to perve.'

'I know, but —'

'Just you remember that everyone here has a job to do and nobody wants to be the one to let the side down.'

Vicky nodded. It made sense. She didn't want to let the side down either.

'You might as well be fully clothed as far as they're concerned. They've got their time cut out concentrating on what they're doing. OK?'

'OK, Sandy.'

'Good girl. Greg's giving you everything. Now you give it back. Off you go and run some lines with him while Ken calls the crew.'

Vicky felt decidedly stronger as she joined Greg. He gave her a wink but said nothing as they sat on the bed and went through their lines. Greg figured the way they handled Vicky's mental block was strictly between Sandy and Vicky.

The girl's got a bit of fight back in her, Sandy thought. That's good. It didn't bother Sandy that she'd lied to Vicky. Of course the crew would perve. Some of the less tasteful would even compare notes down the pub: 'Good tits, great bum.' And it was common knowledge that they ran a points system out of ten on the sex appeal of the female members of the company. What Vicky didn't know wouldn't hurt her.

She still looked a bit tense though. Sandy knew she needed to relax her even more.

'Set up for a take,' she said to Ken and slipped behind one of the flats.

'Positions, please. Next one will be a take,' Ken called.

When each member of the crew was in position, Sandy stepped out from behind the flat. 'Ready to go?'

Everyone, including Vicky, burst out laughing and there was a round of applause. Sandy was stark staring naked.

She let the applause roll as she crossed to a monitor and sat beside it, then she barked. 'OK, that's enough, or the whole crew goes naked.' Another nod to Ken.

'Roll tape,' he whispered to his headphones.

The production team in the control room fought to contain their mirth as they cued up and the studio crew shook their heads begrudgingly. You might not like Sandy but you sure as hell had to admire her.

As the second assistant held the slate up to camera two, Sandy looked at Vicky. Yes, the laugh had done her good.

'Scene 16, Take 1,' the second called.

Ken looked at the cameraman. 'Set,' the cameraman said.

'Standing by . . . and . . . *action*.'

Vicky started to undo her buttons. Her eyes locked with Greg's. Sandy's right, she realised, he *is* giving everything. Go, Greg, go! And she started to give back.

It wasn't a naked Vicky who crossed slowly to the boy. It was a naked Jodie. And the boy was Billy. Vicky felt it all happen and somewhere in the recesses of her brain was the realisation that this was what acting might be all about.

She started to undress him. She fumbled clumsily with the buckle but her eyes never left his. Her hands fought feverishly to free the buckle. She wanted to undress him. She needed to undress him.

And then they were on the bed together. Clasped together. There was a sudden halt to the frenzy as he pulled back and looked at her questioningly. Was this what she really wanted? She raised her head and kissed him. His hand cradled the back of her neck as he responded, gently forcing her head down onto the pillow.

Vicky felt herself thrust her groin against his. Then she heard him moan softly and felt his hand in the small of her back pressing her closer as if to forge them together.

She dropped out of character for a second as she thought, 'Is this what it's meant to be like? Could it be like this in real life?' A cynical voice somewhere said, 'Don't be bloody stupid, this is Mills and Boon, this is soap'. Then another voice said —

'Cut. Check that.'

It was Greg who broke the clinch. He grinned at her and whispered, 'Good girl, great stuff.' Then he threw himself back on the bed. 'God! It's enough to make a man turn!' The crew laughed.

As Vicky donned the towelling robe Ken proffered, delicately averting his eyes, she wondered why she felt strangely empty.

'Very good, Vicky.' Sandy was struggling back into her clothes. 'Every move spot-on. And that added buckle business, talk about a mistake that worked! Good girl.' Sandy patted her on the back. 'Come and watch the playback, we're putting it to the floor.'

As Sandy crossed to a monitor, Vicky thought, why is everyone calling me a 'good girl'? And 'every move spot-on', what did that mean? Then she remembered. The head off the bed for the kiss, the thrust of the groin, Greg's hand to the small of her back, they'd all been plotted in rehearsal. She'd forgotten that.

Part of Vicky felt proud that she hadn't lost a trick even as she had become so immersed in her character, and part of her felt very bewildered. I've got a lot to learn about this acting business, she told herself. And she walked over to the monitor.

Simon didn't need to watch the replay. He'd seen the real thing.

Simon was particularly spaced out that day. After all, he didn't have any lines to remember, all he had to do was to sneak into the studio well before they checked and turned on the 'closed set' lights.

He'd hidden behind one of the unlit sets at the rear of the studio and watched. And as he watched, he fantasised that he was Greg. He was Billy. And when Vicky/Jodie had thrust her groin against Greg/Billy, there'd only been one person who'd really felt it. And that person had been Simon.

He slipped quietly out of the studio while they all watched the playback. Vicky had been making love to him, he knew that, and it wouldn't be long now before she realised it.

Paul turned the sound up on his television set and crouched anxiously before the screen.

' . . . the power of the media to ruin people's lives. And as we promised, here's the perfect example.'

Sure enough, as had been promised at the opening of 'The Five O'Clock Live' show, there was Paul discussing his personal life with a very shallow in-depth reporter. The camera zoomed in on Paul as he wordlessly mouthed a reply to a question and the shallow in-depth reporter's shallow voice-over said, 'Paul Sorell. Fighting for his marriage, fighting for his career and fighting to retain his place in the hearts of the Australian public.'

Paul cringed. Why had he let Mal talk him into this? 'Five O'Clock Live'? Rubbish. All interviews on 'Five O'Clock Live' were prerecorded and cut to ribbons to present whichever view the network chose to present. God alone knew how they'd choose to present Paul.

Mind you, Mal had made a lot of sense last week when he'd said, 'You want to get Barbie back, don't you? You want to get the viewers back, don't you? Then stop closing the doors on the press. That's the way, boyo. You're an actor, for Christ's sake! Give them "I love my wife". Give them "I made a mistake". Give them your soul. Use the media, buddy. Use it!'

And Paul had agreed. Mal had lined up the interview for Paul's day off when the studio was recording the Vicky/Greg scenes. And here he was, only seven hours after he'd recorded it, watching himself 'live'.

'I love my wife. I always have and I always will.'

Paul sipped his Scotch and studied the tired, worn eyes that pleaded directly to him from the screen.

'You know that, don't you, Barbie?' He looked back to the interviewer. 'And the children. I miss the children.'

Paul watched himself look down at his hands, all the while absent-mindedly turning his wedding ring.

'I made a terrible mistake, I know that. But to lose my family . . . ' He faltered, took a deep breath to regain control of his emotions and looked out of the fake window of the interview set, shaking his head in hurt disbelief.

Good, Paul thought, very good. He was going to bury his head in his hands at that point but thought better of it at the last minute. Don't lose the eyes, he'd told himself, and he'd been right. The glint of a tear had worked like magic. And the wedding ring. Good bit of business that, very symbolic.

Paul had meant every word he'd said in the interview and had been genuinely moved. Watching it now he still meant every word and was still moved but the actor in him made it physically impossible not to be aware of what he was doing and watching.

'To lose my family because of one mistake . . . ' his image continued then faltered, again at a loss for words.

One mistake, my arse, Barbie thought. Just the one mistake that caught you out.

When Paul's anguished face had first appeared on the screen, Barbie had wanted to reach out and touch it. He needed her — and God, how she missed him. It took her only a few seconds to register the performance. 'Bastard,' she muttered and reached for the remote control. But she couldn't turn it off. She sat compulsively glued to Paul's image, steeling herself against her desire to believe him. She mustn't believe him. She was her own woman again, at last — with a life, a career all her own. She couldn't afford to believe him. She wouldn't believe him.

But the general public would and did. The channel switchboard was jammed with callers protesting his dismissal from the show and demanding that he be reinstated.

The next day, it was a tight-lipped Alain who called Paul to his office. 'I've decided to give you another chance, Paul.'

'Thank you.' And I suppose you expect me to turn cartwheels, Paul thought. Well, tough. He nodded and said, 'I'm glad.'

Paul didn't ask why he was being reinstated. He knew. It wasn't Alain reacting to public demand. It was someone else. Someone more powerful than Alain. And that could only be Robert Bryce.

He was right. The message to return Mr Bryce's call immediately had been waiting on Alain's desk when he arrived in his office the morning after Paul's televised interview.

'I think you may be overreacting a little, Robert,' Alain suggested. 'It can be dangerous to allow an actor too much power.' There was a disturbing silence from the other end of the line. 'Besides,' Alain continued, 'the general public's memory is short, after three months they'll have forgotten —'

'Bring him back, Alain. Just bring him back.'

Alain was annoyed. More than annoyed, he was angry. And the feeling grew as the day progressed. Bryce had spoken to him in the same dismissive way that Alain himself spoke to his underlings. Alain knew what that meant. No respect. Bryce had no respect for him. He'd given the man the greatest TV hit series of all time. He demanded respect.

Everyone was glad that Paul was back with the show, including Edwina. And she was quite genuine as she congratulated him. After all, he'd learned his lesson, and she'd sated her desire for revenge. Besides, she had weightier things on her mind. Things that had to be sorted out right now.

'What the hell do you mean, conflict?' Edwina demanded as she dumped the advance storylines on Alain's desk. 'That's not conflict! That's assassination.'

'Rubbish, my dear. It's character development — a change of area, change of pace, it helps build the role.'

'Don't underestimate my intelligence, Alain, it's very irritating.' Edwina jabbed the scripts with a manicured fingernail. 'This is the first step to phasing me out and you know it. If the storylines continue this way Jane will end up the key figure and the public won't even notice I've gone.'

'That's not so, Edwina. Not so at all.' Alain was mentally rubbing his hands with glee. This was the moment he'd been waiting for. Edwina Dawling in his power. Edwina Dawling fighting for her career. And would he help her? Well, he couldn't, could he? It was out of his hands.

'I'm afraid there's nothing I can do. They're Evan's storylines and he's been given full rein in the scripting department.'

'By whom?'

'Well, by me, of course, but once one's delegated one can hardly . . . ' He shrugged apologetically.

'I see.' Edwina stood staring at him for a moment — a long moment, Alain thought — before turning and leaving his office.

Alain felt good. Not as good as he would have felt if she'd pleaded. He'd have liked that. Or lost her temper, spat venom and sworn, that would have been a nice fall from grace. Oh well, you couldn't have everything. Maybe she'd squirm more satisfactorily when she learned she was to be killed off. In the meantime, her frustration and powerlessness were salve enough. Salve for a day that had started so badly with Bryce usurping his power. Alain was starting to feel on top again.

Edwina picked up her dressing room phone and dialled. 'Robert? It's Edwina Dawling. You told me to call you if I ever needed anything? I do.'

Power Games

'But the scripts are already written.'

'Then have them rewritten.'

'I think this is a mistake, Robert.' Alain gripped the telephone receiver tightly in his sweaty palm. 'I think —'

'It's immaterial what you think, King.' Alain's thinly-disguised venom had not gone unnoticed and Robert Bryce didn't like it. 'Edwina Dawling is the star of this show and I want you to keep it that way. In fact, start writing that other woman down. She's already getting too powerful.'

'But you need conflict to maintain —'

'Get your goddamn conflict from the other characters!'

It was a direct order and there was nothing Alain could say, but as he hung up the receiver he felt sick with anger. This show was his baby. It had always been his baby. And now Robert Bryce was taking it away from him. He dived for the Mylanta tablets in the top drawer. Alain didn't undergo anxiety attacks often but when he did it was always his stomach that suffered first and he could feel the early growls of a severe bout of indigestion.

He pressed the intercom button. 'Wendy! Get Evan

Ryan in here right now,' he barked. 'And get Kleinberg on the phone.'

He'd teach Bryce a lesson, he thought, as he swallowed the last of the Mylanta tablets. He'd teach him that The King wasn't a Bryce Holdings underling trained to jump on command.

The conversation Alain had with Evan was identical to the one he'd had with Bryce except the roles were reversed.

'But you *told* me to highlight Jane's character. I've been working her up to it for weeks. We can't just —'

'Oh yes we can.'

'Alain, we need the conflict between —'

'Get your conflict out of the other characters.'

'But —'

'Do it, Evan. Just do it.'

The intercom buzzed. 'Mr Kleinberg's secretary on the line. He's available now.'

'Good. That's all, thanks, Evan. I'll expect the new storylines by the end of the week. Thank you, Wendy, I'm ready for Mr Kleinberg.'

Wendy and Kleinberg's secretary confirmed their respective bosses' availability, thereby preserving one from the ignominy of having to wait on the end of the line for the other.

Evan slunk out of the office. What was the use, he thought. Just a hack writer, that's all I am to them. One day, though, he told himself, one day when he'd completed his best-selling exposé novel about the television industry, the novel that he poured into his computer late Sunday nights, he wouldn't have to bow to every whim of self-opinionated producers like

Alain King. And you're in it, Alain, you arrogant shit, Evan thought. You're in it in all your true shades of puce.

'Les! How are you?' Alain poured bonhomie down the line and nodded his appreciation as it was poured back to him. Now this was the way one did business with equals and if Bryce didn't accept him as an equal then Alain had no compunction in offering himself to the highest bidder. And that bidder had always been Kleinberg. Les Kleinberg of Channel 8. Alain and Les had worked on a number of projects over the years and they'd been about to clinch a more permanent deal along the lines of Alain taking over all Channel 8 drama production when Bryce had put up an identical offer with money that was too good to refuse. A realistic businessman, Les had acknowledged the winner and bowed out, but the offer to Alain had remained standing.

'Sure, lunch tomorrow would be fine.' Alain smiled.

The engine roared into life and the power boat surged through the water. Standing in the stern along with the six other businessmen wooing or being wooed within the world of high finance, Alain felt good. He smiled at Les and raised his glass in return to the salute Les offered with his. Yes, they both thought, as the water taxi took off for Doyles Seafood Restaurant at Watson's Bay, this was the way to do business.

As Alain bit into his first Royal Red prawn in

tempura batter and Les cracked the first claw of one of his blue swimmer crabs, Ray Chaplin contemplated the large tin tray of battered fish behind the glass of the hot food section in the Channel 3 canteen. There was always fish on Fridays in the canteen and it was always fried. Ray opted for a sandwich instead.

He wasn't hungry, anyway, he told himself, as he walked to the other end of the bar where the fat lady was piling mustard onto Greg's roast beef sandwich.

'G'day, Ray. You down here for the telethon?'

'Hello, Greg. Yes, that's right. Egg and lettuce thanks.'

They chatted amicably while the fat lady made their sandwiches and agreed that it was going to be a great telethon.

The 'telethon' was every channel's major charity event. An annual competition had developed between the networks to see whose telethon could raise the most funds. It was a big status-booster for the winner.

Actually, Ray was not down for the weekend telethon at all. His instructions were to discreetly ensure that Bryce's orders with regard to Paul and Edwina had been carried out to the letter. Robert Bryce hadn't liked Alain's reactions at all.

Gentle queries had ascertained that Paul and Edwina were indeed being looked after according to Bryce's instructions but the news that Alain was lunching with Les Kleinberg was an added note of interest that Ray thought had made his trip even more worthwhile. He nodded to the security man in the far corner of the canteen and the omnipresent Brian Hopgood nodded a greeting back.

Ray Chaplin accompanied Greg as he joined the 'Glitter Game' cast at one of the centre tables. Ray was aware that it was possible his presence might initially inhibit the actors but that didn't worry him in the least. It was Robert Bryce's policy that his senior directors mingle with all levels of the corporate pyramid.

'Everyone who works for Bryce Holdings is important' was Robert's constant quote. Making people feel important also made them feel committed — something Channel 3's station manager would do well to learn, Ray thought, as he offered his hearty congratulations on the show and pulled up a chair. ('You're going to eat with the actors?' the station manager had exclaimed when Ray had knocked back his luncheon invitation. 'In the canteen!') Oh yes, Robert Bryce would be interested in a reaction like that, Ray thought, as he became aware of Narelle's thigh warmly and naively settled against his own. He'd much rather be with the actors than the tedious network executives anyway. He liked actors. He smiled at Narelle. Narelle smiled back. She thought Ray was a lovely man.

Mandy and Sidney shortly made their apologies. They had a photo call. Sidney had taken to eating sparingly of late and he and Mandy appeared to have called a temporary truce. Yesterday they'd done an interview for a family magazine, today was a colour spread for a feature called 'At Home with the Happy Mature Couple', and tomorrow was the start of the thirty-six hour telethon. Thirty-six hours of giving their all to the public — that is, whenever they'd be able to claw their way to the camera ... so many other stars had made themselves available. Nevertheless, it was thirty-six hours of intermittent starplaying. Thirty-six hours before they had to go home to their little bedsits and empty flats and admit that they were just people, and lonely, ageing ones at that. It created an unspoken bond between Mandy and Sidney.

Paul saw himself in Mandy and Sidney. He recognised the awful, lonely possibility that he could be like them in twenty, thirty and forty years' time. He had his career back, yes, but Barbie was light years away from him. She didn't need him, she didn't love him and without Barbie, what was he? He felt the familiar flood of depression start to wash over him. Then Edwina, seated beside him, clasped his hand comfortingly. He smiled back at her with gratitude. Thank God for Edwina's friendship and support.

As Sandy entered the canteen, there was a general round of applause and a standing ovation from the 'Glitter Game' table. Word had got around about her studio strip during Vicky's seduction scene.

'Wish I'd been there,' Chris said, as he cleared a space for Sandy between Jane and himself.

'You better believe it,' Vicky grinned, trying to ignore Simon's hand under the table as it crept yet again up her knee and into her groin. Every time she slapped it back he giggled childishly. The giggle annoyed her even more than the wandering hand.

'I liked *your* strip better,' he whispered in her ear. There was a moment's silence as Vicky turned and stared at him coldly. 'Oh, you watched the scene, did you?'

Simon missed the warning signs completely. 'Did I what!' he leered.

'And you felt it worked?'

'It sure worked on me, it was a real turn-on.'

'Glad you liked it.' The steel-blue eyes were lethal. 'Shall we find somewhere a bit more private?'

Simon couldn't believe his luck. 'Sure.' And he jumped to his feet. ' 'Scuse us, gang. We're off to run some lines.'

As Vicky and Simon left the canteen together, Chris prayed that it was a sign of improved working relations. Somehow he doubted it though. Vicky's face was thunderous.

'You shit!'

'Eh?'

The moment they rounded the corner, Vicky turned on him. 'You dirty little junkie pervert!'

Simon was totally unprepared for the hand that lashed out and struck him across the side of his face.

'What the hell . . .' Simon gingerly touched his ear. 'That hurt.'

'Listen, you creep. From now on, you keep your distance from me. You keep your hands to yourself, and you keep your pervie little comments to yourself. And I tell you what else, you lay off that junk when we work together.'

Simon was stunned. 'But I—'

'I'm warning you, shitbag, the next time I see you spaced out in the studio, I'm going to report you, and I mean that.'

As he watched her storm off, Simon felt shaken. In his drug-induced state he'd honestly supposed she'd shared his humour, his jokes, indeed, had been flattered by his obvious admiration for her. The slap and her present outrage had genuinely shocked him.

Shocked him even to the point of making him feel vaguely uneasy about his coke habit. Could she be right?

In the canteen, Sandy was just finishing her rave to Chris about the magic of Vicky's seduction scene. Chris agreed that the girl was a director's dream, all right, except when it came to working with Simon.

Jane interrupted. She'd only had a couple of scenes with Simon but found him very difficult to communicate with. 'His energy's too dissipated somehow. He seems to be acting for himself, not the other person. That must be hell for Vicky, she's such a giver.'

One by one the others at the table were drawn into the discussion and, after agreeing that Vicky was indeed a gifted 'natural', the conversation turned towards new young talent in general. It was Sandy who unwittingly struck the first blow.

'What about the preview the other night? The girl in the new Wainwright movie — wasn't she wonderful?'

Jane felt her smile tighten as she nodded brightly at comments like 'greatest Australian film performance ever', 'possibly the first Australian Academy Award'. She told herself that they were the sweeping statements always made by actors with a tendency to exaggerate, but she knew they were right. That was why she hadn't gone to the preview.

They were always getting invited to movie previews and premieres and as usual Jane had knocked this one back, opting for the theatre in preference. Just another 'also-ran' movie, she told herself, knowing full well her true reasons for not putting in an appearance. Every time Jane read an article on Anna Bowrey or saw her picture on a movie billboard, she felt envious. And the envy was turning more bitter by the day. She was starting to feel a distinct dislike for Anna Bowrey. And for Kate Redman. And for Peter Wainwright. And for Alain King for forcing her decision.

Rubbish, she told herself. No one forced your decision, you made it yourself and good luck to your successor – it's hardly her fault that you made the wrong choice. But even as she reprimanded herself, she heard Sandy say, 'When the reviews come out next week the public'll be queuing for miles to see that girl', and a tiny voice in Jane cried out for them to recognise her: 'Don't any of you remember that role was mine? Have you forgotten already that I was the hit of the season?'

'Excuse me.' Jane got up from the table. 'Lunchbreak's nearly up. See you in the greenroom.'

Chris followed her out. 'It's not their fault. They didn't know you were offered the movie,' he said after they'd walked in silence for a few seconds.

But Jane didn't seem to hear. It was only when they reached the doors to the dressing rooms that she turned to him. '*Je ne regrette rien*. The way Piaf sings it,' she said. 'Big and bold. That's always been my theme song. I've always thought you should grab at things as they come along. Sometimes you grab at the wrong thing, sometimes you miss altogether — but in the end it all balances out and as long as you haven't hurt anyone, you can end up having grabbed at a pretty good life. At least one where you're not left regretting lost opportunities.' Chris waited patiently, knowing what she was going to say. 'I didn't grab at this one and I regret it, Chris. God, I regret it! The greatest chance of a lifetime and I went for the safe bet instead.'

It upset Chris to see her so defeated. It was uncharacteristic of his Jane. His Jane the fighter. His Jane the perfectionist. *His* Jane . . . Chris suddenly realised how proprietorial he felt. He clasped her hands.

'There'll be other roles just as good, Jane. And you'll be the one they'll be begging for.' Jane's smile of thanks was lacklustre as she turned towards the door and Chris knew how trite he must have sounded. He pulled her back, squeezing her hands tightly. 'For God's sake, woman, what about this week's storylines? They're building you already. "The Glitter Game" is going to become your own personal vehicle.'

Jane looked back at him. Chris's intensity was impossible to ignore and he was right, of course, the storylines were going just the way Alain had promised they would.

'There's even a rumour of an American network sale. In six months' time you can name the role you want.'

This time Jane's smile was genuine and deeply grateful. 'Thanks, Chris. I needed that. Next time you can smack me on the wrist and tell me to stop dramatising but this time I really did need a boost.'

'I know.' They gazed unwaveringly at each other. Chris had been about to kiss Jane on the cheek but they both knew it wouldn't be enough.

'Keep listening to Piaf. You've got nothing to regret.' Chris gave her hands a final squeeze and walked on towards the studio.

Ray Chaplin had spent a pleasant hour in the canteen. It had been just the sort of animated actors' discussion he enjoyed. He also enjoyed the fact that the actors were uninhibited enough to conduct such a conversation in his presence. It spoke well of his ability to mingle despite his high-ranking position. Ray would never have admitted, even to himself, that, underneath, he was just a touch appalled by their lack of deference. A group of network executives wouldn't have ignored him for one minute let alone the better part of one hour. He smiled paternally. Actors were such a colourful bunch.

Most of all Ray had enjoyed the warmth of Narelle's thigh, the wriggle of her body next to his when the conversation became especially animated and the flash of an excited but slightly querying smile in his direction whenever she made some comment, as if she were seeking his approval. It certainly wasn't deference to his position, and it didn't seem to be a conscious flirtation. What was it? Ray was confused and fascinated. There was something about Narelle. Something elusive, tantalising and utterly erotic.

Whatever the 'something' was, Ray decided he'd better beat a hasty retreat. His erection was becoming an embarrassment. Edwina and Paul had just left and Sandy, Jim and Greg were in deep discussion at the other end of the table leaving Narelle about to turn her full attention on him. He stood, buttoned his suit jacket, and picked up his briefcase.

'Well, goodbye all, keep up the good work.'

'Won't you be at the telethon tomorrow?' Narelle's eyes welled with disappointment.

'Certainly will. That's what I'm here for.'

'Oh, good,' Narelle breathed, with something approaching a sigh of relief. Ray left, rather rattled.

He went out of his way to pass the table where Brian Hopgood was sitting with what appeared to be the same cup of coffee he'd poured himself an hour ago. Ray checked his watch. 'The boardroom in half an hour, OK?' Brian nodded.

Half an hour later, as Alain drained the last of his tawny port and looked across the broad expanse of water to the Harbour Bridge and the approaching water taxi, Ray called out, 'Come in' and thrust the phone at Brian the moment he entered the boardroom.

'Robert would like a word with you.'

To Ray's chagrin even he, 2IC to the man himself, was to know nothing of the conversation that ensued between Robert Bryce and Brian Hopgood. He left the room as Robert had requested.

Although the next day was Saturday, it was still a work day for all at Channel 3. A work day for all but Edwina. Edwina was the only member of 'The Glitter Game' cast who had refused to appear on the thirty-six-hour telethon. She found marathon TV charity events not only hypocritical but bordering on fraud. 'All those phoney performers giving their all for the cause and less than half the money gets to the cause anyway,' she'd complained to Davey many a time. 'You know the networks are actually running commercials during telethons these days! The whole thing's an appalling rip-off.'

Much of her argument was true, of course, but there were always exceptions to the rule. Many organisers, performers and crew did work tirelessly and many charities did benefit as a result.

Greg was as aware as Edwina of the phoney aspects of television marathons but figured they were still worthwhile fund-raisers and had proved himself the best telethon MC and anchor man in the business. This time around was no exception.

'And here it is . . . ! Here she goes . . . ! Watch the lights . . . !' Behind Greg, the two-metre high, four-metre wide screen of lights flashed crazily until they found the sequence they wanted, a fanfare of trumpets rang out, first assistant Ken jumped up and down inciting a riotous reaction from the studio audience and Greg screamed above it all, 'And there she blows . . . *one . . . point . . . five . . . million dollars*!!' Whistles and hooters and streamers, supplied courtesy of Channel 3, were blown, honked and thrown with great abandon as Ken and the crew encouraged hysteria. Everyone was having a wonderful time.

Not even halfway through, Greg thought wearily. Still, he'd have his break in a minute — a full five hours. Bliss. It was three am and he'd been going since midday. There'd been a crew change but Ken had also done the full fifteen-hour stint. Poor bugger, Greg thought, he looks dead on his feet. The fanfare died down and Greg beamed excitedly at camera two.

'Don't go to sleep just because it's the wee hours, though. Stay with us, stay with the fun, get on those phones and keep the money rolling in. Let's go to the phones now and see what's happening.'

As Greg threw to the phone room, Mandy and Sidney, wearing funny hats, leapt into action encouraging more whistles and hooters and streamers.

'One point five million! Isn't that marvellous?' Mandy shrieked girlishly. 'All you marvellous people out there!' She smacked loud kisses at the camera.

Not to be outdone, Sidney held his arms wide in an all-embracing 'thank you' and gave his Donald Wolfit best. 'Wonnnderful! Wonnnderful effort!'

Mandy and Sidney were having the best time. Apart from a couple of appearances on the panel with the rest of the 'Glitter' cast they'd been pretty much ignored during the peak viewing hours when every visiting celebrity and pop star had been available. Now, however, they were 'in demand' and the weariness born of hanging around the make-up department and VIP lounge magically dropped away. Sidney was dangerously boosted by the copious amounts of free Scotch he'd downed in the VIP lounge but he'd managed to stay just the right side of silly.

In the main studio, the relief first assistant took the headphones from Ken and nodded to Greg. 'Well done, mate, see you at eight o'clock.'

Greg gave a thumbs-up to the late night newsreader who was taking over the anchor and headed for the VIP lounge where he quickly downed two double brandies. They hit the hefty amount of gin and tonic he'd been knocking back under the guise of mineral water and gave him an instant boost. Suddenly he wasn't tired. He didn't want to go home to his empty flat and his lonely bed . . . what *did* he want to do?

He slammed his glass down on the table and headed for the car park. He knew exactly what he wanted to do.

Eight hours earlier, as he waited to present Robert Bryce's personal cheque to the telethon, Ray Chaplin decided he was having a pleasant evening circulating among the many performers in the VIP lounge. The television personalities were aware of his position of course but many of the cabaret and stage performers had no idea who he was.

'I beg your pardon, are you talking to me?!' Yvonne looked incredulously at Ray and her voice was loud with contempt.

'Yes,' Ray answered. God, the woman must be deaf. 'Just saying how well the tally's going — looks as if we might make the five million target.'

'Jesus Christ!' she turned her back on him. 'Who's the drab little accountant person?' she asked her leading man who was terrified of her and shrugged nervously.

Yvonne Dupres (born Alma Cox) was presently playing to packed houses in the lavish revival of *South Pacific* at Her Majesty's. She was a big woman. In fact no Nellie Forbush had ever been so big, but the voice was big to match — so big that critics and public alike forgave her and flocked to the production. Just as they had flocked to the last two productions she'd starred in. *The Sound of Music* and *West Side Story* Marias had both been inexplicably big and totally forgiven and it appeared Yvonne could do no wrong in the eyes of Australian audiences. Her head grew proportionately big and she became insufferable.

Ray smiled politely and turned back to the bar. He wasn't a little man. According to statistics he was the exact height, weight and all-round measurements of the average adult Australian male but then he supposed the average Australian male was little in comparison to Yvonne Dupres. Also he saw no reason to be ashamed of his accountant background. Some of the most clever people he knew were accountants. He came to the conclusion that Yvonne was a malicious person and therefore probably very difficult to work with. He must remember to mention that when he and Robert next discussed the series of in-concert specials they were tying up. If the choice still rested between Dupres or Farnham they'd be much better off going with John Farnham. Such a nice man to work with.

'You're wanted on set, Mr Chaplin.' A flustered young second assistant with headphones and two-way radio was at his side. Ray nodded, ignored Yvonne's bulging eyes as her head snapped in his direction, and followed the second. 'OK, OK. Travelling, travelling,' the second hissed to the director's assistant who was nagging him through his headphones.

Oh shit! Oh shit, no! Not *the* Chaplin? Not the Chaplin who is 2IC to Robert Bryce? Not the Chaplin who virtually runs Network Three? Yvonne prayed fervently she was wrong but she had a horrible feeling . . .

'. . . And they feel, without doubt, that the Channel 3 telethon is the most important and worthwhile event on their busy annual calendar,' Ray concluded. 'So on behalf of Robert and Melanie Bryce I'd like to present their personal cheque of $50,000 and their best wishes to all concerned with Telethon 19 . . .'

But the fanfare of trumpets, the flashing lights, the whistles, the hooters and the screaming studio audience drowned him out.

'*And we've hit the big one!*' Greg screamed. 'Just look at that! *One . . . million . . . dollars*!! Six big fat beautiful zeros!!'

That had been at seven pm — prime viewing time — and the director had rigged the presentation of the cheque to coincide with the tally reaching the one million mark. His calculations had been a little out and they were nearly $200,000 over the million but the viewers didn't need to know that.

In the VIP lounge Yvonne had turned her back on the monitor and sunk deep into an armchair. She pushed aside the drink proffered by the nervous leading man. 'You shit. You could have told me.'

'I didn't know, Yvonne, I swear I didn't.'

The flustered second assistant was shepherding Narelle out of the VIP lounge to the studio and a panel appearance when Ray re-entered.

'You were wonderful, Ray.' It was very crowded and Narelle's hand was against his chest. From anyone else the gesture might have been apologetic, saying 'Excuse the contact, I'm being shoved from behind'. From Narelle it was the most intimate caress and Ray couldn't prevent a strangled gasp as his penis leapt to attention. 'You're not going, are you?' she breathed. 'We could have a drink when I get off the panel.'

'Fine, fine. I've got a bit of business to tie up before I go.' He didn't, and had intended leaving immediately for the hotel but his erection seemed to be speaking for him.

'Lovely.' The hand slid away from his chest and she was gone.

Ray couldn't understand it. Nobody had ever had this effect on him before. He was not a man prone to instant erections. In fact he'd always considered his libido to be rather less than normal, probably because he channelled so much of his energy into his work. His wife of twenty-two years had always been grateful for his low sex drive and, after the birth of their two children it was patently obvious she wished he'd lose it altogether.

Not that she'd always hated sex. He could remember their college dating days: his aching spine, the creaking springs in the back seat, the way she planted her feet on the roof of the Holden and met his every thrust. Then suddenly she was pregnant and they were married and they were just nineteen and sex was no longer joyful. Ray wondered with a touch of bitterness whether it had ever been joyful for Penny. He hated to think that her little animal whimpers might have been faked. But as the years rolled by even that didn't matter. It was probably his fault anyway. After all, rocking the back of the Holden and groaning with lust had really only been a release for him, hadn't it? Well, he supposed it had.

Several years after their marriage Ray set out to be unfaithful. A number of times. Purely experimentally. After all he and Penny had been virgins when they met and maybe, if he learned a few tricks of the trade, he'd be able to improve on their sex life. He'd chosen one-night stands and the odd high class call-girl. He didn't want to threaten his family life. But if anything the liaisons had cooled his libido even more. He'd rather be back humping in the Holden.

After that he gave up trying to improve their sex life. Penny insisted they have separate rooms because of his snoring, although he never knew he snored, and he visited her bedroom barely once a month. Until last year. Since last year he hadn't visited her bedroom at all. But Ray didn't want to think about that now.

Now there was Narelle. Narelle, who had this amazing effect on him . . .

Ray caught sight of Yvonne charging towards him

leaving spilt drinks, dropped food and trampled feet in her wake. He turned and fled.

In the corridor he bumped into the second assistant. 'Tell Narelle I'm waiting for her at the staff entrance,' Ray instructed. To hell with caution.

As soon as he'd watched Ray Chaplin present Bryce's cheque, Alain reached across the bed for the remote control and turned the sound off. He toyed with the idea of switching to another channel but decided against it. He'd better be aware of telethon happenings on Monday. After all, he was supposed to put in an appearance over the weekend to show a little support. He had no intention of doing so, of course, and God only knew why he should. It wasn't his department and he had no interest whatsoever in it. Contrary to many peoples' opinions, television charity marathons were not rip-offs by the channels. Well, not profitable ones that is. Of course the channels had to recoup their losses, so not all the monies went to the beneficiaries but in Alain's opinion telethons were a nonremunerative waste of energy and resources.

Unfortunately none of the networks dared back out of the telethon race and leave the others to rake in the kudos, goodwill, philanthropic image and all the other non-money-making incidentals that had become such necessities. Bloody waste of time, Alain thought. If he were Bryce, he'd pull Network Three out of the 'philanthropic image' bullshit and concentrate on making money, concentrate on giving the viewing public what it wanted. Soap, tons of soap, flashtrash, made-on-the-smell-of-an-oily-rag, good old Aussie soap. And that's what he'd do with Les

Kleinberg at Channel 8. By Christ, they'd rake it in.

Lunch at Doyle's had been inspiring. How had he ever allowed himself to be bought by Bryce? He should have taken Les's offer right from the start. They spoke the same language — low budget television with mass appeal.

'If there's one person in this country who knows his market, Les, it's me,' Alain had boasted as the cheesecake arrived. 'And once you know your market you just pick the formula that fits it. And you know the formula we should head for? "The Glitter Game" without the glitter. Thank you, that's fine.' He shooed the waiter away impatiently. 'Who the hell needs the Edwina Dawlings and the salaries they command? Who the hell needs wankers like Evan Ryan and Chris Natteros? When you've got the right format you can get them all cheap. The actors, the writers, the directors. Cheap as dirt.'

Alain reached across to the bedside table for the cocktail shaker and poured himself another dry martini. Yes, everything was going beautifully. He and Les had given themselves six months. He'd wanted to leave Channel 3 earlier, of course, but he was contracted until January and there was no way he could find a loophole in the Bryce contract. There was no way anyone could ever find a loophole in a Bryce contract. 'Not to worry,' Alain had told Les. It would give him time to come up with two hot new series concepts for when he joined Channel 8. The King intended to put their drama unit straight to work.

Les Kleinberg was pleased with the plan. The sooner Alain put his Midas touch to work and created a hit series for Channel 8 the better. Les wanted a return on his investment. Little did Les know that Alain was going to use his time left at Channel 3 to get several new concepts out of Evan. Before he left he'd tell Evan they were useless, order him to wipe them from the computer and start again. Easy. Alain didn't feel the need to admit his creative limitations to Les.

Evan's rewrites of 'The Glitter Game' storylines sat on the bedside table. Alain had already okayed them, a copy had been sent to Rosa Glassberg for Edwina and the rest of the cast would receive theirs early next week. Evan had done as he'd been told: Jane was background material and Edwina centre stage. But even the knowledge that Edwina would think she'd triumphed couldn't kill Alain's elation. Without him at the helm, 'The Glitter Game' would eventually fold anyway. Maybe he could indulge in a little sabotage to help it along. He should be able to come up with something — after all, he had a whole six months to think of it.

The doorbell rang. Alain looked at his watch. Dead on time. 'Door's unlocked, come on in,' he called. He heard the front door open and close. 'Bedroom through here,' he called again.

Alain ran his eyes over her appraisingly as she stood in the bedroom door. She was mini-skirted and wore Dr Martens shoes with saggy socks. Her long hair was streaked and permed. Alain didn't like the way teenagers wore their hair these days — it looked like straw. But who cared? She was young, that was all that mattered. It was the third time he'd used this particular massage agency and they were proving very reliable.

'Talc or oil?' the girl asked, dumping her Rip Curl bag on the bed.

'Oil. Did you lock the front door?' She nodded. 'Good girl.'

Ray was overwhelmed. More than overwhelmed, Ray was in a state of shock.

He'd been overwhelmed when Narelle had said 'That would be lovely' to his suggestion that they have their drink in his hotel suite rather than in the crowded VIP lounge.

He'd been overwhelmed when he'd tentatively kissed her and her lips had opened, warm and moist against his.

But when he'd broken from the embrace, gone to the bar, mixed the drinks and turned back to discover Narelle naked, he was more than overwhelmed. He was in a state of shock. His mind clicked to a darkened room and a female silhouette. Penny would never undress in the light.

Narelle smiled. 'Is that for me? Thank you.' She leaned forward and took the drink from his frozen hand.

Ray was galvanised into action. He turned the overhead light off and started undoing his trousers.

'Don't do that.'

He stopped. 'What?'

'The light. I'd like to see you naked.'

'Oh.' His mind clicked to a time early in his marriage when he'd started undressing prematurely. 'Not with the lights on, Ray,' Penny had said.

He clicked the switch back on and dropped his trousers.

Narelle smiled. 'Is that for me? Thank you.' And she leaned forward again and stroked the rock-hard bulge beneath his underpants.

'Oh God! Oh no! *Stop. Don't.*' It wasn't going to happen, surely. 'Oh hell!' Too late. '*Aaargh!*' It did. Ray was mortified. 'I'm sorry, I really am. It's just that . . .'

'That's all right.'

'. . . just that, for the past couple of hours I've been . . .'

'That's all right. It'll give us a chance to talk before you do it again.'

Do it again? Ray had never ejaculated more than once in twenty-four hours in his life, not even in masturbatory childhood. Suddenly he wanted to leave.

He started to put his trousers on then realised that of course he couldn't leave — it was his hotel suite. What's more, he could hardly clothe himself when there was a naked and hopeful woman on the bed. The least he could do was be polite. He dropped the trousers.

'So let's get comfy and talk, shall we?' Narelle knelt on the bed and started undoing his shirt.

'Narelle, I'm afraid I won't be able to . . .'

'Are you married, Ray?' concentrating on the buttons.

'Narelle, I don't think you . . .'

'Do you have children?' slipping the shirt over his shoulders.

'Narelle, I . . .' Down came the underpants.

'Narelle!'

'Yes?'

'I can't!'

'Oh.' Realisation dawned. 'Well, of course you can't, silly. Not straight away. We're going to talk.'

And they talked. They lay naked on the bed and they talked, Narelle absent-mindedly caressing Ray's body to the point where he found himself absent-mindedly caressing hers back, delighting in the texture and fullness he felt beneath his fingertips.

Narelle was appalled at the sexlessness of Ray's

marriage, appalled at the fact that only six months ago he'd discovered his wife had had a lover for the past five years.

'Yeah.' Ray stopped caressing. 'She can give it to him but she couldn't give it to me and now she wants a divorce. No way!'

Narelle also stopped caressing. 'That's terrible. All those years.' Ray nodded in agreement. 'The poor woman.'

'What!'

'The poor woman! You have to give her a divorce.'

Ray leaned up on one elbow and looked at Narelle incredulously.

'It's not her fault you didn't turn her on.'

He started to get up from the bed, not daring himself to reply but Narelle put pressure on her thigh, the thigh that was hooked over his.

'And it's not yours, either, don't you see?'

It only took a further five minutes of Narelle's philosophies and caresses to convince Ray that no one had been at fault in his marriage, that he would give his wife the divorce she wanted and that he had the hardest, the most controllable, most dependable hard on he'd ever had in his life.

When he entered Narelle, he entered paradise. And as he concentrated on her enjoyment, he realised a power he'd never known before. As Narelle orgasmed repeatedly beneath him, he thought 'Is this what Penny gets from her lover?' If so, who could blame her? Along with the power, he felt responsibility, tenderness, and such a wealth of sensations that he was in a state of delighted confusion. And when he came himself it was like nothing he'd ever experienced. Oh God, if he'd only known how to do it when he was humping in the Holden!

★

The clock on the dashboard said three twenty-five am as Greg's car pulled up outside the terrace house in Sutherland Street, Paddington. He leaned on the bell for a full five minutes before Jim opened the door.

'Greg! What the hell do you want? I was asleep.'

'Can I come in?'

'Sure.'

But Greg was already in. He looked about. 'Upstairs, are they?' he asked.

'What?'

'The bedrooms.'

'Yes.' Jim was wide awake now. He followed Greg up the narrow staircase. 'What the hell are you doing?'

'Which one was Sharon's?' Greg asked as he reached the top and was confronted with two doors. He pushed the first one open to reveal an unlived-in room. 'Don't tell me — this one, right?' He threw himself down on the bed and looked up at Jim. The gin, the brandies and the fifteen hours on air suddenly hit him and he felt tired, very, very tired. 'This is where I want to live. What do you say?'

Jim didn't know what to say. The audacity of the man! But he loved him. 'Go to sleep, Greg.'

'Got to be on air at eight o'clock. Can you wake me in three hours?'

'Sure.'

'The tests came in.' Greg's eyes were closing.

'And?'

'And I'm in the clear.' The eyes closed. 'So far,' he mumbled.

Ray and Narelle made love again at five o'clock in the morning and again Ray felt powerful and in command as Narelle climaxed time and time again beneath him. He wasn't to know that Narelle would have kept herself in check if she'd felt that was what he wanted. She would have taken command herself, straddled him and bucked about like a rodeo-rider if she'd known that would give him pleasure.

Narelle wasn't faking her orgasms. Narelle never faked any form of erotic enjoyment. Narelle's true aphrodisiac was the pleasure she gave to her partner, and the pleasure she knew she was giving Ray was driving her to a frenzy of abandonment.

As they lay, bathed in sweat and the afterglow, watching the sunrise from his twentieth floor window and sipping orange juice, Ray marvelled at the whole process. He was fully aware of Narelle's lack of inhibition and knew that her delight was not due to any extraordinary prowess on his part. But surely if he could please her he could please others. He felt overwhelmed again. Overwhelmed with gratitude. 'Thank you.' He gently brushed her hair back from her face.

She snuggled up to him. 'It was lovely, wasn't it? Do you think you're ready . . .'

'No, I'm not,' he laughed. Then he felt worried for her. 'What are you going to do, Narelle?'

'Well, I have to be back at the telethon in . . .'

'No. I mean with your life.'

'Oh.' Narelle gave a brisk nod. That was easy. 'I'm going to keep giving my body to people. In bed and on television. I like people liking my body. And then when I'm thirty I'm going to have babies. Four of them. I'm going to settle down with a lovely man and use my body to give him babies.'

Ray looked closely to see if she was joking but she wasn't. Life was very simple for Narelle.

Manoeuvres

'Vietnamese boat people!?'

'Yes,' Evan nodded enthusiastically. 'You see, Jim and I thought it'd be a good idea if we started bringing the odd "issue" into "The Glitter Game". Jim wanted to do something around Asian immigration and I reckoned the boat people would be a moving way to go about it — don't you think? Good emotional stuff?'

'Sure, sure, great idea,' Alain agreed. Good God, he wouldn't need to plan any sabotage action at this rate. The quickest way to kill 'The Glitter Game' was to introduce any 'comment'. 'The sooner the better, I'd say,' he added.

Evan smiled excitedly. 'Terrific. I wasn't sure how you'd feel about it. Jim thought we should look at it through the eyes of a fifteen-year-old Vietnamese girl.' Evan warmed to his theme. 'And that's when I thought of the boat people. We have a montage of flashbacks — she's five years old, her family are fleeing Vietnam, they're picked up, she spends years in camps and . . .' Evan broke off with a frown. 'Of course, she'll be hell to cast, not only ethnically, but a teenager . . .' Evan shrugged dubiously.

'Then I suggest you get casting on to it straight away.' Alain rose from the table. 'I'd like to be there at the casting session — shall we make it Thursday?'

Evan was out the door before he knew it. Hell, short notice – the casting department wouldn't like that. But he was pleased. He hadn't thought for a minute Alain would go for such an adventurous and topical storyline.

Alain couldn't believe his luck. Not only were they hellbent on sabotaging their own series, he was to be treated to a casting session of Asian schoolgirls. Today was certainly his day.

It was a good day for everyone. Rehearsals buzzed with the weekend gossip and everyone was thrilled that the telethon had been such a success. Five and a half million! A full half-million above their goal. Channel 3 was riding high.

Greg had the afternoon off and spent most of it lugging his gear around to Jim's. Both of them had monumental hangovers having sat up talking and downing the bottle of sambucca that Greg had brought home with him after the telethon 'finale' at midnight. 'Sambucca seemed pertinent,' he'd said as they started their discussion on where they went from there.

By four am they'd decided that they would share Jim's flat — a strictly platonic arrangement — and see how they got on. Jim needed a flatmate anyway and it was good economics for Greg to lease his flat and share. All in all it was a sound financial move. They were both aware that they were kidding no one.

In-between stints at the telethon, Ray and Narelle had spent the entire Sunday locked in his suite. Narelle didn't have to be at rehearsals till ten o'clock on Monday so Ray cancelled his eight am flight and ordered smoked salmon and eggs Benedict for breakfast. They ate it sprawled naked on the executive suite's king-sized bed — Ray marvelled at the change in him as he dribbled hollandaise sauce on the impeccably laundered sheets and didn't care.

Mandy and Sidney dragged their aching joints through Monday's rehearsals whingeing that they'd been overworked and it was a damn good thing for the channel that they'd been available. Mandy told Sidney he was a grand old trouper and Sidney congratulated Mandy on her professionalism. They felt closer to each other than they ever had before as they refused to acknowledge, even to themselves, that they'd had the time of their lives.

Tuesday the pressure was on again. It was a taping day, and a big one for Jane: first scene up, then every scene till lunch break — twelve on the trot and wordy ones at that. She arrived for make-up at 6.30 am and picked up the large manila envelope with 'Amended Storylines' and her name on it. What the heck did that mean? She flipped through the twenty-odd pages while Tanya did her hair.

The sick feeling in the pit of Jane's stomach grew till she could almost taste the bile. She jumped up and headed for the toilets down the corridor, knocking the hair dryer out of Tanya's hand.

Fifteen minutes later she returned to the make-up department, her face ashen.

'Are you all right?' Tanya asked.

'Fine, just first period day, that's all.' Jane sat back in the make-up chair and concentrated on the mirror.

She knew there was only one person she could talk to and, as soon as she was through make-up and hair, she rang the production department. 'Is Chris working today?'

'Yes, he's editing, but he won't be in for another hour.'

'Would you leave a message for him to ring me in studio as soon as he arrives?'

Jane took a deep breath and tried to close her mind to everything except the work ahead. The first three scenes were two-handers with Edwina who was waiting for her on set, having come directly from her private dressing room. Edwina never used the channel's make-up and hair department. She preferred to do her own make-up and of course Davey always tended to her hair. Tanya and company had been deeply offended, and they'd all decided that Edwina was up herself and they didn't like her — a fact which didn't bother Edwina remotely.

Jane wondered whether Edwina had read the storyline amendments. 'Don't think about it,' she told herself, as she dredged her mind for the lines she'd known perfectly last night. Could Edwina have had anything to do with the drastic changes? 'For God's sake, don't think about it,' she steeled herself as Sandy called for a camera rehearsal.

Two hours later, a note was handed to her. 'Got your message, just read amendments. Meet you 12.35 scheduled lunchbreak, staff entrance.'

She was five minutes late. Chris took her arm and made straight for the car park. 'I checked the schedule — they haven't changed the running order, have they?' Jane shook her head. 'Right, you're third scene up after lunch, so we're safe if we get you back to make-up by 2.30. Let's get out of here.'

Jane didn't say anything as Chris drove. She didn't even notice where they were going. She stared out the window, her mind a blank until suddenly they pulled up at a tiny beach. 'Where are we?' she asked.

'Doesn't matter. I've got a favourite little fish cafe here — thought you might like it.'

Chris led the way into a take-away fish and chip shop overlooking the beach.

Food was the last thing Jane wanted. She'd probably throw up again if she tried to eat. And the place was packed with people queuing up for the fried fish and chips which were being thrown by the bucketful onto piles of newspaper by a large fat man, then speedily salted, wrapped and exchanged for money by a short fat woman. Why on earth had Chris brought her here?

'Eh, Chris!' The woman rattled her metal salt shaker like a castanet and nudged the large man. 'Gio, is Chris.'

Gio dumped a pile of baby squid into the huge frying pan, gave it a shake to coat it with oil, then turned and waved. 'G'day mate, how ya goin'?' The mixture of the heavy Italian accent and the Australian vernacular was almost impossible to understand.

Chris was aware of the baleful looks he was getting from the queuing customers as he pushed his way through to the rear of the shop. He smiled, waved back, then shepherded Jane up the tiny staircase to the two rooms above which had been converted into a restaurant. There were only six tables — all of them were taken.

'Popular place. You can never get in at lunchtime,' Chris said. So what the hell are we doing here? Jane asked herself again. Then she groaned inwardly. The eight people at the large centre table were nudging each other and two other tables were starting to notice the none-too-surreptitious pointing. She'd been recognised.

Chris led her through the archway and across the other dining area to the French windows at the end by which time most of the restaurant was buzzing with 'That's Jane Richmond from "The Glitter Game"'.

'Chris, can we . . . ?'

He opened the French windows to reveal a tiny balcony overlooking the beach. There were two chairs and a table with a 'reserved' sign on it.

'Oh.'

'Take a seat,' he said as he closed the doors behind them.

Jane stood at the balcony and looked out over the still waters of the little bay. Even though they were at the end of autumn there was a bite to the sun. The water sparkled and the sand reflected a brilliant white.

'It's beautiful.'

'Yes, it's a nice spot. I come here a lot. Mainly to get away from the channel — no one at work seems to know about it. Great food, too.'

'I'm sorry, Chris, I won't be able to eat a thing. I'm too . . . '

' 'Course you will. Wait till you try the garlic baby squid.'

'No, honestly. I just needed to talk about —'

'There's nothing to talk about, Jane.' Chris pulled her chair out from the table and gently but firmly sat her down. 'After we've had lunch, we get you back to the channel, you do your three scenes, then we go and see Alain together.'

'But —'

'I've spoken to Jim and to Evan. Neither of them approve of the amendments. The orders for the changes came directly from Alain.'

'So? Alain has the final word, doesn't he?'

'Bugger him, *no*! Not if the writer, the on-line producer and the director all say he's wrong.' Chris looked angry now. 'We'll go over his head if we need to. We'll go directly to Bryce.'

The French windows opened and the fat man from downstairs appeared. Gone was the white apron and chef's hat – he was wearing an outsized grey pin-stripe suit with a red bow tie.

'Ciao, Chris.'

'Ciao, Paolo. This is Jane.'

'Bella, bella! Ciao, Jane.' Paolo kissed Jane's hand.

Chris insisted on ordering a full meal for two, although Jane swore she wasn't hungry, and the only concession he made for her was to skip the garlic squid in deference to her fellow actors during the afternoon.

'How can that man cook and wait tables at the same time?' Jane asked when Paolo had left.

'He doesn't. That's Paolo, the other one's Giovanni — they're twins. Sometimes they swap the chef and waiter roles and the only way you can tell them apart is Giovanni plays the dinkum Aussie and Paolo sticks with the Neapolitan.'

Jane laughed. The mingled aromas of olive oil, lemon juice and garlic suddenly smelled wonderful and she started to relax. Chris was right. Alain couldn't override them all, he couldn't renege on his agreement with her just like that. With Chris fighting for her, everything was going to be fine.

★

But everything wasn't fine.

In fact everything couldn't be worse, Jane thought, as Alain flung his trump card at them.

'Robert Bryce! What do you mean, you'll go to Robert Bryce? It was Robert Bryce who gave the order in the first place!' Alain regretted it the moment he'd said it. Now they knew that he'd accepted directives from Bryce. Alain's pride didn't like that — he liked to be thought of as omnipotent.

He started to feel angry. How dare these nobodies dictate to him? He'd given Chris Natteros some of the best jobs of his career; and where would the girl be if he hadn't offered her the chance of a lifetime? Slaving her guts out in the theatre eight performances a week, that's where. No one became a star in the Australian theatre.

The rave reviews of the Peter Wainwright movie which had premiered that weekend flashed through Alain's mind and he recalled his conversation with Jane six months before. He dismissed them both. One movie. So what? Here today, gone tomorrow. He was offering the bitch much, much more. She should be grateful. A familiar burning sensation rose in the back of his throat and another thought flashed through his mind. He'd run out of Mylanta tablets. He hated Chris and Jane all the more for that.

'What do you mean, it was Bryce's idea?' Chris's voice was disbelieving. 'Why would Bryce want to know about storylines?'

Alain shrugged, wishing he'd never mentioned Bryce. 'Because his wife's a dyke and she's mad about Edwina — how the hell should I know? Stop pushing me, Chris.'

There was a loathing in the way Alain said Edwina's

name that caused a sinking sensation in Jane's stomach. 'It's her, isn't it?'

There was a confused silence. Both men turned to look at her.

'Edwina. She made you do it.'

Another silence. The tension was palpable.

Then Alain spoke slowly and venomously. 'No actress makes me do anything, Miss Richmond . . . '

Chris interrupted. 'Alain, I —'

'No director either. I suggest you go while you've still got a job.'

'I haven't.' Chris crossed to the door. 'As of now. Four weeks' notice.'

'You're a fool. You might never work in this industry again.'

'I'll take my chances. You coming, Jane?'

'I'd like to resign too, Alain.'

'Check the fine print in your contract,' Alain sneered. 'Or if you can't read, get your agent to —'

'I know my contract. I said I'd like to resign too.'

Alain suddenly hoped that Peter Wainwright's film would be the start of wonderful things for the young girl starring in it. 'Oh no, Jane, you've got six months to go. Six months of Edwina cutting you up into so much dead meat.'

After Jane and Chris left, Alain reached for the inner coat pocket where he could usually find the stray Quickeze. There was one left. Then he tried to calm down and convince himself of the positive outcome of the interview.

So what did it matter if Chris Natteros was going? His loss would be a blow to the series. If Alain didn't replace him with a director of equal talent, the series would suffer. And the more the quality of 'The Glitter Game' diminished over the next six months, the more everyone would equate it with Alain's departure. He would have to invent a story for the press — how much he regretted that Channel 3 had not allowed him the artistic freedom to continue the quality production which he had originally created. The show was already rating well in England, and the US network deal would be through next week – all of which would be credited, and justifiably so, to the show's executive producer, Alain King. If everything started to crumble after he left, surely it was positive proof of his acclaimed Midas touch.

Alain's heartburn started to ease.

It was six-fifteen when Chris and Jane entered the pub and 'Happy Hour' was well and truly under way. '*Two drinks for the price of one from 5 till 7*', the sign boasted, which meant that the second 'happy' hour was very noisy.

'Hell, I'd forgotten Happy Hour,' Chris shouted above the din. 'Do you want to go to the cocktail bar at the Hyatt?'

Jane shook her head. If they were going to drown their sorrows, as they'd agreed to, she preferred to do it in private anyway. 'My place,' she yelled back. 'Drinks are on me.'

Jane surveyed the impressive collection of bottles on the lounge room dresser which served as a cocktail bar. 'What say we go for lethal mixes? A dry martini or a sweet cocktail?'

'Hate to have to admit it, but a sweet cocktail.' Chris sat on the sofa facing the open fireplace.

'Me too. Just trying to impress you with the range.'

Jane whirred up some crushed ice and got busy with a cocktail shaker. She wasn't much of a drinker herself but the bar had become a symbol of her success when she'd landed the Wainwright play. Instead of having to offer friends decanted flagon port and instant coffee served from a pot, Jane could now stop pretending and do the real thing. It was important to her.

'Try that.' Chris was jolted out of his reverie. He stopped staring into the fireplace and took the cocktail she handed him.

'Lethal and stunning,' he said when he'd taken a sip. 'What is it?'

'A Scotch mist — Drambuie and Scotch.' She sat on the sofa beside him, with her legs curled up under her.

They sipped their drinks in silence.

'It's winter,' Chris said finally. 'You'll be able to have open fires now.'

'Yes. That was one of the main attractions when I rented the house.' There was another pause as they both stared at the fireplace. Then: 'You shouldn't have done it, Chris.'

The silence broken, there was no stopping them. As they drank through the cocktail shaker and Jane got up to crush some ice and prepare another, it all tumbled out.

Chris was sick of working for the likes of Alain, he was sick of working on series and soaps, in fact, he was sick of working in television. He wanted to go back to the theatre or to features.

'I sold out five years ago, Jane — when I did my first soap for Alain. It was a conscious decision — the kids were little, Helen needed to be home with them. But she's back working now. She wants to be,' he added. 'Now's the time for me to freelance again.'

Jane no longer felt guilty about Chris quitting. In fact she felt envious. 'Oh God, how I'd love to be back in the theatre,' she agreed.

The next two rounds of Scotch mist saw Chris commiserating with Jane over her ensuing six months with 'The Glitter Game' but advising her not to let it get her down. 'Use it, Jane, use the promotion you're getting out of the show.'

'What promotion? I'm not a supporting lead any more, I'm an also-ran member of the cast.'

'Believe me, anyone connected with "The Glitter Game" is big news. The CBS deal I told you about, remember? It's all tied up. They'll announce it next week.'

The final round of Scotch mist led to the inevitable discussions on talent, charisma and commitment and it was agreed that Chris was the most inspired director Jane had ever been directed by and that Jane was the most inspired actress Chris had ever directed and they drained the last drops from the cocktail shaker for their toast, 'To inspiration!'

Then they realised they were drunk.

'My God, how did that happen? We haven't had that much, have we?' Jane crossed unsteadily to the bar and inspected the bottles. They were both half empty. She held them up. 'Oh, yes, we have.'

'Shit.' Chris stood up and looked at his watch. Nine o'clock. 'I'd better ring home and tell Helen I'm on my way — she'll be worried.' He joined Jane at the bar, looked disbelievingly at the bottles, picked up the phone, stared at it for a second, then put it down again. 'What's my number?'

Jane couldn't help laughing. 'Oh hell, you can't drive home like this.'

'No. I'd better stay the night, I guess.'

Their eyes locked for a moment and Jane found she had to look away. 'Yes. The study upstairs converts to a spare room, there's a sofa that pulls out to . . . ' She broke off as she made the mistake of looking back at him. And suddenly they were kissing. Fiercely, hungrily at first, then, when their desperation subsided, tenderly, lovingly, their tongues gently exploring each other's mouths, their hands caressing each other's bodies as they surrendered to the feelings they'd suppressed for the past six months.

When the kiss was over, they held each other close for a long time until Chris finally broke the embrace.

'I feel very sober.'

'Me too.'

Chris picked up the phone and dialled. 'Hi . . . Yes I know, sorry, love, I should have rung earlier but I got drunk . . . Well, one of the cast was virtually written out for no reason so I went in to bat for her with Alain and . . . Jane Richmond . . . ' Chris nodded in agreement and flashed a quick smile at Jane. 'Yes, I know she's the best thing in it. Anyway, the shit hit the fan and we went off and got drunk together . . . '

Jane couldn't take her eyes off Chris and his attention to the phone. She could feel the presence at the other end, she could feel the familiarity, the love and the trust buzzing down the line between them.

' . . . I'm at Jane's place.' He looked at her and time stood still for a second. Then she gently shook her head. Chris breathed an inward sigh, a mixture of disappointment, regret and gratitude. Thank God Jane had made the decision. 'No, I've sobered up,

I'm OK to drive now . . . Yes, I'm quite sure. See you in an hour.'

He hung up and they stared at each other. Jane finally grinned. 'You would have hated yourself in the morning.'

Chris nodded. 'Good luck, Jane. I'll be in post-production until I leave so . . . ' He shrugged regretfully. 'I hope like hell we work together again.'

'So do I.' He moved forward to kiss her goodbye but Jane backed away a step. 'Oh no, we've done that bit.'

'You're right.'

After he'd gone, Jane allowed the alcohol to take effect again and cursed herself as she stomped about cleaning her teeth and removing her make-up. Why did she have to be so damned ethical? Any other woman would have enjoyed a damn good one-night stand and to hell with the rest. But underneath it all, she knew she was proud of herself. The kiss was all she and Chris had needed, an open acknowledgement of their attraction for each other. Now they could get on with a lifetime's true friendship.

Nevertheless . . . You lucky bitch, Helen, Jane thought as she climbed into bed and passed out.

The next morning, Jane woke with only a minimal hangover. It took her a while to remember why she felt slightly strung out and depressed and, when she did remember, she was pleasantly surprised she didn't feel worse. She wondered how she'd feel when she faced Edwina.

No, she told herself, as she turned the cold shower tap on full blast, you will not be bitter, you will not hate Edwina. You can't really blame her, anyway, she's a product of the system. She needs to play the game that way.

Jane continued to convince herself as she stepped into the shower recess and held her face up to the freezing jets of water. Edwina's always been a night-club singer and a recording artist, and now that she's a television star. she needs to kick any would-be contenders off the roost. Jane slowly regulated the shower to warm and started soaping her body. You're an actress, Jane — different ball game. Edwina will never be considered an actress. Let her have her domain; you don't belong there anyway — just serve your six months and get out!

Jane felt very strong when she arrived at the channel. She hadn't been called until mid-morning and she'd had all the time in the world to go through her cold-hot-cold shower routine, do her stretching exercises, jog around the block and eat her raw bran and yoghurt and contemplate how she was going to attack her day.

Then she saw Edwina. And it was face to face, on set, in character — confrontation time. Jane had come from make-up, Edwina from her luxury dressing room and both women had looked only at their scripts during the line run.

'Full rehearsal,' Ken called.

They put their scripts down and were on their own. As cameras, sound, lights, all stood by, Edwina and Jane looked each other in the face for the first time.

The resolve that Jane had built up that morning from the moment she'd stepped into her cold shower was momentarily shaken as she looked into the eyes of the woman who was ruining her career. She felt a flash of hatred. But then her resolve was back, stronger than ever. Edwina can have the flash-trash fame, she told herself. I'm the better actress.

Edwina had been waiting for Jane's response; she read it correctly. She saw the hatred, the resolve and the superiority. And the twinge of guilt Edwina had felt when she'd read the storylines and realised just how much 'background wallpaper' Jane's character had become disappeared in an instant. She was glad she'd pushed Bryce: 'No, I don't want the roles equal, Robert. I'm the star of the show, and that's the way I want it to stay. That's the favour I'm asking.'

Robert Bryce couldn't give a damn who was the star of the show so long as it rated and made money, but he didn't like the demanding way in which Edwina reminded him he'd promised a favour. Robert Bryce always returned favours when he thought they were owed and this time was no exception but, as far as he was concerned, it left a clean slate. No more favours for Edwina.

Edwina was aware that she'd pushed him just a little too hard and she'd regretted it at the time. But not now. Not as she read Jane's face. The woman was most certainly a danger and Edwina had been right to push her out of the race.

'Standing by!' Rehearsals were over; they were going for a take.

'And . . . action!'

The scene was brilliant. There'd been many splendid confrontation scenes between the two female leads. After all, they were the main protagonists of the series. But this time Edwina and Jane outdid themselves as they vied for power over each other.

'Cut!'

The crew broke into spontaneous applause and Sandy came down from the control room to congratulate them. There was mutual respect in the look shared between Jane and Edwina, until Jane raised an eyebrow slightly, as if to say, 'Look what you're missing out on — no more scenes like this after I'm shoved in the background'.

The mask was back on Edwina's face in an instant. 'I'll be in my dressing room,' she said to the first. And she said it with the knowledge that hers was the only luxury dressing room in the entire channel, reminding everyone, 'I'm the star and don't you ever forget that'.

'Scene 27, day two. Vicky, Jane and Greg. You've got a wardrobe, hair and make-up change, Jane.'

When she reported back to make-up, Greg was leaning over the make-up chair having just fed Vicky the punchline to a joke. Vicky was cracking up, Max, the make-up artist, was stamping his foot in a queenly rage and Greg was looking very satisfied at the havoc he'd created. Jane looked at them fondly. It really was impossible to take oneself too seriously with such a good-humoured pair.

'Hi, Greg, Vicky.'

'Hello, Magic,' Greg whirled around. 'Got the best one . . . '

Jane took one look at Max fighting a losing battle with Vicky's make-up, a mascara wand in one hand and a cotton bud in the other.

She shook her head. 'Bugger off, Greg, they're waiting for us on the floor.' But she smiled as she sat and nodded to Tanya, and of course Greg took no offence.

'Humorous, humorous, what's happened to

humorous? Come on, girls, chop chop! On set, please, we're waiting for a line run.' Greg was out of the make-up room and into the studio, his voice wafting back to them before the soundproof door closed gently behind him.

Jane and Vicky smiled at each other, sat back in their respective hair and make-up chairs and let Tanya and Max get on with it.

Vicky hadn't been sure whether she should bring up the subject. After a few moments she decided, what the hell. 'I read the new storylines, Jane. They can't be for real!'

'They are.' Oh don't,Vicky, please, Jane thought.

'But you're going to do something about them, aren't you? You're not just —'

'There's nothing I can do.'

Vicky was outraged. 'Oh, come on, there must be. We'll all —'

'You'll all nothing. Leave it, Vicky, it's done.'

'But —'

'I said, leave it.'

As Vicky sank back into her chair, Tanya and Max exchanged glances. They couldn't wait to read the storylines.

Jane regretted the edge to her voice. 'Thanks, love. There really isn't anything that can be done, but thanks.'

'It's a bummer,' Vicky scowled.

'Yes,' Jane smiled back. 'It's a bummer. There is a favour you could do me, actually.'

'Sure. Whose head do I smash?'

Jane laughed. 'Spread the news that I don't want to talk about it. It's done and I want to get on with the job. OK?'

'OK,' she said. Shit, she thought.

'Hi, stars.' It was Simon, poking his head around the make-up door. 'Want to run some lines, Vicky?'

'Not just yet. I've got one scene before ours.'

'Oh. Sorry.' Simon looked very contrite as he crossed to the running schedule pinned on the make-up supplies cupboard. 'Are we behind time?'

Max gave an irritated moue as he held a tissue for Vicky to blot her lipstick. 'Nearly an hour down, dear, isn't it a bugger? Upsadaisy pet, you're done.'

'Found the car yet?' Vicky jumped out of the make-up chair and grabbed her script.

'I'll know tonight.' Simon had been on the hunt for a 1960s M.G.B. 'I'm looking at one after work. The guy reckons it's in great nick. He's a mechanic and he restored it himself.' He held the studio door open for her.

'Good one,' Vicky grinned. 'I hope it's red.' The door closed behind her.

'Thanks, Tanya.' Jane nodded approval at the restyled hair and slid into the make-up chair vacated by Vicky. 'You two seem to be getting on well now, Simon. That's great,' she said, as Max started changing eye shadows.

Tanya nodded to Simon to take a seat.

'Yes,' he said, closing his eyes to avoid the fine jets of water being sprayed into his hair. 'It just took me a little while to settle in, that's all. My fault.'

When Jane left for the studio, Simon settled back to the drone of the hairdryer and the chatter of Tanya and Max. He congratulated himself as he thought back over the weekend. Yes, Jane was right, he and Vicky were getting on well.

It hadn't taken him long to talk Vicky round. Of

course she made it easy, she was a forgiving sort of girl, a sucker for an apology.

Simon had used the telethon and the endless hours of waiting around between panel and phone rooms to get to her, and he'd gone easy on the coke before he did.

He didn't think he'd be able to win her over at first. His abject apologies had been met with a cold but polite, 'It's OK, Simon, forget it'. It was only when he admitted that he'd let the coke get out of hand and he hadn't realised how much until she'd told him and . . . It was only then that Vicky had become putty in his hands. She was glad that Simon was giving up the coke. She'd seen the damage it could cause physically and emotionally, the personality changes. As she warmed to her subject, Simon knew he was home and hosed. Hell, he was a schoolboy again, convincing his mother that the fifty dollar note she'd given him really had been stolen from his sports locker. Talk about naive. It was so easy.

Simon was right. Strangely enough, Vicky was naive. She'd been observing social users and junkies since she was twelve years old and she thought that meant she knew them. But Vicky had always been a loner. She may have 'mixed with' but she'd never 'lived with' and that made her naive.

The comfortable, middle class families who had contended with a junkie son or daughter — the families to whom Vicky had always felt a condescending superiority — knew far more about addiction than she did. They knew more about the devious, secretive, schizophrenic behaviour of the addict than Vicky could have ever known.

Having accepted Simon's remorse, Vicky would have been shocked to learn that he'd followed her

home from the channel on Friday evening and that
he'd been parked outside her flat first thing on Saturday morning. She would have been appalled to
know when he approached her at the telethon that
same afternoon, that it was his first step in a carefully
considered plan of attack.

That morning Simon had observed Vicky going
about what appeared to be a routine Saturday, a
routine so mundane that Simon was surprised. Her
first stop had been the laundromat. What on earth
was a television star doing at a laundromat? The only
concession she made to disguise were an American
baseball cap and a pair of dark glasses.

While her laundry went through the washing
machine Vicky visited the supermarket, and as it
dried, she called into the greengrocers and the
chicken shop.

Two hours later, as he watched her give her all to
the millions of Australian viewers, Simon felt very
close to her. They don't know, he thought, but I do.
And next weekend I'm going to know more. Much,
much more.

'Wake up, Simon, you're done.' Tanya gave his
fringe a tiny blast of hair spray and whisked the
plastic cape off his shoulders.

'Next!' Max stood aside, camping it up as he gestured to the make-up chair. He'd always fancied
Simon.

As he was being powdered down, Simon looked at
the monitor. Greg, Jane and Vicky were giving their
all.

Twenty minutes later it was Jane watching the monitor. This time Simon and Vicky were giving their all.

She was in the greenroom, sucking back the fifth coffee of the day and telling herself what a foolish industry it was that she had been caught up in. Then she caught sight of Vicky's face in close-up on the greenroom monitor. The girl was certainly good. There was an energy about her that refused to go unrecognised. Admittedly, it was raw and needed to learn when to hold back, but if Vicky stayed in the game and kept fighting, Jane was sure she could make it to the top.

Jane liked Vicky — a lot. Although they came from vastly different backgrounds they had a great deal in common. Vicky reminded Jane very much of herself at that age: the same fierce independence, the same desire to do battle.

'Hi, Jane. Edwina in her dressing room, is she?'

'Hello, Paul. Yes, I think so.' As he left Jane switched back to the monitor. Poor bloke, she thought. She knew that Paul's marriage had collapsed. Mind you, his wife was probably better off — according to the social pages, she was making a killing with her return to the fashion world.

When Paul had studied the schedules, he'd been pleased to discover that Edwina had a four-hour break between her first scene for the day and the five scenes she had to do with him during the afternoon. It gave him an excuse to suggest they have lunch together while they went over some lines. It also gave him a reason to get out of his hotel room and go into the channel early.

Paul was desperately lonely. He'd given up ringing Barbie. Mostly he got the answering machine anyway and, on the rare occasion that Barbie answered, she was pleasantly remote and spoke only about the children. The day he'd visited the house to see the twins she'd made sure she was out and had left Jamie in charge. Paul fought to keep himself in check all that afternoon, but when he got back to his hotel room, he burst into tears. No more trips to the house, he promised himself. He'd only seen the children once since then. Jamie had brought the twins to the hotel and Paul had taken them all to a football match. That had been upsetting enough.

Davey opened the door to Edwina's dressing room.

'Paul,' Edwina looked surprised. 'You're not called for hours. What are you doing here?'

'I thought you might want to go over this afternoon's lines.'

'You're keen,' Edwina smiled. 'What time is it, Davey?'

'Nearly one o'clock. Liza's due any minute.'

'Sorry.' Edwina shrugged regretfully and Paul turned to go. Four hours sitting in the canteen. God, he felt depressed.

'Paul, wait.' Edwina exchanged a look with Davey as Paul turned back. 'I don't really feel like a heavy dose of Liza in the middle of a taping day. Why don't you come back when they call lunchbreak and Davey'll bring us something up from the canteen?'

Paul smiled with relief, saved from his own company. 'OK, great. What time are they calling lunch?'

Edwina looked at Davey. 'One-thirty,' he said.

'Make it one forty-five.'

Paul gave a salute and left. Davey closed the door behind him. 'Liza expects to lunch with you. Don't you think it's a bit rude?' he asked.

'Probably. But I know she's going to start angling for the "Edwina Dawling inside story" and I can only fob her off for so long.'

Davey shook his head disapprovingly. 'Honestly, Edwina, it was sheer madness to make that promise in the first place.'

'I know, I know.'

'Well, what are you going to do?'

'Avoid the subject as much as possible and if she doesn't give up, tell her to bugger off.

'Why the hell did you agree to this appointment with her, anyway?' asked Davey

'I didn't. Rosa did.' Edwina gave a sigh of irritation, and Davey countered, 'Well, she doesn't know that you owe Liza one for the Paul Sorell expose, does she?'

Edwina was about to snarl back at him when there was a knock on the door. 'Moral support, Davey — don't you dare go away.'

'Hello, Liza, come in.' Davey ushered Liza into the room and gestured to one of the leather armchairs.

'Hello, Davey, Edwina.' Liza sat down and looked around her appreciatively. 'What a beautiful dressing room.'

'Yes, it's very comfortable. Tea or coffee?'

Liza looked slightly taken aback. 'Coffee, thanks. Black.'

Edwina nodded to Davey. 'Same for me thanks, and bring us some of that lovely shortbread.'

Liza's smile was slightly fixed as Edwina turned back to her. No lunch, she was thinking, I'm about to be fobbed off. So Rosa must be right.

Liza was well aware that Rosa Glassberg hated her guts but of course they played the game with each other. When Davey had gently fielded Liza's last two phone calls, saying that Edwina had a very heavy work week and would get back to her, Liza had worried that he was being a little overprotective and that her messages might not have been relayed.

She decided to go through the more official channel of Edwina's agent and she was glad she had. In an effort to glean as much inside information as possible, Rosa had been most helpful. Yes, she had Edwina's schedule in front of her – there was a four-hour break on Wednesday. Edwina would be only too happy to meet over lunch.

'Now, is there anything I can do?' Rosa had asked. 'What angle are you taking on the story? As her close friend and agent I'm sure I could give you an added insight.'

'Yes, I'm sure you could, Rosa, but it's not really an interview I'm after this time. When we get around to doing the Edwina Dawling life story I'm sure you'll be a great help.'

Damn you, woman, Rosa thought, if it's not an interview you're after, then what the hell is it? And as for Edwina's life story . . . well, that was a laugh. 'I doubt whether you'll find Edwina agreeable to a life story, Liza.' Rosa didn't even attempt to disguise the sneer.

'Oh, she's already agreed. We made an arrangement quite a while ago.'

There was a pause while Rosa fought to regain her composure. What 'arrangement'? What was the favour in return for which Edwina had promised a story Rosa knew she would never give? But most important of all, why had Rosa not been told? The anger she felt towards Liza turned full bore against Edwina. The ungrateful bitch — how dare she?

'Congratulations, Liza. That's quite a coup. And when you get around to writing it, I'll be only too happy to help. Don't forget I know Edwina better than anyone. In fact I know *all* about her and I'd be only too willing to share it with you.'

The woman is furious, Liza thought as she hung up. Furious with Edwina. That could be very helpful.

As Liza sat in Edwina's dressing room and realised she was about to get the full run around, as she watched Edwina cross her long, elegant legs and flash one of her dazzling smiles, Liza thought, yes, Rosa, I'm sure you could be very helpful indeed.

'Now, what can I do for you, Liza?'

'It's more a case of what I can do for you at the moment, Edwina.' Might as well play the game back for a while, she thought.

'Oh?' Edwina pushed the small china plate which Davey had placed before her to the centre of the table. 'You must try one of these shortbreads, they're marvellous.'

'Thank you.' But Liza ignored the biscuits and lit up one of her rare cigarettes. Menthol, 0.4 milligrams of nicotine. She'd kicked the habit ages ago. She only carried the pack in case she was hit with the odd occasion which called for a cigarette, so that she wouldn't have to bot one with a higher nicotine content. That 'odd occasion' was always prior to a showdown, and Liza had a definite feeling that a showdown was imminent.

Nevertheless, she continued to play the game. 'I wondered if you knew that the CBS deal had gone ahead? They intend to announce it next week.'

Edwina hadn't. She gestured for Davey to open a window and bring an ashtray. 'I knew they were negotiating, but . . . next week! How did you find out?'

Liza gave a self-deprecating shrug. 'Trade secret — no one but a couple of people close to Alain know but I thought you might want to act on the advance news.'

'In what way?' Edwina looked shrewdly at the journalist. What was she angling at?

It was the question Liza had counted on. 'Well, a new agent for starters. You want to be well and truly set up with an American manager before the show goes to air in the States.'

'So? Thank you, Davey.' Edwina offered the sugar bowl to Liza as Davey set the coffees down before them. Liza ignored both. 'Why a new agent?' Edwina continued. 'Rosa can liaise with whoever I choose to represent me in the States. In fact, she could probably arrange an American manager for me.'

'Rosa?' Liza's face said, You're joking. 'Come on.'

Edwina stopped trying to figure the journalist's angle as she realised that the woman was right. Rosa would be totally out of her league mingling with the big American negotiators and was bound to stuff up any deal which might present itself. And more than anything else, Edwina wanted stardom in the United States. Liza was right.

Edwina made a snap decision. End of favours time: Rosa was out; better representation was most certainly required. She decided to give credit where it was due.

'That's good advice, Liza. Thank you.'

Liza knew she had a foot in the door, and decided to go for broke. 'Of course, there's another area you should be looking at, Edwina.' She stubbed the cigarette out. It tasted awful but it went hand in hand with the familiar showdown feeling and was therefore somehow comforting. 'You need a promotion campaign for the States. I want to do it for you. And I want the life story of Edwina Dawling.'

Edwina gave a gentle, resigned sigh. It was what she'd been expecting. She'd have to play it gently, evade the issue. 'Liza, in my experience, you are the best television journalist in the industry . . . '

Liza seethed at the term 'television journalist'. Didn't the woman realise she'd been one of the country's top investigative reporters?

' . . . and as such,' Edwina continued, 'you would be my immediate choice should I —'

'I want what you promised Edwina!' Liza stopped hedging. 'I want the inside story and nothing less.'

'And if you don't get it?' Edwina's eyes flashed danger. Was Liza daring to threaten her?

'You owe me, Edwina.' Liza glared back with equal intensity. She knew it was the wrong thing to say and that she was burning her bridges by saying it but she'd compromised herself for Edwina and now Edwina was trying to renege on the deal.

Edwina felt something strangely akin to fear. She wanted to look at Davey for support but didn't dare — it would weaken her position. Instead she stared back into Liza's coal-black eyes.

'I don't owe you a thing, Liza.'

As Liza walked through the channel's reception area, a sharp pang of neuralgia flashed up the side of her face and she realised she'd been grinding her teeth. Damn! Her teeth hurt, her face hurt, her hands hurt. Damn Edwina! But Liza felt a certain grim satisfaction. Edwina would pay. She'd pay, all right.

Liza looked at her watch. Yes, there was just enough time.

Rape

'*You bitch*! You fucking hypocritical bitch!' It happened so quickly there was nothing Edwina could do. Her dressing room door was flung open and Paul was standing there screaming at her.

He slammed the morning paper down on the table and her eye caught a flash of the headline: DAWLING v. SORELL: IS IT WAR? She didn't need to read the leader — '*Edwina Dawling's bid to destroy Paul Sorell*' — to know that Liza had spilled the lot.

'Who the fuck do you think you are, Edwina?'

Edwina was frightened. Paul was a strong man and his anger was approaching madness. She tried to placate him, wondering where the hell Davey was.

'You don't know the full story, Paul, you're overreacting —'

'*Overreacting*!' Something in Paul snapped. He grabbed Edwina by the neck and she felt her back crack dangerously as he slammed her against the side of the dressing table.

'You ruin my marriage . . .' he snarled, his fingers sinking deep into her throat, 'you turn my wife against me . . .' deeper and deeper, 'you take my children away from me . . .' The words were now being hissed from behind clenched teeth as he tightened his grip on her throat.

He didn't hear the bathroom door open. He didn't see Davey pick up Edwina's handbag from the sofa. He didn't see him take out the .25 calibre Colt pocket automatic pistol she always carried.

It was only when Paul could sense that Edwina was near her last breath, when he could feel her back about to break against the dressing table that he became aware of the steady pressure of something metallic against his left temple.

'That's enough, Paul.'

Slowly Paul's head started to clear. Edwina's terrified bulging eyes were only centimetres from his. He still wanted to see her dead but a shred of commonsense restrained him — and he gradually released his hold, as the metal barrel continued its relentless pressure against his temple.

'I said, that's enough.' Davey's voice was as steady and as cold as the gun he held and Paul suddenly dropped his hands, leaving Edwina holding on to the side of the dressing table, her chest heaving.

'Go into the bathroom, Edwina.' Davey kept his eyes on Paul. Edwina nodded and, still gasping, fumbled her way to the bathroom door.

When he heard the lock turn, Davey slowly lowered the gun. Paul turned to face him and the two men looked at each other for several seconds before Paul spoke. 'Tell her to watch her back. Tell her from now on she'd better watch her back.'

'Don't be a fool, Paul.'

Paul made for the door, then turned back to Davey with agony in his eyes.

'Why, Davey? *Why?*'

Davey couldn't return Paul's gaze. He shrugged and looked away. He'd never been able to understand

Edwina's thirst for revenge and the lengths to which she'd go to satisfy it.

The question went unanswered.

As Paul left the room, Davey returned the gun to Edwina's handbag and tapped on the bathroom door. 'OK.'

The door opened and Edwina stood looking at him, her hand to her throat.

'Are you all right?' he asked.

'You took your time.'

Davey ignored the retort. She was still badly shaken. He sat her at the table and pointed to the newspaper. 'Want to see the damage?'

'The maniac,' Edwina said, still massaging her neck. It hurt to swallow.

Davey had opened to the story. It was anonymous, of course. The newspaper had received verification from a reliable source that Edwina Dawling had been responsible for disclosing Paul Sorell's sordid background and for bringing it to the attention of the press. The article went on to surmise the reasons for Miss Dawling's vicious attack. Unrequited love, perhaps? Professional jealousy over Sorell's increasing popularity? The entire article was a slur on Edwina's character and worded so cleverly that it would be impossible to make a libel suit stick.

Davey read out every word, painstakingly slowly. Whatever damage Edwina may have wanted to do to Paul in originally releasing the story was nothing, nothing at all, compared to what she now wanted to do to Liza.

When Davey had finished reading, Edwina continued to stare down at the open newspaper. 'Bring me the telephone,' she said at last.

Alain cradled the receiver on his shoulder as he held a photograph in each hand. 'That's entirely up to you, Edwina. You're the one who wanted the woman to handle you exclusively. If you don't want her any more, then just say so.'

He squinted at the photos. One girl was Chinese, the other Indonesian. Both were eighteen but looked younger and he couldn't make up his mind which he preferred. He was momentarily distracted as he realised that Edwina's request was more far-reaching than he'd realised.

'Why do you want her off the show altogether?' Alain had a vague idea — he'd seen the early edition. 'She has a contract with us, you know.'

As he listened to the voice, which was just bordering on self-control, Alain smiled down at the photographs. Yes, the Indonesian, he decided, although it was really neither here nor there — he'd be able to judge them in the flesh in half an hour. He dumped the photos on top of the pile of other hopefuls lined up for the auditions and concentrated on the phone.

'If you put it like that, Edwina, how could I possibly refuse?' Alain resisted a chuckle. He felt positively gleeful. Edwina was giving him thinly-veiled threats about contacting Bryce. Hell, no! Bryce had countermanded his orders in favour of Edwina's before, why shouldn't Alain automatically accept the fact that the man would do it again and therefore immediately acquiesce to Edwina's demands? Particularly as Edwina's demands were in direct conflict with the wellbeing of the show. Tim Arnold and the Channel 3 publicity department didn't have access to the quality publications that Liza had, and their work lacked Liza's class. If Robert Bryce ever wanted to know why he'd sacked the best in the business, Alain had only to shrug and say 'You created the precedent, Robert. You said "What Edwina wants, Edwina gets". '

Alain couldn't believe how easy it was to sabotage this show. There was no need for him to do anything — they were doing it themselves. He looked back at the photographs. A ridiculous storyline about Vietnamese boat people, Chris gone, Liza gone. Hell, the only thing left up to Alain was to rip off some ideas from Evan, and that part was easy. Evan was already slaving away over three new concepts under the misguided belief that Channel 3 was going to give birth to one of his embryos and that he would be heralded as the creator of a new hit series. Things couldn't have been going better for Alain. And Alain couldn't have been nicer or more agreeable to Edwina.

Yes, of course he would demand that the paper print an apology for any unintended slur upon Edwina's character. And, yes, of course, he assured her, it would be easy to undo most of the damage. They'd had their headliner story and no doubt would be quite willing to make reparation in exchange for some tawdry bits of smut Tim Arnold could dig up about stars from rival networks.

As she hung up, Edwina allowed herself a moment's confusion. Why had Alain been so amenable? Then the rush of hatred for Liza returned. What the hell did it matter? He'd agreed; Liza was out. Now all Edwina had to do was spread the word elsewhere.

As he watched her pick up the phone again, Davey felt powerless. What drove Edwina when she felt this need to destroy? As a friend from childhood, Davey knew every reason for Edwina's need to fight, but to destroy? Davey shrugged to himself and stood by, helpless. There was no stopping her.

Alain settled back in the semidarkness and sipped at his coffee. In front of him a camera was trained on a small lighted interview set and Chris was chatting to the Indonesian girl. She was even more beautiful than her photograph but Alain was no longer interested. He'd seen what he wanted.

On his way to Studio D, Alain had popped his head into the greenroom to have a quick glance at the Asian talent.

'Hello, girls. I'm Alain King, executive producer. Just thought I'd wish you good luck.' There were ten of them, all lookers, and there was the Indonesian girl. Yes, she was the pick of the bunch. But who was that standing behind her? A shy face peeked around the girl's shoulder and Alain caught his breath.

She was petite and fragile and very, very young, with gleaming blue-black hair. She knew his eyes had sought her out and she smiled a shy, gentle smile in return. She must have been fourteen, fifteen at the outside.

'Yes . . . well, good luck, everyone.' Alain backed out before his desire became too obvious. What was her name? How come there hadn't been a photo and biog on her? Not to worry, he'd make sure she got the part and then . . . Alain pushed the door open to studio D . . . all those research sessions!

After the Indonesian girl, there was a Chinese, a Malay, a Thai and then . . . There she was. Alain tried to keep his voice steady as he muttered to Jim, seated beside him, 'Right age'.

'Too young.'

Jim was rifling through the photographs and biographies. He didn't notice the sharp look Alain gave him and it wouldn't have worried him if he had.

Ever since Chris had told him that he was leaving, and the reason why, Jim's attitude to Alain had changed. He'd put up with Alain's arrogance in the past because of the man's talent, but Alain no longer seemed to care about the quality of the show and Jim found that unforgivable.

Jim remained outwardly civil, of course. He couldn't afford to lose his job. He didn't want to — he still cared very deeply about the show.

Jim watched with admiration as Chris took the auditionees through their paces. Many of them were very inexperienced but even the most nervous relaxed with him.

The girl's name was Tran and she was Vietnamese. Chris looked questioningly at Jim. Jim shook his head.

'We don't seem to have any details about you, Tran. Who's your agent?' Chris asked.

'No agent.' The girl's voice was barely a whisper.

'How did you know about the audition?'

'Friend of mine. She was going to come. Then decide not. She tell me I should smash audition.'

Chris laughed. 'Crash. She told you to crash the audition?'

The girl smiled back. 'Crash. Yes.'

'How old are you, Tran?'

The girl looked nervously towards Jim. She'd witnessed the communication between the two men and sensed that it was Jim who was making the rules.

'Seventeen.' There seemed a slight question mark at the end and Chris again glanced at Jim. He gave a slight shake of the head and Chris agreed. There was no way this girl was seventeen.

'I'm sorry, Tran, you're just a little bit too young for this part.'

The girl's look shifted to Alain. It was a direct plea and again he felt his pulse quicken with desire.

'If you'd like to leave your name and phone number with the man at the door — the man with the headphones — we'll get in touch with you when we're after someone a little younger, OK?' Chris was ushering her gently towards the door as he nodded for the next girl to be called.

'He's not even going to run the camera on her, for God's sake,' Alain hissed to Jim. 'Call her back.'

'She's too young, Alain.'

'Jesus Christ! The part's written for a fifteen-year-old.'

'To be played by someone over sixteen. We don't want to have to arrange guardianship and everything.'

'She said she was seventeen.'

Chris joined them. 'Like hell. And she can't act. Did you hear that voice? She can't speak above a whisper.'

Alain wanted to run after the girl. 'I still think we should test her.'

Both men looked at him with loathing. They knew.

'Hello, Suzie, isn't it?' Chris consulted his list and walked over to the Chinese girl who was looking a little lost in the middle of the studio floor.

With the exception of the ninety minutes it took to

tape two short scenes, Edwina had spent all afternoon on the phone and was well satisfied with the damage she'd caused Liza. The woman would find it very difficult to get a job in this town again. Well, Edwina shrugged, maybe she could go back to art gallery openings, but that was about it. There was one final phone call to be made.

'Liza was right about one thing,' Edwina said to Davey as she dialled. 'It's time to get rid of Rosa.'

Davey felt a sudden chill down his spine. Was Edwina going mad? The damage Rosa could do! 'Edwina, I think . . . '

'Hello, Rosa? It's me.'

'Edwina, darling!' The voice poured sympathy down the line. 'I've called you about twenty times, ever since I read that dreadful article but —'

'Yes, I've been on the phone.'

'You poor thing, you must be —'

'I've decided to leave the agency, Rosa.'

Well, that shut her up, Edwina thought, as Davey cringed in the background. She waited a long time for Rosa to say something but there was only a stunned silence.

'The show's sold to the States,' Edwina resumed 'and I need an American agent, so —'

'Liza Farrelly's idea, I take it?' The gushing bonhomie was gone and the voice cut like a knife.

'Why Liza's?'

'Because you've been pissing in each other's pockets for months now and the bitch wants me out, that's why.' Rosa's true vulgarity showed itself whenever she was cornered. 'Well, I'm not going to let you do it, Edwina.'

'I don't see there's much you can do about it. I'll

call around and collect my files and tapes tomorrow morning.'

'Like hell you will. Tell your friend Liza fucking Farrelly to come and get them for you — she can collect a nice juicy story while she's here.'

Rosa slammed the phone down and sat staring at it, breathing heavily, beads of sweat popping out on her brow. Liza Farrelly had convinced Edwina Dawling to leave the agency! Between them they were about to ruin her. She hated them both.

'Are you all right?' It was Dee at the door, all ready to leave.

'Yes. Go, go.' Rosa forced a smile. 'You go home, dear. I'm working late tonight — I'll lock up.'

As the door closed behind Dee, Rosa picked up the receiver again and dialled Liza Farrelly's number. Yes, she thought, Liza could come around and see her — she'd give her a few home truths, all right. Rosa felt a rush of uncontrollable hatred. Come on, come on! Answer the phone, cunt.

'Good night, Mr King.'

Alain didn't acknowledge his secretary as he stormed out of his office. It had been an irritating afternoon. He'd questioned the first assistant about Tran but evidently she'd left no contact phone number. He'd tried to date the Indonesian girl with a hefty hint that if she was nice to him the part was hers. The bitch had led him on. She'd nodded politely which at first he took to be encouragement, then stupidity, which perfectly suited his purpose. Finally, deciding that actions spoke louder than words, particularly when dealing with a dumb woman, he put his arm around her waist and started shepherding her to the door.

'Let's discuss it over a drink, shall we?'

The Indonesian girl stopped nodding and stood her ground. 'You realise this is sexual harassment, don't you?' The voice was beautifully modulated with perfect enunciation and the eyes gleamed with an assurance that put her way out of his league. She was a brown version of Edwina. Alain dropped his hand. 'Now, piss off,' the girl said, 'before I call the police.'

'Good night, Mr King.' Alain didn't acknowledge the receptionist as he stormed past the front desk. He looked at his watch and wondered if it was too late to call the massage agency. The decent girls were probably all booked out by now. The automatic doors closed silently behind him.

'Mr King?' The voice, barely a whisper, came from amongst the ornate potted palms which lined the drive to the main doors of the channel. Alain stopped, confused.

'Mr King?' It was Tran. 'I can see you? Please?' She made as if to step out from behind the palms but Alain signalled for her to stay where she was. He darted a look up the end of the driveway where Brian Hopgood was stationed in his gatehouse office.

'Stay where you are. I'll get the car.'

Trying very hard not to break into a run, Alain walked briskly to the Mercedes waiting in his VIP parking space and drove down the drive to the main doors.

He parked the car so that it was masking Tran from the gatehouse, got out and walked around to the boot.

'Get into the passenger's seat,' he muttered, opening the boot and pretending to look inside. 'And make sure that the man up there doesn't see you.'

Tran ducked into the car. Alain slammed the boot and glanced in the direction of Brian Hopgood, who looked up, caught his eye and waved. Damn! He couldn't have seen anything but he'd be wondering why Alain had driven back to the front doors.

Alain strode into reception. 'Get my secretary on the phone and remind her I need that report first thing in the morning, will you?' he barked to the receptionist. Then he turned on his heel and left.

'Keep down,' he hissed to Tran as he got back into the car.

She glued her tiny body to the car seat, gripping his upper thigh for support. As she did so, her hand brushed his penis. Surely it wasn't an accident, he thought, glancing down at her. But it was impossible to tell with her face turned away, cheek pressed against the car seat, black hair strewn across his leg.

Alain chose the exit lane farthest from the gatehouse. From there it would be impossible for Brian to see below the window level of the car. He acknowledged the man's wave as the boom gate was raised and he drove through.

He waited until they'd turned the corner nearly half a kilometre down the road.

'It's all right now,' he said.

The girl slowly raised her head, her chin gently touching his thigh, her hand once again brushing against his penis. This time Alain was sure it was no accident. He shivered in anticipation.

Her breasts were still gently touching the car seat and her back was straight as she looked up at him. She was as supple as a cat, he thought.

'Thank you.' Her voice was the merest whisper, her

eyes deep with gratitude and her hand stirred slightly as if asking a question.

Alain now had a rock-hard erection and he could feel himself starting to quiver as he nodded to her.

He kept his eyes on the road ahead. The girl unzipped his fly. As she withdrew his penis, he clenched his teeth and gripped the steering wheel till his knuckles turned white. He was on the verge of ejaculating.

But he didn't. Tran was an expert. She brought him to the edge time and time again, and knew just when to stop and how to stem the tide enough to start all over again.

By the time they reached his apartment block, Alain was on fire. Even during the fifteen floor elevator ride the girl didn't leave him alone.

Once inside his apartment, Tran continued to take control. She undressed him, then undressed herself, kissing him, stroking him, caressing him — never speaking, except for tiny whimpers and moans. She gestured for him to lie down and then, assiduously avoiding his genitals, she started to massage every inch of his body. Not just with her hands — with her breasts, her tongue, her groin.

Finally she turned her attention again to his penis, locking it between her vice-like thighs and sliding up and down against him. And when she opened her legs and slid him into her, Alain's orgasm was more powerful than anything he'd ever known before.

He lay gasping and dizzy as the girl rolled off him. He barely noticed her get up from the bed and leave the room. He barely noticed her several minutes later when she returned with a bowl of warm water, soap and a flannel.

She made gently shushing sounds as she washed

him, tenderly, rhythmically, until he was lulled into a blissfully deep sleep.

Friday had not been a good day for Liza. She'd accepted with equanimity her dismissal from Channel 3 — she'd more or less expected it. But the following day, when she tried to line up alternative work, the general reaction from within the industry took her by surprise. She was met with a succession of refusals.

One editor, with whom she'd had a particularly good relationship in the past, was honest enough to give her a straight answer. 'If I offer you a job, Liza, I can kiss goodbye any story on Edwina. She's the hottest television property in this country right now and she's promised to give us an interview.'

It appeared that after twelve months of refusal, Edwina had suddenly decided to play ball with every magazine in town and was agreeing to give interviews to all and sundry with the one proviso, a ban on Liza Farrelly.

'I can give you some straight freelance stuff if you like,' her friendly editor suggested tentatively. 'No by-line and no individual style. But frankly, I think you should go back to newspapers. Edwina doesn't carry as much weight with the press.'

Liza hung up the receiver, looked at her hand and tried to ball it into a fist. She couldn't, and the pain was intolerable. So much for newspapers. Newspapers wouldn't employ a secretary for her like the channel had and magazines would. Edwina had certainly been busy, she thought.

Liza tried to quell her rising hatred. Emotionalism was unproductive; she must be clear-headed to plan her counter-attack. And she certainly had the ammunition – it was just a case of when to fire the guns.

Liza decided to lie low for a while. Logie time would be as good as any. The darling of Australian television would certainly be the headliner then. Top of the bill in both magazines and press. That was when Liza would strike.

Davey rang the channel on Friday to say that Edwina was unwell and would not be coming in to the studios.

It was uncharacteristic of Edwina, Alain thought. And she certainly hadn't sounded ill when she'd insisted on Liza's dismissal the day before. But what the hell, it was yet another nail in the coffin of 'The Glitter Game'. Picking up ten scenes in next week's heavy taping schedule would cause chaos.

Besides, Alain couldn't be bothered trying to figure out her motives — his mind was preoccupied with other matters.

Tran had brought him coffee in bed that morning and scrubbed his back in the shower. 'Tonight? I stay?' she'd asked as he was about to leave.

Alain tried to look as if he were giving the question serious consideration but the thought of a repeat of last night's performance allowed for only one answer.

'All right,' he said finally, telling himself he'd kick her out on Saturday morning.

There was the minor dilemma of letting her stay in the flat while he went off to work but he decided, so long as she couldn't get to the safe, there really wasn't much else of value. He locked the study door and left.

Due to Sandy's efficient and highly professional

direction, and the tireless labour of the girls in the coordination department, Edwina's absence on Friday wasn't nearly the production disaster Alain had expected. New schedules were drawn up incorporating ten scenes which were to have been shot the following week and Sandy blocked the actors' moves and camera shots on the spot.

Mandy, Sidney, Greg and Vicky were the actors to cop the added workload and, except for a bit of a grizzle from Sidney at having to swat up on extra lines, they handled it beautifully.

Most of Edwina's scenes had been with Paul who now discovered he had the day off and was extremely relieved. He assumed that Edwina had reported sick because she was scared to face him the day after his attack. Well, she was damn right to be scared, he thought. He himself wasn't sure how he'd react to being confronted by her — the mere thought of her made him feel sick with anger. At least now he'd have three days to regain control of himself. But if he ever got her alone again . . .

He rang Jamie and arranged to have him bring the twins around on Saturday.

Friday's 'state of emergency' rescheduling meant that the production girls had phoned direct. Agents had been by-passed while frantic questions had been flung at the actors: 'Can you get in two hours earlier and stay three hours later? . . . Can you handle the lines for scenes such and such if we fly them in the afternoon and you have lunchtime to look at them?' Agents, money, overtime, special considerations — all could wait till the crisis was averted.

As a result of this, it was Friday lunchtime before

Vicky remembered she was booked for a store promotion that afternoon and she'd never make it because she and Simon had five scenes on the trot. What the hell, Rosa would probably bill the channel for the full fee, the cancellation being due to the lack of rescheduling notice given and Vicky hated store promos anyway. She rang her agent.

'Oh, Vicky, hi,' Dee answered. 'I tried to ring you an hour ago but they told me you were in the studio. I bet it's chaos out there.'

'Oh, they've told you all about it, have they?'

'You're joking,' Dee laughed. 'Disaster means the agents are the last to know. They rely on the actors' old "show must go on" mentality to get them out of the shit. No, Davey rang to say Edwina wasn't going in. Well, I mean gulp, gulp, at that bit of info, and when I rang the production office to say how terribly sorry we were that our client was so mortally ill, they told me they were rescheduling.'

Vicky smiled and shrugged an apology to Simon who was waiting to go to the canteen with her for lunch. Dee always rabbited on when Rosa wasn't there, particularly with the younger clients, but she was good enough at her job.

'Anyway,' Dee continued, 'I cancelled this afternoon's promo and I warned the channel that Rosa would probably bill them for the full amount.'

'She's not in, then?'

'No. She hasn't been in all day. But she often doesn't come in on Friday if she's worked late on Thursday. She says Friday's a lousy business day, anyway, everyone living for the weekend and knocking off early. It's a bit of a bastard' for me though. I mean, I've got to —'

'Thanks a lot, Dee. Gotta go — we're on a short

lunch break.' Vicky hung up the phone, gave a mock wipe-of-the-brow and grabbed Simon's hand. 'Let's eat!' she said. 'I'm starving!'

Simon had taken as little dope as possible that morning. A half-line first thing and a quick top up in the loo at tea break. If he snorted another half-line after lunch, the afternoon should go as well as the morning had. Vicky was in the palm of his hand, and tomorrow . . . Well, it looked as if tomorrow everything would work out exactly as planned.

They worked hard over lunch, running lines and discussing scenes. As they were about to return to the studio, Vicky said to him. 'So, when do we see the car? You pick it up tomorrow, don't you?'

'Yep. But you'll have to wait till next week. Gotta big weekend.'

Vicky nodded, happy for him. 'Is it red?'

'Wait and see,' he grinned back. She's panting for me, he thought. Well, tomorrow, baby, tomorrow.

Saturday morning Alain again experienced one of the most erotic encounters of his heavily indulged life. Because he didn't have to dash off to work, he was able to give Tran free rein. Go for it, baby, he thought, as he lay back and surrendered to the pressure of her hands and the texture of the oil.

Friday night had been exciting but exhausting and, in the sated aftermath of Saturday morning, he would have been quite happy for her to leave quietly without disturbing him. But, as he drifted in and out of sleep, aware of her hands and her mouth and her sleek black hair drifting across his groin, Alain didn't want Tran to go. Ever.

So she wanted to be his slave? Fine. She could

move in with him. Just so long as she behaved herself. Just so long as there was no talk of bringing family out from Vietnam. Just so long as she kept well out of his public life. Where was the harm? He'd even pay her a healthy allowance. After all, he'd be saving a heap on massage agencies.

They didn't talk about it much. Alain gave her a hundred dollar bill and ordered her a cab. He figured that she'd either be back with her gear in an hour or he'd never see her again. Either way it didn't really matter.

So why was he trying hard not to stare at the front door two hours later? he asked himself as he paced the kitchen with his fifth cup of coffee.

He stopped. The door opened and Tran stood there, tiny and lost, a battered suitcase in each hand. She smiled shyly. Alain smiled back. He couldn't help it.

Vicky woke up happy that it was Saturday. She always liked Saturdays.

A large plastic bag full of washing sat by the front door, and a shopping list lay on the bench which separated the kitchenette from the bedsitting room.

In the seven months since 'The Glitter Game' started, Vicky's life style had altered very little. She continued to live in the same Darlinghurst bedsit, with a bathroom down the hall, while her weekly pay cheque was deposited via the Rosa Glassberg Trust Account directly into a high interest-bearing deposit account. A small allowance found its way to Vicky and, although this was twice her previous income, it only allowed for the added luxuries which most people considered necessities.

For the first time she could remember, Vicky was enjoying the bite in the air and was actually looking forward to midwinter evenings locked up in her cosy bedsit. Her new electric fan heater would be turned up full blast and she'd curl up in bed with her new electric blanket and watch herself on her new television set. Roll on winter, she thought gleefully.

Each month Vicky would go to the bank and look at her account statements. At the end of the first year of 'The Glitter Game' she figured she'd have enough for a deposit on a small flat. Each Saturday afternoon she'd walk around the inner-city areas which boasted the cheapest real estate and fantasise about which would be her dream home. Her choice was always a cute little stone cottage or a tiny terrace house with iron lacework balcony but she knew she'd never be able to afford them. No, her future probably lay in the groundfloor back flat of one of the unimaginative red brickwork blocks of apartments but it wouldn't really matter. It would be her own! It would be a dream come true!

Vicky pulled a large soft wool beanie low over her brow. It was a gawdy green and red and gave her a clownish look but she'd found that, with some form of hat and a pair of dark glasses, she managed to escape recognition for the most part. The main trick was to concentrate on where she was going and what she was doing. By paying no attention to others she called less attention to herself. She'd observed Mandy and Sidney skulking around corners and darting furtive glances at people in a bid to go unrecognised. It meant they always were, of course. It took Vicky a little while to realise that Mandy and Sidney wanted to be recognised.

She locked the door, slung the laundry bag over

her shoulder and bounded down the wide, central stairway to the street.

Simon had parked the yellow MG well out of sight in a small lane behind Vicky's apartment block. He was quite sure it was an unnecessary precaution. He knew exactly which direction she'd take as she came out of her front door.

He'd been leaning against the brick wall three doors down from Vicky's for nearly an hour when she appeared, turned right and headed up the hill towards Oxford Street and the shops. Simon decided to follow her on foot just to ensure she stuck to her itinerary. When she'd finished at the supermarket and was queuing at the chicken shop, he'd dash back, get the car and be accidentally cruising past in his new MG as she was walking home. Perfect timing to give her a lift home with her shopping bags.

Sure enough, just before she got to Oxford Street, she dumped her laundry at the laundromat. A slight change in procedure — she didn't put it in the machine herself but arranged for the attendant to do it for her. She looked at her watch and nodded, obviously telling the girl what time she'd collect it, then popped into the milk bar next door and came out sucking on a chocolate heart. Then she turned the corner into Oxford Street. But instead of going into the supermarket, she crossed the road and waited at the bus stop.

Shit, Simon thought, as he dashed off to get the car. He wouldn't be able to make a right-hand turn into Oxford Street, he'd have to go around the block, and what if a bus came along in the meantime? But when he drove round the corner he saw that she was still there.

'Want a lift?'

'Simon!'

'Hop in.'

A girl in the queue three people ahead of Vicky had recognised her. She nudged her boyfriend and whispered, 'It's Jodie!'

'But where are you going?' Vicky asked, keeping her back to the girl and her boyfriend.

'Wherever you're going.' Simon patted the dashboard lovingly. 'I'm taking her for a spin. Isn't she beautiful?'

'And that's her brother, whatsisname,' the girl hissed, pointing at Simon. Several other people in the queue were starting to stare. Three cars had pulled up behind Simon. One of them tooted.

'She's not red,' Vicky grinned, 'but she'll do. Annandale OK?'

Before Simon could open the passenger door, Vicky had swung herself over the side of the open convertible and snuggled down into the seat beside him. 'Actually, I prefer yellow,' she said as Simon revved up impressively. 'Red's too aggro.'

'You live around Darlo, do you?' Simon asked casually.

'Yep. Palmer Street.'

The wind grabbed at their voices and they had to yell to each other. Vicky was in danger of wearing her chocolate heart so she hurled it at a passing rubbish bin and missed. Then she pulled off her beanie before she lost it. She was exhilarated and loving every minute of the drive.

'What's in Annandale?' Simon yelled.

'Do you know Nelson Street?'

Simon nodded. 'I think so.'

'Head there and I'll show you. Number 88.'

Number 88 had a 'For Sale' sign up and there was an 'open for inspection' placard on the footpath outside. The moment Vicky saw the cottage she fell in love with it. And the moment she saw it, she also knew that it was way out of her league. She wasn't too disappointed — it was all part of the fantasy game that happened every Saturday.

She told Simon about her regular weekend hunt and smiled wryly at him as they closed the wooden gate and got back into the car. So how come she hadn't gone on the hunt last weekend? Simon wondered to himself. Then he realised — the telethon, of course.

Vicky had another three places marked in the *Herald*, all in the same area and all too upmarket.

'I pick a different area each week,' she explained 'and cover it by foot. Everything's so damn expensive though, there's no such thing as cheap suburbs any more. Not inner city ones, anyway.'

'So? Why bother buying cheap? You'll sign up for another year of "The Glitter Game" at the end of the season, won't you?'

'Sure. If they want me.'

Simon roared with laughter. 'If they want you! Hell, Vicky, you'll be able to name your own price. You're a star, mate, you've got to start thinking like one.'

'OK,' Vicky grinned back. 'Take me house perving — find me a star home.'

They spent the next two hours driving around the wealthiest harbourside suburbs and, while Vicky happily 'house perved', Simon did his own surreptitious perving on Vicky. Every time she nudged, pointed and lifted those electric eyes to meet his with a 'Cop that one!' Simon felt a chill down his spine. God, how he wanted her! But he kept telling himself to play it cool.

Vicky refused lunch, apart from a Coke, and, by two o'clock, was insisting she go back and pick up her laundry.

'So, this is where you live.' Simon looked up at the apartment block that he already knew so well.

'Yeah. Real star material, eh?' Vicky swung herself over the side of the car and heaved the bag of laundry off the back seat. 'Thanks, Simon. I've had a great time.'

She wouldn't let him carry the laundry upstairs for her but he wasn't the least bit fazed by that. He'd downed a couple of Dexedrine with his Coke and he felt good, strong and confident. 'How about dinner, then? We could rage on to a couple of discos afterwards.'

'Nah. I'll skip dinner, thanks.' Vicky slung the laundry bag over her shoulder. 'Tell you what, though, I wouldn't mind a bit of a rage. Start at the Hard Rock?'

'You're on.' Simon swung the car out into the traffic. 'Pick you up at ten.'

'Flat 4D,' she called after him.

He waved acknowledgement without looking back. Tonight they'd rage all right.

And rage they did. From the Hard Rock Cafe to Bobby McGee's, to Metropolis, to Site, and finally to the Bourbon and Beefsteak where three am saw them drinking tequila slammers and eating nachos.

'Isn't it funny how you can drink so much on a rage night and end up not feeling remotely pissed?' Vicky remarked, her mouth full of melted cheese and chilli. 'It's all the sweating you do on the dance floor, I guess. Hell, that chilli's hot.'

Simon offered her his beer chaser. He wasn't feeling pissed either. He wasn't feeling anything. The cocaine was meeting the alcohol which was meeting the Dexies he'd been downing all evening and he was floating.

'Let's drive to Watson's Bay and look at The Gap,' he said.

It was dark and it was chilly but it didn't matter. They felt very comfortable together as they sat looking out over the Sydney Harbour heads and the vast expanse of black beyond them. Simon took Vicky's hand and she didn't resist. She smiled at him and he kissed her, very, very gently. As their lips parted, Simon wanted to cry. He'd never felt himself so overwhelmed with love. It wasn't lust at all, it was an all-consuming love the like of which no one had ever felt before. He dropped her hand and looked out to the ocean. He mustn't say anything to her about it — he might frighten her off. But he wanted to know her, everything about her. And he wanted her to know him. So he started to talk.

Vicky's heart went out to him as he talked about his family. He'd had everything that money could buy. Nannies, boarding schools, holidays at exclusive riding schools, everything that money could buy — except parents.

Vicky realised that Simon was probably a bit maudlin with the drink — after all, he'd put away twice as much as she had — but he was so sad, so sincere. Besides, they had more in common than she'd realised. She hadn't had parents either. And before she knew it, Vicky was telling Simon her own background. Then they were kissing again. Still gently, so gently. Finally it was Vicky's suggestion. 'Shall we go home? To my place?'

She'd never offered herself to anyone before. Simon nodded and helped her up.

Vicky had no idea how it happened. One minute they were lying on her bed, kissing, Simon's hand beneath her shirt tenderly caressing her breast. Then the kiss became a little too insistent and his teeth were biting into her lip, and his caress became a little more brutal. He was starting to hurt her. She tried to pull away, to signal that he was hurting her. But when she did, he dug his teeth savagely into her mouth and ripped her bra apart, twisting and kneading and bruising her flesh.

She managed to push him away from her and leapt up from the bed. 'Simon! What the hell's the matter with you?'

'Come here, bitch.' The eyes that stared back were mad, demented. He sprang at her, grabbing both her wrists and pinning her against the wall.

'Stop it, you're hurting me.' She tried to sound in control, as her mind sought frantically for a defence plan. Should she reason with him? Get angry with him? Scream, to scare him off?

'Take your clothes off bitch.'

Vicky decided to buy time. 'It's a bit impossible with no hands.'

He released her hands and stood back watching her every move. As she slowly undid the buttons of her shirt, he unbuckled his belt.

Vicky decided to reason with him. 'Come on, Simon, give us a break. Be fair.'

'Faster.'

'I'll scream. There's a lot of people in this building.'

'I said, faster!'

What the hell, Vicky thought, she might as well give it a go. She knew damn well that the tenants of Darlinghurst bedsits didn't answer screams in the wee hours of the morning but maybe it would scare him off.

Her scream rang out for a fraction of a second before Simon's backhander slammed into the side of her face and she fell to the floor, momentarily stunned, her elbow cracking against the side of the bed.

He grabbed a fistful of her hair and dragged her to her feet. That was when Vicky knew there was only one way out. 'OK, Simon, you win.' The stranger's red, angry eyes stared at her disbelievingly. 'I said, you win. OK?' She nodded for him to let go of her. He did, once again stepping back and watching her like a hawk.

Vicky undressed and stood before him, trying to read which way he wanted it. Standing up? Bending over? Lying down? Hurry up, hurry up, her mind was saying. Get it over and done with and don't hurt me any more.

Simon didn't bother to undress. He pulled his jeans and underpants down over his buttocks and gestured for her to lie on the bed. He entered her painfully and continued to thrust violently, desperately, for what seemed like hours to Vicky. She felt her fingernails bite into the palms of her hands and she could taste the blood from her torn lip as it seeped between her clenched teeth. Oh God, when would it stop? She had heard that junkies often had trouble ejaculating. She had to come up with another plan.

Simon himself was tiring now.

'Why don't we take a break?' she said. 'You want a joint?'

He looked at her suspiciously. 'I thought you weren't into dope.'

'I'm not. Just grass. It's good stuff, too.' She gestured to the dresser. 'In the bottom drawer.'

Simon rolled off her with a groan. 'OK. Get it.'

She hurled herself at the door.

'You cunt!' Simon threw himself at her just as she managed to wrench the door open. She felt him grab at her hair then let go as she slammed the door behind her, catching him heavily on the shoulder.

She tore down the hall to the bathrooms at the far end. She could hear him thundering along behind her, cursing as he pulled his jeans up.

Not daring to look back, she dived into the door marked 'Women' and slammed it shut just as Simon's full weight landed against it. By the time he'd opened it, she'd ducked into one of the cubicles and bolted the door.

'I'll get you, bitch.' The voice sounded thick, drugged and unrecognisable as Simon backed out of the women's bathroom.

She stood there naked, panting and frightened.

Murder

Vicky sat shivering on the rim of the bath. She'd long since stemmed her bleeding lip with cold water but the bath tap kept slowly trickling and she continued mechanically dabbing at her lip. The sound of the water and the repetitive act of dabbing were strangely comforting to her.

She wondered why she wasn't frightened any more. She was worried, certainly. She was worried about how she was going to get help in her naked state — the public phone was in the front foyer on the ground floor. And she was sore. Her head, her face, her shoulder were all throbbing, and there was an insistent pain between her legs.

But she wasn't frightened. She was more depressed and disappointed than anything else. Hell, she sure could pick them, couldn't she? The first person she'd ever wanted to make love with, a junkie! She of all people should have known better. She was disappointed in Simon, she was disappointed in herself, she was disappointed in life, and, for the first time in her seventeen years, Vicky was depressed.

She'd been a fool. She'd broken all her rules and she bloody well deserved to be raped! Well, back to square one, she told herself. Keep your nose clean, don't get into trouble and don't get involved with anyone. Damn it, she'd relaxed far too much lately. She'd concentrated on work and fun and dropped her guard completely.

Gradually her strength and self-esteem returned as her resolve strengthened, and she started to form a plan of attack. She looked at her watch. Seven o'clock. She'd been sitting there for an hour and a half. If Simon was still in her flat, who could she trust to help her get rid of him? She certainly didn't want to call in the police. Better to just get him out and pretend the whole episode had never happened.

The thought of having to face Simon at the studio next week was of no great concern to Vicky. If he was this far gone, he wouldn't keep his job much longer anyway. No, the immediate problem was how to get rid of him. Nothing else mattered.

Vicky suddenly thought of Greg. He was the only one she could trust. Yes, she'd ring Greg.

She started pulling metre after metre of paper towelling out of the dispenser. God, how embarrassing, being caught at the front foyer phone wrapped in paper towelling.

'What did you bring the shampoo for? You haven't got time to wash your hair.'

The door to the 'Womens' opened and Vicky recognised the voices of the two lesbians from Flat 6 across the hall. She jumped up and turned the bath tap on full blast.

'Oh, shit,' she heard Maxie hiss, 'someone's running a bath.'

'There should be a sign up.' Val's voice was deliberately loud. 'People shouldn't be allowed to take baths in the morning.' There were only two cubicles per bathroom on each floor of the apartment block.

'Forget it,' Maxie answered dismissively. 'We'll share a shower.'

'But it's downright rude. People should have more —'

'I said, forget it. Skip the shampoo and we'll share a shower.'

Vicky waited until the shower had been running for a full two minutes before she unlocked her cubicle door and peered out.

Draped over the top of the cubicle door opposite were two bath towels. Steam was billowing above the door and Vicky decided to risk it. She flicked one of the towels off, wrapped it around herself and stole out into the hall.

She was about to creep down the steps to the front foyer and the phone but, when she looked down the hall to her flat at the end, she noticed the door was ajar. What the hell, she'd risk that too. Maybe he'd gone. Maybe he'd fallen asleep or passed out. She crept towards the door.

When she was nearly there, her heart started to thump. You silly bitch, she told herself, what if he's sitting there waiting for you? He'll be angry. You don't want to be hurt any more. Turn around, go back to the bathroom.

The simple solution of getting the lesbians to ring Greg flashed through her mind but she just as quickly dismissed it. The law of Darlo bedsits was that everyone minded their own business. She'd got herself into this one, she'd get herself out with as little help from others as possible. And if Simon had gone, she wouldn't even need to ring Greg.

She eased the door open a few centimetres. From the little she could see through the gap, the room was in utter chaos. Here goes, she thought, and she kicked the door wide open, turned and started sprinting down the hall.

She slowed as she reached the bathroom door. There were no following footsteps. She turned. No one there. The door to her flat was wide open and there was no sign of anyone inside.

Mr Blackman from Flat 8 at the other end of the hall appeared, toilet bag and towel in hand. He looked disapprovingly at Vicky in her semi-naked state as he made his way to the 'Mens'. Mr Blackman was eighty-eight and always looked disapprovingly at Vicky. He saw her picture regularly in newspapers and magazines and knew she was in some sort of television show but, as he couldn't afford a television set, he didn't own one. And as he didn't own one, he didn't approve of television. And television was never around in his day anyway. And in his day all actresses were sluts. So the sight of Vicky now merely confirmed his views and he continued to mutter his disapproval as he hobbled into the 'Mens'.

Vicky breathed a sigh of relief. Thank God. Simon had gone. She'd clean the flat, soak in a hot bath and pretend the whole thing had never happened.

But Simon hadn't gone.

There was no sign of him as Vicky closed the door and surveyed the havoc about her.

She righted the overturned heater, switched it on and dressed hurriedly in front of it, rubbing the warmth back into her body.

Then she stopped as she heard a noise from behind the kitchen bench. She waited. There it was again. A sort of choking sound. And she realised Simon was still in the room.

Vicky edged back towards the door, opened it and

kept it ajar as she finished dressing. Then, poised for flight, she called out, 'Simon?'

Nothing. She crossed to the bench and peered over to discover Simon passed out on the kitchen floor. He was lying on his side, his jeans pulled up but his fly wide open. A small pool of vomit lay on the linoleum next to him.

He stirred. There was another choking sound and a further thin stream joined the pool. He coughed and the cough caught in his throat, making a strangled noise. For a moment Vicky thought he was going to choke on his own vomit and instinctively she dived forward and shook him. 'Simon! Wake up! For God's sake, wake up!'

Simon's eyes snapped open and he was instantly alert. 'Vicky. G'day. Are we having a good time?' He noticed he was on the floor. 'Hey, did I pass out?' Then he noticed the pool of vomit at his elbow. 'Oh shit.' He looked genuinely remorseful. 'I didn't know I'd had that much to drink. Hell, I'm sorry.' He scrambled to his knees. 'Can you get us a cloth? I'll clean it up.'

Vicky found herself automatically obeying him and, having handed him a dampened tea towel, she watched in fascination as he efficiently cleaned up the elbow of his jacket and then the floor, chatting amicably all the while.

'God, how gross. I really am sorry. It must have been all that fresh air up at The Gap. Bloody embarrassing. I don't normally throw up on people's kitchen floors, you know.' He grinned up at her engagingly. 'Well, not on a first date, anyway.'

Vicky stared at him, stupefied. It was quite obvious he didn't remember a thing.

'What's the matter?' Simon asked as he stood up

and crossed to the sink. Then he looked down at his jeans and his unzipped fly and stared back at her in horror. 'Did I try something on?'

'You could say that, yes.'

Simon dumped the tea towel, rinsed his hands as quickly as possible and zipped up his jeans.

'What'd I do?'

He seemed genuinely concerned and, although Vicky felt she was in no immediate danger, she cautioned herself nevertheless. Use your sense, girl. He's obviously schizo and if you tell him to leave he's just as likely to turn on you again. Don't say anything. Call Greg.

'What'd I do, Vicky?' he asked again.

'I'll tell you in a minute,' she answered, collecting some change that had spilled from her handbag, along with everything else, to the floor. 'I've got to make a phone call first.'

'Hey.' Simon suddenly noticed. 'What happened to your lip?'

'Tell you about that too.' And she left.

Vicky didn't say anything to Greg about the rape. Given Simon's memory loss and apparent normality, she wasn't sure what to say to Greg. But there was one thing she was sure of. She was no longer going to keep quiet about Simon's drug addiction.

'What do you mean, you're scared to ask him to go?' Greg queried when she was halfway through her story. 'Just tell him. The cheeky little bastard. Tell him it's poor form to pass out and throw up on people's floors and you want him to get out. Easy.'

'You come and do it. I don't want to risk him turning on me.'

'Why should he turn?'

'Because he's a junkie.'

There was a pause. Then, 'He's what?'

'It's true, Greg. He's already flipped once and I'm worried he'll do it again. He's totally schizo.'

'I'm on my way. Be there in fifteen.'

Vicky went to the bathroom and examined her face in the mirror. It didn't look good. The lip was puffed up and black with congealed blood and there was what promised to be a healthy bruise on her right cheekbone. Her scalp hurt where he'd ripped out a fistful of hair. In fact, now that the pressure was off and she could allow herself to relax, Vicky realised that she ached all over. She patted her face with cold water, dried off with a paper towel and slowly walked back to the bedsit.

In the ten minutes that she'd been gone, Simon had somehow managed to put the entire room back in order. Table and chairs were righted and the table-cloth returned to its place, a broken glass was swept up, handbag contents were returned. He was picking up the doona from the floor and about to make the bed when Vicky came back.

'Borrowed your toothpaste, hope you don't mind,' he said, dumping the doona on a chair. 'Hey, you don't have a bathroom here.' His movements were frenetic and his voice was brittle as he desperately tried to avoid meeting her eyes.

'No, it's down the hall.'

'Down the hall.' Something flashed in Simon's brain, something about running down the hall. He willed it away, refusing to recognise it.

'Bit archaic, isn't it?' He picked up the bed sheet which Vicky had dragged to the floor when she fell.

There was another flash as he stared at the sheet in horror. 'There's blood on this.'

He couldn't will the flash away this time. It wasn't an image so much as a feeling of violence. Something awful had happened. He didn't want to think about it. Get out of my head! But it wouldn't. Violence, it kept flashing. Violence.

'Don't worry.' Vicky shrugged at the bloodied sheet. 'I wasn't a virgin.'

He looked at her for the first time and Vicky was shocked by the expression on his face. She'd never seen such agony.

'It was just . . . ' she tried to give a nonchalant smile but winced as her lip cracked. She gave it a gentle tap with her finger. 'Just the lip, that's all.'

Simon kept staring at her. Then, without a murmur, he fell to his knees, his eyes still fixed on Vicky's face. Her poor battered face which he was seeing now for the first time. And the flashes started again.

Flash. He could feel his teeth grinding into her lip. Flash. He saw the back of his hand smashing against the side of her face. Flash. He felt the texture of her hair as it ripped away from her scalp.

'No! No!' But no matter how hard he tried, the flashes wouldn't go away. He buried his head in his hands.

Vicky watched him for nearly a minute as he rocked backward and forward on his knees, whimpering like a frightened animal. Finally she couldn't stand it any longer. She knelt beside him. 'Simon, stop it! I said, stop it, do you hear me?'

'I'm sorry, I'm sorry, I'm sorry,' he moaned.

'I'm OK,' Vicky reassured him. 'Really. I'm tough

— I'll get over it.' Gradually, the whimpers subsided but he kept his head buried in his hands. 'You need help, though, Simon. You know that, don't you?'

He allowed her to take his hands away from his face. Tears were coursing down both cheeks as he looked back at her. Then he averted his eyes.

'You know that, don't you?' she insisted.

'What did I do?' His voice was barely a whisper.

'You name it. Just about everything.'

'I didn't . . . ' He couldn't bring himself to say it and the pain in his eyes was intense, begging a denial.

What the hell, Vicky thought, he'd raped her and he deserved to know. 'Yes. That too.'

For a moment he looked as if he were going to break down again but he didn't. He took several deep breaths, fighting for control, and when he finally spoke, his voice was distant, emotionless. 'I don't remember it.'

'I know.'

'I remember The Gap. I remember what we talked about. And we kissed.' He put out his hand and touched the bruised cheek. 'And you asked me back here.' She nodded. He touched the broken lip so gently she could barely feel it. 'And I —' he broke off. 'That's all. That's all I remember.'

Even the flashes had left him now and Simon felt empty. Riddled with guilt and remorse for what he knew he must have done, but empty. There was no way to make amends, but Simon wanted to talk. He wanted to tell Vicky the truth.

'I've been spying on you for the past two weeks. Planning on how to get you into bed. Bumping into you this morning wasn't an accident — I'd decided today was the day it was going to happen.'

Vicky didn't dare move for fear of breaking the flow.

'I've wanted to sleep with you from the moment I first met you,' Simon continued. 'But I never meant . . . It was a game. Just a game. I was so crazy about you I don't think I even expected it to come off but I was getting a real buzz out of just planning it. Then, last night . . . ' He paused. 'Last night was magic, everything was magic. The dancing, the laughing, the eating and drinking. And then we were at The Gap and we were talking and that was the best part of all. And when we kissed and I knew you wanted me too . . . ' As he turned to her his face was aglow with the memory. 'It wasn't a game any more. I loved you, Vicky. I loved you more than I thought I was capable of loving anyone.' The pain returned, he looked away again. 'And that's all I remember.'

Vicky took his hand in hers and he held it tightly as if it were a lifeline.

'I swear if there was any way I could undo what's happened, if there was anything I could . . . '

'There is,' Vicky interrupted. 'Get off the drugs. Go to a clinic, Simon — sign yourself in, get help, you need —'

'Anybody home?' There was a tap on the door and Greg peered in.

The noise startled Simon and he gripped Vicky's hand so hard it hurt.

'Come in,' she said.

Greg pushed the door open to reveal Jim standing beside him.

'Hello, Jim.' Vicky stood up, still holding Simon's hand and Simon struggled to his feet beside her.

'My God! What's he done to you?' Greg stared at her, horrified.

'I thought you were coming on your own,' she hissed.

'Don't be ridiculous, Vicky.' Jim took over. 'Let's get you to a doctor, then we'll —'

'No.' Jim had made as if to usher her to the door but Vicky pulled away, still holding onto Simon's hand. Jim and Greg exchanged puzzled glances.

'What the hell's going on here?' Greg demanded. 'You said he's a junkie and he turned on you and now —'

Simon interrupted before Vicky could reply. 'I am and I did.'

There was an appalled silence as they all turned to look at Simon. He glanced briefly at them then looked down at the floor.

'But I didn't . . . didn't . . . didn't . . . '

The veins in Simon's neck stood out in dark ridges and his face was flushed. He was gagging on the words.

'Simon.' She squeezed his hand but he shook her off and clenched his fists tightly as he forced the words out. 'I didn't mean to do it.'

'Do what?' Jim demanded threateningly.

'Nothing.' Vicky jumped in again. 'He freaked out a bit and we had a fight and he landed a punch, that's all.'

Simon was still staring at the floor, breathing heavily as he fought to maintain control.

'You're a bastard, Rothwell. We should take you straight to the police.'

'Greg, listen,' Vicky begged. 'He knows he's got a problem and he wants to sign himself in for treatment.' Greg and Jim looked uncertainly at each other.

'He does. Honest! Don't you, Simon?'

Simon nodded at the carpet.

'So, if we took you to the Drug Centre now you'd let them start you on a programme, book you into a clinic?' Jim asked.

Simon raised his head and looked at Vicky. His voice was steady and he was in control. But only just. 'I'll do whatever Vicky wants me to do.'

One good thing about living in Darlinghurst, Vicky thought three hours later as she eased her aching spine on the hard wooden bench, you were right next door to the inner-city Drug Rehabilitation Centre.

Even on a Sunday; or maybe especially on a Sunday — Vicky was too tired to wonder about it for long. The Centre was busy. They'd waited two hours for a doctor. Simon's examination and interview had taken forty minutes and now they were waiting while arrangements were being made to book him into a private clinic.

When they'd first arrived at the Centre, everyone in the waiting room had recognised them. It didn't look as if it would present any problems though. In fact the addicts and their accompanying families recognised Simon's obvious symptoms and kept their distance. Some family members even smiled sympathetically, as if to say, 'We've all got our problems, good luck.'

Then the receptionist entered from the surgery, took one look at Greg, shrieked, and demanded an autograph. Grabbing him by the elbow, she dragged him to the counter and thrust a pen in his hand. Jim tried to interrupt but there was no distracting her. Greg shrugged, signed as quickly as he could then called her attention to Simon. 'We'd like to see the doctor —'

Another shriek as the receptionist recognised Simon and he too was dragged to the counter and a pen thrust in his hand.

But Simon was rapidly going under. His hand dropped to his side, the pen clattered to the floor and he stared glassily at the receptionist.

She knew at once and her face clouded, first with disappointment, then disapproval. A 'Glitter Game' star and he was just another junkie! With a mild shake of her head she circled the reception counter and produced an enrolment form.

'Name?' The voice had its customary edge, its customary brittle, bored edge. Then she looked up momentarily and caught sight of Vicky standing to one side of the men.

'Jodie!' she shrieked. 'You're Jodie!'

'And you're a cunt,' Vicky answered.

There was a stunned silence before the woman attempted to stammer a reply but Jim interrupted. 'Just fill out the form ... '

'Please,' Greg added, glaring a warning at Vicky.

And now, as they waited for the receptionist to make the arrangements with the private clinic, the air was thick with disapproval. The receptionist couldn't wait to tell everyone about her run-in with the stars. 'Rude they are,' she'd tell her friends. 'Up themselves, all of them. And rude, very rude.'

The private clinic would cost, the doctor had told them. After all, Simon wasn't a cot case. His type of drug control programme was normally conducted on an outpatients basis. But if he could afford the option, well . . . The doctor shrugged. The early with-drawal days were always handled more easily if the patient were kept well away from the source of supply.

'That's what he wants.' Vicky jumped in without even referring to Simon. 'The private treatment, special clinic — he can afford it.'

The doctor nodded dismissively. Bully for you, boy, he thought. He was tired. It had been a long shift.

It was agreed that the doctor would give Jim a medical report to the effect that Simon was under-going treatment for a severe nervous disorder and would not be available for work till further medical notice.

It had taken every ounce of Vicky's persuasive power to convince Jim that the channel need not know of Simon's addiction.

'What's the point?' she hissed, taking him aside. 'It won't make any difference whether they know or not.'

'For God's sake, Vicky, you don't owe him any-thing.'

Vicky looked at Simon as he sat pathetically accept-ing his fate and she felt the weight of responsibility, knowing he'd abide by any rules she set. 'Somebody owes him a chance.'

Jim eventually agreed and even he showed a touch of pity when Simon, who had arranged for the clinic fees to come via his parents, said in reply to the querying looks, 'It's OK, they won't want to know what it's for.'

Greg and Jim wouldn't let Vicky go to the clinic with them.

'There's nothing more you can do, love,' Greg insisted. 'Look at him. He's just about ready to pass out.'

Simon was indeed nodding off in the corner, his head jerking up intermittently to look around in bewilderment at the unfamiliar surroundings.

'We'll collect his gear and take him to the clinic after we've dropped you home.'

Simon was still half asleep during the drive home but he snapped awake as soon as Vicky got out of the car. 'Will you come and see me?'

Vicky was sore, tired and emotionally drained. She suddenly wanted to cry. Tomorrow she'd feel fine, she knew, but what about Simon? How would he feel tomorrow?

'Will you?' The eyes pleaded.

'Yes.'

Greg got out of the car and took her arm.

'No, don't come up with me.' He looked as if he was going to insist but Vicky was too tired to argue. 'I don't want you to.'

'OK.' He gave her a soft peck on her unbruised cheek. 'Go straight to bed, you look bloody terrible.'

She smiled weakly and glanced at Simon before turning to go.

'Promise?' he whispered.

'I promise.'

As Vicky lay back in the tub groaning with relief at the soothing effect of the hot water on her aching body, Narelle was leaning back in another tub only a few kilometres away. She was also groaning but not in pain. She was in the throes of ecstasy.

With a final glorious shriek, she disappeared beneath the bubbles to re-emerge spluttering and giggling with delight. 'Oh, that was heaven, Darren. Absolute heaven!' She tugged at the head immersed between her thighs and Darren rose from the froth and foam, breathing heavily. 'My turn, my turn, lie back,' she squealed.

Darren did, and Narelle's head disappeared from view.

With a playful smile, Darren turned the jacuzzi on. 'That'll teach you!' he called down to her.

But it didn't. Narelle soldiered on, paying no heed to the roaring in her ears and the jets of water forcing her upwards. She locked her elbows against the sides of the jacuzzi and refused to give in until Darren's erection forced him to admit defeat. He hauled her to the surface and kissed her deeply. This would make the fourth time in two hours. I'm forty-three years old, Darren thought, that's impossible. But it wasn't.

Narelle had been to the dentist on Friday. She didn't have a filling in her head but Charmane had always insisted she have six monthly checkups and, since her mother's death, Narelle had continued the practice.

It was the same surgery that Charmane had booked her into when they first moved from Strawberry Hills. It was only five minutes from their new harbourside flat and had even better water views, she told Narelle. Charmane reasoned that if a dentist had water views he had to be good.

It was immaterial whether old Mr Potger was a good dentist or not as even the occasional cleaning treatment of Narelle's mouth was a token gesture. In fact treatment was so unnecessary that Mr Potger rarely charged her, preferring to sit and chat instead.

When Narelle turned up for her appointment, she had no idea that old Mr Potger had died three months before. Notification cards had gone to regular patients, not only informing them of Mr Potger's death but extolling the virtues of the dentist taking over the practice. Why not? It was the least Ethel Potger could do — she'd got a damn good price for the Double Bay practice. Ethel, twenty years Mr Potger's junior, had really only married him to be a dentist's wife and a Double Bay one at that. She instructed the secretary to send the notifications to $1,000 and over patients. Ethel figured that setting the criteria at a moderate amount would cover not only worthwhile clients with chronic decay and cosmetic obsessions, but also the old faithfuls who'd been treated by Mr Potger on a regular basis.

The monetary qualification meant that Narelle, who'd been seeing old Mr Potger twice a year for five years, didn't receive a notification.

'Hello, I'm Darren Farrell.'

'Where's Mr Potger?' Narelle asked the beautiful looking man in the white coat. How lovely that old Mr Potger was employing male nurses, she thought. Very modern of him too.

'Mr Potger died three months ago. I'm your new dentist.'

From that moment on it was impossible for Darren to attempt an examination of Narelle's teeth. She was crying so much that every time he tried to open her mouth she started to gag.

'Poor old Mr Potger. Why him? What did he ever do to anyone?' Narelle sobbed.

'He was seventy,' Darren tried to point out, but it didn't make any difference.

'Exactly. How could he do any harm? Why him?'

Darren decided that she was in shock and instructed the nurse to call Narelle's home and tell someone to come and collect her. He was heavily involved in fitting a complicated piece of bridgework when the nurse informed him Narelle had no family.

'Put her in the waiting room and give her a coffee,' he barked.

Thirty minutes later, Darren bumped into Narelle on his way to buy a sandwich for lunch. She looked very subdued.

'I'm sorry,' she said. 'Thank you.'

'What for?' he asked, confused.

'I'm sorry for making such a fuss. It was just the shock.'

'Of course, don't worry,' he smiled. 'But why the thank you?'

'Your nurse got me four cups of coffee. She was very nice.'

There was not a shred of accusation in her voice but Darren felt riddled with guilt nonetheless. 'Have you had lunch?' he asked.

That was how it started and two days later there they were, still in the flat above the surgery with the harbour views that Charmane would have killed for.

Darren was yet another in the endless stream of men who'd never met anyone quite like Narelle. But there was one big difference. Narelle had never met anyone quite like Darren.

Life had been easy for Darren. He'd breezed through university on a scholarship, managed to captain the first grade rugby team and lead an extremely active social life without jeopardising his studies too disastrously. It meant that, instead of topping his year as he easily could have, he came in sixth. Darren figured it was a small price to pay.

Since then, nothing had really changed. An only

child, his doting middle class parents had set him up in his own practice and he'd been a successful dentist for nearly twenty years.

The rugby had become golf, the socialising was now more on a one to one basis than the uni bashes, but the concentration on the good life remained the same.

As in his university days, women remained top priority. Darren was devastatingly attractive to women and they were devastatingly attractive to him.

Not that he considered himself promiscuous. In fact, he believed implicitly in monogamy. Whether an affair lasted a week or six months he remained faithful to his lover. Six months was roughly the limit to which his interest could be maintained and, in the past few years since he'd turned forty, he rather regretted that fact.

He'd never married and, during his thirties, he had felt a touch superior to many of his friends who were going through the traumas of divorce. Since turning forty, though, he'd noticed that those same friends were happily remarrying, usually fellow divorcees, and that the few friends who'd managed to weather the youthful marital storm were now happier than they'd ever been in their lives.

Darren began to feel there was something missing in his life. Was it perhaps time for him to contemplate marriage and children? He started to view each affair in a different light and several times even asked his lover to move in with him, an arrangement he'd assiduously avoided in the past. Each time it was a disaster. Within a month she was making a nest, spontaneity went out the window and days became programmed. Worst of all, the endless preoccupation with sex that had been the basis for the relationship started to take second place to so many things which Darren considered mundane.

The more his friends told him that he simply hadn't met the right person, the more Darren was convinced that he was the problem. Most of the friends were women and most of them were ex-girlfriends. Darren always remained friends with his ex-lovers, all of whom had the perfect advice. 'If you can only learn to hang in there after the first flush of sexual delirium, Darren, you'll find it's replaced by something far deeper, far more meaningful.' All of his ex's were extremely fond of him but their fondness was tainted by a touch of superiority. Superiority at the fact that they'd had the wisdom to outgrow him. Even those whose hearts he'd unintentionally broken at the time.

Darren couldn't understand why the first flush of sexual delirium should ever have to go but he tried to act on their advice nevertheless. He hung on desperately to the next several affairs way beyond the time he felt they'd died a natural death. He discovered no miracle replacement though. Neither did the women. They appeared to be just as dissatisfied with the living arrangements as he was and eventually were only too happy to move out.

After two years of serious spouse-seeking, Darren gave up, accepting the fact that he would never be a father and that he could anticipate a lonely old age but deciding that between now and then he'd continue to have fun. Somehow though, the merry-go-round wasn't quite as satisfying as it used to be and Darren was forced to admit that, every now and then, he was just a little bit lonely.

'What do you want out of life, Narelle?' he asked, gently tweaking her nipple. It wasn't a leading question, just idle interest — Darren had never met a screen sex-goddess before.

It was late on the Friday night and they lay naked in delicious exhaustion on the queensize circular bed looking up at the mirrored ceiling.

'Nothing really,' she answered, idly playing with his penis. 'Just to keep doing what I like doing.'

'And what's that?'

Narelle thought for a second, then became aware of the penis in her hand. 'This. Making love. Using my body for pleasure.' Darren's penis started to swell. 'Again? Already?' Narelle smiled at him delightedly. 'And then one day I'll use my body to have babies.' She threw her body across his as if by way of demonstration. 'I'll settle down with a lovely man and have four babies.'

As he engulfed her breast in his mouth, Darren gave a sigh of happiness. It appeared that life was just as simple for Narelle as it was for him.

For the next two days, they loved and laughed and continued to delight each other and by late Sunday afternoon, as they climbed out of the jacuzzi, Darren had decided that he was the man to give Narelle her babies and that Narelle was his ideal mate. He'd take it slowly at first, though, he didn't want to frighten her off.

'Would you like to move in with me for a while, Narelle?'

'Oh, that would be nice.'

He'd give it a week, maybe two, and then he'd propose.

George Glassberg pressed the remote control button, watched the twin garage roller door close then started his weary walk up the terracotta tiled pathway lined with the tubs of cumquat trees, Rosa's pride and joy.

It had been an exhausting four-day business trip to Melbourne and he didn't need the added irritation of discovering that Rosa wasn't home. She knew he was booked on the six o'clock flight. It was dark, too; she should have left the house lights on if she knew she was going to be out this late. George was tired but he didn't dare put himself to bed before she got home or there'd be hell to pay.

Mind you, he was also hungry and Rosa was a superb cook. She was bound to have something special lined up. He peered in the oven, nothing there. No saucepans on the stove, nothing exciting in the refrigerator.

Then he realised. That was it. Of course! She was out buying takeaway at their favourite Thai restaurant. George felt much happier at the thought and poured himself a large Scotch, turned on the television and settled back to watch the news.

It was nearly midnight when George awoke. On the television screen, an earnest, spindly man with an American accent was talking enthusiastically about movies. Rosa still wasn't home. George wondered if he should start to worry. Whom should he call? He always kept well out of Rosa's social life and he had no idea who her special friends were. They were all connected with the agency, clients and casting people and ... Yes, of course, that's who he'd call. Rosa's secretary, Dee. She'd know if Rosa was out feting some important client. Mind you, if she were, why hadn't she left a note?

'Hello, Dee? ... George Glassberg here ... Very well thank you, and yourself? ... Good, good ... I'm so sorry to ring you so late, but I'm a little worried. You see ... You were? Oh that's good, I'm glad I didn't wake you ... You see, I just got back from a business trip and Rosa hasn't left me a note which isn't really like her and I'm presuming she's been detained at some business meeting and I thought you might ... you *what*?!!' George nearly dropped the phone. 'Since Thursday!'

As Dee raved on, saying she'd presumed that Rosa had taken Friday off, George's mind raced. The car had been missing since Thursday evening too, Dee had said. Then it had to be a car accident. But why hadn't anyone got in touch with him? Should he ring the hospitals first or the police? Four days, for God's sake! She'd been missing for four days! He'd ring the police.

And the nightmare began.

It was three weeks before they discovered Rosa Glassberg's body. Her Alfa Romeo was hidden in thick bush well off the beaten track in the Blue Mountains. Rosa was slumped over the wheel. A garden hose led from the exhaust pipe to the driver's side window. The petrol tank was empty, the ignition was in the 'on' position and the police naturally assumed suicide. The pathologist was quick to correct them. Rosa Glassberg's neck had been broken.

Discovery

The murder of Rosa Glassberg shocked the industry and for a month general gossip took second place to endless conjecture as to who the killer could be.

Three months after the event, when the initial horror had died down and the word 'murder' aroused only an impersonal reaction, it became more or less a party game to play Rosa Glassberg 'whodunits'.

Finally, six months after the murder, the police were no closer to solving the mystery despite endless harassment of half the entertainment industry. Indeed the police had virtually closed the books on the Glassberg case and Rosa barely rated a mention any more.

After all, it was the end of the non-ratings period. The long hot summer was at its height, soon it would be Academy Awards time and not long after that, the Logies. Certainly not the season for discussing sordid murders, particularly long-unsolved ones.

This year the Academy Awards were being discussed with particular interest. After all, Australians were hot contenders in two of the major categories: Peter Wainwright for Best Screenplay and Anna Bowrey for Best Actress.

And as for the Logies, Australian television had

certainly come of age. The British ITV conglomerate had bought the Logies telecast and for the first time the UK would witness an Australian television awards ceremony.

The success of 'The Glitter Game' was acknowledged as being responsible in no small measure for this. Not to mention the fact that 'The Glitter Game' had also sold to CBS and had been to air in the States for two months now. Who could say, maybe next year the Americans would also want the Logies telecast? Whatever the outcome, Australian television was on a high.

And if Australian television was riding high, then Edwina Dawling was undoubtedly its high priestess. She was the name on the nation's lips. The international recognition accorded her was also phenomenal. The sales of her LP had broken all records in the UK when 'The Glitter Game' had gone to air and, at her request, the network was only too happy to send her to London for a fortnight's promotional tour. Any promotion of her record could only further the show's popularity, and the fact that she was willing to break her trip for a frantic three days of promotions in America en route home was an added bonus.

The network didn't know that Edwina was interested in only one interview in the States. The interview pertaining to a release through the CBS network of a potential vehicle written for and starring Edwina Dawling.

A CBS spokesperson had contacted her immediately after 'The Glitter Game' special had gone to air in America. It was around the time that every client on Rosa's books, including Edwina, was being endlessly questioned by the police and she'd had to arrange special dispensation to leave the country but the concept breakdown CBS has sent her certainly appeared to make the whole process worthwhile.

When she'd approached Robert Bryce about her 'availability' (a euphemism regularly employed by stars meaning 'I want') to do a UK promotional trip, he had been surprisingly amicable. She'd decided to bypass Alain, of course, but was not prepared for Robert's effusive welcome of her approach directly to the top. She was sure she'd crossed him when she'd reminded him of 'favours owed' and demanded Jane's downgrading.

But Robert couldn't have been more amenable. 'Any time you feel you want to bypass normal channel procedure, Edwina, do come to me. I'd like to think we're all one happy family after all and that we don't have to stick to any particular form of protocol.'

The King would have been furious to know he was being dismissed as 'normal channel procedure', Edwina thought. She remarked to Davey that Alain must have crossed Robert Bryce, but then gave it no further thought. She was only too happy for the chance to get out of the country for a while. Not only to chase up the American deal but to get away from the pressure of working with Paul.

Fortunately the relationship of their characters had drifted a little so that they weren't working together on a daily basis but, when they were, it was an untenable situation and, as soon as 'cut' was called, Edwina dived for the shelter of her dressing room. As soon as the next scene was called, she would breathe a sigh of relief. Paul's hatred seemed to grow daily and Edwina was in fear of being caught alone with him. Even though Davey stayed with her at all times, her hand kept darting to the pistol she kept in her purse whenever there was a knock on the dressing room door. Yes, it would be a relief to be out of the country, albeit for only a fortnight and, quite frankly, it would be a relief to be out of 'The Glitter Game'. Roll on CBS, Edwina thought.

Tim Arnold, the queen of the publicity department, had been none too happy with Alain's peremptory manner. 'It's all very well to say "Do it Tim",' he complained, tapping the desk top, 'but an international promotion campaign! I mean, you know what that costs? I mean, what sort of budget do I have? I mean, what about Princess Davey, does he go? Personally I don't think she'll wear it without him. And do they travel first or business? And is accommodation four star or five? I mean, it's all budgetary and I need to —'

'Fuck the budget. I said, do it!'

Tim was torn between two reactions, shock at hearing an executive producer say 'Fuck the budget' and genuine offence at Alain's tone.

'Very well, fuck the budget it is.' And he sailed out of Alain's office, all three chins quivering with offended dignity.

'The Glitter Game' had made life confusing for Tim Arnold. He'd been a Channel 3 marketing influence for years. He'd been a publicity demigod, held in terror by the transitory soap 'stars' he could make or break. But the unprecedented success of 'The Glitter Game' had totally undermined his power.

Right from the start he'd been offended by the special status accorded Liza Farrelly as personal publicist to Edwina Dawling. It was rare that Channel 3 employed stars of the status of Edwina Dawling and, as head of Channel 3 publicity, it was Tim Arnold's privilege to serve her.

Tim's double standards were extreme. While maintaining it his right to condemn many young actors and ruin their chances with chilling comments like 'No charisma, pet' to his many mates in the press, Tim considered it his duty to glorify the Edwina Dawlings of the world. Just as he'd glorified the Joan Crawfords and the Judy Garlands when he was a young man. There were certain stars, he maintained, that lightened the firmament of the entertainment world and should only be handled by those who fully appreciated them. Naturally if a Crawford or a Garland beckoned, Tim Arnold would be there. Just like he'd be there for Edwina Dawling.

So when Tim had to come to terms with 'old vinegar tits' Farrelly's appointment, it certainly hadn't been easy.

As it turned out, though, the huge success of 'The Glitter Game' had one compensatory aspect for Tim Arnold. The ingratitude of the actors in refusing to agree to an across-the-board merchandising deal offered by the channel meant that there was a massively lucrative business in pirate merchandising. Of course Tim didn't dare to be too bold, but the discreet release of various production stills for illicit use in magazines, portrait photographs for T-shirts and badges, and details on stars' personal lives for swap cards guaranteed a healthy income and, so long as he dealt purely with the overseas market, such transactions were virtually untraceable to him.

Indeed, so lucrative was his business sideline that Tim's offended sensibilities at Liza's appointment were completely repaired and, by the time Liza was given her walking orders, he had to entirely rethink his position. He didn't have time for Edwina Dawling and star treatment now. He didn't even have time for the show. Indeed, 'The Glitter Game' had become its own self-promoting publicity machine and didn't need his constant input. He was halfway through compiling a pirate magazine, *'The Game Behind The Glitter Game'*, for a fifty-fifty split with a British tabloid journalist who was willing to put his name to it.

And now he had to organise the Edwina Dawling promotional trip. Life really was becoming complicated and the workload was altogether too much. Tim called a conference.

The junior assistants were put in total control of the 'treadmill' areas: the handing out of current storylines to soap mags, the TV and radio promos, the daily press ads and competitions and all personal appearances. Tim then set specific tasks for his assistants, Lois and Val, thereby leaving himself apparently free to handle Edwina and the promotional tour but, in actuality, to get on with *'The Game Behind The Glitter Game'*.

'Val, you take over the *TV Week* feature article on Jane,' he ordered. 'They wanted Edwina but she's refused so they've agreed to take second best. It's a cover story so you'll have to work a half-day photo session around her taping schedule.'

Tim's dismissive attitude toward Jane had only developed over the past few months since she'd been demoted to semi-background. Pity, he thought. She'd certainly looked like power material at the start of the show and Tim would have been only too happy to hitch his wagon to her and cry 'star'. Now that her storylines were diminished, he'd decided she was wimp material instead and he couldn't be bothered.

'And what're the latest polls on Mandy and Sidney?' he barked at Lois. 'Are they being axed? Have you checked with Evan?'

Lois nodded. 'The storyliners want to keep them.'

'I know that, pet,' Tim snapped impatiently, 'we all know that. But Evan's been told they're down on points lately — he's been told directly by the producers to isolate their storylines and prepare to kill them off. Why the —'

'Well, he hasn't,' Lois interrupted. She was a feisty little thing and, when Tim's irascible temper came into play, she had difficulty controlling herself. 'And it's probably just as well,' she continued before Tim could reply, 'their popularity points have picked up ten per cent.'

'Does Alain know?'

'Yes, he said to hold back on "sad to lose them" press but he won't renew their contracts until the next survey — if their popularity count isn't up by then he'll kill them off.'

'Oh, Mother Mary, what a farce. Why not send the tired old farts over a cliff and be done with it?' Tim heaved a weary sigh. 'OK. Give them a miss for a fortnight. That'll force the issue. No press and their points are sure to be down.' He noted Lois's disapproving look. 'Don't give me girly-glares, pet; someone's got to take some positive action around here.

'Narelle!' Tim snapped his fingers. 'We'll do a before and after on Narelle, change of image routine. Any one of the women's mags'll want that. Give it to the one that'll run a cover.'

'Before and after what?' Val asked.

'Wedding, you twit. Wedding. Marriage. Nuptials.' Val still looked bemused but Tim didn't notice. He never did when he was on to a hot new idea. 'Get Big Sally to line up top designer label gear, sophisticated stuff. Set up a photo session. Then look out the horniest shots from any sex scenes we've got: "The Idol of Erotica turns Double Bay Darling". '

The conference didn't last much longer. Tim decided that Vicky had been given a lot of press lately since Simon had been killed off and they could afford to give her a brief rest. 'Just a tasteful reminder that Jodie's still lamenting the death of her brother,' he instructed. 'A good one-liner'll do. They'll all assume Vicky's in mourning herself so she'll get the sympathy vote.'

He decided Paul could be given a miss altogether. The man was becoming positively unbalanced. One never knew what he'd say to the press. 'Frankly, I don't know why the producers don't get rid of him,' Tim said, as he turned to go. 'Now, hop to it. Don't forget Jane and Narelle are our big guns this week.' He sailed out of the conference room.

Tim was wrong about Narelle. Marriage had changed her very little. Apart from being strictly monogamous, her sexual activity remained as strenuous as it had ever been, thanks to her equally active husband. Life was still the great adventure that it always had been for Narelle and everything she saw about her held the same source of wonderment it always had. And her body! Her body was a greater delight to her than it had ever been. Narelle was two months pregnant.

The Narelle Farrell wedding had been the media event of the season. Channel 3 had televised the entire ceremony for their 'Hello Australia' morning programme, every major news report had shown clips, and magazine colour spreads and front-page newspaper shots had appeared all over the country.

Darren had encouraged and enjoyed the hype just as much as Narelle had — in fact, probably more so. His pride in Narelle was overwhelming and the thought that the whole country would be able to feast its eyes on his luscious bride was thrilling to him. He didn't seek the nation's envy, he didn't seek to boast his 'prize', he merely wished to bask in the admiration she inspired. And if she also provoked lust in the hearts and groins of many, as indeed she must, then what taste the 'many' showed, Darren thought approvingly.

Although the wedding dress was skintight and slit to the hip, although the décolletage was daringly low and displayed her breasts to their fullest advantage, the overall effect was delightful and not in the least offensive. And the fact that the dress was white seemed entirely appropriate. There was something about Narelle's healthy animal sexuality that was strikingly innocent; she was as proud and as joyful as any virgin had ever been. And who could dispute Narelle's purity? Certainly no one would have been able to convince Narelle herself that she was anything other than a virgin. After all, she'd never been married before, she'd never had babies before. Hers was a virgin mind and body, reborn, as she'd planned it would be one day, to devote itself to one man and to the birth of children.

Darren's and Narelle's wedding was flamboyant and, to some, not in the best of taste, but their love for each other was so evident that even the media's most hardened cynics, while taking witty cracks at them, couldn't help but wish them well.

In fact, six weeks after the wedding, when Narelle announced that she was pregnant and was terminating

ing her contract with 'The Glitter Game' and resigning from the industry to devote herself to her family, thousands of fans went into mourning at the imminent loss of their favourite sex symbol. So much so that Darren felt guilty at depriving the Australian viewing public and made Narelle promise that, when the baby was a year old, she'd let him get a live-in nanny and that she'd continue to make television guest appearances.

'The Glitter Game' had been in production for nearly a year, and major contracts were due for renegotiation. Both Jane and Vicky had announced they were not renewing.

Alain had expected Jane to get out as soon as possible, of course, and was only too glad to hold her to the last week, day and minute of her contract. He'd made her a star and she'd tried to renege — the girl was an ingrate.

Vicky was another story altogether and Alain was dumbfounded when a simple 'availability' query to her new agent revealed that no negotiation was necessary. Vicky had decided to leave the series regardless of the deal offered. Obviously the girl had no idea that her character was extremely popular and that she had them over a barrel, Alain thought. He despised her for her stupidity but secretly he was delighted. It was another blow to the show. The days of 'The Glitter Game' were numbered. The thankless girl could go back to the streets with her newly-acquired junkie friend and in all probability acquire her own habit and go on the game to support them both, Alain thought. She was certainly about to blow her chances.

But Vicky wasn't about to blow her chances at all. Simon was the best thing that had ever happened to her. In fact, Simon was the only thing in Vicky's life she'd ever really cared about.

At first she'd made her visits to the clinic out of a sense of duty. A promise was a promise, after all. But, several weeks later, Simon's dog-like devotion was replaced by a genuine desire to beat his addiction and, as his willpower took over, his wit, his humour and his good spirits returned. He was no longer the pathetic creature she'd so pitied.

It started with his exuberant plans for the future. 'Law, Vicky. I'm going to study law. Full time.'

'But it's a five-year course. What are you going to live on?'

Simon roared with laughter. 'Are you kidding? Do you know how much my olds have been forking out for me to shove up my nose? I'll give away half in uni fees and live well on the rest.'

'Won't you miss acting? I mean, you must care about your career, you trained for three years.'

'Only because I thought it was the best way to be the centre of attention and it might mean an easy buck. Besides,' he sent himself up with a wry grin, 'if I'm what's supposed to be an "addictive personality", this is probably the worst business for me to be in.'

'Why law? Why's law such a big deal?'

Simon considered the question seriously. 'I think deep down I've always wanted to go into law. I've got an uncle who's a lawyer and he's the only relative I liked as a kid — well, respected anyway.' Simon grinned. 'He's still the only relative I like. Good bloke.' He shrugged. 'Then it became more important to be noticed so I opted for drama school. I don't know why, Vicky, I just know that it's right.'

The day Simon was released from the clinic, Vicky arranged to have the afternoon off. Well, she spoke to Jim and he arranged it for her. True to his word Jim had kept quiet about Simon's problem, simply informing Alain that the doctor's report said 'a stress-induced nervous disorder'. Then Jim had instructed Evan to come up with an open-ended departure for the character. 'We want to be able to bring him back once he's medically in the clear.'

No one knew how the story leaked, but a week after Simon had committed himself for treatment a gossip column in a tabloid newspaper carried the full story. Presumably a member of the staff at the clinic had talked. Vicky was convinced that it was the bitch at the front counter of the drug rehabilitation centre. Whoever it was, the story created a furore within the network.

Robert Bryce was livid that any employee of Bryce Holdings was involved in any way with narcotics. He'd always looked upon the anti-drug campaign as his own personal crusade and he was appalled that Alain had not only allowed a junkie to be employed in the show, but had somehow let the press get hold of the story.

The gap between Robert Bryce and Alain King widened even further as Alain hung up the phone, stinging with humiliation at Robert's invective.

'Kill the little prick off,' Bryce had said, 'and make a press announcement that everyone connected with the show had no idea that —'

'They didn't, Robert. No one knew, I swear.'

'Then they fucking well should have. Stop whining, get off the phone and do the job I pay you for, King.'

Alain dived for the Mylanta, crunched through

three tablets and downed two Dispirin before ringing Jim.

'I didn't know, Alain,' Jim said. 'None of us did.'

'Then you fucking well should have.' And so it went on.

Two weeks after the episode in which Jodie got the news that her brother had been killed in a head-on collision between his sports car and a semitrailer, the public was well on the way to forgetting Simon's character entirely, such was the ephemeral life of a television soap star. And the day Vicky took Simon home from the clinic, the cab driver, who recognised her immediately, said to Simon, 'And what do you do, mate?'

'I study law,' Simon replied, giving Vicky a wink and a nudge.

Simon's large airy flat was one of four units in a converted mansion overlooking Centennial Park. It would have been extremely impressive if it hadn't been in such a mess.

'God, you're a pig,' Vicky complained as she set about stacking the dozens of dirty plates in the sink. 'Look, they're congealed. Didn't you ever wash up?'

'Sure, when there wasn't any clean stuff left. Anyway, I was a sick boy, remember?' He gave her his sickly pathetic look and she threw the wet dishcloth at him.

'I'll collect the junk, you start washing.'

'In a minute,' He picked up the restaurant courier directory. 'What do you fancy? Italian, Greek, Thai, Japanese?'

'Whatever you reckon.' Vicky disappeared on the hunt for further dirty dishes. 'A pizza'll do.'

Simon was on the phone for a full twenty minutes

making call after call. 'Done!' he said finally.

'That's one helluva pizza. Are you sure you weren't talking to "Dial a Prayer"?'

'What do you mean?'

'Well, it's obvious you'll do anything to get out of cleaning up.'

'Oh, yeah? Watch this.' Simon leapt to his feet, grabbed the dishcloth from her and started frantically washing up. 'We've got half an hour before the food arrives. Come on, move it!'

Half an hour later Vicky collapsed on the sofa. 'OK. We made it, now where's the food?'

The doorbell rang. 'Right on cue,' Simon said as he pressed the buzzer. 'Upstairs, the flat to the left,' Simon instructed as he pressed the front door release button.

It took the courier two trips to cart the food up. Along with two bottles of Moët et Chandon vintage, Simon had ordered a sushi selection, spicy Thai soup, fettucine marinara, a barbecued Greek seafood platter, and strawberry pernod pancakes for dessert.

'You couldn't make up your mind so I ordered my favourites,' he explained as he tipped the courier. 'You've no idea what that bloody clinic food was like.'

Later Vicky swore that it wasn't the champagne but the spicy Thai soup that led to their lovemaking.

'I've never had it before,' she said. 'That is the horniest taste sensation I've ever experienced.'

When they'd finished eating, despite the fact that Vicky swore she'd never eat again, she kept going back for sips of the Thai soup as they dawdled over the second bottle of champagne. When Simon started kissing her gently, not only did it seem the most natural thing to respond but Vicky found herself taking the initiative. She started to undress him even before he put his hand on her breast. For the first time in her life, Vicky felt sexually aroused.

When they finally rolled naked and giggling off the couch on to the floor, their lovemaking was uninhibited and joyful.

At one stage, as Vicky became aware of an immense sense of sharing, of an overwhelming desire to give, Greg's face flashed through her mind. It was 'Billy's' face really — the seduction scene when she'd wondered for a second whether it could be like that in real life. Whether it could ever be genuinely loving. Well, it could. It could be better, much, much better, but why the hell was she thinking about acting now? Damn — it was the 'third eye' again. The 'third eye' Jane had taught her about that time they'd discussed the craft of acting. If that was what acting was all about, she didn't want it. She didn't want to be outside looking in. She wanted to lose herself in Simon, she wanted Simon to lose himself in her. She wanted to take, she wanted to give. Take. Give. Take. Give. And suddenly Vicky was lost. Lost in herself, lost in Simon, lost in time and, as Simon's groans reached a peak, she flung back her head and heard her own involuntary cry of fulfilment.

They talked, gently nibbling and caressing each other's flesh. They dressed and walked through the park. In the evening they ate some more of the food without even bothering to heat it up and they went to bed and made love again. This time gently, consciously exploring each other's bodies. Vicky was once more outside herself, observing, thinking, 'Is this really me?' and once more chastising herself for being so analytical. And then once again she became lost, once again he became part of her and once again, as she clutched him to her, she heard herself cry out.

Two days later, Vicky sought out Jane at the studio. She needed someone to talk to.

Jane was surprised and touched. She and Vicky were genuinely fond of each other and had developed a great camaraderie and a respect for each other's talents but they hadn't mingled socially and their conversations were invariably about work or acting in general. Now here was the girl discussing her intimate life and crying out for help. Jane felt maternal and protective but also a little inadequate. Hell, who was she to give advice on sex, lovers and affairs of the heart? She'd well and truly stuffed up that area of her own life.

'Honestly, Vicky,' she admitted. 'I don't know what help I can give except to say that, if you honestly love Simon then I think you should go for it. If you back off because you're scared of getting hurt or scared of interfering with your career then you could end up never loving anyone.' Jane recalled that someone had given her that piece of advice at one stage when the importance of a lover was threatening her career. It had made sense to her in theory but she'd got rid of the lover nonetheless.

'No, it's not that,' Vicky protested, 'I'm not scared of giving, I'm scared that I can't give enough.' Jane looked puzzled. 'It's the third eye, Jane — it's always there.'

Jane remembered the conversation they'd had a couple of weeks ago about her 'third eye' theory. It

314

had become quite an excited debate over the canteen's Tuesday loin chops.

'Everybody has a "third eye", Vicky,' she explained. 'You know, that really weird feeling of looking at yourself from the outside. Often when you least expect it.' Jane looked down at her plate as she continued. 'I remember when I was about fourteen my dog was hit by a car. I was nursing the poor thing in the middle of the road and I don't know who was screaming loudest, me or the dog, but all the time I was telling myself that this was what it was like to feel panic, terror, grief. All of that. I've used that memory a lot since.'

'You knew you wanted to act when you were fourteen?'

'Oh, sure. I knew when I was ten.'

Although Vicky was a 'natural' and had been hitting upon many performance techniques instinctively, it was the first hint of an acting lesson she'd ever had and it fascinated her. She let her favourite loin chops solidify on the plate before her as she and Jane talked for the whole lunch break about analysing one's emotions and behaviour.

'We're different people, depending on who it is we're relating to at the time,' Jane said. 'Whether it's family, lover, employer, workmates. It's useful for an actor to analyse that.'

Vicky identified with much of what Jane was saying. She'd used the many facets of her personality for years. To lie to prospective landlords, to get jobs for which she wasn't qualified or was underage, to fool the authorities. Her existence had been consciously chameleon-like for most of her life, but she hadn't analysed why or how she chose her particular 'performances'.

After that conversation, Vicky's 'third eye' became a predominant part of her life and she found it endlessly interesting to observe her own reactions to situations and the effect she had on people and they had on her.

But now there was Simon. He'd taken her by surprise and Vicky was in a dilemma. 'I don't want the third eye to take over, Jane. I don't want to be on the outside looking in. How do I stop it?'

'I don't know, love. A lot of actors can't.' Jane shrugged. 'One of the hazards of the business, I guess.'

It was then and there that Vicky decided to quit acting.

Jane was appalled. 'You're mad. You can't!'

'Why not?'

'Quit the business! Just like that!'

'Oh, I think I'll stay in the business. Go into the production side or something.'

'But . . . you're a star. The whole country knows you.'

'Yeah. That's one of the parts I hate.'

'Fair enough,' Jane nodded. 'But you're so talented. You're a natural. I mean . . . ' It was beyond Jane's comprehension that anyone, having established themselves and having experienced the challenge of acting, could ever give it up.

'So?' Vicky grinned. 'I'll just have to discover another talent and be a natural at that.'

'God almighty, I hope Simon's worth it.'

'I'm not doing it for Simon, Jane, I'm doing it for me. If Simon disappeared tomorrow I'd still do it.' Jane looked at the girl blankly. 'Don't you see?' Vicky continued, 'Simon's made me realise that I can accept somebody else as being important in my life. That I can actually 'love', I guess. I never thought I could. I mean like . . . ' Vicky fumbled for the words, 'like love in the general sense. I can love friends, I can love family.' She gave a wry smile. 'Well, I could if I had any. I can love anyone or anything, not just Simon. He's only been the . . . the . . . '

'Catalyst?' Jane prompted.

'Sure. Catalyst, that's it. He's been the catalyst.'

'So why do you have to give up acting?' Jane vaguely knew the answer but she asked anyway.

'Because the third eye's too easy for me, Jane. I've been acting all my life, only I never knew it. I want to quit before I see myself through a camera lens all the time. I want to quit before this analysing business takes over and I can't think of anyone but me and who I am and . . . oh, all that shit, you know?'

Jane knew only too well and she felt a sudden rush of envy. Yes, Vicky was getting out in time. Too late for me, Jane thought, knowing full well that she was no longer able to be subjective. Everything was observed, noted and filed for possible use in a future performance. It took Jane only a few seconds to shrug off such negative feelings though. So what? She and Vicky were different people, after all. Vicky obviously didn't have the commitment to be an actress, she didn't want to risk paying the price. Well, Jane did. Each to their own.

'I wish you luck, Vicky,' she said and meant it.

Following on the heels of the death of Simon's character and the news of Narelle's pregnancy, Jane's and Vicky's announcements that they were quitting the show meant that the ranks of 'The Glitter Game' regulars would be sadly depleted and of course Alain couldn't have liked it more. There was only one continuous thorn in his side. Robert Bryce.

After the irritation of being overruled several times in production decisions that should have been totally his domain, Alain had to face the humiliation of the bad press about Simon and Bryce's reaction to it. Then to top it all off, there was Bryce's peremptory order for Alain to make all arrangements for Edwina Dawling's promotional trip. Good God, Alain thought yet again, the man's treating me like a lackey.

And so Alain had found himself barking, 'Fuck the budget, do it,' at Tim Arnold. This time, though, it didn't take Alain long to get over the insult. He only had to remind himself that Robert Bryce would be regretting his actions in a very short time. 'The Glitter Game' would be a dead horse, which no amount of whipping would be able to resurrect unless perhaps the whip was wielded by the Midas of soaps, the King himself. And the King himself would be happily ensconced at Channel 8.

Yes, what was the point of allowing Robert Bryce to upset him? This was the most peaceful, relaxing time Alain could remember in his entire life of fighting, scratching and clawing to get to the top and stay there. He had only one week left with Network Three, having officially handed in his notice a month ago, informing Bryce Holdings that he was departing on the very day his contract expired.

Robert had not announced Alain's successor. Indeed, he'd requested that Alain himself keep his departure a secret. Alain understood. The press would not be kind about Channel 3's chances in the local drama stakes, and 'The Glitter Game' ratings would be bound to plummet when it was announced that the King was leaving. It was the least Alain could do, and one never knew when one might need Robert Bryce again. Alain agreed to keep the secret.

Although he'd been adamant about his decision, Alain had been a little disappointed that Robert Bryce hadn't fought harder to keep him. Maybe their recent conflict had irritated Bryce to the point where the man was willing to cut his own throat. Because cut his own throat he certainly had, Alain thought with satisfaction, by not coming up with an offer too good to refuse. On the other hand maybe Bryce was losing interest in his television assets. After all Bryce Holdings had acquired two more mining leases in the year of 'The Glitter Game'.

Whatever the reason, Alain decided he couldn't care less. And his indifference to anything pertaining to the network gave him the most precious gift he'd ever known. Time. Time for himself. Time that didn't belong to the media, the network, the ratings war. Time to indulge. Time to concentrate on the home front. And indulgence and the home front meant the same thing now. Tran.

Tran had become an integral part of Alain's life, as necessary to him as his favourite armchair or his home computer. Their relationship was still highly sensual, but the sex itself had become more of a daily ritual, one which Alain was only too happy to take for granted, to lie back and let Tran do all the work. It was far less exhausting than the obsession he'd had for her body in the first few weeks.

Tran's role as a release factor was just as important to Alain on an emotional level as it was on a sexual one — in fact, possibly more so. He would pour out all the pent-up frustrations and angers of a day at the studio while she stroked his brow or massaged his feet. She rarely answered but made sympathetic clucking sounds with the back of her tongue or small popping noises with her lips or simply hummed in a soothing tone. She seemed to have a language completely her own, designed solely to calm him.

And it did — to the point where Alain found himself talking to her endlessly. Even when he wasn't stressed, he'd chronicle the day's events as if he were writing in a diary, merely to hear the crooning noises in return.

Apart from simple board and lodging, Tran seemed to require nothing in return for her endless attention. She never asked for money or gifts or for outings to expensive restaurants. The same selflessness eradicated Alain's fear of public exposure as, apart from stealing out via the service entrance once a week to do the shopping, Tran was quite happy to stay at home. These trips were always conducted midweek during working hours and the shopping was delivered later that afternoon when Alain could arrange to be home to accept delivery. It was Tran's idea to organise things that way and Alain was grateful for her discretion.

After all, he had more to fear than mere public ridicule. Cohabiting with Tran would carry a hefty charge. She still wouldn't tell him how old she was. Every time he badgered her she would giggle shyly, look away and whisper, 'No matter'. Indeed, her reluctance to admit her age was such that Alain thought maybe he'd be better off not knowing. Despite her sexual knowledge, Alain's assessment of her age remained at around fifteen. But what if she really were younger? A lot younger? He thrilled at the thought, but he also worried. What if he were found out? No. It was better not to think about that — better not to know.

In the meantime, with the exception of incoming phone calls which were attended to either by Alain or the answering machine, Tran handled all household affairs from cleaning, cooking and washing, to accounts and maintenance. Alain had no secrets from Tran. He didn't feel it necessary to teach her the combination of the safe, of course, but he no longer locked the study door or banned her from looking through desk drawers for any papers she might need for maintenance records or the like. He even taught her how to load and cock the gun he kept in his bedside cabinet should she need it for her own protection when she was alone. All in all it was a perfect domestic situation.

It was fitting that the first day of Alain's final week at Channel 3 should be a sparkling blue glorious day. Fitting because it matched his mood. Alain and the day were both happy.

He kissed Tran goodbye and she too glowed with happiness. He didn't kiss her very often.

And everything ran to schedule at the station — no particular dramas, no phone calls from Robert Bryce, no rantings and ravings from overreacting queens. Tim Arnold obviously had Edwina's trip all under control.

Alain picked up the pile of trade magazines and papers his secretary had left on his desk and leaned back contentedly in his plush leather chair. Every Monday Wendy left the magazines and every Monday Alain had time for no more than the quickest flick through the most important business articles on figures and projected ratings surveys. Today he intended to luxuriate. Today he intended to read about his favourite comedy team and catch up on media gossip and trivia. Today he had time.

He tossed the *Financial Review* to one side and Jane's face stared up at him from the cover of *TV Week*. Good looking girl, he thought. And that touch of defiance. Could have been a star. Oh well, he'd given her the chance — it wasn't his fault if the stupid bitch had knocked it back. He tossed the magazine on top of the *Financial Review*, not bothering to look at the article. The *Bulletin* was next. And who was that on the cover? Shit! More star quality — and how! Who the hell was she? Alain read the leader: 'Is this the face of the first Australian actress ever to win an Academy Award?' Of course. It was that new girl, what was her name? 'Anna Bowrey', he read. 'Anna Bowrey, Academy Award Winner?' Well, good luck to her, Alain thought. Nice to see Aussies do so well in the international market. He'd helped put so many there himself, it made him feel very proud.

Jane also had both magazines in front of her. She was sitting in the canteen having arrived early to go through some lines.

When she'd called in at a newsagency en route to the channel specifically to pick up the *TV Times* and read her article, she'd caught sight of the *Bulletin*. The words on the cover of the top magazine leapt out at her: ANNA BOWREY, ACADEMY AWARD WINNER? There was a sick feeling in her stomach.

She felt even worse when she'd finished reading both articles. The probing questions in the Bowrey interview were well-fielded and left the girl looking good, particularly supported by the beautifully framed and lit stills from the movie.

By contrast, the stills of Jane and Edwina glowering at each other looked harshly-lit and posed, and as for the article itself . . . Jane cringed. 'Jane's star sign is Aries with Pisces rising . . . No, there is no particular man in her life at the moment but if there were she would love him for his mind rather than his body . . . Her favourite colour is bright yellow' . . . Jane dumped both magazines in the rubbish bin and left the canteen.

The rest of the day was a battle for Jane. A battle to keep her venom at bay. There was a war raging inside her and she knew she mustn't let it show. She reasoned with herself until she had successfully persuaded herself that it wasn't Alain's fault. He was a deadshit, sure, but he'd been doing his job when he'd talked her around to 'The Glitter Game' in preference to the Wainwright offer. He was a clever man. Good luck to him. It was Edwina who'd killed Jane's chances. Jane would still be starring upfront, impressing the international market, but for Edwina. And no amount of reasoning could persuade her to forgive Edwina.

At midday when Edwina arrived on set for her first scene of the day, she knew immediately what was going through Jane's mind. She'd read both articles herself and had fully expected a violent reaction. The fact that she was met with seething hatred was a measure of Jane's self-control and Edwina respected the girl for that. But even as she thought 'Good for you, dear, you're showing great style', Edwina didn't regret a thing. She'd done what she had to do. The name of the game, dear, the name of the game.

Nevertheless, it made working conditions most uncomfortable, Edwina thought. She could see and feel venom all about her, Paul on one side, Jane on the other. Oh well, she sighed, only two more days and she'd be out of the country. Thank God!

The day had held no such tension for Alain. At six o'clock he left the channel in as buoyant a mood as he'd been in that morning. One day down and only four to go, he told himself.

'Good night, Alain,' Brian Hopgood called as he raised the boom gate and Alain drove through. But even the audacity of a security guard calling him by his first name failed to irritate.

'Good night, Brian,' Alain called back.

It was two o'clock in the morning when gunshots rang out and alarm bells screamed at Channel 3.

Brian Hopgood whirled about, dropped to one knee, and pointed his gun at the sound he'd heard behind him. It was Frank, the young security assistant who was also on patrol that night.

'He got away,' Brian said, rising to his feet and holstering his gun. 'The bastard got away.'

Frank looked around at the offices of the drama unit. Everywhere was chaos. Paperwork spilled out of dozens of open filing cabinets, drawers were upended, their contents strewn over the floor, and tables and chairs were covered with open files and computer discs.

'Shit!' he said.

Betrayal

The press heralded the news of the Channel 3 burglary in the early editions the following day.

'. . . valuable discs containing top-secret guidelines for future television series, detailed storylines for the next twelve months of "The Glitter Game", intricate marketing plans and merchandising deals . . .' the list went on. All stolen. The whole industry was guessing. Had a rival network had the audacity to stage such a burglary? If so, it must have been purely an act of sabotage. Apart from destroying it, what could they do with the stolen material? To use it, even in disguised form, would court discovery. The entertainment world and the media in general buzzed with excitement at the boldness of such strong-arm tactics.

The drama unit was closed that morning while Brian Hopgood and two police officers sifted through the carnage and examined the bullet holes in the walls, one of which came from the assailant's gun, and one from Brian's return of fire.

Nevertheless, it was business as usual at Channel 3.

'I don't know how the hell they're still hanging in there,' Alain barked. He'd called a meeting with Jim and Evan and they were discussing Mandy and Sidney. 'They haven't had key storylines and there hasn't been any press on them for a month. So how come their popularity points have picked up another fifteen per cent? That's twenty-five per cent over the last two surveys, for God's sake.'

'Well, as I mentioned before, Alain, the writers like writing for them — they're warm, humorous characters.' Evan tried hard to keep the smug edge out of his voice but he wasn't entirely successful. 'This is obviously conveying itself to the viewers.'

Apart from a derisive snort, Alain didn't deign to reply to him, but turned to Jim. 'What do you think?'

'There's something in what Evan says,' Jim agreed, ignoring Alain's glare. 'They're certainly providing the bulk of the show's humour.' He shook his head. 'But, to be quite honest, I've no idea why they're reaching the public the way they are.'

'All right,' Alain barked, 'renew their contracts — another six months. But only the basic increase.'

'Ten per cent it is.' Jim glanced at Evan. 'We'll ask for a six-month option on top if that's OK. The writers might want them for a full year.' Evan nodded vigorously.

'All right, all right,' Alain gave a dismissive wave, 'so long as the option's our way only. But make it clear, no negotiation. If they don't like it they can piss off.'

Jim paused. Should he say anything? The Jim of old certainly wouldn't have. But something had happened to him lately that had given Jim a backbone he never knew he had. And that something was Greg. Greg's humour and laid-back attitude were having an undeniable effect on Jim. 'Tell them to get rooted, it's only television,' Greg would say. Or 'They need you, sport, stick it up them. Go for what you want.' If Jim were to diagnose Greg's contribution more seriously it could be read as 'love and support'.

'I'd rather allow them a small area of negotiation, Alain,' Jim said.

Alain didn't answer. He couldn't. He stared back in a state of shock. The man was a producer, for Christ's sake. What was he saying?

'You see, they've been with the show for a full twelve months on pretty basic money. I think the goodwill we'll create in allowing them a minor area —'

'Fuck goodwill!' Alain exploded. 'They're actors! They're lucky we're giving them a job! What's happened to you?'

Jim smiled. Alain was so readable there were times when he even liked him. 'If we get them for ten per cent for the first six months, then allow them to negotiate a small increase for the second . . .' Jim spelled it out carefully, '. . . bearing in mind that the option for that six months is on our side only and that they have to negotiate that increase now, then we'll end up with goodwill for the latter half of the year just when tempers are getting frayed. And it'll have cost us peanuts. It's not a bad policy. What do you think?'

'Oh, do it, do it.' Alain waved him away. Of course he could see the sense in it, that was why he'd employed Jim, after all. Jim was one of those line producers who always managed to get on with his actors. But it was all so petty! Alain couldn't be bothered.

Jim smiled and left. Alain looked at Evan and wondered why he wasn't leaving too.

'I wanted to have a word with you, Alain.' Alain raised an eyebrow. 'About the burglary,' Evan continued. Alain raised the other eyebrow. Evan cleared his throat. 'A heck of a lot of stuff was stolen.'

'I know.' Alain nodded sympathetically. My God, he asked himself, how much more disaster can 'The Glitter Game' take and survive? Very little, he answered himself with pleasure.

'You'll have your work cut out, won't you, Evan?'

Evan nodded. 'I'm not too bad with "The Glitter Game" storylines, I've got a lot of those on old discs at home.'

Pity, Alain thought.

'But all the breakdowns and treatments for the new season's series were in the Drama Unit, including the family sit-com pilot.'

'Oh dear,' Alain feigned anxiety.

'Exactly. We were due to start preproduction on the pilot next week.'

'I know,' Alain feigned worry.

'So I wondered if we should give "Lolly's" a go. I know you said we should shelve it because the family sit-com would cost less but we've got the first three episodes written plus the complete —'

'We haven't.' Alain feigned utter defeat. 'Wendy erased the disc last week.'

'My God!' Evan's face was ashen. 'Why?'

'A mistake. I told her we were shelving "Lolly's" indefinitely. She misunderstood me and wiped the disc.' It would always be his word against Wendy's should Evan pursue it and as Wendy cleared discs daily, it wouldn't be difficult to convince her that she'd inadvertently made a mistake.

'Lolly's' was a sitcom set in an Australian confectionery factory with a colourful cast of migrant factory workers — it would be a breakthrough comedy series. Alain had recognised it as a winner the moment Evan mentioned the vague outlines of his idea.

328

From that moment on, Alain had worked as closely as possible with Evan to the point where it had become impossible to say who had contributed what. He made sure all meetings were solely between Evan and himself and indeed Alain's input was such that, if challenged, Evan may well have found himself confused to the point of admitting it was as much Alain's work as his. This had been Alain's intention from the outset. Writers were such a naive bunch, it was like taking candy from a baby. Alain had pulled the same trick many times before.

'Lolly's' was presently sitting in Alain's safe at home, along with two other Evan Ryan concepts. It would see the light of day as a Channel 8 production a year down the track. The character names and title would have to change of course. What a pity, Alain thought — great title, 'Lolly's'.

Alain spent five minutes consoling Evan then ushered him out of the office and leafed through the paper work on his desk. Greg MacNeil's contract was there. Pity he couldn't have stuffed that one up. Greg had agreed to renew. For megabucks of course; he was a sharp man and knew his worth. Alain respected him for that.

Paul's contract was also there, signed, sealed and delivered. Paul was still popular but a few more months and the booze would solve that one. Nobody loved a drunk.

Edwina's contract remained not only unsigned but unnegotiated. She refused to discuss it until her return from overseas. By then her promotional trip would have set the world on fire, and she would undoubtedly demand the earth. Thankfully, Alain would be gone by then and wouldn't have to witness her triumph.

With Greg and Edwina re-signed, 'The Glitter Game' might limp on for possibly another year, but it would definitely be on the way out by the time 'Lolly's' hit the screens. And then Alain would be responsible for the next Australian hit series — this time for Channel 8.

The increase in the popularity of the characters played by Mandy and Sidney was only a minor concern, a passing public fad that would make no difference to the destined death of the show. Bit of a mystery though, Alain thought as he buzzed Wendy to get him a coffee.

Mandy's and Sidney's success wasn't really a mystery. It was the result of damn hard work. The veteran actors had been pushing for months to raise their stakes in the popularity polls.

They both knew only too well that, until the end of the second year to air, contract renewal time in a series meant severe pruning. And if there were any members of the original cast likely to be considered dead wood, they were it. Mandy and Sidney both felt the familiar sense of panic. No, don't do it to me, don't send me back to the bottom of the heap. Not now, for God's sake. 'Not now' meant 'not at my age', although neither of them would have admitted that.

If they could only get to the end of that second year! After the first two years of a series, it was unlikely for management to sack any of the original cast members who by that time were firmly entrenched with the viewers.

They never talked to each other of their fears, being unwilling to admit their insecurity, but they both grabbed at every possible opportunity for self-promotion. And, as the comic elderly couple, their 'Glitter Game' characters were always identified together, so that each promotional appearance invariably involved the other. If Mandy scored a gala charity event, she was asked if she could bring Sidney. If Sidney scored a store promotion he was asked if he could persuade Mandy to appear as well.

And then there was the Saturday shopping. That had become the biggest promotional gig of all. After thirty years of assiduously avoiding each other around the streets of Kings Cross, Saturday morning shopping had become a shared ritual.

It had happened by mistake. Both Mandy and Sidney had become masters of the art of noticeably struggling not to be noticed, which meant they managed to call a remarkable amount of attention to themselves.

So the day they accidentally bumped into each other at the pastry shop they'd both acquired a number of gawking passers-by.

'Mandy, my dear!'

'Sidney! Sidney, darling!'

A smattering of applause broke out as they hugged each other and people picked up small white paper bags from beside the cake stands, hunted around for pens and demanded autographs.

A small band of loyal followers trailed behind them from the pastry shop to the butcher, the greengrocer, and the supermarket. By the time they reached the newsagency, they were being followed by a veritable army of admirers and their hands ached from signing autographs.

That was just the beginning. Since then they'd

shopped together every Saturday. They never arranged to meet. It was a tacit understanding that ten o'clock on Saturday mornings saw them at the pastry shop.

The Kings Cross residents knew this and each week there was an increase in numbers as the locals brought their families and friends and their kids brought their classmates. And Mandy and Sidney always managed to have an adequate supply of Channel 3 photo fan cards of themselves to hand around.

The pastry shop man loved Mandy and Sidney. He did a thriving trade in pies, sausage rolls and chocolate eclairs as the crowd lolled about outside his shop waiting for their 'Glitter Game' celebrities.

Then one day, Mandy varied the routine. Her agent had rung late Friday and asked if she'd be interested in calling in at the Central Mission House on Saturday afternoon. The Reverend Tom Spence evidently wanted a few celebrities to make a brief appearance at a funding drive being held in aid of homeless children.

'There's no money involved,' the agent said, 'but Central Mission's only around the corner from your place and there's some press coverage so . . . '

'It's for homeless children,' Mandy interrupted. 'Of course I'll be there.'

So it was that Mandy suggested Sidney accompany her to the Central Mission House. They were at their final port of call, the newsagents, and Sidney naturally thought it was an excellent idea. 'When we can do a little something for homeless kiddies it makes our foolish industry truly worthwhile, doesn't it?' he commented. Mandy nodded her agreement and suggested they leave their shopping with Don the newsagent. Sidney agreed. It certainly wouldn't look good, stars arriving carrying plastic bags of sausages and laundry powder.

Don was only too happy to be of service. The weekly invasion of soap-watchers always saw a rise in the sale of comics, Mad magazines and Mills and Boon books.

Mandy and Sidney turned out to be the fund raiser's main attraction. The Reverend Tom hadn't managed to score the services of many celebrities — the event wasn't high profile enough. In fact there was only a faded ex-quiz show hostess who now hosted a regular five minute flower-arranging segment on Channel 3's morning show and a stand-up comic who still trotted out John Wayne impressions but was very popular with the RSL clubs.

As Mandy and Sidney wandered through the exhibition of handiwork done by reformed streetkids from some of the halfway houses run by Central Mission, they were filmed briefly for a possible late night news human interest segment. Then they posed for a few publicity shots with one of the reformed streetkids.

His name was Nathaniel, Nat for short, and he was the pride and joy of Reverend Tom. 'Nathaniel's background is terrible,' he explained. 'A severely underprivileged boy. That's what makes his talent so remarkable. Show them your work, Nat.'

Nat led them to the section of the exhibition displaying T-shirts. Screen-printed T-shirts, T-shirts which were tie-dyed, hand-painted or beaded, T-shirts in every possible style of original design. There must have been hundreds of them.

'It's one of the most popular art-forms in the workshops,' Reverend Tom said. 'And Nat's the star talent.' He gave Nat a hefty pat on the back which nearly sent the scrawny boy sprawling. The Reverend was a big, thickset man who, on first meeting could have been taken to be a heavyweight boxer which was understandable enough because ten years ago he had been. Since declaring himself a born-again Christian he'd kept in training and the children, particularly the boys who were mostly aspiring Jeff Fenechs, worshipped him.

At the Reverend's suggestion, Nat showed Mandy and Sidney the computer room where he designed his computerised, screen-printed T-shirts.

'We've only got the one computer, though, so I only get to use it two hours a week,' Nat whined. He was undersized for his age, looking at least two years younger than his fourteen years, but he had a wiry body which could have appeared quite fit, if it weren't for the stoop of his shoulders and the defeat in his eyes. He looked so sad Mandy wanted to cry.

'That's one of the things we're raising money for,' Nat continued, 'another computer.' He looked from Mandy to Sidney and back again. 'Don't want to contribute, do you?'

Mandy and Sidney were shocked. Contribute? Contribute *money*? Stars were never asked to contribute money. Time, yes. And, after all, time was money, wasn't it? But ready cash? They looked at Reverend Tom but he obviously didn't think it was too impertinent a question. He should have known better and they both thought he should have corrected the boy but nevertheless Mandy found herself diving into her handbag. That poor pathetic child.

Sidney scrounged around in his coat pocket for a two dollar coin. 'Sorry, my boy, seem to have come out a bit short, that's all I can do.' Mandy handed Nat a ten dollar bill. 'Now if there's anything else we could do,' Sidney continued, 'by way of giving our time, personal appearances and all that, we'd be only too happy to . . . '

'Could I use your photos for a T-shirt?' Nat asked and, for the first time they saw a touch of animation in his face. 'I'd only make a few,' he added hastily. 'Just for me and me mates at the home.'

'Naturally, Nat,' Sidney said, which sounded so silly that he was relieved Mandy said, 'Of course you can, dear' at the same time.

'We'll get the Channel 3 publicity department to send you out —' But Mandy was interrupted.

'It's OK,' Nat said, 'I've got a camera. I can do them now.'

'Oh. Well . . . ' Mandy demurred, unsure of her make-up.

'I think it might be best if . . . ' Sidney balked, aware that natural daylight didn't show him to his best advantage.

'Great idea, Nat. Grab your camera and let's go.' The Reverend Tom shoved them out the back door into the harsh midsummer day and, before they knew it, Mandy and Sidney were squinting into a ferocious Australian sun. Click. Click. Click. Before they'd had time to reposition their faces from the shock of the glare and before they'd been able to make further protest, Nat was grinning from ear to ear.

'Hey, bizarre! Thanks heaps.' And he disappeared around the corner of the building, a different, jaunty set about his shoulders and a clearly defined swagger to his walk.

'Thank you so much for giving us your time.' Reverend Tom shook their hands effusively, severely bruising several knuckles, and then he too disap-

peared, leaving Mandy and Sidney alone in the back
yard of the Central Mission House. They found the
side entrance and wound their way through several
back alleys to the newsagent where they collected
their shopping. Nobody saw them, nobody followed
them and it was all a bit of a let-down after such a
successful start to a Saturday.

A fortnight later, in fact, the day after the Channel 3
burglary, two things happened that had a marked
effect on Mandy's and Sidney's future standing in the
industry.

Firstly, there were the phone calls from their
respective agents. Channel 3 was renewing their contract, with a ten per cent salary increase for six
months, with a possible six month option to be discussed.

After their initial relief, which knew no bounds,
Mandy and Sidney told each other how insulted they
were at the contract conditions. But both knew
neither of them was going to make waves. They knew
that a whinge was necessary to retain their dignity
and each was grateful the other was there to whinge
to. Mandy and Sidney were actually beginning to like
each other.

The second thing that happened on that Tuesday
was the arrival of two parcels from the Central
Mission House, Kings Cross, addressed to Mandy
Burgess and Sidney Meredith, c/o 'The Glitter
Game', Channel 3. Inside each was a personal note
from the Reverend Tom Spence:

> Hope you like the enclosed. Nat's done a good
> job, don't you think? The cheeky young bloke
> conned the use of another computer and he's

worked around the clock for the past fortnight to get these out to all the Mission sales outlets. There's hundreds of them around already and he's not stopping till he's flooded the market. All proceeds, bar the twenty-five per cent necessary for Nat's expenses, go to the Fund and, on behalf of Central Mission I'd like to thank you most sincerely for your generous contribution.

It's donations of time and energy like yours and Nat's that make our purpose so worthwhile.

Thank you once again,

Yours, Tom Spence.

Inside each envelope was a large white T-shirt. Emblazoned boldly across the chest were the words 'THE OLDS' in black, and there, underneath, were Mandy and Sidney.

They gazed at the T-shirts in horror. How had the boy managed to get so much detail onto a screen-printed T-shirt? No one had ever looked that old!

'Ladies first,' Sidney said as he handed Mandy the phone. And for the first time, they rang their agents together. They were a team now and there was strength in numbers.

Both agents said the same things and made the same points. Firstly, Mandy and Sidney had given permission for their photos to be used so it was hardly illegal. Secondly, it would be dreadful for their images to withdraw permission from a money-making concern which was benefiting homeless children. And thirdly — this was the only point made that Mandy and Sidney ultimately remembered — a potentially huge fan club had been set up from Central Mission House and was already running hot through all the Mission halfway houses and sales outlets.

The Mandy Burgess/Sidney Meredith Official Fan

Club had been started by a Nathaniel somebody, they were told. The National Headquarters of the club had been set up at the Central Mission House, Kings Cross; branches were opening up at halfway houses all over the country and fan club kits complete with 'THE OLDS' T-shirts, badges and biographies were presently being parcelled for distribution in the UK.

Mandy and Sidney appeared to be the only employees at Channel 3 not obsessed with the endless burglary discussions that day. While everyone asked 'who, why and how', Mandy and Sidney couldn't have cared less. They were flying.

So was Alain as he prepared to leave the channel that afternoon. He was knocking off early today, bugger it. After all, there were only three days to go. Only three days, then goodbye 'Glitter Game' and hello 'Lolly's'.

It was going to be a steamy, hot summer evening. The heat always made Alain extra horny and Tran was waiting — he couldn't have been happier. He stopped on the way home and bought a chilled bottle of chardonnay and a bunch of pink roses. He'd give Tran a special treat. She deserved it.

Robert Bryce looked out the portside window at the eastern coast of Australia only five hundred feet below. He'd instructed the pilot twenty minutes ago to drop from forty thousand feet as he neared the coastline. And here it was.

Robert never tired of air travel. Sometimes he missed the four-seater Cessna Skyhawk he'd cut his teeth on. And of course he missed being in the cockpit himself. He still managed a couple of fun-flying hours a week at the controls of his Beechcraft

Baron but he was resigned to the fact that time and business dictated he employ a professional pilot to fly his Citation. Besides, corporate image demanded it.

The white beaches stretched endlessly from bay to bay and the ocean glistened a vivid aquamarine over the sand and a deep blue over the weed. Robert wished Melanie were with him. They'd be sipping Dom Perignon, holding hands and telling each other that nothing mattered, except life, the beauty of it, and each other. Looking at the world from five hundred feet always did that to them. And they inevitably fantasised about ditching the entire corporation and flying away together in a little single-engine Cessna.

'Fuck Bryce Holdings,' they'd say to each other. 'Who needs Lear Jets and forty thousand feet?' The jet set could have their mile-high club; the world at five hundred was all that Melanie and Robert required.

Of course as soon as they touched down the fantasy bubble would explode and it would be business as usual, but if Mellie were with him right now, Robert thought, at least they'd have had the fantasy.

As it was, all Robert could see beneath him was the beauty of the eastern coast of Australia and all he could feel inside was a weariness at the unpleasant business ahead. I miss you Mellie, he thought.

'For me?' Tran was thrilled with the roses. He'd never bought her roses before.

Alain was glad he'd gone to the trouble because Tran had been out shopping and bought him his favourites for dinner. Avocado, king prawns, a chicory salad — it would all go so well with the chardonnay. But first things first, he decided, as he led the way to the bedroom.

Alain never got to eat his avocado and king prawns. In fact, he hadn't even pulled the cork from the bottle of chardonnay when his world started to crumble.

After their sex, Tran had washed him down as usual and helped him into his towelling robe. Then she brought him the wine, corkscrew and two glasses on a small tray with a dish of mixed olives. It looked very pretty, but then Tran always did things delicately.

As Alain picked up the bottle, they heard the first rap at the door. They looked at each other in surprise. It was eight o'clock at night — who could it be? No one ever called at the flat. Any contact out of office hours was strictly via the telephone. Even before the days of Tran, it was a rule Alain had always enforced. Meetings outside the channel were conducted in restaurants, cocktail bars or other people's boardrooms, never on home ground.

There was a second rap at the door. It was an authoritative rap and Alain felt a rush of intense irritation. Who the hell was it and how bloody dare they?

He jerked his head toward the bedroom and Tran disappeared, quietly closing the door behind her.

When Alain opened the front door he discovered Brian Hopgood, hand poised, about to knock again. A man who was obviously a police detective stood beside him. They shared a quick glance and Brian gave a barely perceptible nod.

'Alain King?' The detective flashed his badge, not waiting for any form of acknowledgement. 'Detective Sergeant Dalton. Mind if we have a word with you?' Dalton was already easing his way into the flat.

Alain glared at Brian. 'What the fuck's going on, Hopgood?'

'Hello, Alain. Sorry about this,' and Brian also stepped inside, closing the door behind him.

Alain was dumbstruck at the audacity of the man. 'Exactly what do you think you're —'

'I have a search warrant, Mr King,' Dalton interrupted, 'but it'd be much easier all round if you simply cooperated.'

Alain took a deep breath. He mustn't overreact, this was obviously some ridiculous mistake, but by God, he'd make Hopgood suffer. He didn't give a stuff what the man's connection with Robert Bryce was, he was a fucking security guard and it was time he learned his place, time he learned to pay some respect to his superiors. 'I'd be only too happy to cooperate, Sergeant, if I knew what this was all about. Perhaps Mr Hopgood could enlighten me?'

'It's about the burglary, Alain.'

'What *about* the burglary, Brian?' Alain's voice was heavy with a sarcasm that seemed to entirely escape Brian Hopgood.

'I'm afraid investigations have revealed some evidence that could seem to implicate you and . . .' Brian's voice was deeply apologetic and he gave a shrug that seemed to say everything was beyond his control.

Alain stared at the two men for a second then laughed loudly. 'What utter bullshit!'

'Do you possess a Smith and Wesson .38 revolver?' Dalton barked.

'Yes, but what's —'

'I'd like to see it, please.'

Alain shook his head in disbelief but led the way

into the study nonetheless. He might as well get this farce over and done with.

He took the revolver from the desk and handed it to Dalton who smelled the weapon and checked the chamber, then nodded briskly and looked about the room. 'Now the safe.'

Alain suddenly started to feel a little uncomfortable, although he didn't know why. "What about it?'

'I'd like to see the contents of the safe please.'

Alain knew it was useless to argue. Besides, there was no threat to him. There was no way he could be involved in the burglary. The 'Lolly's' disc wasn't on the list of stolen property and if word got out that it was in Alain's possession, so what? An innocent mistake. He'd unwittingly brought it home with the load of work that he regularly carted to and from the office. Nobody could prove a thing.

So why was he feeling so vulnerable? he wondered, as he clicked through the final combination number and opened the safe door.

Then he froze. The safe was stacked high with files, discs and video tapes which he'd never seen before. Brian Hopgood took them out and handed them one by one to Dalton who methodically ticked off a list in his notebook.

Alain sank into an armchair, his stomach churning. It was a set-up. But how the hell had they done it? The first half-dozen items had been laboriously ticked off Dalton's list before Alain spoke. 'All right, I get the message.'

Dalton flicked his notepad shut. 'We'll check the rest out down at the station.'

'And the gun. What about the gun?' Alain already knew the answer.

'It's been fired recently, of course, and I'm sure ballistic tests will find it matches the bullet we dug out of the wall at the channel.'

'Yes, I'm sure they will,' Alain muttered. Apart from the churning of his stomach, he felt numb. He looked dully at Brian Hopgood.

'We won't take any action until we've discussed it with Mr Bryce, Alain,' Brian said reassuringly. 'He'll be at the channel tomorrow and, who knows, he may decide not to press charges.' Alain nodded wearily. 'In the meantime,' Brian continued, 'Sergeant Dalton will keep hold of the gun and the channel property.'

Brian crossed to the door. 'So if you'd like to present yourself at the boardroom at eleven tomorrow morning, Mr Bryce will be expecting you.' He opened the door for Dalton and there was an undisguised air of complicity as they exchanged smiles.

Dalton left and Brian Hopgood nodded sympathetically to Alain. 'Mr Bryce has advised me that nothing about this is to be mentioned at the channel until after your meeting. I'm sure he wants to save you from any embarrassment until arrangements have been agreed upon.' He turned to go.

'How did you do it, Hopgood? How the fuck did you do it?'

But Brian had gone.

Alain didn't sleep that night. At seven in the morning he was pacing the kitchen with his third cup of coffee, counting the minutes till he could leave for the channel. The sooner he got the whole thing sorted out the sooner he'd know how to fight it.

The hour between his arrival and his eleven o'clock

appointment was tortuous but he went through the motions of a normal morning. He glanced at the mail that Wendy had carefully scanned and accepted the coffee she handed him.

'Mr Bryce is in the channel,' she said.

'I know, I know.' Alain noticed his hand was shaking slightly as he took the cup.

'He called to say he'd like to see you in the boardroom in an hour.'

'I know that, too.'

Wendy left in a bit of a huff. It was customary for initial contact to be made between Mr Bryce's secretary and herself. It was not only a common courtesy but what on earth were personal secretaries for if they were to be so overlooked?

Alain stood outside the boardroom door for a full minute wondering whether he should knock or just walk in. He'd never knocked on the boardroom door in the entire time he'd been at Channel 3. But circumstances were different this time. He knocked.

Brian Hopgood opened the door. 'Good morning, Alain.'

Alain didn't answer. He stepped inside and Brian closed the door behind him.

Robert Bryce was seated at the end of the boardroom table but Alain barely saw him as his eyes focused on the diminutive figure standing beside him. It was Tran. Head bowed, eyes fixed on her feet, hands clasped over her tiny flat stomach. Alain gasped involuntarily.

'Alain.' Robert Bryce's voice was authoritative but not unfriendly. 'Come in. Sit down.'

Alain's tongue froze against the roof of his mouth

and he swallowed the breath that had been about to call her name. He crossed the room and sat in the chair beside Robert. He looked directly into the man's eyes but all he could see were Tran's tiny breasts only inches away from Robert's left ear.

'Hello, Robert,' he said.

'You sit down too, Tran.' Robert indicated the chair to his left and the breasts disappeared from Alain's peripheral vision to be replaced by the gleaming blue-black crown of Tran's head. 'And relax, dear,' Robert continued. 'The performance is over.'

Robert Bryce turned his full attention to Alain but all Alain could see was the head slowly raising itself to look at him.

'You know Tran, of course.' Robert was forcing Alain to look directly at the girl. He did. And he saw betrayal.

The eyes that looked back at him were not Tran's eyes. The lips, already curving into a remote smile, were not Tran's lips. Apart from the fact that the cool, self-possessed creature sitting opposite him was a child-woman, there was nothing that reminded him of Tran. Nothing.

'Say hello to Alain, dear.' Robert's instruction was courteous and friendly.

'Hello, Alain.' And the voice! Accent-free, bold and distinct. Not even a touch of malice.

Somehow that helped Alain. He forced aside his sense of personal betrayal as he told himself, 'So that's how they did it. Of course'. Tran would have smuggled the gun out of the flat so that Brian Hopgood could use it to fire that incriminating shot during his staged 'burglary', then she would have smuggled it back again. Just as she would have smuggled the tapes, discs and files into the safe. Or easier still, simply been there to let Hopgood in and open the safe for him. Alain had never told her the combination but she'd watched him open the safe often enough. Clever little thing, she'd worked it out and memorised it easily.

It was all so simple. And of course, he'd told her everything. Every devious little trick he'd pulled to undermine 'The Glitter Game'. Every stolen idea. Alain's rush of realisation stopped there. So what? he asked himself. Everyone stole ideas, everyone undermined other network's shows. Why was Robert Bryce out to ruin him for doing what was common practice?

Alain realised that Tran's face had become a blur. He'd been focusing on the space somewhere between Tran and Bryce as his thoughts raced to make sense of it all. Now her face appeared sharply before him again as he asked himself 'why'.

He turned to Robert Bryce who smiled back at him. 'You didn't really think I'd let you go, did you?'

'That's why?' Alain was incredulous. 'But you accepted my resignation.' Robert shrugged. 'You didn't try to outbid Channel 8.' Robert shook his head. 'But why didn't you just buy me? Why didn't you make a better offer?'

Robert studied the top of the boardroom table for several seconds. 'Contrary to popular belief,' he said slowly, 'I'm not of the opinion that one can always buy loyalty. Sometimes one can of course,' he said looking at Tran who accepted the innuendo without a shred of offence, 'but not always. Sometimes, in quite rare cases, one simply relies upon the personal integrity of a man.' He gave a quick nod in Brian Hopgood's direction. 'But more often than not I've found it necessary to let a man hang himself, just a little, in order to make him aware of where his loyalty is best placed.'

Robert leant forward over the boardroom table and for the first time in their interview, there was an edge to his voice. 'And I'll tell you why your loyalty is best placed with me, King. Because I'm the best there is at what I do.' He sat back and smiled winningly. 'And you're the best there is at what you do. So I suggest you let me look after the rise and fall of networks and you concentrate on giving the viewers the television they want.' He shook his head like a kindergarten teacher chastising a child. 'You really have let things go a bit, haven't you?'

Robert opened up a manila folder which lay on the table in front of him. 'Here's a contract I'd like you to have a look at. It ties you to Network 3 for five years but I think you'll find it more than generous in all areas and we can always chat about the bits and pieces, can't we?' He closed the folder and pushed it towards Alain. 'I'll be staying at the Regent for the next two days. You can reach me there.'

'Once it's signed and sealed I'm sure we can persuade Brian to return your gun and forget the whole unfortunate burglary business. You're far too valuable an asset to us to spend ... ' he looked at Brian for affirmation ' ... ten years?' Brian nodded. 'Ten years in prison.' Robert pushed back his chair, rose and extended his hand. 'I think that just about covers it.'

Alain also rose, automatically accepting the handshake. 'I'll certainly look at the contract, Robert,' he said. He knew he was trapped and he knew he'd say yes but his mind was whirling at such a rate that he also knew he could concentrate on nothing but getting out of that room. He turned to go, but he couldn't resist a parting glance at Tran. It was as if she didn't see him. It was as if her mind was miles away.

It was. Tran's mind was in Cabramatta, the outer-Sydney suburb known as Vietnamatta to many. It would be nice to be living at home again with her mother and two little brothers instead of having to rush there several times a week during office hours. This had been a long job and she was tired. The rest would do her good. It would be a whole six weeks before Mr Bryce needed her again. Six weeks with her friends and family, and it was her birthday next week. She wished she could persuade her mother to move to a more upmarket suburb. They could afford it. Mr Bryce gave her a generous monthly allowance even when he didn't need her to service or set up one of his clients. But ever since they'd arrived in Australia from the Hong Kong transit camps in 1979, Cabramatta had become home to her mother.

Lost in her own thoughts, Tran didn't even hear Robert call to Alain just as Brian Hopgood was about to open the door for him.

'And Alain . . . ' Alain turned back. 'Carnal knowledge of a minor is also a pretty hefty charge, not to mention what it would do to your standing if it got out.'

Alain felt small beads of sweat pop out on his forehead. No more, please!

'I'd like to think that you could concentrate on the matters in hand without unnecessary worries on your mind.' Robert gave his warmest smile. 'So to put you at ease on that score, Tran turns twenty-six next week.'

Brian Hopgood opened the door and Alain left.

Survival

The next fortnight was the greatest challenge of Alain's career. The day after his meeting with Robert Bryce he woke feeling sick, a negative, depressed sickness, beyond the restorative powers of Mylanta, a sickness the like of which he'd never known. After months and months of plotting and scheming to undermine Channel 3 and to kill off 'The Glitter Game' he was expected to undo all the damage . . . overnight?

He lay on his sleepless bed and stared up at the ceiling, his head dulled by the rare Mogadon he'd taken at two am which hadn't really worked anyway. Where did he start? It was hopeless.

He looked at his watch. Seven o'clock. Just the time Tran would have been trotting in with his pot of tea on a tray with two slices of toast and little glass dishes of butter and orange marmalade. She'd put the tray on the bedside table, humming gently, slowly open the drapes, so that the shock of early daylight wouldn't be too sudden. Then she'd sit on the bed beside him and pour his tea.

She'd never speak a work until he'd had the first sip. Then, 'You sleep well, yes?' She never called him by his name. Well, she had once, hadn't she? 'Hello, Alain.' The direct, impersonal stare flashed through

349

his mind for the hundredth time that morning and the clear, confident enunciation again rang shockingly in his ears.

Alain forced himself out of bed, crossed to the window and threw the drapes aside. The morning light streamed in. He looked down at the busy city below. The view was exciting, spectacular, it was why he'd bought the penthouse in the first place.

Alain could still remember the public outcry nearly twenty-five years ago when the block of luxury apartments had been built. 'There should be laws protecting harbour frontages from high rise,' the lobbyists had cried, 'particularly residential frontages overlooking the city.' Alain had been barely twenty at the time and was already making himself known as a bright light in the field of market research. He disagreed with the lobbyists. They were only fighting harbour frontage development because they couldn't afford to buy into it themselves. Go for it, he willed the developers. Go for it, and one day I'll buy it. I'll buy the penthouse first and then I'll buy the whole damn block.

It was brash youth talking, of course, and he no longer even wished to buy the block — real estate wasn't his game, after all. But twelve years ago, on the day that he'd signed the contracts on the penthouse, Alain had proved something to himself. He'd proved that he could do anything he set out to do and from that moment on his belief in himself had never wavered. Until now, he thought, as he watched the endless stream of early morning commuters crossing the harbour by car, bus, train and ferry.

It had been a long time since he'd looked out of his window. It had once been a daily ritual to draw his power from the city. I own this town, he'd tell himself. Every person in every one of those buildings watches the television I make. I'm the most successful producer in the country.

So why hadn't he been drawing his power from the city lately? He knew why. Tran! He'd been drawing his power from Tran. Stupid! You never relied upon people, you used people.

Alain felt a tightening of his buttocks and something strangely akin to an erection. He knew the signs. It was the call to battle and he hadn't felt it for years. Things had been too easy for too long now. His only thrills had come from humping promiscuous schoolgirls or fighting for a ten per cent better deal. Where was the challenge in that?

The challenge was back now. With a vengeance. The challenge was his survival, his fight for life. Alain felt a surge of triumph. 'The Glitter Game' would make television history. Not only did he know it, but Robert Bryce knew it. What had he said? 'You're the best at what you do, Alain.' That's what he'd said. And he was bloody right.

Would he have given Alain as much rope as he had without knowing the man's power to fight back? No way. He'd be making a noose for himself too if that was the case, and Robert Bryce was far too clever for that.

'Get this to Robert Bryce.' Alain slapped a sealed envelope down on Wendy's desk. It was the contract, fully signed. 'He's at the Regent.'

Wendy nodded. 'Good morning, Mr King. Isn't it a lovely —'

'Get Les Kleinberg on the phone then line up a midday meeting with Evan, Jim and Sandy.'

'Would you like me to bring in your —'

'Yes. Black with two sugars.'

Wendy looked dumbfounded at the door Alain had just slammed in her face. She wasn't remotely surprised at his rudeness, but black coffee with two sugars? In all the time Wendy had been working for him it had been white and none.

Alain wasn't disturbed by Kleinberg's threats to sue. He knew he wouldn't.

'Sorry, Les. Got to go.' Les Kleinberg was still talking when Alain hung up.

He called Chris Natteros on the private line.

'Chris. Alain King.'

'Oh. Hello, Alain. How's things?' Chris' voice was blurred with sleep.

'Got a proposition for you. Can you come in to the channel this morning?'

'Christ, Alain, it was opening night last night. Can't it . . . ?'

'Sure, sure,' Alain had read somewhere that Chris was directing a stage show. 'It can wait till this afternoon. Two o'clock, OK?'

Alain hung up and Chris drifted back to sleep. The bastard hadn't even asked how opening night went, he thought. Typical.

Exactly one hour later, Wendy announced Brian Hopgood with a special delivery from Mr Bryce.

Brian entered Alain's office and placed a dozen large bulky envelopes on his desk. 'Mr Bryce thought you might be able to use these, Alain. They were dumped not far from the channel and the police haven't been able to come up with who did it.' Brian's shrug and smile suggested that it was unnecessary to bandy any story other than that about the station. 'Your personal property's here too.' He patted the smaller padded bag on top.

'Mr Bryce said, welcome back. He told me to tell you he's delighted you've decided to stay on. He goes home tomorrow but he said anything you need, just ask.'

When Brian had left, Alain took the gun out of its padded bag, put it in his desk drawer and checked the rest of the material.

It was all there. Files of 'Glitter Game' storylines, the family sitcom, discs, videos, marketing plans.

He took a deep breath. The fight was on.

'Sandy, you'll be directing with the second unit crew from now on. I'm sacking Mike.'

Sandy, Evan and Jim were assembled in Alain's office. They looked from one to the other. What was wrong with Mike? He was inexperienced, sure. Fresh out of the Film and Television School, with only one trade doco and two episodes of a second rate soap to his credit — everyone had been amazed when Alain had insisted on his appointment. But he'd proved his worth since then and was a nice enough bloke.

'Why?' Jim asked.

'And who'll be directing the first unit?' Sandy demanded belligerently.

'I'm bringing Chris back.'

'When?' Jim looked amazed.

'As soon as possible.'

'But Mike's contracted till —'

'We'll pay him out.' Despite Alain's confidence, he

was praying inside that Chris didn't have a solid commitment. The play had opened, thank God, but if there was another deal lined up, Chris was the sort of man who would honour it.

It didn't occur to Alain for one minute that Chris might turn down his offer. Chris was a family man and in Alain's experience, family men could also be bought. It would cost, but Chris was worth it.

Jim was offended that he hadn't been consulted in an area that was directly his domain and he was insulted that Alain was now announcing his decision in front of Evan and Sandy. 'Just a minute, Alain. I think we should —'

'Evan, I want you to ditch the boat people storyline.' Alain didn't even appear to notice Jim. 'Are the scripts completed?'

'They're not even started.'

There was a silence. Scripting was nearly six months in advance, the boat people storyline should have been about to go into production. Alain now looked to Jim, and his look demanded an explanation.-

'They were shelved a month after we held the auditions, Alain.'

'Why wasn't I told?'

'Well, to be quite honest, you weren't taking your usual interest in the scripting department and I thought you didn't give a damn.'

Alain's face was thunderous. He didn't like Jim's recently acquired backbone.

'Besides,' Jim said, 'Robert Bryce told me not to mention it.'

Another fractional pause. 'What did Robert Bryce have to do with it?' Alain asked slowly, although he already knew the answer.

'The boat people storyline was Melanie's idea. She rang Evan herself. She thought it was a moral issue we should cover.' Evan was nodding his vigorous agreement. 'But when Robert quelled it a month later,' Jim continued, 'he told me it was one of Melanie's aberrations and it was an embarrassment and the less said about it the better. I must say I agreed with him and . . . '

'I didn't.' Evan's face was flushed with annoyance. 'It was a damn good storyline and I'd put a lot of work into it and I still think it could work if —'

'Shut up, Evan,' Alain snapped. Of course it had all been set up to plant Tran but Alain didn't have time to think about Tran now. He didn't have time to cringe with embarrassment at Melanie's involvement in the plot. There was far too much to be done.

'The police found this dumped near the channel.' He pushed the pile of envelopes over the desk at Evan. 'It looks as if everything's there. Take it with you, get on with those storylines and keep them tight.'

Evan peered into the top envelope then looked at Alain in amazement. 'It's the stuff that was stolen.'

'Well, it obviously wasn't, was it?' Alain snapped. 'It was obviously dumped.'

Evan, Jim and Sandy exchanged incredulous looks.

'But why? Who would have done it?' Jim asked.

'Oh, Christ, Jim. I don't know! The police don't know! A junkie covering his tracks, who cares? We've got the stuff back, now let's get moving!'

After he'd got rid of Evan, Jim and Sandy, Alain called a meeting with Tim Arnold and his assistants. He announced that 'The Glitter Game' publicity budget was to be increased by half again and a massive promotion campaign was to be mounted leading up to the Logie Awards night.

Alain waited till Lois and Val had left the office and Tim was about to close the door behind him. 'Oh, and Tim.' He watched the PR man turn. 'Didn't want to mention it in front of the girls, but those pirate deals of yours. Give them a miss.'

Tim's face was suddenly ashen. 'Alain, I don't know what —'

'I said, give them a miss.' A thin smile. 'If you want to stay in this industry, Tim, just remember your place.' A pause. 'Which is really nothing in the scheme of things, is it?' The smile was gone. 'Now get out.'

Alain's meeting with Chris was as successful as he knew it would be. Of course they played games to start with. 'We were a little premature I feel, Chris.' Alain's golden rules when rectifying a mistake were to never apologise and to use the royal 'we' whenever possible. 'We fully appreciate your worth and we'd love to have you back in the family.' Alain's smile was warm and generous. 'Now, what are your commitments and how can we go about this?'

Chris smiled back. He knew exactly the game Alain was playing and he knew, even before he answered, that he'd allow himself to be bought. But for a good price, he told himself. Helen and the kids deserved it. 'I don't have any firm commitments after the play, Alain.'

'Which opened last night?' Chris nodded. 'So, you're in the clear as of now?'

'Except for policing the show. I like to go to every second performance.'

'Of course, of course,' Alain nodded, thinking the man was a workaholic. Few other stage directors went to those lengths. 'But if we made sure you weren't involved in night shoots you could start back immediately, right?'

'That depends, of course.'

'Double the money?'

Chris was used to Alain's games. This was a new approach and he was suddenly taken aback. What had happened to the foxing around and bargaining?

Alain read his reaction. 'No point in messing about, Chris. You know me too well. Will you take it?'

'I'll take it.'

So far so good, Alain thought, after Chris had gone. Writers, directors, publicity were all tied up. Now for the difficult part. The actors. How was he going to repair the damage there?

Ironically enough, the major damage in that department hadn't been caused by him at all. Edwina's insistence that Jane Richmond be relegated to the background had been the first big mistake and Alain had protested it at the time. Also, he could hardly have prevented Narelle's pregnancy or Vicky's choice of lover over stardom. But he knew that if he hadn't been willing the destruction of the show he would certainly have found a way to keep them. Oh well, it wasn't too late. He'd talk them around, it wouldn't be difficult.

Narelle's pregnancy could be disguised till the last minute and she could be filmed in tight mid-shots and close-ups when it was really showing. She'd only need a few weeks out. Then the channel would supply a full-time nanny. Not that that idiot dentist husband of hers couldn't afford his own fleet of nannies but it was good to appear caring.

Of course! The idiot dentist husband! That was the way to get to Narelle! Alain punched the intercom button. 'Wendy, send a memo to all cast. Friday week. Dinner. Husbands, wives, boyfriends, girlfriends welcome. It's to say thanks for a great team effort, ratings are well up, we want to congratulate our Logie nominees and wish them luck, etc. etc.'

'Yes, Mr King.'

'And book somewhere upmarket — Pruniers, Le Trianon or whatever. I want them all there.' He released the intercom button without waiting for Wendy's reply, then punched it again as he remembered. 'And get Vicky Fraser in here as soon as possible.'

'I don't think she's in the studio today, shall I —?'

'Tomorrow, then.'

'Mr King!' Wendy leapt in before he could release the button. 'Edwina Dawling isn't due back from overseas until the week after the cast dinner you're planning. Would you like me to organise it for the following Friday?'

Alain paused only momentarily. 'No. Chances are she wouldn't show anyway.'

As he leaned back in his chair and drew breath, Alain realised he didn't want Edwina there. It would be a work night for him, he must be on his mettle and the woman continued to unnerve him. What was it about her that made him feel so self-conscious?

Alain felt a pang of regret as he remembered his original plan. If everything had gone accordingly, Edwina would be out of the show by now and Jane would be starring.

Feisty little number that she was, Alain would have had no trouble controlling Jane. He knew her type. All he'd have to do would be to maintain strong storylines for her and keep telling her what a good actress she was and how the show couldn't survive without the skills of such a fully-trained professional. All that shit and she'd be eating out of his hand. They were a dime a dozen, these 'committed actors' — they felt themselves superior to soap and needed that superiority acknowledged. It used to irritate Alain in the old days until he realised just how easily manipulated such purist egos were. If only Edwina were so easily manipulated. If he tried the professional flattery on her, she'd give him that arrogant stare that said 'So what? I know that,' and wait for him to go on.

Alain toyed with the idea of tempting Jane to stay but dismissed it quickly. He'd have to give her good storylines and Edwina wouldn't take that. Like it or not, it was the Edwina Dawling show now and Alain couldn't risk losing her. It was a pity, but Jane was out.

Who next? Paul. Alain would have to get him off the booze before the viewers discovered they were idolising a drunk. That pretty wife of his who'd made an impressive comeback in the fashion world recently — what was her name? Barbie Nelson — she'd be able to do the trick. Again the intercom button.

'Find me any recent stuff on Barbie Nelson.'

'Paul Sorell's wife? She's on the cover of *Woman's Day* this week.'

'Get it. Oh, and call Mandy Burgess and Sidney Meredith's agents. I want their contracts signed and back on my desk first thing tomorrow.'

The rest of the day went smoothly. Alain made an appointment with Barbie, via her agent, for the following afternoon. They were to discuss a possible ongoing fashion segment in Channel 3's morning programme.

'I was most impressed with the televised "Night of Stars" wool fashion parade she hosted,' Alain explained to the agent. *Woman's Day* had said it was Barbie's latest showy gig.

'Yes, it was good, wasn't it?' the agent agreed enthusiastically. 'Barbie's always been the best in the business at —'

'Around two-thirty, three o'clock be all right?'

'Yes, fine, Mr King.'

'Good. Tell Barbie I'm looking forward to meeting her.'

Alain hadn't bothered to check with the producer of the morning show to see whether a fashion segment could be incorporated. It was immaterial. These things took months to finalise and by the time Barbie was informed that the deal had fallen through, Paul would hopefully be ensconced once again in the loving bosom of his family and off the bottle.

The only real irritation of the day came at four forty-five as Alain was preparing to leave the office.

'I've just had a call from both Mandy Burgess' and Sidney Meredith's agents,' Wendy said.

'Right. Are they couriering the contracts over?'

'No. They say their clients are no longer happy with the conditions and they'd like either you or Jim Avalon to get back to them.'

'They *what!*'

'They want more money,' Wendy said, then ducked out before the explosion.

It was those fucking stupid T-shirts, Alain thought,

and that fucking stupid fan club. Mind you he had to admit it was good for the show.

He was buggered if he was going to make the contact though, he'd puke if he had to negotiate with those old farts. He grabbed his briefcase and opened the door. 'Tell Jim to get on to the Burgess, Meredith agents and give them what they want. Burgess Meredith! Oh Jesus,' he snorted, 'even their fucking names are a joke.'

Alain's interview with Vicky the following afternoon was the first hiccough he'd experienced in his reparation process and he didn't like it at all.

'Sorry Alain, no way!'

Alain was taken aback. As soon as Vicky had told him nothing could sway her personal reasons for leaving the show, he'd assumed it was a bargaining ploy. The girl learns fast, he thought with a touch of admiration.

He recalled her manipulation of events during their original 'research session'. Yes, he'd recognised her as one of his breed from the very start, he told himself. One of those who, like him, used people and situations — one of those who never allowed others to get too close. So what was this 'personal reasons' shit she was giving him?

'All right, Vicky.' Alain didn't even bother laying on the charm. 'Say we double the money. What happens to the "personal reasons" then?'

And that was when she came out with the reply. There wasn't even a split second's consideration. 'Sorry, Alain, no way!'

He allowed himself only a momentary surge of anger before he dismissed her. She obviously wasn't going to budge and he didn't have time to waste. There were too many other things to be done and the Sorrell wife would be here at any minute.

'That'll be all, Vicky,' Alain said. 'You're a fool,' he added as she rose to go.

'Maybe, maybe not.' The electric blue eyes sparkled and the grin was unimaginably cheeky.

Alain wanted to hit her. 'Ungrateful little bitch,' he whispered through clenched teeth as the door closed behind her.

Vicky didn't hear him but she might as well have. She knew exactly what Alain was thinking. When she got out into the corridor, she threw her head back and laughed out loud. She'd never felt so happy. She no longer needed to use and be used. She no longer needed to put up walls and stand guard.

She was nearly bowled over by Jim as she turned the corner into the front foyer reception.

'What's the joke?' he asked, and Vicky realised that she was still grinning from ear to ear.

'Alain's reaction to the big "no",' she answered. 'Hey, where have you been? You smell like a brewery.'

'Only a bottle of red and a couple of cognacs. You need at least that much when you're wining and dining two agents simultaneously.'

Vicky cocked a knowing eyebrow. There was no way the Jim Avalon of old would have consumed alcohol in the middle of a working day. She approved of the change. 'Well, don't drink yourself under the table before tonight. It's going to be a big one.'

Greg and Jim were spending the evening watching the Academy Awards telecast with Simon and Vicky. Simon was already at home putting the champagne on ice and preparing endless food treats.

Along with Vicky, Greg and Jim had helped Simon through his rehabilitation and since then the four had become great friends.

'Don't worry, I'll keep myself nice,' Jim promised. 'You haven't heard anything, have you?' They were all praying for Anna Bowrey to pick up the award and Simon had even bought little Australian flags to wave when the Best Actress category came up. But of course the telecast went to air hours after the actual ceremony so it was essential to close ears and eyes to late afternoon radios and newspapers which carried announcements of the winners.

'Not a word. Wendy tried to tell me when I was waiting for Alain but I screamed and covered my ears.'

'Good girl,' Jim grinned. 'See you tonight.'

'Six o'clock and don't be late!' Vicky yelled, as Jim disappeared down the corridor on his way to Alain's office.

'Don't! Don't!' Jim turned Wendy's afternoon paper face down and put his hands over his ears.

'I wasn't going to,' Wendy snapped. She'd been very put out by Vicky's behaviour and certainly didn't expect a similar exhibition from someone as responsible as Jim Avalon. 'It's not in the paper yet anyway, it was on the radio news . . . '

'Don't care, don't care, don't want to hear it,' Jim intoned, his hands still over his ears. Wendy caught a whiff of cognac and thought, 'So that's it'. 'I'll tell Mr King you're here,' she said. 'He has an appointment in,' she looked at her watch, 'five minutes, though.'

'I'll only be one.'

'I take it you've locked in Mandy and Sidney,' Alain demanded the minute Jim's head appeared around the door.

'That's what I'm here for.'

'And?'

'A couple of placatory minors like better dressing room allocation and hire cars instead of cabs but basically we're looking at a fifty per cent increase.'

'Oh.' Alain looked pleased. 'Could have been worse — they could have wanted double.'

'They did. The dressing rooms and hire cars talked them down fifty per cent.'

Alain also caught the whiff of cognac. 'Have you been drinking?'

Jim nodded. 'I took them to lunch. And I tell you, you need a drink when you're jointly wooing the Burgess, Meredith agents.' Jim gave a hoot of laughter.

Alain looked irritated. 'It isn't like you, Jim —'

But Jim interrupted. He was irritated back. Bugger Alain, not a word of congratulations on a deal well done, and now he was being reprimanded like a schoolboy. 'Oh leave it Alain, alone.' He gave another hoot as he realised what he'd said.

Alain watched him leave and wished yet again that Jim had remained in the closet.

'Miss Nelson is waiting to see you,' Wendy announced through the intercom. 'Shall I send her in?'

Alain flung the door open, beaming, his hand extended.

'Barbie! Come in, come in. Coffee or tea?'

'Coffee, thank you.'

His handshake was warm and effusive and he flashed the smile of the perfect boss at Wendy as he ushered Barbie in.

'Coffee would be lovely if you have a moment, Wendy.' He closed the door and gestured to one of the comfortable armchairs beside the coffee table. 'Sit down, sit down.' He pulled the other armchair up beside her, casting a sideways glance as she crossed the elegant legs and smoothed down the tailored skirt. Good looking woman, he thought. Easy prey, too. Oh, she was playing the poised figure of fashion to perfection but he knew that it was a cover-up. He could sense the tiny heart racing beneath the smart linen George Gross jacket.

It was true that Barbie was nervous. When she'd kicked Paul out of her life, the anger and the hurt that remained had lent fire to her confidence. Enough fire for her to forge a new career. But there were times lately when she was painfully aware that the career was no more than a distraction from the ache for Paul. There were times when she felt the tough exterior crumble and then the desire to run back to the comfort of being a housewife and mother would return with a vengeance. This was one of those times.

She'd felt nervous even walking through the foyer of Channel 3. What if she bumped into Paul? The prospect of meeting Alain King had made her feel even worse. The stories she'd heard over the years of The King and his dealings were intimidating to say the least. And now, seated beside him, she was intimidated by the man himself as she felt him see through her composed facade. Hang in there, Barbie Doll, she thought. Whenever she was in a tight corner these days she unconsciously talked to herself as Paul used to. It helped.

They exchanged pleasantries. The coffee arrived. Alain talked about the fashion segment in broad terms. He'd discuss the specifics with her agent, he said, the main purpose of their present meeting was to ascertain her own interest and commitment.

Barbie's instinctive reaction was the same as it had been when her agent had phoned her yesterday. She didn't want the job. The thought of working under the same roof as Paul, even if she could continually avoid him, was more than she could bear. But the agent had convinced her that it would be the biggest career boost possible and Barbie had reluctantly agreed.

It was after Wendy had cleared away the coffee cups and the plate of uneaten Scottish shortbread that Alain decided to make his move. 'Well, I think we've covered all we can at this point, Barbie. I'll arrange our next meeting with the on-line producer and then we can really get down to the business of format, budget, etc.' Barbie was about to make her farewell when Alain suddenly remembered. 'Oh, there was just one thing.'

'Yes?' Barbie sat back and recrossed her legs.

'I hope you won't think I'm being too personal.'

Barbie didn't say anything. His words sounded ominous. One of the lessons she'd taught herself was, when in doubt, keep quiet.

'At Channel 3 we're one big happy family, you see,' Alain continued expansively, 'and I like to protect that as best I can.' Confused, Barbie nodded. 'And with your husband working here on "The Glitter Game" . . . ' Alain shook his head compassionately. 'Well, I'd like to think . . . '

'There wouldn't be any friction.' Barbie couldn't stand it any longer. 'I'd avoid him at all costs, as I'm sure he would me.'

'Oh no, my dear, you misunderstand me.' Paternalism flowed from Alain. 'As I said, we're one big happy family. I would love to think that it was Channel 3 that brought you two back together again.' His brow furrowed with worry. 'You see, Barbie, Paul's drinking heavily — he has been for months now. We're very fond of him at Channel 3 and we don't like to see him do this to himself. Or, indeed, to his career.'

Alain contemplated taking Barbie's hand in heart-felt sympathy but the woman looked as if she were in a state of shock and he wasn't sure how she'd react. He'd let the voice do it instead. 'He loves you, Barbie,' he crooned, 'and I know your love for him and the warmth of his home and children would bring him back to the fold.' Alain sat back, the proud patriarch. 'And then we can all be a happy Channel 3 family, can't we?'

He waited for a reply but Barbie remained frozen so he continued. 'If, between us, we can get Paul back on the straight and narrow it could be a big year for him, Barbie. It hasn't gone to press yet, but,' he lowered his voice conspiratorially even though they were alone, 'he's been nominated for a Logie and we're confident he'll win.'

Ah, finally a reaction, Alain thought as Barbie's eyes flickered. He took it as encouragement and pressed on. 'Not the public "Most Popular" vote either. He's up for "Best Actor", Barbie, and I don't have to tell you what that would mean to him.'

Alain rose and Barbie automatically followed suit. 'I look forward to seeing you and Paul reunited, my dear. And I'll contact your agent in a week or so about our little morning segment.'

'Don't bother.' The head was held high and the voice was sharp but the glint of a tear behind the eyes belied the confidence. 'You can't buy me, Mr King.'

It wasn't the reaction Alain had expected at all and, in the brief pause before he could come up with a rejoinder, Barbie had made it to the door and escaped.

Alain looked at his watch. Twenty minutes he'd wasted on the bitch. He'd seen the tears glinting in the eyes. She'd be well and truly bawling by now. Well, serve her right! Fancy letting her mousey little pride deny her the best job opportunity she was ever likely to get. God, how he detested fools.

Alain was right about one thing. Barbie was bawling. She made it to the ladies toilets near the foyer, fought against throwing up, washed her face in cold water, then locked one of the cubicle doors and sat on the lavatory fighting to gain control.

Alain had been way off mark about everything else. If Barbie were now to spare a thought for the job offer it would be relief at not having to take it. But she wasn't sparing a thought for the job offer. She wasn't sparing a thought for anything but Paul.

So Paul was hitting the bottle. What did that mean? It didn't mean anything particularly new. Paul had hit the bottle with dependable regularity for years. But Barbie couldn't fool herself. She was painfully aware that it did mean something new. In all the years they'd been together Paul had never drunk dangerously when he was working. In fact Paul had never drunk dangerously at all. The 'dependable regularity' of his drinking had always been part of his 'between jobs' self-dramatisation. As he moped about declaring he'd never work again, that the industry had wiped him, that he was washed up, tumblers of Jack Daniel's and ice seemed to go with the image. The moment he was working again the bottle disappeared. It was a moderate Scotch at the end of the day, a couple of glasses of wine with dinner and not even that if the following day's studio call was an early one.

So why was he drinking now? Was Alain right? Was Paul really that unhappy? If so, he certainly never let on to the children when he saw them.

Barbie felt her resolve strengthen. She couldn't afford to give in now — she'd worked too hard to become her own person again. She was no longer Paul's doormat. Besides, she told herself as she gave her face a final cold water splash, he didn't need her. Logie for Best Actor? Voted in by his peers? Hell, Paul wouldn't need anybody. That was all he'd ever wanted. He'd had the adulation of his fans for years but to be taken seriously as an actor of note . . . !

Barbie attacked the paper towel dispenser. He'll be fine — you look after number one, she told herself as she studied the pale face in the mirror. With the make-up gone and only a smudge of mascara left she looked very wan. But not pathetic, Paul, no, not to be walked over.

Vicky, Simon, Greg and Jim had a great time watching the Academy Awards. They were slightly drunk and very raucous.

Then, suddenly, as the presenters for the Best Actress category were halfway through their inane preamble, Greg announced that Anna Bowrey had lost out.

'What?' Jim looked at him dangerously.

'Yeah. Sidney told me.'

There was a stunned silence before Vicky screamed at him. 'What did you tell us that for, you deadshit.'

'Oh, come on.' Greg's smile was patronising and irritating to the extreme. 'You didn't really think she had a chance, did you? She's up against Meryl, for God's sake.'

'That's not the point, Greg.' Jim looked just as angry as Vicky. 'We agreed. We've been avoiding the news all day.'

'It's not my fault,' Greg shrugged. 'Sidney told me. I couldn't shut him up.'

'That doesn't mean you had to tell us.'

'Doesn't matter, doesn't matter,' Simon interrupted. 'We'll wave the flags anyway.'

' ... *and the winner is* ... ' Jim and Vicky glared at Greg as the presenter gave a toothy grin right down the barrel and took just a little too long over the dramatic pause. ' ... *Anna Bowrey*!'

While Vicky, Jim and Simon stared at the screen in disbelief, Greg jumped to his feet wildly waving his flag. 'She did it! She did it!'

A slow smile spread over Simon's face. 'You cheeky bastard, you didn't know, did you?'

''Course not. I had no idea! Isn't it wonderful?'

Then they were all on their feet, waving flags, pouring champagne, belting Greg and generally feeling a patriotism they'd never known was in them.

Jane wasn't feeling patriotic at all. She was trying to. She was trying desperately to tell herself that the main thing was that an Aussie had won an Oscar. But it wasn't working. 'Which Aussie?' a little voice kept asking. And another little voice kept answering, 'It should have been me, it should have been me, it should have been me ... ' until she felt like screaming.

Jane had known since mid-afternoon that Anna Bowrey had won. She'd made a point of finding out as soon as possible. The news had left her with a dull, sick feeling that she knew was going to grow and fester. And that night she didn't even attempt to quell the masochistic drive that compelled her to watch the Academy Awards. She needed to witness the triumph that should have been hers.

Only seconds after Anna Bowrey's acceptance speech, Jane punched the 'off' button and sat staring at the blank screen. She felt such hatred! But it wasn't directed towards Anna Bowrey. The girl had grabbed at the main chance after all, just as Jane had grabbed at hers. But the girl hadn't had an Edwina Dawling around to cripple her. God, how Jane hated Edwina Dawling!

And the following day, when the headlines, the media news programmes, and the radio DJs all screamed 'Aussie wins Academy Award', Jane felt her hatred grow.

Within the television industry though, the excitement was short-lived. The Logies loomed near and, by the following Friday, Academy Award fever came to an abrupt halt when the press announced the nominees for the Logies.

There was a triumphant Channel 3 party that Friday night. 'The Glitter Game' had scooped the pool.

Not only was Edwina nominated in every category for which she was eligible, but it was considered quite possible that she might win all three.

Paul's Best Actor nomination was a surprise announcement but very well received and the only person with reservations about Mandy's Best Supporting Actress vote was Sidney who, while being effusive in his congratulations, fumed with jealousy inside. Mandy understood and, underneath her gracious acceptance, felt genuinely sympathetic. Sympathy was easy for Mandy. If the roles were reversed she knew she'd feel exactly the same way.

The Best Newcomer nominations were no surprise to the viewers. All three nominees were highly popular and it would be anyone's Logie.

Jane found it ironic that, after nearly six years in the industry, she should be nominated for Best Newcomer. It meant all those TV guest roles she'd sweated over had gone unnoticed and even rave reviews for leading stage performances meant nothing to television viewers. It was a further bitter pill to swallow on top of Anna Bowrey's triumph. Some substitute for an Academy Award!

Jane hoped desperately that Vicky, the other 'Glitter Game' nominee, would win. The third nominee was a ten-year-old cutie with freckles and plaits who'd recently moved in as the resident GP's niece in the Channel 8 doctors' soapie and Jane couldn't bear the thought of her taking out the award.

It was a 'closed' cast, production and friends party. No press or general network executives were present and, after the opening congratulations to the nominees, everyone was encouraged to let their hair down.

Alain resolved the Narelle situation early in the festivities. The guests hadn't even been called to the table but were still milling about the bar when Alain sought out Darren. 'Darren!' They pumped hands effusively. 'I haven't seen you since the wedding. You look fighting fit. Married life agrees with you, I take it?'

Darren nodded vigorously and cast a goofy look at Narelle who was giggling in a corner with Vicky and Simon.

'She's one in a million, all right, isn't she?' Alain continued. This was the way to talk to Double Bay dentists, he'd decided. Clichés. Darren would respond to clichés.

'She certainly is.' Another goofy look.

Alain looked troubled. 'She belongs to the world, though, Darren. You know that, don't you?' Darren dragged his eyes away from Narelle and looked at Alain. 'Her public needs her,' Alain said by way of reinforcement.

'Yes,' Darren agreed. 'She's very popular.'

Darren kept nodding as Alain outlined his plan — the channel would help Narelle through a comfortable pregnancy, supply every form of postnatal aid and thereby save the public from a substandard viewing existence, otherwise cheated of their favourite pet.

He was still in mid-flow when Darren interrupted. 'Yes, I think that'd be great.'

'You do?' Surely it wasn't going to be this easy?

'So long as Narelle's happy.'

'Oh, she will be. She will be.'

'Yes. Her fans are very important to her and she enjoys her work.'

'She won't regret it, Darren.' Alain patted his shoulder. 'Neither of you will. She has a gift that belongs to the world.'

It was time for Alain to circulate. 'Now you let your hair down, kick up your heels, enjoy yourself.' And he set off to dispense bonhomie, pleased with a job well done. 'The Glitter Game' had retained its number one sex symbol.

Darren watched Alain circulate. Narelle would be pleased. In fact, just this morning their postcoital conversation had evolved around how much they'd both miss the bright lights and adulation. What a strange man Alain was, though, Darren thought. Did the man always speak in such clichés?

Alain was adding up his debits and credits. Vicky was a big loss admittedly but he'd find another street kid and make another star. Paul hung in the balance, dependent upon Barbie, the booze and a Logie — all things beyond Alain's control. Now there was only Edwina to go. She'd be back on Monday. He'd give in to whatever astronomical fee she demanded, of course, but he wasn't going to enjoy the negotiations. He heaved a sigh at the thought.

'You're *what*?'

'I said, I'm leaving, Alain. Right after the Logies. I'm not renewing my contract.'

'But, you said . . . '

'I know what I said, but I didn't sign, did I?'

'Edwina, the show will —'

'The show will just have to get on without me.'

Alain felt a sense of panic. Could the show survive without Edwina? Normally, yes; anything could be rigged, given time. But could the show survive without the six months' preparation which would normally be planned for the departure of such an important character and the introduction of a new one to take over? Could Edwina now undo all his hard work in one fell swoop?

'I'm disappointed in you, Edwina.' He tried a last-ditch appeal to her better nature. 'I would have thought your sense of loyalty . . . '

Edwina laughed. 'Listen to yourself, Alain. Just listen to yourself.' She was still laughing as she opened the door.

The Logies

Sydney looked good. The Opera House gleamed white against the night sky and the floodlights of the Harbour Bridge tinged the giant coat hanger a magic blue. Multicoloured lights bounced off the black water and brightly-lit ferries scuttled across Sydney Harbour.

Searchlights fanned the sky around the Regent Hotel, flashbulbs popped blindingly and fans screamed by the thousands.

The television magazines had been boasting for weeks now that it was to be the biggest and most lavish Logies night on record. And it was. After all, the budget was triple that of any preceding award night because of the delayed telecast of the Logies to England.

Edwina's limousine pulled up and the fans went wild. It was obvious whose night it was going to be.

There were other triumphs, of course. Mandy's was of global proportions as she collected her Best Supporting Actress award and she glowed, even as Sidney spat his congratulations at her from between his Terry-Thomas teeth. Poor old sod, she thought, and sincerely hoped that next year would see an award for him. Well, she corrected herself, for both of them; it was only fair.

When Vicky took out the Best Newcomer award, the auditorium went wild. Everyone approved. Everyone, that is, except the precocious ten-year-old nominee from Channel 8. And when Chris Natteros was voted Best Director for the pilot of 'The Glitter Game', the Channel 3 tables gave their favourite director a standing ovation.

Alain accepted the Best Television Series award for 'The Glitter Game' with his customary humility and many grateful acknowledgements to production team, cast and crew. He'd made acceptance speeches into quite an art form. Not too short, not too long, he mentioned all the necessary people, made two good gags and got off the stage while they were smiling. He left the podium to a healthy round of applause, caught Edwina's polite smile and genteel handclap and thought, 'You cunt, Edwina'. He'd corner the bitch alone and give it one more go.

Edwina knew what Alain was thinking and it didn't bother her. Neither did Jane's malevolence. She had felt Jane's eyes burning into her when the Best Newcomer nominees were announced. Tough, she thought. It's the same old name of the same old game.

She'd felt a twinge of something, maybe a slight regret, when Paul failed to carry off the Best Actor award. He looked so broken. But then she'd caught his eye and seen the flash of unconcealed hatred. Well, too bad, she thought, and dismissed him as well.

Edwina decided to ignore them all. It was her night and she was going to savour her victory to the fullest. Then two things happened to mar her enjoyment.

Liza Farrelly was the first. Liza hadn't come near

Edwina for months. In fact, not since Edwina had ruined her career. Strange. Liza was a formidable adversary and Edwina had been prepared for some form of battle, or at least a protest. But there had been nothing. Why? Then suddenly the confrontation that night, right after Edwina's first acceptance speech. Cornering her like that on her way back from the stage. And again as Edwina was accepting the Gold, again there was Liza, gloating. Yes, that was the worry. The woman seemed triumphant in her hatred. What was she planning? Why did Edwina feel a flash of fear?

And then there was Davey. Halfway through the evening he'd suddenly looked so ill. But the more Edwina asked, the more he insisted he was fine, that it was just the smoke. But he asked whether they could leave early nevertheless. Eventually Edwina found herself feeling irritated. How dare he get ill on her big night? As the MC was announcing the final dance spectacular, over which the credits would roll, she finally snapped. 'For the last time, no! We cannot go home. Now will you shut up about it?'

Edwina never said 'shut up'. She considered it extremely rude and tantamount to heavy swearing. As Davey looked away, tired and defeated, she felt guilty. 'I'm sorry, Davey.' She squeezed his hand under the table. 'I have to go up on stage for the press photos after the show, and then we'll leave. I promise.'

Davey nodded and smiled back. His hands were sweaty. He really is sick, Edwina thought.

Davey felt more than sick. His stomach was knotted, his head was pounding and waves of dizziness were threatening to engulf him.

He could barely remember a thing after his meeting with Liza in the foyer. The remainder of the evening drifted by in a kind of haze and he was only vaguely aware of Edwina accepting the Best Actress award and then the Gold Logie.

The dancers wound up their athletic finale amidst smoke machines, laser lights and revolving sets, signalling the end of that year's Logies award presentations.

The following onstage press barrage was completely chaotic and Edwina, being the centre of attention, copped the brunt of it, with British and Australian photographers and journalists all vying for prime shots and comments.

She eventually signalled Davey to rescue her and they weaved their way through to the hotel foyer.

'I'll go to the Ladies while you organise the car,' she whispered.

It wasn't that easy. During the press session, most of the Logies guests had left the auditorium and were milling about the Gothic foyer area where they could be seen through the huge plate glass windows by their fans who were being held back by a cordon of police.

Robert and Melanie Bryce were the first ones to corner Edwina.

'Congratulations, Edwina, what a victory.' Melanie shook her hand first, then Robert took over.

'Yes, it's been a big night for you, hasn't it?' But his voice was steel. 'Just a quick word, if I may?'

There was no way out. In a united move which was quite graceful, Melanie turned on her heel to block Davey while Robert wheeled Edwina into a corner beside a huge display of flowers.

'What a night of triumph,' Melanie was smiling at Davey. 'We're so proud of her.'

'I'd like you to reconsider leaving the show.' Robert was grim-faced. 'In fact, I'd take it as a personal favour if you decided to stay.'

Edwina felt a little unnerved but she met his eyes and answered strongly. 'Not a favour I can oblige you with, I'm afraid, Robert. I've signed the deal with CBS.'

'Oh, you can leave us to find a way around the legal aspect. I'd give it serious consideration if I were you, Edwina.' Davey was now once more at Edwina's side. 'You might regret a hasty decision,' Robert added. He smiled coldly, nodded, and rejoined Melanie.

Once again Edwina felt a chill down her spine. Two people had frightened her tonight. Robert Bryce and ... As she turned to Davey she caught Liza's eye across the foyer. The woman made a move as if to join them.

'Organise the car, Davey.' Edwina backed off to the corridor leading to the women's toilets.

Davey followed her far enough to see her enter the door marked 'Ladies', and watched long enough to see Jane follow, but when Liza crossed the foyer and also made a beeline for the toilets, he cornered her. 'There's no need to bother her any further, Liza. I gave her your message.'

'I'd like to check her reaction out for myself, if you don't mind.'

Inside the women's washroom, Edwina had applied fresh lipstick and was opening her powder compact, all the time aware that Jane was standing beside her. Jane was looking in the mirror and combing her hair.

But she wasn't looking at herself, she was looking at Edwina.

Finally Jane couldn't bear it any longer. 'How do you live with yourself, Edwina?' she demanded. 'How the hell do you live with yourself?'

Edwina had had enough. What with veiled threats from Robert Bryce, the menace of Liza Farrelly, not to mention Alain King and Paul Sorell both breathing down her neck, the last thing she needed was a jealous actress out to twist the knife. She didn't even glance at Jane but threw her make-up in her bag and stormed to the door. It was her night, for God's sake — why couldn't they all leave her alone!

She threw the door open only to collide with Liza.

'Davey said he gave you my —' Liza started to say but Davey was there immediately.

'I've signalled a doorman,' he said, hurrying Edwina to one side as Jane appeared beside Liza. 'I'll tell him to bring the car down to the car park so that you don't have to go through the crowds.'

Edwina kept walking. 'I'll meet you down there. I've got to get out.'

'But it'll only take a minute. Why don't —'

'I'm not waiting a second, Davey. I'll see you in the car park.' Davey watched as Edwina crossed the foyer and disappeared around the corner to the lift which serviced the underground car park.

'Have you seen Paul?' A voice startled him. It was Barbie. She was in jeans and a sweatshirt and looked very out of place among the formal evening wear. But Davey didn't notice. His head was beginning to ache again.

'No.' He started to move off, then noticed how odd Barbie looked and wondered vaguely if there was anything wrong. Barbie was a nice woman and he regretted being brusque. 'Sorry, I haven't seen him for ages.'

They both looked around the crowded foyer but Paul was nowhere in sight.

The party in the foyer dispersed to various executive suites and private rooms in the hotel. Political power games and general brown-nosing went on in the executive suites booked by the channels and fornicating went on in most of the private rooms booked for the stars. Everyone was having a great time until the body was found.

No one knew how it had happened or who had done it. In fact it was only when the police arrived and started their endless rounds of questions that it became known who had made the actual discovery.

It had been a Japanese couple, tourists not even connected with the Logies, who'd found Edwina's twisted body lying on the concrete floor of the car park. She'd been shot with her own gun, a .25 calibre Colt automatic pistol she always carried with her.

Revelations

The next day the banner headlines made lurid reading: GOLD LOGIE WINNER FOUND DEAD IN HOTEL CAR PARK ... A BLOODY END FOR AUSTRALIA'S DARLING.

Billboards all over the city were plastered with huge blowups of a triumphant Edwina, holding her Gold Logie aloft, as if to say, 'Today Australia, tomorrow the world!' Suicide? On her night of victory? Surely it had to be murder. The nation was in a state of shock and conjecture was endless.

The police interrogations after the Logies had been ruthless. Guests had been rounded up like cattle and forbidden to leave the hotel until they'd given a full report of their actions during the evening. To many the questions were an embarrassment and a number of people lied, which didn't make things any easier for the police.

Melanie and Robert Bryce were interviewed first thing the following morning. They hadn't been available at the hotel as they'd evidently left the Regent shortly after the presentations to supper quietly alone.

Paul Sorell had also left the presentations early. The police had ascertained that he had spent the night at his estranged wife's home and was still there.

As the homicide detectives left Melanie and Robert
to interview Paul, Davey handed a twenty dollar note
to a cab driver in Glebe. He waved away the change,
got out of the car, and started walking.

Davey couldn't recall much of the previous night.
He vaguely remembered searching the Channel 3
executive suites asking everyone whether they had
seen Edwina: 'I was supposed to meet her in the car
park but she's not there.'

Then her body was discovered. When the police
arrived and the guests were detained for questioning
all Davey could say was, 'I was supposed to meet her
in the car park. I was supposed to meet her in the
car park.'

He'd refused to stay the night with Vicky and
Simon but accepted a lift home from them. The
police doctor had given him a sedative and he sat
numbly in the back of the car, staring out of the
window. He hadn't let them come inside and he
couldn't remember how he'd spent the night. Sitting
in a chair, he knew that much, but whether or not
he'd slept, he really didn't know.

The same bewildered look was in his eyes as he
wandered the streets of Glebe — his face was expres-
sionless but his eyes screamed, '*why?*' His wandering
wasn't aimless. He knew where he was going. He had
somehow wanted to feel his body moving so he'd got
out of the cab several blocks before his destination,
but he knew where he was going, all right.

Arthur Burton had been a pathologist with the Police
Department for twenty years but he didn't behave
like one. He never cracked black jokes about 'stiffs'
or played macabre pranks on his workmates. Despite

this, and despite the fact that he liked reading poetry and cried at sad movies, he was a true professional. To him, a body was the same piece of meat it was to the next pathologist or the next seasoned cop. However, even Dr Burton had been deeply disturbed by the body of Edwina Dawling.

The case being a possible murder, he'd been called in to the City Morgue immediately upon delivery of the body and so hadn't been at home to see his wife's reaction when she opened the early morning paper which was delivered daily. She and both the kids had been such avid fans of Edwina. And he had to admit, he'd always fancied her himself.

And here she was, lying on the slab in front of him, with a bullet through her temple. He pulled the sheet back over Edwina's face and heaved a sigh. Time to get on with the paperwork. It was definitely no suicide, of course. He'd already phoned his findings in to Homicide, but now there was the lengthy report to get on with. He always hated that part of the job. Maybe he'd make himself a cup of tea first. But he stopped. Someone was standing in the doorway.

'How did you get in? What are you doing here?'

'I've come to say goodbye to Edwina,' Davey answered, his eyes fixed on the slab in the centre of the room.

The man was drained, defeated, numb with grief. Arthur studied the face, and he suddenly knew. 'You did it.' It was a statement rather than a question.

Davey was startled. 'What?' He shook his head as if to clear his brain and there was a spark of recognition in his eyes.

'You did it. You killed her.'

A shocking flash of revelation rushed through

Davey's mind. Yes, of course. He nodded. 'Can I say goodbye?'

It was a pathetic question and Arthur was moved. He knew that the man posed no threat. He closed the door behind Davey and crossed to the wall phone. 'I'll tell them you're here,' he said and he started to dial. Then he turned away as, very, very slowly, Davey walked towards the slab.

Pictures flashed through Davey's brain. Fire escape steps. Running down the fire escape steps to the underground car park. Throwing the door open.

'Oh! Davey.' Edwina's startled gasp. 'You frightened me.'

Taking her evening bag from her. 'I can't find my car keys.' Feeling the weight of the pistol through the fine fabric. Then kissing her gently. 'I was very proud of you tonight. I love you.' Kissing her again.

Then his mind went blank. He stood staring down at the sheet. As he reached out to pull it back, there was another flash.

Taking the service elevator to the top floor of the hotel. The smell of food. The view of Sydney Harbour. The sense of surprise that he didn't want to jump, that he didn't want to end his own life. Not that he cared what happened to him — he didn't care if they found him. He'd simply done what had to be done. What was the name of that film? Susannah York's face had danced through his mind. Yes, that's right, *They Shoot Horses, Don't They*? that's what he'd done. But how? How had he . . . ? Again his mind went a blank.

Slowly, Davey eased the sheet back. Apart from the neat hole in Edwina's temple, she looked as beautiful as ever. As beautiful as she'd looked when he'd kissed her for the last time and held the gun to her head.

Davey eased the sheet back unthinkingly as the final moment came to him. The feel of her soft white neck as he'd drawn her face to his for that last kiss. 'I love you,' he'd said.

The sheet was now drawn down to Edwina's waist and the small firm breasts were exposed. Arthur Burton hung up the phone and turned to Davey — then turned away again, embarrassed. He didn't want to see any more. He didn't want to see again that, despite the obvious years of hormone treatment, Edwina Dawling was still a man.

But the sheet remained at Edwina's waist as Davey once more caressed the white neck. There were no regrets — he'd had to do it. Liza Farrelly's voice rang in his ears and he could see her black eyes, burning with triumph and hatred. 'I know, Davey,' she'd said. 'I *know*. And so will the whole country tomorrow. Tell Edwina the story's already in print, thousands of copies are just waiting to be distributed. The billboards are going to read "Edwina Dawling is a man!" Tell her that. I'd like to think of her sweating out the night. Tell her, Davey! Tell her!'

As he bent once more to kiss her, Davey knew that, even without Liza's discovery, Edwina had been destined for destruction. They'd both been living on borrowed time ever since that day in Rosa's office.

Poor, foolish Rosa. Davey hadn't believed for one minute that Rosa would carry out her threat to tell the world if Edwina left the agency. He'd been wrong. Very wrong. She had already told the world. She'd told Liza Farrelly that very afternoon. But Edwina wasn't to know that as she leapt at Rosa, her anger bordering on insanity.

Ten years ago Davey himself had been the recipient of one of Edwina's insane rages and she'd nearly killed him. She was strong, very strong, and Rosa didn't stand a chance.

When Rosa was lying in a crumpled heap on the floor, her neck broken, Edwina had become hysterical and it was left to Davey to clear up the mess, to make the plans, to drive Rosa and her car to the Blue Mountains. It was all Edwina could do to follow in their car.

Ever since then their days had been numbered, and Davey had known it. Now, with the awful realisation that it was all over, he felt a sense of relief.

His kiss was as gentle as it had been the night before when he'd pressed the muzzle of the gun to her temple. 'I was very proud of you tonight,' he'd said. 'I love you.' Then he'd kissed her again. 'I'll always love you, Edward.' Then he'd pulled the trigger.

Epilogue

The news of Edwina's murder, rapidly followed by the disclosure of her true identity, made journalistic history. Edwina died as she'd lived: centre stage.

But the television industry ground along remorselessly. Careers soared or crashed or plodded on regardless of lurid headlines.

Jane went back to the theatre — a fringe production with an experimental group working out of a converted warehouse. She'd been offered the lead in a British farce opposite a big TV star from the UK, her 'Glitter Game' profile guaranteeing bums on seats for the management, but she'd knocked it back in favour of fringe. And she didn't regret it. She felt as though she'd come home. Bugger the big time, she'd decided. They could keep the fame and the money — she'd go for the challenge instead.

Paul was glad he hadn't won the Best Actor Logie. When Barbie arrived on his doorstep that night she admitted to him that she wouldn't have had the courage to come to him if he'd won. She'd been watching the ceremony on television and when he lost she'd picked up the car keys, walked out of the house and had driven straight to the Regent. If he'd won . . . well . . . he wouldn't have needed her.

Barbie had never seen Paul cry. Not really cry. He

put his elbows on the table, his hands over his face and gritted his teeth to stifle the noise. It was the very lack of sound that moved Barbie more than anything. Could this be her show pony, Paul? Why was he being so quiet?

'Come home, Paul.'

She was standing beside him and he suddenly clutched at her, sank his head into her breast and let out a howl of anguish. He needed her, he wailed. Oh God, how he needed her!

Barbie smiled. Yes, that was more like her Paul. He stank of Jack Daniel's but he'd be fine in the morning.

'Come home.'

Liza left the television industry altogether.

After the initial shock of Edwina's death, all she'd felt was anger at the sheer waste. How could that silly little bastard Davey honestly have thought there were thousands of newspapers exposing Edwina's sordid secret sitting in a warehouse just waiting to hit the stands the following morning?

Good God! Liza hadn't breathed a word of it to anyone, let alone sold the story. Now Edwina was dead and the whole sordid truth had been made public.

All Liza had wanted was her career back. And it was rightfully hers to demand — she hadn't even considered her threat as blackmail. If Edwina had come halfway Liza would have taken her secret to the grave.

But Edwina had been intractable. She had met Liza's request with an icy smile. 'I'll send Davey to the foyer,' she'd said. 'He'll be only too happy to relay any message you may have, Liza.'

And Liza had burned. Oh no you don't, you don't send me your lackey. I'll make you sweat the night out for an insult like that. You fraud.

The fact that Edwina was a fraud was the biggest insult of all to Liza. Rosa's bitchy disclosure that afternoon in her office all those months ago had been the greatest shock of Liza's life.

She'd lain awake most of that night trying to come to terms with the fact that Edwina Dawling was a man. It explained everything, of course — Edwina's mystery, the importance of Davey in her life. But did it explain the strange attraction that Edwina held for women? Did it explain the affiliation Liza had felt, and which she knew was reciprocated, that first day they lunched at Darling Harbour? She and Edwina had recognised a common bond that day, a bond of style, ability, strength and, unbelievable as it now seemed, femininity. Liza had felt her anger grow. How dare this vulgar fraud cheat her way into Liza's esteem when few real women could?

It was only after Edwina's death that Liza came to terms with the truth, that there was no need to take Edwina Dawling as a personal insult. No one could have known, no one. And Liza realised that Edwina was just as fascinating and just as alluring in death as she had been in life.

During Davey's trial, when the truth of the Rosa Glassberg murder came to light, Liza finally wrote her story on Edwina. Davey himself was quoted in the story as saying that Edwina had been living on borrowed time since Rosa's death, and that her madness was self-devouring so Liza had felt vindicated enough to write it.

Her tribute to Edwina Dawling was the last television story that Liza Farrelly ever wrote. Liza thought the article was the least she could do — she wouldn't admit that it was something she needed to do. Then she left television altogether.

Alain King didn't. The challenge of churning out successful television soap remained the motivating force in his life.

And true to that purpose, the week after the Logies it was storylining as usual. He'd called a special meeting with Evan Ryan, Jim Avalon and Chris Natteros.

'Now, how are we going to use this?' he said. 'Transvestite. Great storyline.'

Evan was innocent enough to nod; he could see the possibilities. Chris and Jim were appalled at Alain's lack of taste.

'Why don't we get an Edwina look-alike and bring her in as her own sister?' Alain continued. 'Well, *his* own sister,' he laughed.

Alain had pressed the button for Evan. 'Yes, yes,' Evan cried, lights flashing. 'But six months later we find that it's not his sister, it's really him. Only he faked his own death so that he could go away and have a sex change and come back and no one would know it was really him.'

'My idea exactly, Evan, well done.' Alain turned to Jim and Chris. 'Get on to the casting agents. We're looking for an actor who looks like Edwina.'

Chris wondered about returning to the theatre then remembered Helen, the kids, and his whopping salary. He nodded.

Jim grinned. 'What about an actor who looks like

Edwina would have looked if she'd had plastic surgery to not look like herself?'

Alain knew Jim was sending him up but it didn't worry him. This was hot, they were firing, and the challenge was being met.

'I've got it!' He nodded to Wendy who was taking notes. 'Get Tim Arnold in here. We'll start a nationwide hunt for the right actress — the right height, the right colouring and one who's willing to have plastic surgery to look like Edwina.' Alain walked to the drinks cabinet. 'It'll be bigger than *Gone With The Wind*! Wendy, we need more ice.'